AT THE PLEASURE OF THE MARQUESS

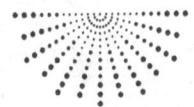

SOFIE DARLING

OLIVER
HEBER
BOOKS

COPYRIGHT © Sofie Darling

Published by Oliver-Heber Books

0 9 8 7 6 5 4 3 2 1

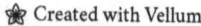 Created with Vellum

PROLOGUE

*T*he girl observed the two boys from the other side of the dirt square that served as the airing court. Noon now, it was crowded with fifty other children out for their daily dose of sunlight, what little of it filtered through the dense blanket of clouds enshrouding London.

The one boy, she knew. *Ned*. He wasn't much to think about. It was the boy on the other side of the crack in the wall who interested her.

The one with his freedom.

With a will of their own, her feet began moving, her scrawny form navigating the frenetic lot, careful not to make eye contact or engage with the other children. She wouldn't get pulled into any of their scuffles or, worse, games.

Once she'd drawn near enough, the other boy said, "Well, if ye ain't got the nerve fer it..." He shrugged indifferently.

"Ain't got the nerve for what?" the girl asked.

Both sets of eyes swung around. Ned's were wide with guilt, the other boy's narrow with assessment. A fraught moment lapsed before he said, "The matron got a strongbox in 'er room. Flick Doyle wants it knicked."

1

"Flick Doyle?" asked the girl, not one to be put off easily. "Who's that?"

"Never ye mind," he said.

The girl felt jittery and excitable, as if coins jangled through her veins. "What's he want it for?"

"To see if ye got what it takes."

"To do what?"

The boy sucked his teeth. "To join us."

"And who is *us*?"

The boy expertly spat a gob, quick and efficient. "Ye'll find out, or ye won't."

The boy was shifty, but she was determined. "When do you want it?"

"Midnight."

"Tonight?"

"Now wait a minute," said Ned. "Ye think ye can just come 'ere an' take me chance?"

The girl, shorter than Ned by a foot and slimmer than a shadow, squared up to him, fists planted on her hips. "Yeah, that's exactly what I think. And no grassin'. You keep your mouth shut."

With a neat pivot on her heel, she stalked away, only to return twelve hours later beneath a black sky, a far-away clock ready to strike midnight. As she lugged Mrs. Ditch's strongbox across the dark, empty yard, it occurred to her that this could be a jape, for she detected no sign of the boy, or anyone for that matter.

Then she heard it, a hissing sound. She squinted into the night. A pale, squiggling hand appeared through the crack in the wall and caught her eye. She scurried toward it as fast as her legs could carry her beneath their heavy load. Upon reaching the wall, she shoved the strongbox through a freshly dug hole at its base and scrambled beneath in quick pursuit. The strongbox wasn't leaving without her. She came up on the other side dirty, damp, and...

2

Free.

"That'll make ye one o' us, then," said the boy.

"And who is *us*?" Maybe she would get an answer now.

"Eels." The boy must have read confusion on her face, for he continued, "As in slip'ry as one." His thumb dug into his chest, proud. "'Is lucky eels, that's what Doyle calls us."

"Lucky eels," the girl repeated, testing the words in her mouth. They didn't feel bad. Not at all. They felt like freedom.

"Come on, then. Ye'll see. Yer the first gel we ever 'ad. What's yer name?"

The girl almost said Amelie but stopped herself on the *ahh*. "Hortense," she said instead, her middle-given name, so not a complete falsehood. Not that she minded lying to suit a delicate circumstance, but she needed a name she would answer to.

Instinct told her she couldn't enter this new life as Amelie, the name Papa and Maman had called her with such affection. An Amelie was soft and sweet. An Amelie could be hurt.

This instant, and going forward, she was Hortense, a hard, nervy sort of girl.

The sort of girl who could slip as one with the shadows.

The sort of girl the world couldn't touch.

It wouldn't dare.

CHAPTER ONE

WESTMINSTER, LONDON, APRIL 1827

*H*ortense rounded the corner from Bowling onto Little Peter Street, and out of habit, she scanned both directions to gauge the state of the thoroughfare. It stood empty of all but one other night skulker on the opposite side, back to her and keeping to himself. She stuck tight to the midnight shadows, her tread light. Always better to stay unnoticed.

Her boardinghouse lodgings at Number 11 lay just one more street ahead. Already, she was anticipating the comfort of her bed after yet another night of tracking the movements of a philandering husband. The third such case this week.

Ever since the informal spy network she'd been part of disbanded two years ago, her former handler and mentor, Lord Nicholas Asquith, had introduced her to aristocrats in need of tact and her expertise. From there, her discreet investigation outfit servicing London's elite had naturally formed by word of mouth. Nothing was too mundane or, conversely, too sordid. Mostly, it was infidelity that filled her coffers. Lost and stolen items, every so often. It wasn't the glorious, seductive spy craft that saved nations on the sly, but it did pay the bills, and then a little to put by.

Her boot heels should be the only *click-clack* echoing off uneven buildings to either side of her. But an unaccounted for *click-clack* joined hers, its tread heavier and quicker. Someone was gaining on her.

Her heartbeat kicked up a notch, and the blood whizzed through her veins. She overshot Number 11 and, half a street up, rounded a corner into a dark, fetid alley.

Back flat against the damp stone wall, heart pounding in her throat, breath hitched in her chest, she waited. *Nothing may come of it*, entered the clear voice of reason. The man might stride past the alley, blithely unaware of his role in this little drama of her own creation. It was a possibility.

Yet it was a different potential outcome that had her crouching low and her hand wrapped around the dagger strapped above her boot. Silently, she counted backward from ten. She reached zero, and no one had passed, not even a rat. Doubt niggled through her. Mayhap the paranoia that was never far out of reach was clouding her judgment, and the man—or woman, but likely man—had turned onto a different street with nary a thought for her.

Again, she counted slowly from ten to zero.

Again, nothing.

She drew a shallow breath and squeezed the hilt of the dagger, her hand shaky with anticipation, before poking her head around the corner. Not ten feet away, a still figure shrouded in shadow stared out at her. In an instant, her body was flooded with the twin thrusts of fear and readiness.

Recognition hit her, replacing fear with a relief so acute she could sag to the ground with it. "Asquith?"

Lord Nicholas Asquith stepped forward into a dim ray of the waning moon. "You know to call me Nick these days."

"Old habit." Annoyance flared. "You could have announced yourself."

A sardonic smile twisted about his mouth. "How else could I have tested your sharpness?"

"And?" She couldn't resist asking, the urge to win her mentor's approval rooted deep after all these years.

"As ever."

She snorted. "You're lucky I didn't knife you."

"I'd have deserved it." He jutted his chin toward the empty street. "Let us walk."

She pushed off the wall and joined him. They didn't walk side by side with arms locked, like a couple. Theirs wasn't, and never had been, that sort of relationship. "I'm guessing you'll state your reason for seeking me out tonight?" she asked at last.

"I would like to hire you for a job."

Alarm streaked through her. "You don't suspect Mariana of—" She gulped down the last word, unable to speak it aloud.

Nick and Mariana were the rare aristocratic couple who were perfectly suited to one another. Well, after they'd sorted through the first ten years of their marriage. Their connection could almost convince one to believe in the sort of love that lasted.

"Infidelity?" He waved dismissively. "Nothing like that."

She could sag with relief. "What's the job?"

"My brother."

She knew of the older brother, but Nick never spoke of him.

"You'll recall," he continued, "my mother and father died in a carriage accident five months ago."

She nodded and kept her silence at the cold distance in his voice. The few fragments of rumor and speculation about the Marquess and Marchioness of Clare that had drifted her way over the years—indiscriminate affairs by both parties, public screaming matches—painted them in a depraved and loathsome light. Nick wasn't the sort of man to be close to such people.

"As the firstborn son, Jamie inherited the title."

She detected no bitterness. Second sons knew their lot was to be the spare to the heir. And if the heir survived to inherit, well, the spare received naught all for his trouble.

"I haven't seen my brother since the reading of the will four months ago. As far as I can tell, he hasn't left Asquith Court in all that time, and he won't let anyone in. I've tried."

"What do you need from me?" she asked, the bud of anticipation blossoming, impossible to resist. It had been so long since a job truly interested her.

"I need to know what state he's in." Nick met her gaze for the flash of a second, but long enough for her to detect uncertainty, and concern. "If he's dead or alive."

She inhaled the sigh that wanted release. "*Blast.*"

He cut her a hard glance. "You won't do it?"

"Of course, I shall." She couldn't refuse Nick anything. "But, just once, I would like to wear a silk dress instead of a maid's uniform."

He snorted, a wry smile playing about his mouth. "When the job is finished, Mariana will take you to her dressmaker. A new silk dress as a bonus payment."

Her eyes rolled toward the uncommon indigo sky above London. "And where would I wear such a garment?"

He shrugged. "Life rarely lets us know where it's leading us before the fact. It has a habit of simply arriving. One should ever have one's silk dress at hand, in case."

They walked on a few steps. "When do you want me to start?"

8

"At your earliest convenience."

In fact, she had another job set to begin on the morrow—a lady whose precious terrier had been kidnapped by a former lover. This lady happened to be married to a well-known member of Parliament and required the deed done discreetly. Another job that was simply a variation on the tired theme of infidelity. But Nick was the one person in the world for whom she would drop everything. He'd loosed her from Doyle. The debt she owed him commanded utter and complete loyalty.

They had circled back and were quickly approaching Number 11. "I can start in the morning."

"It shouldn't take more than a handful of days."

"Any other pertinent facts I need to know?"

It was a standard question, but Nick's brow creased into a deep furrow. "My brother," he began, haltingly, "struggles with drink. You should be aware of that."

She gave a curt nod. He need say no more. His primary concern was that his brother was drinking himself to death. "I shall contact you in a few days' time."

"My thanks." He nodded and pivoted on his heel, continuing up Little Peter Street, a muted whistle trailing in his wake.

Hortense ducked down the narrow alley that ran alongside the boardinghouse. Her key slid into the lock of an unobtrusive black door. Once inside, she turned the lock behind her and climbed the straight staircase to her attic rooms. This private entrance was the deciding factor for having chosen this place. A useful feature for those nights when she returned in the early hours of the morning, like tonight.

It had taken quite a bit of searching to find a respectable landlady willing to accept her two conditions. She would be allowed to keep her own hours. And no questions would be asked.

Ever.

For this arrangement, Mrs. Hayhurst charged double the rent. The landlady might not ask any questions when Hortense placed prompt payment in her hand every Thursday, but her pinched mouth and knowing eyes did her talking for her. The woman could think what she liked.

Inside her rooms, she gave more thought to the conversation with Nick, specifically the part about his brother. Actually, she'd seen him once. It was last year at an exclusive gaming hell. He'd been deep in play and his cups. She didn't remember much about him, beyond his dark hair, rangy form, and general sardonic mien, as he hadn't been her mark that night. He'd been someone else's mark as it turned out, which triggered a series of events that ended with Lord Bertrand Montfort shot and Lord Percival Bretagne wed. She doubted very much the lofty Marquess of Clare—then the Earl of Pembroke—was aware of any of it.

Yet she wondered what the man was like. He and Nick would differ in temperament, of that she was certain. Nick was disciplined, patient, and loyal. So, what did that imply about the brother?

A marquess and a drinker had been said. *Wastrel* had been left unspoken. *Right.* Plenty of that variety of lord charging about London.

Temptation pulled her toward the bed, but she resisted. Instead, she lit the single candle on her bedside table and disrobed down to her chemise, which a quick sniff revealed might need a wash after a long day of striding to and fro about crowded, noisome streets. Due to her early start this morning, she hadn't a chance to do her exercises. There wasn't a day she skipped them, not even when she was tired down to the marrow of her bones. Especially then, for that was the moment her guard could slip.

And that wasn't an option.

She crouched deeply and sprang up, her arms thrusting upward and her toes lifting off the floor for the space of a second. She repeated the sequence one hundred times, like every other exercise in her rotation. She came to the floor and on her stomach, rising to her hands and toes, with arms extended straight. They released and bent at the elbows, lowering her body to the floor, before she pushed up again. Once she reached one hundred repetitions, she flipped to her bottom and lowered her torso until her back nearly touched the floor, then she curled forward. Next, she picked up the lead shot wrapped in burlap and began moving in a variety of extending, curling, and crouching motions. Half an hour from the time she started, she completed the full sequence.

Now, she could sleep.

Years ago, early on when she started working for Nick, she'd learned a valuable lesson about readiness the hard way, the specific memory of which she kept tucked in the deepest corner of her mind. The lesson was this: she would never be bigger or stronger than her adversaries and quarry, but she could be quicker and smarter.

No one would ensure her safety for her. She must do it for herself.

She blew out the candle and slipped her weary body between the covers of her welcoming bed. Sleep, however, eluded her.

She'd missed the odd midnight surprise rendezvous with Nick. These last few years, she'd felt...

Untethered.

Sure, every Monday, she visited Nick for dinner, which included Mariana and their twins, Geoffrey and Lavinia. But that was in the bosom of his family. It was the relationship they'd had to forge when Nick decided

11

to step out of the spy game, taking her with him. She still hadn't grown entirely accustomed to it. She didn't quite think of herself as lonely, but she had been living a solitary life.

Not that she thought she could build the same sort of family life as Nick. What man would have a woman like her? She had no interest in homemaking, or any of the activities that made a woman a woman in the eyes of a man.

She had two goals, really. The first was to continue to build her investigating business. With every month, she added a few more clients. The thought of her second goal, however, made her heart double in beats, for this goal was absolutely vital to the success of her first goal. Simply put, it was to put herself out of reach of Flick Doyle, permanently.

During her years of spying for Nick, she'd thought she had. Then, about a year after her return to London, Doyle had demonstrated how very wrong she'd been when one sunny afternoon he'd sent one of his lucky eels around to summon her. He'd then explained to her the "taxes" he would be collecting from her forthwith. After all, he was *allowin'*—his word—her to conduct her business in London, his turf.

"This ain't the Continent, as those nobs like to put it. All yer fancy new clients wouldn't be so quick to pay a jumped-up guttersnipe to be prowlin' 'round their palaces, nosin' into their affairs, if they knew yer past. One of them gossip rags would gobble that story right up."

Of which past he spoke was clear. Her past before Nick. Her past with *him*.

And his threat was doubly obvious: if she didn't pay her taxes, he would destroy her business.

Like that, he'd pulled her back into his web.

But now, a year on, she had to disentangle herself.

Before Nick caught wind of it. Before Doyle's "taxes" ruined the good name she was trying to build, for he didn't require payment in coin, but in baubles. A bauble didn't have to be fine or expensive, but rather personal to the aristocrat she nabbed it from. She would eventually get found out. It was only a matter of time.

And, tonight, Nick had given her a job. Doyle didn't need to know about it, for she wouldn't be stealing from Nick. She had a line, and there it was.

With that assurance to herself, which might not hold in the stark light of day, her head sank into her pillow, and her eyes drifted shut as she succumbed to the pull of an exhausted, and hopefully dreamless, slumber.

The same hope as every other night.

13

CHAPTER TWO

*O*nward, night ticked steadily into the small hours of morning. Jamie attempted to settle into the wing chair. The width of his shoulders, however, wasn't exactly compatible with the narrowness of its confines. He took the letter from the Bow Street Runner he'd received yesterday and marked the book on Parliamentary procedure he'd been attempting—and failing—to give his attention. Neither the subject of the book nor that of the letter held the urgency of the matter at hand.

Tonight, he had a thief to catch.

Outrage strummed through him at the very idea. The damned bloody cheek.

Not much in his life was by his choosing, save this room, his private study. Every servant in Asquith Court knew not to enter without his express consent. Yet someone had, indeed, dared.

In truth, he hadn't yet found anything missing, only items disturbed. Three days ago, the first indication had been the inkwell. The angle of it hadn't been square to the corner of his desk, and it was *always* square to the corner of his desk.

Every day since, he'd found a different item angled

oddly. The only logical conclusion was that someone was rifling through his belongings in the night. The belongings, it was worth noting, of a marquess. Whatever this person was seeking, they would soon understand it wasn't worth the price.

A slow, creaking noise sounded at the opposite end of the room. A sliver of light widened along its oak length as the door cracked open, and anticipation surged through him. In slipped a form so slight it could be mistaken for a passing shadow.

His heart accelerated into a gallop as the shadow crossed the room on footsteps that made not a sound. Eyes squinted, he attempted to make out any features or details of this person beyond their slight build. Dark trousers. Dark shirt. A lad, mayhap a hall or stable boy.

What stupid daring for a boy who only had everything to lose if he was caught. Which he was. Another sort of anger shot through Jamie. This time for the utter waste of a young life.

The lad stopped before an imposing cabinet and swung both doors wide. Fists planted on his hips, he looked up and down, evaluating its contents from top to bottom. Commandeering a nearby chair, he started at the top. Thoroughly, *systematically*, he searched the contents. Curious that.

Jamie kept quiet. Clearly, the lad was after a specific item. What could it be?

That cabinet contained naught more than century-old scientific journals, essays, treatises, bric-a-brac from various parts of the world, tomes about any number of subjects ranging from landscape gardening to the proper care of one's livestock to Parliamentary procedure—such as the book on his lap—and a musty old blanket in the bottom drawer.

The lad was now refolding and replacing the blanket, which had made him sneeze twice. He pushed the cabinet doors shut, carefully, so as not to make a sound, and exhaled a sigh. That sigh held the frustration of the thwarted. He hadn't found his prize.

On impulse, Jamie said, "If you would simply tell me what you're searching for, mayhap I could be of some assistance."

Though the room was lit only by a low fire in the hearth, he was able to catch the instant the lad's body went rigid. Shoulders tensed, his fists clenched and unclenched at his sides. A trio of heavy heartbeats thudded past before, at last, he turned.

The intruder had black hair pulled back and tied at the nape. Delicate chin and jaw. Red rosebud mouth. Smooth, dewy skin...

Shock traced through him. If he wasn't very mistaken, this person was no lad, but was, in fact, a...*woman*.

She stared out at him from beneath straight black eyebrows. Firelight flickered and offered a glimpse of extraordinary blue depths. He might have expected fright or, at least, sheepishness, in those eyes, but standing before him was a woman decidedly unflinching and unapologetic.

The outrage that had grown too familiar these last few days surged. What audacity. "What are you looking to steal?" he asked in a tone that implied no quarter would be given.

"Steal?" Was that amusement he detected in her voice? "Nuthin'."

"Then for what purpose have you been despoiling my study these last three nights?"

"Where do ye keep 'em?" she asked.

What a strange conversational turn. "Keep what?"

"Yer bottles o' brandy. Or whate'er it is ye soak yerself in."

"*Bottles of*—" Suspicion lifted its head. He sat for-

16

ward and rested his hands on his knees, his entire being focused on this woman. "Who sent you?"

Her head cocked, surely a perfect mirror of his. "You know who."

If he'd been a dog, his ears would have pricked forward at the sudden change in her speech. Not *ye know 'oo*, but *you know who*. She'd stopped dropping her aitches, going from Cockney to refined in an instant. Yet he detected an inflection within, too. A softness he couldn't quite place.

That instant, he knew. *"Nick."* His brother's name had barely crossed his lips when the next question followed. "Why?"

"He hasn't seen you in months."

"It's not unusual for us to go that long without seeing each other." It was only the truth. Realization sank in. She'd been searching for bottles, which meant... "He thinks I'm drinking myself into the grave."

"Aren't you?"

At last, he recognized the accent hiding behind the woman's perfect English. *French.* An intriguing detail, admittedly, but one he wouldn't allow to divert him. "I was," he admitted.

Why did he feel compelled to explain himself to this singular woman? He was a marquess. He need only explain himself to the king.

The woman shrugged. The gesture poked at him. The past tense of his admission was important. It meant he'd stopped using spirits to speed himself unto death. It might not make a lick of difference to her, but it was something to him.

It was time to put an end to this farce. "Your service in this household is terminated immediately."

Disbelief marched across her face, a second held, then she laughed. Not the response he'd expected. He'd witnessed more than one man quake in his boots when he'd employed that particular tone, a fine blend of entitlement, arrogance, and anger.

Not this woman.

"You cannot terminate my employment. *You* do not truly employ me."

He'd never met such a saucy minx. "Tell Nick—"

"Tell him yourself," she said. "That's what this is all about."

He couldn't escape the feeling that she wanted to finish her sentence with *you dunderhead*, and he experienced the prick of truth. He'd been wrong to shut his brother out of his life these last several months, but he'd had no choice. Or, at least, that was how it felt. It was as if his very life had depended on him retreating from the world after his parents had unexpectedly died and he'd taken over the marquessate, his rather vague plan to have drunk himself into an early grave before the eventuality of inheriting the title, a failed effort.

"You may leave." He gave a flick of the wrist, the gesture intended to convey highhanded, aristocratic indifference, even if the opposite veered closer to the truth.

"Thank ye, milord," she said on a small, mocking curtsy, the Cockney accent returned. On silent cat feet, she crossed the room and was pulling the door open when she stopped. She pivoted and pinned him with her striking blue gaze that cut through the shadowy light. "Would you like to know something?"

"Likely not," Jamie replied, honest.

He'd never spoken to a woman thusly. But then, neither had one ever spoken to him like she did. Before he'd become an actual marquess, he'd been a future one and the Earl of Pembroke, which had afforded him no small measure of awe and respect, particularly from those of lower rank and class. This woman clearly didn't give two figs about his title or the awe and respect due him. He braced himself for whatever words were about to spill from her pert mouth.

"You are Nick's brother."

"An established fact, I believe."

"I thought—" Her head canted, and an assessing light glinted in her eyes. "I thought you would be more impressive."

With that, she exited the room as silently as she'd entered it. Her words, however, stayed behind and permeated the air like a noxious flume, crawling through Jamie and filling him with their poison, so all he could do was steam and stew, even as he wanted to roar with frustration.

He was a lord. Lords were impressive. Therefore, *he* was impressive. Everyone knew it.

But she'd been speaking of a different sort of impressiveness, or a lack thereof.

Her disdain wakened a primal animal inside him. He tried to tamp it down, but to have a woman—any woman, but especially that woman for some cockeyed reason—speak those words to him—a marquess, a *man*—well, they made him want to spring up from this chair and prove to her exactly how impressive he was.

He shoved back in his chair and released a rough breath. He stared into the low fire and attempted to let its calm seep into him. Most nights it worked, as this study was his retreat, the only room in this sprawling mansion that felt like his. The rest of it, well, the rest of it felt like *theirs*.

He snorted. Not *theirs*. Not anymore. Ghosts didn't hold possessions. Those possessions and titles were passed down to first sons, whether they cared to have them or not.

He cast an eye toward the empty brandy decanter no more than ten feet away. Five months ago, he'd drained it to the last dregs, on the night Father and

Mother's carriage hadn't successfully negotiated a hairpin turn and careened off a cliff.

Dead in each other's arms. An awed light had entered the magistrate's eye when he'd related that detail. Jamie had accepted the words stoically and refrained from informing the man that his parents would rather spend eternity in the seventh circle of hell than a single minute locked in embrace.

Jamie had emptied the brandy decanter, gulp by bitter gulp, that night.

And, the next day, he hadn't refilled it.

Or the next.

Or the next after that.

Oh, it had been a temptation. Every night, hands shaking, he'd unstoppered the decanter and inhaled deeply of sweetish, heady fumes with their promise of oblivion, if only he would have it filled. He'd been a wastrel as the heir. Why not now as the master? It wasn't as if the Marquess and Marchioness of Clare had left behind a legacy worth preserving.

Quite the opposite. To say they would be missed or mourned was a lie.

The hate Father and Mother had borne one another was an inheritance of a more malicious sort. For that sort of hatred reached long tentacles and poisoned all it touched, including any relationships their two sons had ever formed. Nick's marriage to Mariana had suffered for a decade beneath the burden of it, until, somehow, they'd worked their way through it.

Jamie didn't begrudge Nick his happiness, for he understood like no one else the courage it must have taken to attain it. In fact, in a highly unusual move that had caught the attention of the gossip rags, Jamie had split all unentailed properties and monies down the middle with Nick. It was only fair, that was what the rags didn't know. Nick had suffered through the same wretched childhood as Jamie, full of all the humiliation and neglect two self-centered and uncaring parents could offer. Nick had earned his share.

His eye caught on the Bow Street Runner's report keeping the place in his book. It replaced the lie—a lie that had come directly from Father's mouth—he'd believed of Mollie Rafferty these last fourteen years with the truth. Every time he so much as glanced at the thin slip of paper, he felt gutted and betrayed and like the world's biggest fool all over again.

Mollie hadn't taken Father's money and run. The report in his hands attested to that fact. Instead, she'd suffered a fate much different from the one he'd imagined all this time.

Anger and shame roiled in his gut, turning it to acid and eating him from the inside. He was finding it difficult to live with this new information that he was powerless to change. It wasn't so long ago that he would have found the bottom of a brandy bottle and not come up for air for a fortnight.

He snorted. He didn't right understand why he hadn't imbibed yesterday or today. After all, drink was a known numbing agent for anger and shame. He knew from experience, however, it didn't cure either condition. Better to keep sinking into his role of teetotal recluse, a role he had no intention of climbing his way out of. Except…

Now that he was no longer a wastrel heir, he wasn't precisely sure what to do with himself.

He scanned the floor-to-ceiling bookcases on the opposite wall. The library had been filled by one of his forebears a few generations back as its stock of scientific journals, essays, treatises, and tomes reached as far as two centuries in the past. Not much else to do these last several months, he'd taken to reading through it. But one could only maintain so much interest in the lambing ease, high fertility, and plentiful milk yields of the Black Welsh Mountain variety of sheep and similar, yet disparate, topics.

Still, he couldn't help feeling the time was fast approaching when he would have to venture out of Asquith Court and fashion a life for himself as the Marquess of Clare, one with some semblance of meaning, possibly. It was a life that could easily carry him along on its current from one obligation to the next, if he would simply allow it and leave the past be. Why was he resisting? Why had he stirred the waters and sought out information about Mollie Rafferty after all these years?

On a burst of agitation, he shot to his feet and strode to the window overlooking St. James's Square. And, now, there was the matter of his recently departed visitor.

Nick had hired the woman to spy on him.

And she'd left here thinking Nick's brother wasn't an impressive man.

That his blood didn't boil at the very notion. He should dismiss and forget it. Why bother about what some slip of a woman he would never see again thought of him? Her opinion amounted to nothing.

Yet, somehow, it did. The woman didn't hold him in awe. A fact he found both annoying and strangely enlivening.

And those extraordinary eyes of hers, they might see through him.

Nay, not *through* him. *Into* him.

And they found him lacking?

The question poked at a place deep inside him that he never let others see, and rarely even himself. His entire life, his titles—past, present, and future—had been all that had given him distinction in the world's eyes. But behind that façade, he suspected a different truth.

There wouldn't be enough to him without them.

And that woman, well, she'd seen him—the true him —and it wasn't a flattering likeness, but one rather unimpressive.

His eye caught on a figure crossing the square. A slight figure. No thicker than a shadow…

Her.

Of course, she was leaving. He'd demanded as much. But…

Where was she walking with such a sure step?

Where did a woman like her go?

He started moving without consciously willing himself to do so. Within a minute, he was inside his dressing room and shoving one foot into a boot, the other hastily following. Then his arms were sliding into his greatcoat, and he was placing a topper on his head.

On his way out of his bedroom, he snatched a few cuts of meat from the late supper board near the door. As his appetite had been erratic these last few months, his butler, Stinton, had taken to placing various bits of food around to tempt him. The house would be teeming with rats soon if Jamie didn't put a stop to the practice. Tonight, however, he was grateful, for he was ravenous of a sudden.

He hadn't the faintest notion what he would discover about that blasted woman, but no matter. For the first time in months, curiosity moved through his body, invigorating him, spurring him forward. As the firstborn son and wastrel heir, his world had been limited to the pursuits of his rarified set, which had mostly amounted to drinking and carousing. A life that wasn't nearly as exciting as it was made out to be. Then once he'd inherited the title of Clare, his small world had shrunk even smaller to the four walls of Asquith Court in his self-imposed exile.

Tonight, he found that neither world suited him.

Tonight, he wanted to experience a different world.

Her world.

The very idea made his heart race and the blood rush through his veins.

He felt alive.

CHAPTER THREE

*H*ortense charged across the near-empty thoroughfare of Piccadilly, the street as quiet now as it was busy during the day, her feet a blur of motion mirroring that of her mind.

She was rattled.

By that man.

Since she'd been hired into the household by the housekeeper, Mrs. Blanche, tonight was her first interaction with the Marquess of Clare. Certainly, she'd caught glimpses of him from afar about Asquith Court as she'd scrubbed marble floors, dusted porcelain vases, and replaced wood in cold, needy fireplaces, invisible to him as any other servant. Which had been fine by her. She would much rather slink about the shadows. From experience, she understood that to be noticed by a master only invited trouble of one sort or another for a servant.

Tonight had been no exception.

Blast.

She'd allowed complacency to set in, assuming that since the master hadn't remained in his study the last three nights, he wouldn't tonight. What had Nick always told her?

Past doesn't predict future.

The possibility existed that an additional factor had lulled her into a false sense of security. The man was Nick's brother. How dissimilar could they be?

As different as black from white, it turned out.

Not if one went by their looks, however. The men shared a similar height and leanness of person. Dark hair that wanted to curl at the tips. Inscrutable, stormy gray eyes. Straight nose. Cheekbones and chin chiseled from marble. In short, *handsome.* Nick's handsomeness had never affected her one way or another. But the brother's...

His handsomeness was an altogether different matter, one it wouldn't do to examine too closely.

But, oh, how different in personality was this brother. *Arrogant. Condescending.* A rich, spoiled lord was all he was. *A marquess.*

And didn't he know it.

The impulse to provoke him had come all too naturally. *I thought you would be more impressive.* Oh, the fire that had sparked in his eyes. What had possessed her to speak such words to the man? She should have simply vacated the room and been done with him.

Yet she knew why she'd spoken thusly.

Because he was rich and spoiled and arrogant and condescending and had his life cinched up in a tidy bow for him. That such a man could get one over on her, well, it rankled. He'd caught her, and she'd lashed out, wanting him to feel the sting he'd delivered to her. For, she could admit to herself, the man possessed a natural impressiveness, an intelligence behind his eyes. She would wager he'd read every book, essay, and treatise in that study.

And about his arrogance, well, she'd always found a bit of arrogance about a person attractive. Not the

26

overweening sort. But an arrogance confident in its own abilities and able to deliver.

The condescension in his low, gravelly voice, she could do without entirely.

Anyway, she was clear of him, having left her uniform folded on the narrow maid's bed and decamped with naught more than the clothes on her back. She traveled light when on a job. Tomorrow, she would report her findings to Nick—his brother was alive and hadn't drunk himself to death—and that would be the end of it. Never again would she think about that man whose arrogance and handsomeness might turn her head a bit too much. Under different circumstances, of course.

Tonight, she had Lady Fortescue's terrier to rescue from a disgruntled former lover. She'd assured the lady that she would have the dog returned to her within a week, the end of which was tomorrow.

She lifted the collar of her rough, woolen jacket and tucked her chin into her neck to brace against the bite of a sudden north wind that April could produce. The townhouse she sought in Berkeley Square was only a few streets over.

Her ear picked up a night sound that wasn't quite right. Footsteps that had the surety of intention. She glanced over her shoulder. *Nick*, was her first impression. Then came another quick on its heels. No, it wasn't Nick rapidly closing the distance. It was the brother.

The marquess.

On the count of three, she whirled and planted her feet wide. He stumbled to a stop so as not to collide with her at full tilt. At close range, she was again struck by how remarkably like Nick he was.

"Clare," she said, her voice pitched low and hard. Over the years, she'd made more than one person rethink their choices with the narrowing of her singular blue eyes. Witch's eyes she'd heard them called.

He didn't flinch. "Call me Asquith."

His lordliness held no sway over her. "Your brother is Asquith."

"Then Jamie."

Mild shock ran through her at the suggested familiarity. But then lords had their own rules and tended to make them up as they went along. "How about I call you nothing?" she retorted. "We won't be in each other's company long enough for it to matter."

His head cocked. "No?"

What was the blasted man playing at?

"Why are you following me?" She might as well get to it. "I can assure you I didn't abscond with the family silver."

He snorted, cool, dismissive. "As if I care about the silver."

She mirrored the cock of his head. "A curious point." She allowed a loaded beat of time to pass. "What is it you *do* care about?"

Even in the near dark, she detected a shadow pass within his eyes. He cared about something or someone. Or *had*. She tamped down her instinct to pursue the line of intrigue. "Can you, at least, answer the first question? Why have you followed me?"

"I saw you leaving."

"That is generally what a servant does when she is dismissed from her master's employ."

The suggestion of a smile tipped at his mouth. "You said it yourself. You were never my servant."

She wanted to unleash a frustrated sigh, one she refused to indulge. He would likely enjoy it too much. "Which continues to beg the question."

"You're an associate of my brother's."

She was near enough now to notice the thick fringe

of black lashes encircling his gray eyes. They would strike the heart of any woman green with envy. "A fact established in your study."

"You're one of his spies," he stated with perfect certainty.

She was beginning to take a genuine dislike to this brother of Nick's. "Simply a favor for an old friend," she bit out.

One side of his mouth curved, imbuing his face with a saturnine cast. "You're too young to have old friends."

The cheek of the man. "Neither my age nor my whereabouts are of any concern of yours. Now, I really haven't the time or inclination to involve myself in sibling politics. So, if that is all, I have matters to attend and a night to get on with." An efficient pivot of the heel, and she was on her way.

"Wait," he called.

With great reluctance, she stopped and half turned, her eyebrows lifted in silent question.

He gestured up and down the length of her person. "Why are you dressed as a lad?"

Her body reluctantly followed the turn of her head. "A man, you mean. As a woman, I would be dressed as a man."

A dry laugh sounded through his nose. Maddening condescension radiated off him in waves. "Have you glanced in a mirror? You appear no older than a lad of ten years."

"Is that all?" she ground out. She didn't have to stand here and be insulted, even if she half suspected his words were true.

He gave his head a slow shake. "You haven't answered my question."

"I don't owe you an answer."

"Would you consider giving it for free?"

Was that a flash of playfulness she detected in his

serious gray eyes? "Everything in life is transactional," she said, the words the truest she'd spoken all night. "I bid you good evening, Clare."

She spun around and bolted up the sidewalk. Immediately, his heavy step began dogging hers. *Blast.* The man might be rich, spoiled, arrogant, and condescending, but he was tenacious, too.

"Where are you walking with such purpose this late at night?"

"You won't leave me be, will you?" she asked, beyond exasperated.

With annoying ease, he used the advantage of his longer stride and drew abreast of her. "I rather doubt it."

She shot him an incredulous glance and laughed. She couldn't seem to help it. The man was too much.

"What is your name?" he asked.

"*Ahh,*" she began and stopped, shock tracing through her. She'd almost blurted *Amelie,* a name she hadn't uttered in a dozen years. "Hortense," she said, righting the course.

His eyebrows crinkled together. "Are you certain? There seems to be some doubt."

"*Hortense.*" Most definitely Hortense.

She sewed her mouth shut before she could say—or *almost* say—some other unsettling thing.

She'd very nearly told him her name, her true name, the one Papa and Maman had called her. Why? Was it because he so resembled Nick? That couldn't be it. She'd never shared that name with Nick.

"Hortense is a French name, *non?*" Clare asked.

He was deducing rather a lot about her. Her earlier observation had been correct. He was a sharp one. She would do well to remember it. "I'm growing bored of this game and have a job to complete."

"Like the job you did for Nick tonight?"

"A different sort of job," she said, tart, but also a little sheepish. His question pricked. "One that has naught to do with you. So, if you will leave me be—"

"The way I see the matter, you owe me."

Another disbelieving laugh startled from her. "I owe you nothing."

"You've been creeping about my house for days and spying on me."

"It was a job, and nothing personal."

"Yet it had to do with my person. You're lucky I didn't call the night watch and have you arrested."

"You cannot be serious," she said, meeting his eye. She saw he was.

"However," he continued, "if you allow me to accompany you tonight, I shall forgive your debt."

She only just realized her mouth had fallen open. She snapped it shut. But, truly, this lord had some brass. "I owe you nothing," she repeated.

When he opened his mouth, surely to refute her statement, she held up a staying hand. The man was determined, and the job ahead of her, well, it wasn't a difficult one. Clearly, this spoilt, entitled lord was looking for a lark, and she was meant to provide it. With the rare exception, wasn't that how all lords viewed women like her?

"I'll allow it," she relented. "On a single condition."

"Name it," he said, his reply the vocal equivalent of a shrug. What sheer, bloody confidence the man possessed.

"That you leave me be after this night."

"You have my word."

She snorted. "And how do I know what your word is worth?"

Long, masculine fingers wrapped around her upper arm and pulled her to a stop. His gaze had gone dark and intense. She'd seen that expression before, on his brother, but never had she been its recipient.

"Are you implying that I am not an honorable man?" he all but growled.

She looked him square in the eye, though an unsettled shiver ran through her body. The free hand that could reach for the dagger strapped to her ankle clenched and unclenched, ready. "Unhand me."

He glanced down at his hand still clasped around her arm and released it.

"I am saying I don't know you," she continued, her voice careful and steady. "Therefore, I haven't the faintest clue as to the sort of man you are. And being of the aristocracy doesn't spontaneously confer honor onto a man. If anything, quite the opposite."

He held her gaze, revealing nothing of his thoughts, until, at last, he relented with a slow nod. Men and their stupid honor. Honor was usually what got them killed. She had no use for it.

"Right," she said, all business, her feet on the move again, leaving that shaky feeling in the dust. "Let's get on with this night, shall we?"

Somewhat mollified, Clare asked, "What part of town is this job?"

"Berkeley Square."

"And the job itself?"

"We're, um—" She almost didn't want to speak it aloud, but the man would know sooner rather than later. "We are rescuing a kidnapped dog."

Clare's eyebrows shot together. He was wondering if he'd heard her correctly. The next moment, a smile spread across his face, his mouth losing its sardonic curl. He was a man transformed by that smile of his, no longer the brooding marquess, but an altogether different man. One possessed of humor. One appealing and beautifully handsome.

32

She had to look away. That smile rendered the man too attractive by half.

"A kidnapped *dog*?" His laugh echoed off the limestone townhouses to either side of them.

"Shush," she chided, holding a finger to her mouth. She didn't need a startled resident calling out for the night watch. "Jobs come in all forms."

"And species." His rakish smile hadn't abated a whit.

A responding smile twitched about her mouth, but she suppressed it and kept placing one foot in front of the other, navigating the few remaining streets in silence, until, at last, they arrived at a discreet black iron gate.

She crouched and bid Clare do the same. Her voice pitched low, she said, "The garden has a guard, so follow me closely and—" She held a finger to her mouth, hoping he would understand the time for talk had come to an end.

She pressed her face against wrought iron bars and peered through, scanning garden grounds cast in myriad shades of night grays and blacks. At last, she located the guard a good twenty yards in the distance. Limbs relaxed, head tipped to the side, the man was settled on a bench, stealing a nap. The ex-lover had neglected to collect the key to his private garden from Lady Fortescue upon their final parting. Hortense pulled the silver key from her jacket pocket, twisted it in the lock, and pushed the gate open only wide enough to permit first her, then Clare.

Even in the dark, it was a beautiful garden, spring blossoms of all varieties bursting into various stages of bloom. People like her—the *hoi polloi*—had access to a few public gardens, but nothing like this, ones filled with marble and bronze statuary, rare roses, and whimsical trails. A garden like this was for the rich, and only the rich.

Like the nob currently dogging her step.

"Does this job involve Sir Archibald Winthrop?" he whispered at her back.

Her eyes lifted toward the sky. Of course, this lord knew Sir Archibald Winthrop. All lords knew each other.

She held a finger to her mouth and continued creeping along the perimeter of the wall in a low crouch, hoping with every movement not to wake the guard. Fortunately, the townhouse was both dark and the last in its row, making it the nearest. Still, they would need to break cover to access the set of glass double doors.

She pointed down at their feet before crouching to remove her boots. She indicated that Clare do the same. His eyebrows drew together in question, then disbelief once he'd intuited her meaning.

"It's best to enter a house on stocking feet," she explained in a rushed whisper. Truly, the man was a bit of trouble.

She waited for him to balk at the idea—even hoped he would, so she could bid him farewell. But a few heartbeats later, he followed her lead.

She retrieved another key from a different pocket, flashed another quick glance toward the guard, whose soft snoring was barely audible across the grassy distance, and broke cover, Clare fast on her heels. Key at the ready, she slid it into the lock and twisted.

Or attempted to twist. The mechanism didn't budge.

"What is it?" came an urgent whisper, moving closer with each syllable.

"'Tis nothing." She tried again, putting all her weight into it. It refused to do as bid. A worry came to her. "The guard. Has he moved?"

"Dead to the world." A beat passed, and she felt

Clare draw closer, so close she could hear the intake of his breath, feel the heat of his much larger body. "Let me try."

"She must have given me the wrong key."

"Here," he said, using his larger mass to nudge her aside.

"I beg your pardon," she hissed, even as she accepted she might have to concede his point. He was larger and stronger. Further, he might be right.

She was beginning to give way when his hand covered hers. She startled back, but his fingers only gripped tighter. Her head whipped around, and she met the cool gray of his eyes.

Her heart, already at a quick trot, kicked into a full gallop. In sudden need of a deep breath, she inhaled flowery scents of the garden, but also, *him.*

Woodsy and warm, he smelled expensive, but not in an overbearing way, not perfumed like so many men of his class. It was a subtle aroma that made her want to draw nearer and nearer—which wouldn't do. Even so, he was the most delicious-smelling man she'd ever encountered.

He swallowed, and her eye followed the undulation of his throat. When her gaze lifted, what she detected in his eyes froze the breath in her chest.

Knowledge.

Oh.

He felt it, too, then.

35

CHAPTER FOUR

*H*e should release her.

Jamie understood that.

But he couldn't seem to loosen his fingers enough to allow her freedom.

A beat of the heart, then another, her hand and her spectacular blue eyes remained his captives. Her pink tongue gave her full bottom lip a quick lick. His mouth went dry.

What was happening, here, with this woman?

Of a sudden, in the way one ripped off a bandage with a single swift motion, he unclenched his fingers. She yanked back, but her eyes remained locked on his. "Give it a try before the guard wakes," she said, her voice a rasped whisper.

Jamie nodded and suppressed the unexpected flare of desire that had made his trousers go tight. He felt strangely caught out. As his fingers tightened on the key, he gave it his all, the muscles of his forearm straining with the effort. Just as he became concerned the key might break in the lock, the stubborn tumblers began to shift and, at last, released on a muted click. The woman—*Hortense*, she'd insisted, even though he sensed a half lie in the name—grabbed the handle and pushed the door open a crack, wide enough for her to slide through. She was like mercury, so liquid and quick was her movement. How easily she could slip through one's fingers.

Once inside, back pressed to the glass-paned door, it took him a moment to ascertain that they stood behind thick velvet curtains which had been drawn closed, only a few feet of space to either side of them. With two people within its dark confines, this was an intimate space.

Attuned to her, that was how his body felt. Deuced inconvenient was what it was.

She inched forward and used a single finger to part the curtain a sliver before peeking out. "The room is empty."

She stepped through the opening, and he followed into a drawing room that would have been cast in complete darkness if not for the banked fire in the hearth. It was an elegant room that also managed to have the look of a bachelor's residence, its colors muted, the woods dark, a lack of flowers and general femininity. It was a space Jamie understood well.

Hortense jutted her chin toward the fireplace. Before it, dozed a small, tan-and-white furry form curled up on a blanket. The kidnapped dog. A little terrier, by the looks of it, who was watching them with one eye open.

Disappointment shot through Jamie. This job looked to be an easy one, which meant they would be finished in a matter of minutes. Then he would return to Asquith Court.

That dread didn't fill him at the thought.

One careful step after another, Hortense crept toward the little dog. His head popped up and tipped to the side as he silently observed this human advancing upon him.

"*Dog*," she whispered.

The terrier's light brown ears pitched forward. Mayhap this wasn't going to be so simple.

"*Dog*," she tried again.

The animal showed his tiny white teeth and gave a little growl.

"Don't you know his name?" Jamie asked.

A curt shake of her head was all the reply he got.

"Try a sing-songy voice," he offered. "Like"—he cleared his throat—"*Dah-ogg*."

Well, that was silly, wasn't it?

Her gaze flashed to meet his, humor shining in her eyes. The woman was most definitely stifling a snicker. She opened her mouth to possibly laugh him out of the room when the dog shot to his four feet and began a sustained growl, one that shook his compact body from head to paw. He wasn't having it.

The sudden slam of a door at the front of the townhouse drew all three sets of eyes. Next came the rustle of silk skirts, followed by the low, cajoling rumble of a masculine voice and a delighted feminine giggle.

Sir Archibald Winthrop had returned home.

With a paramour.

And judging by the increasing volume, the couple was approaching this room.

Hortense jerked her chin toward the curtains. Before Jamie knew what he was about, he'd grabbed her hand and pulled her into the alcove with him. And in the nick of time, too, as the party of two, who sounded no small bit tipsy, entered the room.

He glanced down to find wide eyes staring up at him, expectancy in their depths. "What is it?" he whispered.

Her gaze lowered, and he felt it land on his hand still grasping hers. His fingers released her slender hand that instant. He couldn't seem to keep his hands off hers.

What a strange and puzzling night this was turning out to be. He wasn't certain he even *liked* the woman, yet he seemed to be drawn to her in ways that had naught to do with his conscious mind.

"Shall we go?" he asked, seeing no other option.

Her gaze hardened to steel. "Leave if you like, but I never give up on a job. That dog will be caught."

She parted the curtains an inch and pressed one eye to the gap. Over her head, Jamie was just able to make out Winthrop on the other side of the room pouring a pair of brandies. Those two weren't going anywhere soon. A barely perceptible groan of frustration released with Hortense's breath. She crouched low and waggled her fingers through the slit in the curtains. From his nest of blankets, the dog observed her with a guarded eye and moved not a muscle.

Jamie's ear picked up a sound, both familiar and predictable. The smacking of wet flesh on flesh. Winthrop and his companion, they'd begun—*deuce it all* —a rather amorous bout of kissing on the chaise longue.

He dropped to a crouch beside Hortense and waggled his fingers alongside hers to entice the terrier. He understood the direction of Winthrop's night, and he had no intention of being here for it.

Unfortunately, his efforts had the opposite of the desired effect upon the dog. Clearly wearied of this game, the feisty pooch barked once, twice, until it turned into a full-on yapping. As one, Jamie and Hortense startled backward.

Winthrop, thinking the dog was barking at him, shouted out, "Oh, shut it, you little pest," and threw a pillow in the general direction of the animal. The pillow hit wide of the mark both literally and figuratively, for now the terrier was directing his animus toward Winthrop.

"I take it this is the first time you've attempted wooing a dog away from its kidnapper?" Jamie whispered, his mouth an inch from the whorl of Hortense's ear.

Her jaw tensed.

He detected a reluctance to provide a truthful answer in the movement.

"Might be." The confession sounded pulled from her as easily as an extracted tooth. "Winthrop was supposed to be out until dawn. Now, shush, and let me think."

Another feminine giggle wafted across the room, this one pitched lower, emerging from deep within the woman's throat. This giggle left no doubt where the next few minutes were leading. Next sounded a released sigh with a little moan at the end. Items of clothing began to be discarded at a rate both alarming and haphazard.

Face pale, Hortense's eyes flashed up to meet Jamie's, panic clanging in their depths. And something more, too.

Awareness.

The intimate space behind the black velvet curtains suddenly halved in size. It became warmer, too.

Nay, not merely warmer. *Hot.*

He swallowed and found himself loosening his cravat.

Then came other sounds. Rhythmic sounds accompanied by a noise that resembled the mewling of a cat.

Oh, lord. What he needed was a glass of water.

Or a dunk in it, more like.

Hortense's gaze broke from his and found her feet. He wasn't sure he could endure this.

The moans.

The groans.

The *oh's*.

The *ah's*.

The sound of one naked body sliding against another.

The couple fornicating on the chaise longue weren't the only ones sweating in this room. Awareness blossomed into full effulgence.

Awareness of his body.

Awareness of her body.

Awareness of his body in relation to her body. His was rangy and hulking compared to her small, graceful form. Yet he suspected they would join together in a perfect fit.

She bit her lower lip between her teeth, and his overriding thought was that he wanted nothing more than to test its delicate plumpness between his own teeth. *Cherries*, he decided. She would taste like cherries.

He summoned the last shreds of his willpower. When had he last experienced desire? Months? *Years?*

A particularly strident screech jerked him back into reality. The sexual interlude on the other side of the curtains was only getting louder and rowdier and shoutier.

And the interlude that had begun to play out in his head with the woman at his side, well, best stop at lips and cherries.

"Don't you think it would be wise to go?" he asked. Wisdom, that was what the moment called for. The wisdom of Solomon. His cock, however, had other ideas as it stretched hard against the superfine of his trousers.

The stubborn woman at his side shook her head. "Not without the dog."

Jamie inhaled a groan of a thousand frustrations, but one in particular. "Have any ideas come to you?"

"We need…" Her gaze screwed up to the ceiling as if she might find the answer there.

"What?" he asked, jumping on her words. He needed her to save him from himself. "We need *what*?"

"We need…" she began again. "We need something to lure him."

"A lure?" Jamie patted his coat pocket. "Like food?" he asked, the idea only just coming to him.

Black eyebrows crinkled together, questioning. "Um, yes."

When he dug a small cut of bacon from the pocket, her mouth gaped open for the split of a second. No small amount of gratification coursed through him. He suspected it was bloody difficult to shock the woman.

Decision entered her eyes, and she stepped forward —so close her subtle scent reached his nose. *Fresh… clean…lemon*—and reached up. He went rigid in anticipation of her touch. Perhaps a brush of his cheek. Or mayhap her slender fingers would slide around his neck and curl into his hair. He didn't think he would mind very much.

Or at all.

Her hands, however, stopped at his neck and began tugging at his cravat. "Pardon?" There was no mistaking the scratch of desire in his throat.

"I need this."

Words his body yearned to hear, but not about his cravat.

Her clever fingers made quick work of the garment before sliding it off his neck. She tied one end around the bacon and parted the curtain the necessary inch to cast the meat like a fishing lure. It landed with a soft thud, too muted for the couple to hear, caught up as they were in what sounded like a competitive shouting match.

The little terrier's nose started working, then his head popped up. In a flash, he sprang to his four legs and, nose to the floor, began following the trail of meat as Hortense pulled the cravat, careful to keep the bacon just out of reach.

Jamie parted the curtain only wide enough to admit the cantankerous canine. Hortense snatched him up and offered the meat on her open palm. The dog gobbled it in a single bite. His little face stared up at her for more, all innocence. "Greedy beast," she muttered.

Jamie felt a smile threaten to release. Those kept trying to escape. He suppressed the betraying muscles of his mouth and made himself useful by pushing the exterior door open. "After you."

She poked her head out and glanced both ways, presumably checking for the guard. Then she swept through the narrow doorway, her shoulder brushing his arm in the tight space. An unexpected trace of electricity streaked through him. What a novel effect this one small woman had on his person. He shoved the thought aside and followed, joining her in the shadow of the perimeter wall where they'd left their boots.

"Do you have any more of that meat?" she asked in a rushed whisper.

Jamie glanced down and found the little terrier growling up at him from her arms. He felt around his pocket, located another cut of bacon, and extended it. The dog took one cautious sniff, then another, before snapping up the savory treat.

Hortense tucked the terrier deeper beneath her arm, while he remained somewhat content, and again hugged the perimeter wall as they scurried out of the garden at a fast clip. They didn't speak again until they were half a street away.

"I must ask," she said, not slowing her step. "How did you happen to have bacon with you?"

"Stinton leaves trays of food lying around as my appetite has become somewhat capricious." Why couldn't he curb this tendency to reveal himself to this woman? "Then I hied off after you. Hence, bacon."

That pulled a reluctant smile from her. That he felt so gratified by it was perplexing. "I should thank you for saving the job," she said.

"You can if you like. I won't stop you."

She snorted. Her lips pressed shut, no such thanks forthcoming. She slowed her pace to one more reasonable, one that invited conversation.

"That was," he found himself saying, "*fun*." The word emerged like it was a new experience. "We could do it again."

Incredulous eyes rounded on him. "That was not our agreement."

"Agreements can be amended."

She would never agree to such an arrangement, so why was he pushing her?

Because something inside him couldn't resist.

"Not ours," she said, firm, definite. "Now, this is where we part."

He glanced around the neat rows of townhouses stretching to either side of them. "You reside in Mayfair?"

"Of course not."

"I shall see you to your lodgings." His lordly tone brooked no disagreement.

"That is quite unnecessary." She resumed walking, clearly intent on leaving him in her dust.

He held his tongue and allowed his feet to carry the conversation for him as he drew alongside her. He would see her to her lodgings. He was a gentleman, after all.

On they strode through London in silence. Even the little terrier kept his peace and hardly tugged at the lead she'd fashioned from the cravat. They traversed streets, byways, and alleys, exiting the tame environs of Mayfair into the heart of the city many in his social strata never experienced firsthand. London was never completely asleep, but this was as close as it got, few others crossing their path, and the ones who did, giving them not a moment's notice.

In the deep reaches of Westminster, her step slowed, and she indicated a building ahead. "This is where we part ways."

He gave the edifice a once-over—nondescript gray, black trim, its only decoration the number eleven. "You live here?"

He was stalling. Why?

An answer forwarded itself, one he didn't especially like. An answer that explained why he'd said they could do this again.

She glanced up, a glint in her eye. What an extraordinary blue they were. As if the Mediterranean Sea had been hit with a lightning bolt. The terrier at her feet pinned him with the exact same look, except his eyes were brown. "I have a question for you," she said.

"Go on."

"How did you know I'd been in your study? I was careful."

At this reminder of the reason for their first encounter—no more than two hours ago—his outrage made an attempt to flare up. But its former ire could muster not much more than a fizzly spark.

"The inkwell," he said.

She frowned. "Pardon?"

"The inkwell wasn't at its usual angle."

Her brow lifted. "And you noticed?"

45

"Aye."

"Huh."

"What?"

She gave her head a curt shake, as if trying to clear muck from it. "You're not so different from your brother, are you?"

"As day from night."

"And which are you?"

He opened his mouth and shut it. In truth, he wasn't certain.

Without another word, she scooped up the little terrier and ducked into a narrow alleyway that Jamie only just noticed. His eye followed her until she disappeared through a doorway.

And all the while he kept his feet firmly rooted in place, for if he gave them leave, they might try to follow the frustratingly interesting woman.

Something in him didn't want to let this night go.

But it was no use. He commanded his feet to move, away from her street, away from her neighborhood, one step in front of the other.

He attempted to hold on to the feeling that had started humming through his body tonight at the very first sight of her. It was one he hadn't felt in months, years, maybe his entire life. Yes, there had been the outrage, but what had followed was singular. Excitement, yes, but something more.

The air around that woman held a brightness, an unpredictability.

Hers was an unusual life, one he'd never understood in all the years Nick had engaged in it. But, tonight, he'd been given a glimpse, and he'd be damned if he didn't want more.

For some deuced reason, he wanted to be impressive to that woman who he suspected was quite impressive herself.

You're not so different from your brother, are you?

When she'd asked the question, again, he'd felt it. *Seen.* He didn't quite understand it, but this woman *saw* him. Strangely, it mattered.

At last, his feet led him to St. James's Square, and his mausoleum of a mansion. Dread sank to the pit of his stomach, as with each stride, the night faded further behind him.

Ahead lay his future, the opposite of tonight. *Predictable...dull...*

Alone.

Except... What if it didn't have to be? What if...

Of course.

What if he had a use for her?

His cock twitched.

Not *that* use.

At the end of his report, the Bow Street Runner had asked how Jamie wanted to proceed. He'd delayed his reply, weighing whether or not to let the matter of Mollie Rafferty drop. But he understood now that he was being disingenuous with himself. He'd raised the dead, and though fourteen years had passed, he needed to know how, why, and what happened to her.

Tonight, he'd met just the person to find the answers to those questions.

Convincing her to agree would be an entirely different matter.

CHAPTER FIVE

$\mathcal{T}$he lead in Hortense's hand pulled taut and yanked her to an abrupt halt.

A now familiar frustration took flight inside her. This was the tenth stop in the last fifty feet. She'd been counting. Who knew such a little dog could be so strong and so very curious?

She was accustomed to an economy of movement that involved traveling from one place to another in as efficient a way as possible. The little terrier—and his bold nose—had other ideas, which involved exploring interesting scents to his thorough satisfaction and then relieving himself on them. She'd taken to calling him Sir Bacon, due to his penchant for the savory meat and his aristocratic upbringing. For a blue-blooded pet, however, he certainly displayed a variety of uncouth manners.

Speaking of aristocrats, it was from Lady Fortescue's Mayfair townhouse they were now returning. An unproductive trip, to say the least, for Sir Bacon remained at her side, his tiny legs matching her longer stride five steps to her one, when he was walking and not sniffing. The terrier's energy was boundless, as was his bladder, for last night he'd piddled twice on her bedroom floor and once on the bed. Truth told, she hadn't minded him so much once he'd settled and curled next to her in sleep.

What did bother her exceedingly was that Lady Fortescue hadn't been in to receive him today. The woman wasn't even in London. She'd up and sped off to her Hampstead estate and wouldn't return for an indeterminate number of days. This fact had been relayed to her by a kitchen maid who hadn't bothered hiding her delight.

Initially, Hortense had shrugged at the unexpected development—she could collect payment another day —and extended the dog's lead toward the maid. With a decided shake of her head, the girl took a hasty step backward, then another for good measure. "Oh, no. With 'er ladyship gone, I don't fancy cleanin' up after this scoundrel."

The kitchen door had closed in Hortense's dumbfounded face, and that was it. Sir Bacon would remain her charge for the foreseeable future. She spared a glance for the terrier. He did possess a certain charm with his short, jaunty stride and proud bearing.

His nose drew him to a stop. Yet again. "Oh, Sir Bacon. Can't you see number eleven is just ahead?"

She calculated a distance of one hundred feet to her destination. Which meant twenty vexatious stops between here and there.

Of a sudden, a feeling prickled across her skin. She glanced about until she found a pair of eyes steadily trained upon her from across the street. Crouched into a nondescript corner, the boy was scruffy and clothed in rags and unlikely to be given a second glance, precisely as all eels wanted it. Having caught her attention, he unfolded his lanky form and stood. Then he tipped his cap and scurried off, the message sent. Doyle expected a tax payment tonight.

She had his tax. A small brass horse rearing on its hind legs—Doyle had a penchant for both brass and horses—that looked to receive the dusting feathers but twice a year. In other words, such a bauble wasn't likely to be missed by Winthrop.

A quiver of ice shot through her. But for how long? How long could she keep this up? How many times would "this time" be the last time?

In front of near the boardinghouse, she noted a magnificent dapple-gray horse, whose reins were being held by a rather smart groom, drawing the eye of every passerby. Such an animal wasn't often seen in these parts.

Her gut churned. It was a sight more familiar in locales like, say, Mayfair and St. James's Square.

Intrigued, but mostly suspicious, she decided to enter the boardinghouse by the main front door, instead of taking the alley entrance directly to her rooms. She was reaching for the handle when the door swung inward. Dead center in the opening stood Mrs. Hayhurst, tall, erect, and dressed in her customary head-to-toe black. What wasn't usual was the frantic look in her eyes. "You have a caller," she said, her voice a rushed whisper.

"Oh?" Hortense remained calm for the sake of the other woman.

Mrs. Hayhurst's gaze dropped. "What is this?"

"A dog." She'd known this confrontation was coming.

"But...but why is it *here?*" The landlady's eyes narrowed. "While I do tolerate your eccentric requests and odd hours, a mongrel in my house is quite out of the—"

Hortense held up a hand to stay the remainder of Mrs. Hayhurst's scold. "This mongrel is Sir Bacon. You and I will speak about him—and fitting recompense —later."

The other woman exhaled a *harrumph*, but an avaricious glint had entered her gaze at *fitting recompense*. Sir Bacon's stay could be negotiated for a price. Hortense suppressed a sigh. The world could be such a predictable place.

"Now," she said, "you were saying about this caller?"

Mrs. Hayhurst blinked, and the harried look returned. Her voice lowered a confidential octave. "'Tis a *gentleman* caller. I've shown him into the communal drawing room."

Hortense gave the landlady a nod, and she and Sir Bacon brushed past. The visitor was likely Nick, and the horse outside was his. Early this morning, she'd sent a note informing him that a report on his brother was ready at his earliest convenience.

Yet one detail niggled at the back of her mind. Nick had never entered the front door of Mrs. Hayhurst's establishment, always opting for the back stairwell directly to her rooms when he'd needed to see her.

Hortense poked her head inside the drawing room and was relieved to see she'd been correct, for there at the opposite end of the room stood Nick staring out the window that overlooked Little Peter Street. She considered the wild possibility it could be the brother.

She gave herself a mental shake. She couldn't think about the brother. Because if she thought about the brother, she would think about last night and the job. And if she thought about the job, well, she might think about the couple beyond the curtains going at each other like a pair of badgers in heat...and the man stuck with her in hiding. And his delicious scent and his long, masculine fingers and the deep, attractive rumble of his voice and the unbearable heat that had streaked through her at the combination of all of the above.

The fact was simple. The man held an attraction for her.

She was no virginal miss, but neither was she the sort who tupped every man she found attractive. That behavior only got a woman in trouble, of either the family variety or the diseased. Neither option held an ounce of appeal.

So, yes, it was a very fine thing that it was Nick who was paying a call.

Sir Bacon leading the way, she strode confidently into the room, a greeting on her lips. He turned at her approach, and she stopped dead in her tracks. Her mouth snapped shut.

It wasn't Nick at all.

It was the brother.

Lord James Asquith, the Marquess of Clare.

Jamie, as he'd requested to be called.

And, somehow, he was more attractive in the light of day, dressed in the typical finery of the London gentleman: gleaming Hessian boots, buff buckskin breeches, hunter green morning coat, and impeccably knotted white silk cravat. Yet the way he filled out the finery with his broad shoulders and muscular thighs was, well, anything but the usual.

And she'd called *this* man unimpressive?

By contrast, 'twas she who was unimpressive, with her dull gray dress, dull gray cloak, and dull brown boots. All clean, but decidedly plain, as they were intended to be. She didn't dress to attract attention. Quite the opposite. So why should she feel shabby? She'd never cared before; why should she now?

She cleared her throat, even if her mind was less easily ameliorated. "To what do I owe the pleasure of this visit?" Her tone implied anything but *pleasure*. "I believed our association with one another to have reached its natural conclusion." Irresistibly, she added, "Again, I didn't abscond with the silver."

He jerked his chin toward Sir Bacon. "He is still in your care?"

"Indeed." Impossible to mask her pique.

"And I see my cravat continues to serve its new purpose."

Her gaze landed on the length of white silk. "Oh."

Of course, he would want such a fine garment returned. She dropped to a crouch and began tugging at the knot at Sir Bacon's neck. The feisty canine gave a fleeting growl but submitted. "Let me just—"

"There is no need."

The knot was proving its mettle and not giving. "I'll have it off—"

"Keep it."

Her fingers stopped. Simple, quiet, and sure, Clare's command wasn't to be nay-sayed. She glanced up and found him watching her. Was that a glint of humor in his gray eyes? Warily, she rose to a stand.

"You never did thank me last night for wooing this beast," he said.

"I put it down to luck."

"I put it down to the slice of bacon I happened to have in my pocket."

She shrugged one shoulder, as if indifferent, when, in fact, she was well aware the blasted man had rescued the job from certain disaster. But that didn't mean she had to like it. Or thank him for it. "The nature of the business can be fickle."

His eyebrows lifted in disbelief. "You truly are going out of your way *not* to thank me."

"Why are you here?" she asked, ready to put him as wrong-footed as he'd done her.

All traces of humor fading, he made his way to the room's lone settee, lowered to its threadbare cushion, and crossed one leg over the other, as if he owned the place. The man was aristocratic, no doubt about it, but his movement wasn't stiff or inhibited. He had a natural ease about him.

He pinned her with his stormy, arrogant gaze. Another beat of time passed, this one interminable. She wouldn't shift on her feet and show her discomfort. She simply wouldn't. Would he never state his business?

"I would like to hire you," he said, at last.

Shock, sudden and jarring, flashed through her. What in the—

Then she remembered. He was a *marquess*. In short, a nob having a lark. He'd gotten a taste for adventure last night, and it wasn't yet out of his system. "I make a terrible maid. Your household can do better," she said, deliberately obtuse. Mayhap it would discourage him from whatever mad proposition he was about to put forth.

All it did was pull a sardonic grin from him. "How droll."

If that was all he had to say, so be it. Unwilling to smooth the way for him, she gave silence permission to fill the air and create a bit of discomfort. Let him encounter a few bumps in the road. Likely, no one ever threw those his way.

"I am here to retain your investigative services."

"Missing a dog?" she asked.

"Hardly."

"Cheating lover?"

He snorted. If a snort could sound lordly, his did.

"Why me?" she asked. "A Bow Street Runner would likely serve your purposes, whatever they are."

"I've already gone down that road."

"Go down it again."

He gave his head a slow shake. "I don't want a runner." He uncrossed his legs and sat forward, elbows on

54

his knees. Of a sudden, he took up all the space in the room. "I want you."

The breath vacated her lungs. That he could speak such words...

"For the job, of course," he amended, but not sheepishly so.

She gathered her composure. And her wits. "My calendar is full."

"This is a matter of some delicacy," he continued, as if she hadn't just refused him.

"Do I strike you as delicate?"

His head cocked, and his eyes narrowed in assessment. "In truth?"

Something in the sound of that question made her nerves perk to life, but she nodded anyway.

"You might be."

Her lungs felt suddenly too full of air. She could ignore those three words. She must. Otherwise, she might wonder what else he saw in her.

"What's the job?" she asked against her better judgment. She would be drawn in if she wasn't careful.

"I need you to uncover what happened to a woman."

Of course, came a cynical thought. *Delicate matters* always involved women. "The women in your set aren't too difficult to trace, and you'll find servants are usually willing to part with information for a bob or two. There only a few places your lady could be."

"She wasn't my *lady* in the strictest sense."

"Her London townhouse," she continued, ignoring him. "Or her country estate."

"To be clear, she wasn't from my social set."

Again, the past tense. Further, she'd caught a note in his voice, a note that lingered for an instant in his eyes. Was that...*pain*?

She must ignore whatever emotion she detected in

his eyes, which was surely none of her concern, and refuse him, for three simple reasons.

He was Nick's brother.

He only saw her as a means to a lark.

He set her nerves ajangle with a mere glance.

"I have quite a few jobs in the queue that will fill my time for the foreseeable future."

She had one job lined up. And one to finish. She glanced down at Sir Bacon, sitting at her feet, licking parts that should remain private. He truly had no manners.

"Now, if that is all," she said, hoping to speed this encounter to its inevitable end. "I do have a day to get on with." She inched toward the door.

The man didn't move a muscle. "I'll pay double your going rate."

The words about to fly from her mouth fell to the floor. *Double?* Temptation, sly and beguiling, lifted its head and posed a question. *What if—*

She didn't allow it to finish. She must refuse. She simply could not get mixed up with Nick's too attractive, aristocratic brother who might make the blood fizz in her veins. "While I appreciate the generosity of your offer, I must decline—"

"*Triple.*"

The reasons for her refusal grew hazy. *Triple?* How difficult could it be to find one woman who, by the sound of it, wasn't alive?

"But you don't know the amount you are tripling," she said, giving him another opportunity to regain his senses and see the ridiculousness of the situation.

Face set in inscrutable granite, he stood and strode —did the man walk any other way?—to the escritoire, which had seen better days, judging by the deep scratches and scuffs scarring its surface. He began rifling through drawers until his hand emerged holding a scrap of paper, which he immediately set about scribbling upon. Then he strode to where she stood and stopped not three feet away, paper extended.

His scent reached out and enveloped her in its now familiar notes of birchwood and patchouli. Resisting the urge to inhale deeply of his delicious aroma, she took the scrap.

"That is the sum I'm willing to pay if you agree to the job."

She glanced down, and her pulse ticked up into a full tilt run. Could that number be true?

She blinked. The sum remained the same.

It could, and it was.

The number on this insignificant scrap of paper represented a year's worth of spying on aristocratic men's cheating wives, and vice versa. He'd made it impossible to refuse, and his arrogant expression said he knew it.

His cool gray gaze narrowed. "I have two conditions."

Her body went rigid with tension. *Conditions.* Of course. There always were when dealing with powerful men. They were so very accustomed to having their every thought and desire catered to. Why should he expect anything less in this instance?

Well, he would see.

She crossed her arms. Sir Bacon, sensing the change in her demeanor, gave a little growl. "The first condition?"

"Nothing nefarious, I can assure you. It's simple, really."

She braced herself.

"I accompany you."

"Accompany me?"

"I take part in your investigation," he explained, rather too patiently.

"But why?"

He shrugged and flicked a piece of lint off his otherwise impeccable sleeve. "Call it a whim."

"A whim?" She scoffed. "You're not a whimsical man."

"And what more do you know about me?" he asked low and hard. Only last night he'd caught her sneaking into his study. She knew a few things about him.

Even as butterflies fluttered about her insides, it was vital she stand firm and give back the same as she got. "I hardly know you at all, but I know that much."

Again, his sardonic smile appeared. "I am involved every step of the way, understood?"

She should say no. She should say no. *She should say no.*

Instead, she held up the paper. "Double the figure."

He snorted, as only a lord could. He would refuse, she knew it. Then his hand shot out. "You have a bargain."

She swallowed before taking his hand. It was warm and masculine and possessed of a firm, assured grip. If his eyes didn't convey the message decidedly, his handshake did. She wouldn't be backing away from their bargain. Her fate was sealed.

She experienced a pang of misgiving. She'd always been able to handle any situation and any eventuality, with few exceptions. She had a reputation for it. But now, with this man, she wasn't so sure.

What had she done?

She made to pull her hand back, but his held fast. "When do we start?"

"Tomorrow."

"Why not today?"

A laugh startled from her. "Contrary to what you were likely taught since birth, you are not the sun around which the universe orbits." With those words came a return to her senses and her customary mettle as she reclaimed her hand with a neat, little jerk. "What is this woman's name?"

"Shall we sit while we confer?" He waved toward the settee.

She swept around him, perched on the edge of the chair opposite, and waited while he sat. "Her name?" she asked, rattling off the first question of any new client interview.

"Mollie Rafferty."

"Irish?"

"Her parents came over from Ireland when she was a babe."

"Where did you meet her?"

"At Pett's Coffeehouse in Covent Garden."

"And where did you last see her?"

"Her apartment rooms on Honey Lane."

"Cheapside? Decent neighborhood." But not Mayfair. A picture of the woman and Clare's relations with her was beginning to form.

He held her eye. "It was the flat I let for her."

And here it was, the clear picture. Mollie Rafferty had been kept by him. Hortense couldn't help feeling a bit disappointed. It was always this sort of business with lords. Yet she'd thought this one might be different.

"And when was your last meeting?"

"Fourteen years ago."

"What did the runner tell you?"

"That she is dead."

Although she'd suspected it, a trace of shock ran through Hortense at the bluntness of the statement. It was as if he had to speak the words in a gruff manner to hide...what? She didn't know this man, or the way he should be speaking such words. *Right.* "Dead people tend to stay in one place," she said. "She shouldn't be too difficult to locate."

"I want to know how, why, and what happened to her." A heavy beat of time loped past. "I need to know."

She would ignore the note of emotion that had strayed into the word *need*. He wouldn't appreciate it being acknowledged. She knew that much, too. "Have the runner make further inquiries."

"Again, I want *you* to make them."

"Did the runner tell you where she died?"

"Bermondsey."

Acid swirled in the pit of Hortense's stomach. It was the same every time she heard the name of that place. "A large area to cover. Did he narrow it down at all?"

"A workhouse."

She willed steadiness into her voice. "St. Mary Magdalen?"

"That's the one."

There it was, as her gut had suspected. It would be that workhouse. The walls of the drawing room began to shrink in size, narrowing with each quick inhalation of her lungs.

Clare's eyes formed into slits. "Are you well?"

She willed her body to calm itself, even as emotion rioted through her. After all these years, St. Mary Magdalen held a power over her. Yet that past had naught to do with the job at hand. "Quite," she croaked.

"I don't believe you."

The words hung in the air, her gaze latching on to his as if for a lifeline. Was that *concern* she detected between the spaces of those four words? And why did they sweep the panic from her body?

"You don't have to believe me," she retorted. It was what she would say.

And it succeeded, for he gave another of his lordly

snorts and settled back. They both understood she'd recovered herself.

"Are we off to the workhouse now?" he asked, again trying to gain his way.

"No."

"Why not?"

"It's not the correct time of day."

"I don't see why that—"

"Not today," she said, willing authority into her tone. Vital when dealing with an aristocrat. "Tomorrow."

His jaw tensed and released, but his eye remained ever watchful upon her. At last, he nodded.

Equilibrium mostly recovered, she began issuing a series of instructions. "Arrive here tomorrow at three of the clock. Ride in your coach and four. You do have a coach and four, don't you?"

"Of course." He sounded mildly offended.

"And wear your absolute finest togs. Something with brass or gold thread."

His eyebrows lifted in question.

"To get someone at St. Mary Magdalen to talk," she explained, "you're going to need the full weight of your pomp and title." She remembered something else they would need. "And coin. Bring a pouch full of it." She sat back in her chair. "That's everything."

A sudden smile lit up his face. The one that rendered him a touch too attractive. "Am I dismissed?"

He wasn't wrong. She had, indeed, dismissed him, a marquess. It was likely a novel experience. One she was only too happy to provide. "You are."

Smile slipped but a few notches, he stood and offered her a shallow bow. "Until tomorrow, Miss Marchand."

She began to reply and stopped. *What had he just*

called her? "How do you know my surname? I haven't given it to you."

"Your landlady is perhaps not as discreet as you would prefer."

The blasted man was about to sweep from the room when she remembered something. "Clare?"

Hand on the door handle, he half turned. "Yes?"

"Your second condition? You never said."

The sardonic glint returned to his eye. "I stipulate that you call me Jamie."

"Highly irregular," she said, as she must say something. She didn't want to call him Jamie. It was too familiar, and familiarity only bred more familiarity.

"Indulge me," emerged from his mouth on a low, velvet rumble that very nearly stole her breath away.

Luckily, she held on to both her breath and enough sense to say, "Therein lies the problem."

"What problem is that?"

"Haven't you been indulged all your life?"

He gave another of his lordly snorts by way of reply and vacated the room.

And she was alone. Well, not quite. She had Sir Bacon for company. However, the little canine had begun sniffing around one of the chair legs in a most suspicious manner. "Oh, no you don't."

She scooped up the terrier and rushed him through the boardinghouse, shouldering past a flummoxed Mrs. Hayhurst in the narrow corridor. Once outside, she deposited the dog on the ground and pointed. "Here."

He shot her a skeptical glance before sniffing out a suitable piddling spot. Her eye caught on the magnificent dapple gray receding up the street with Clare sitting astride with total instinctive ease. Only a man with position, power, and privilege sat a horse that naturally. It struck her afresh how different in station he and she were, a consideration that struck close to the heart of what niggled at her about their arrangement.

In short, an imbalance of power existed between them that didn't weigh in her favor. She wouldn't be the one in control, no matter how she might snipe and pick at him. That unpredictability had her stomach twisted into a knot. In every job, she was the one in control. Even during her years with Nick, she'd been an equal.

But the marquess? She wouldn't be able to control him.

By agreeing to take his money and to the terms he demanded, she'd ceded him all power. And if her intuition about the man was correct, he would use every bit of it. She would be at his pleasure.

Yet the man insisted on being called—not by his title as surely did every other lord in the land—by his given name. Nay, not even that, for he wasn't insisting on being called James, but rather *Jamie*.

Even so, those considerations weren't what had her stomach roiling with portent.

St. Mary Magdalen.

She'd vowed never to return.

And tomorrow she would.

Here it was, an example of her inability to maintain her self-determination when her path intersected with Clare's. How many more ways would she lose control before their dealings reached their conclusion?

That a frisson of dread raced through her at the thought was expected. It was the other feeling accompanying it, however, that gave her pause.

Excitement.

There was no other word for what pulsed inside her when he was near.

Blast.

She might be in trouble.

When she visited Doyle tonight, here was yet another job she would keep to herself. Clare was connected to Nick, and she was determined that Doyle have no opportunity to corrupt that relationship.

She was definitely in trouble.

In more ways than one.

CHAPTER SIX

*J*amie attempted to settle himself into his coach and four's leather squabs, but it was no use. His well-sprung carriage was no match for London's pitted thoroughfares. The wheels rattled through a new trench every twenty feet as they made their way toward Little Peter Street.

He adjusted his cravat for the dozenth time and smoothed back the errant lock of hair determined to flop over his right eye. He hadn't been this concerned with his appearance in months, and it wasn't simply that he was dressed extravagantly enough for presentation at King George's court.

It was that woman.

She had an effect on him.

The truth was he'd been on tenterhooks since they parted ways yesterday. The possibility that she would change her mind and renege on their bargain had been turning into a very real probability in his mind. He'd even considered adding another condition to their agreement: that she reside in Asquith Court for the duration of the job.

She would never agree to such an arrangement. He may have known her for fewer than forty-eight hours

—could it possibly have been such a short amount of time?—but even he understood the high value she placed on her independence. The fact was, even with her pert tongue and cynical eye, the air around her shimmered with vibrancy.

He wanted more of that air, and he'd never been all that disciplined about curbing his desires. She would say it was because he'd been brought up as a future marquess, and she'd be correct, mostly. But once he decided on a path, he committed to it fully, never a half measure with him. Which was how he'd fallen into drink for so many years—and, no doubt, he'd fully committed to becoming a wastrel. But, then, it was also how he'd as quickly walked away from the habit five months ago. Not that it had been easy, but his mind had been made up.

A carriage wheel plonked into yet another deep rut. As he steadied himself, he questioned not why he'd set out on this course—he understood that only too well—but rather the course itself. After all these years, why had he begun the search for Mollie Rafferty?

Sobriety. That was the short answer. No longer was he numb to the past lodged deep within. But, also, boredom—the sort that came of being too much in his own thoughts—had played a role. And once he'd thought of Mollie, a curiosity set in, which had led to the hiring of the Bow Street Runner.

Now that he had a few answers—she'd died, in a workhouse—he needed more. He needed answers to the how, why, and what had happened to her. Why had she ended up in a workhouse? Why hadn't she come to him for support? If she had, he'd have given it to her, freely, without question.

Again, he felt ten times the fool. He'd taken Father's word for the truth—that she'd gone on her merry way with a little money in her pocket—when he now knew his father's word for a lie. If Mollie had funds, she wouldn't have gone to the workhouse. When he'd been informed of Mollie's departure, however, his judgment had been clouded. All he'd seen was a rightness in its inevitability. Of course, she would leave him for Father's coin. When had he ever been enough for anyone to truly love? For anyone to stay?

His parents had certainly never chosen him. Nor had any lover. Why would Mollie have been different?

Now, with years passed and emotions clear, he needed to understand. It was only natural that he would employ Hortense—he couldn't think of her as Miss Marchand—for the job. He had the power and resources. It was his prerogative.

The carriage began slowing as Number 11 rolled into view. He checked his pocket watch. Three of the clock, precisely. Just as he was pushing the door open, he caught sight of a jaunty little terrier barking his head off at a passerby who had ventured too close. He followed the length of the white silk lead to find Hortense at the other end, standing back from the road in the shadow of an alcove.

His gaze made its slow way over her. As was usual, her clothing was nothing to speak of, but her person— it struck him anew how small she was. And young, too. She couldn't have yet reached her twenty-fifth year. More than a decade his junior in years, if not in life experience. Sobering thought, in more ways than one.

He couldn't help noticing something more. With her delicate chin and cheekbones, clear pale complexion, raven black hair, sharp Mediterranean blue eyes, and cherry red mouth, Hortense was a beauty. He intuited why she dressed in plain, dull colors and without ostentation. To mask her attractiveness. He couldn't imagine it fooled anyone.

She glanced up from fussing at the dog—a full time

job, no doubt—and met his eye through the window. The storm cloud on her face didn't diminish one bit. She and the feisty little dog rushed forward. She scooped up the canine and deposited him unceremoniously on the floor before pushing inside to settle on the bench opposite Jamie. She patted her lap, and the dog hopped up and curled into a tight ball. The two of them had clearly made terms with one another.

Jamie gave the ceiling three sharp raps, and the carriage lurched into motion. "Have you named him?" He had to ask.

"Sir Bacon."

A laugh startled from him. "A more fitting name, there isn't."

Her eye roved across him in a slow up-and-down assessment. "You listened when I told you to wear your best."

"Is the velvet too much?"

She shook her head. "You look—" She gave a sheepish laugh. "You look, well, magnificent." Was the appreciation in her eyes for the clothes? Or him?

Unsure what to do with the comment, he didn't address it. Her gaze slid away, a light blush staining her cheeks. She looked... "Lovely."

Her eyebrows met, forming one long questioning line. "Pardon?"

He'd spoken his opinion aloud. Deuce take it. "You look lovely."

She picked at her skirt, a small laugh escaping her. Full of jitters, that laugh. "I'm not here to look lovely."

"Loveliness has nothing to do with intention. Loveliness simply is."

Her gaze fixed on London passing them by outside the window, presenting him with her, yes, *lovely* profile. As they went, the sounds of the city teemed all around: the carriage wheels rolling across noisy cobblestone streets; the shouting of vendors plying their wares; animals barking and clucking about; children whining; parents scolding... And the list went on, for London was a place with myriad varieties of people and experiences being lived at any moment. It was the wildest of cities, lest anyone forget it to their peril.

The coach and four rattled across London Bridge, the Thames a murky brown in the cloudy afternoon light. Hortense discreetly wiped her palms on her skirts for the dozenth time. An indication of nerves, that gesture. He had a subject to broach, and he had the distinct feeling she wouldn't like it, so he allowed silence to prevail for a time, his gaze mostly resting on the river flowing below, but also flicking toward her every so often.

When the carriage rolled onto solid land again, he decided he could wait no longer. "You seem to know rather a lot about St. Mary Magdalen."

She inhaled a subtle sip of air, but he caught a trace of the nerves she hadn't quite been able to control yesterday at the first mention of the workhouse. "Aye," she said.

"From your investigative work?"

"No."

He detected unsteadiness in that single syllable. She didn't want to say more, and he had no right to ask.

"I vowed never to return," she said.

Her confession had been spoken so softly, he could have imagined it. One word, however, jolted him. "Return?"

Her mouth pressed into a firm line, as if she'd said one word too many, and she picked at her skirt. "I'm wearing my best." An abrupt, self-conscious laugh escaped her. "My best dress, best bonnet, best spencer, best boots. Well, my only boots."

"I meant it when I said you look lovely."

A scoff scraped across her throat, a bitter shard. "I am nothing to you."

"Clothes are hardly the measure of one's magnificence."

She nodded, pensive. "True."

He exhaled a slow breath of relief. She appeared to be returning to her usual pert self.

"Do you have coin?" she asked.

He pulled a plump bag from an interior pocket of his greatcoat.

"The sort of person willing to run a workhouse is impressed by titles, finery, and coin. All of which you, the Marquess of Clare, possess in abundance." Her cool appraisal told him she'd most definitely returned to herself. "Can you be the haughtiest lord the world has ever known?"

"I believe myself equal to the task." He spoke in his loftiest voice. Which sounded disconcertingly like his usual voice.

She didn't react. "May I speak plainly?"

"Do you ever not?"

"Be a pompous dunderhead."

He snorted. "And you?" he asked. "Who are you to be?"

"They won't dare ask, not while they're in awe of you."

"But you have a role worked out, don't you?" He couldn't resist asking. This woman was an expert at her vocation. She wouldn't leave such a detail to chance.

"Of course."

"Humor me."

"I am the niece of your old nanny, a servant now in her dotage, but who remains dear to you. A beloved cousin of mine fell on hard times some years ago, and you have taken an interest in the matter."

"That's a rather convoluted story."

"If you can't make a lie simple and close to the truth, then make it difficult for others to remember."

A second ticked by. "You're rather excellent at this."

She glanced away. He could see she didn't want to feel anything at his praise, but the twin patches of pink staining her cheeks betrayed her.

She clenched her fists, and her resolve steeled before his eyes. "You will take the lead." She hesitated. "But don't let on that you know Mollie Rafferty is deceased."

"Why not?"

"You'll put them on the defensive if you do. They'll close ranks, and you'll get nowhere."

"And what will you do?"

"I will appear overwhelmed by the whole situation and won't speak a word. Who is the most pompous and overbearing lord you've ever met?"

He snorted. "It would take a while to whittle it down to just one."

"Be him," she said.

Through Southwark streets the carriage rattled, its air a little more rancid, its buildings a little more moldered, its citizens a little more hard-bitten. This was a London as far from the civilized drawing rooms of the West End as one was likely to find. The carriage rounded onto Russell Street, and the grounds of St. Mary Magdalen rolled into view. Jamie sensed a return of Hortense's tension. On impulse, he reached out and touched her knee. Startled eyes met his. "You are not truly returning."

He wanted to say more—*as long as I'm alive*—but he held it inside, taken aback by his fervency of feeling on the matter.

A war in her eyes, she, at last, nodded, and he pulled his hand back. The carriage slowed to a stop, and he pushed the door open. His feet hit uneven cobble-stones, his gaze casting about this new environ.

Hortense settled Sir Bacon on the squabs beside her and met his brown gaze. "You shall remain here. Try not to make too much of a nuisance of yourself." She tucked the lap blanket about him. "Now, stay."

About to hop to the ground on her own, she noted Jamie's outstretched hand and hesitated. "A marquess doesn't help his old nanny's niece alight from a carriage."

"I'm a rather odd marquess. I do as I please."

Still, she didn't move. She was tempted not to accept his assistance. The woman wasn't accustomed to men acting like gentlemen, that much was clear.

The contact lasted no longer than a trio of seconds as she descended. Her hand delicate within his, the woman weighed no more than a bird. But it was a different weight he felt, one peculiar and unsettling, one that traced down to his toes.

Desire.

It had been dancing around the edges of their inter-actions, but the way it hit him just now was troubling.

Then her touch was gone, and she swept past him, and he was left feeling not unlike a fool. Never had he been affected this way by the fleeting touch of another person. When it was the two of them, he was able to forget who he was—a lord, her employer. As such, he had a responsibility to her. That was what he'd been taught all his life about his position, not by Father of course, but by teachers and by observing men better than his father. Never once had he dallied with those in his employ, and he wasn't about to start now.

She turned to shush Sir Bacon, who had taken to barking through the window.

"He's going to yap the entire time we're away, isn't he?"

"Very likely." She faced Jamie, ignoring the feisty terrier. "Are you ready?"

Skepticism formed a wall around her. She didn't hold an ounce of faith that this endeavor would yield a positive outcome.

He squared his shoulders, drawing himself up to his fullest height and summoning every last one of his aristocratic forebears, both patrilineal and matrilineal, and arched an exaggerated eyebrow. "Have you any doubt?"

Snobbish and supercilious, he was every inch a lord not to be nay-sayed. An amused light flashed in her eyes, and she bobbed her head before murmuring a meek, "No, milord."

Hortense's transformation into submissive servant took Jamie slightly aback. He understood she wouldn't be breaking from her role until they returned to the carriage.

Together they faced St. Mary Magdalen. Rising above the black gates was a plain brick structure that held little appeal. A small side door cracked open, and out shuffled a man possessed of a distinctly officious air, presumably the porter. "What can I do for ye, milord?"

"How can I know that? I haven't yet asked you a question," Jamie retorted without so much as glancing at the man. "Your superior," he stated, embodying the worst sort of aristocrat. The sort who didn't ask questions but made demands.

"Erm, will ye be wantin' the gent's or women's wing?"

"Women's."

"Ye'll be wantin' the matron, Mrs. Ditch."

"She's still here?" asked Hortense, her face gone a few shades paler than usual.

"Between you, me, and the birds," said the porter, "I reckon she'll be 'ere forever, seein' as 'ow she's too mean fer the devil to take." He began moving. "This way."

As they followed the porter's slow, shambling gait, Jamie took the opportunity to gauge his surroundings. Upon closer inspection, the building didn't improve as they navigated its narrow warren of dimly lit corridors lacking all pretense toward cleanliness. Quite frankly, it was the filthiest place he'd ever encountered, and he'd spent the better part of a decade exploring the lowest gaming hells London had to offer. It was saying a lot.

The filth extended beyond its atmosphere and toward its inhabitants, he saw, peering into open doors whenever the opportunity presented. And the stench... The noxious fumes were potent enough to bring tears to a grown man's eyes.

All the while, he kept half an eye on Hortense. The change he'd noted earlier had come over her again. Now, however, her skin held a distinctive pallor. This woman who he'd thought composed of unshakeable self-possession had a jittery air to her. Whenever he tried to catch her eyes, they skittered away. A rawness of feeling radiated off her, a feeling she didn't want to share with him, and it was because of this place.

I vowed never to return.

He now understood that vow more clearly. His jaw clenched with a sudden and unaccountable anger. She hadn't simply been here. She'd lived in this horror.

The porter stopped before a closed door at the corridor's end. "This'll be Mrs. Ditch's room," he explained before giving the door two tentative raps. One could only guess at the harridan on the other side.

"Oh, what is it?" came a woman's rough voice.

The porter pressed his mouth to the door. "Ye 'ave visitors, ma'am."

Suddenly, the door swung open, and the porter stumbled, nearly falling over. Battle-ready, the woman strode forward, arms akimbo, a set-down ready on her lips, when she noticed Jamie. Her face tumbled through myriad expressions—wrath, confusion, befuddlement, before settling on obsequiousness—as she took in the finery of the aristocrat standing before her.

"How may I be of service to you, milord?" she asked, her gaze sweeping rakishly over his person. She descended into a deep curtsy that wobbled only slightly to the left.

"You are Mrs. Ditch, I presume."

"That's the name the dearly departed Mr. Ditch—bless his soul—bestowed on me thirty years ago," said the woman, bringing a soiled handkerchief to decidedly dry eyes.

Jamie strode through the open doorway, leaving Mrs. Ditch no choice but to stand aside and allow him entry. It felt ungentlemanly, but it was how many a lord would conduct himself. He sat in a rickety wooden chair that threatened to give way beneath his weight and waited for the matron to take her place at her desk, which was strewn with the remainder of her afternoon tea and a rather large cup of spirits he smelled from five paces. Every cell in his body clamored for another sip of that air. He turned his head to the side, denying himself what he so craved, and found Hortense hovering at his side. "Sit," he commanded.

She lowered to a perch on the only other chair in the room, her eyes cast down.

He ignored the contents of Mrs. Ditch's cup and gave the woman the full brunt of his attention. "I am here to inquire about a woman who may have been in your care fourteen years ago."

"Well, I've been matron for the women and children these last twenty years." It had been a hard twenty years for the woman, if the lines crisscrossing her face were any indicator. The spirits she'd hastily shoved out of view likely had something to do with that. A suggestive smile played about her thin, dry lips. "Anything I can do to help. *Anything.*"

He would ignore that last bit. "She was my old nanny's favorite niece's cousin from her father's side of the family." He decided to further complicate the lie Hortense had concocted.

The matron's eyes went wide. "We shall do our utmost to assist you, my lord." Her gaze did a sly sweep over Hortense. "And this is the cousin?"

"The niece."

Her gaze narrowed into appraising slits. "Do I know you, dearie?"

Hortense kept her eyes cast to the floor and shook her head.

Jamie cleared his throat. "This chit isn't your concern."

Mrs. Ditch's gaze lingered. "There ain't a gel I don't remember." She tapped her forefinger to her temple. "I once knew a little Amelie. Took something of mine. She woulda grown to look exactly like you, come to think on it."

"There is no Amelie in this room," murmured Hortense, avoiding Mrs. Ditch's searching gaze. It was her eyes. Their cerulean hue was that striking. Anyone who had met those eyes once would remember them.

"The cousin's name is Mollie," Jamie cut in.

"More than one Mollie round here, if you don't mind me sayin'," said Mrs. Ditch, her gaze at last straying from Hortense. "Too many, if you ask me. Difficult to keep 'em all fed, as coin bein' hard to come by."

She couldn't have pronounced her message more clearly. Jamie pulled the bag of guineas from his greatcoat. An avaricious light entered the woman's eyes as he plucked out one coin and plunked it on the desk. "As I said, she was here fourteen years ago."

"So many Mollies over the years." The woman flipped the bright coin between forefinger and thumb. "Do you have a last name?"

"Rafferty."

"Mollie Rafferty," she repeated. "A name that hangs just on the edge of memory."

Jamie withdrew another coin. He understood the game. Hortense kept her gaze trained on the floor, but her head had canted to the side ever so slightly. She was taking in every beat of the conversation.

"Ah, sweet memory returns," cooed Mrs. Ditch. "A beauty of some remark, that Mollie Rafferty."

"Tell me where she is," Jamie demanded, his mask of cool, aristocratic indifference slipping, now that they were on the brink of discovery.

Mrs. Ditch gave her head a shake. "You'll not find her here, milord."

Impatiently, he flung another guinea on the desk, its thud loud and final. "Where?"

She spread her hands wide. "Where so many of them end up."

His gut began to churn. He knew what she wasn't saying. He wished she would out with it so they could get to the how, why, and what.

He managed to catch Hortense's eye. This wasn't going to end well, her gaze was telling him. She'd known it all along.

"If you will enlighten me, Mrs. Ditch." He needed the answer spoken aloud, and it was that need that gave him away. Another coin hit the table, hard.

"The Cross Bones," said the matron.

"The Cross Bones? Was she taken by pirates?"

This brought a mean smile to the woman's mouth, but before she could reply, Hortense said, "It's a burial ground for prostitutes—"

"Prostitutes?" He didn't bellow. He remained very still, even if his blood shot thunder through his veins.

"—and paupers," finished Mrs. Ditch. "Not too far from here."

His stomach plummeted to his feet, and it was as if someone had plugged his ears with cotton. He gave his head a shake, but he couldn't deny that here it was, the inevitable.

Mollie was buried in a grave with paupers and prostitutes for her eternal company. A sadness, a hopelessness, washed over him, but so, too, did an emotion with more force behind it. *Fury.*

He'd believed a lie—more than one—and that was why Mollie lay in a pauper's grave. His gaze narrowed on Mrs. Ditch. "And you're certain?"

"As can be." The woman gave an indifferent shrug. "You want to know what killed her?"

At last, they were getting somewhere. He smashed all the remaining guineas on the desk. "Tell me." There was no mistaking the menace in his words.

A canny light entered the woman's eye. "Childbirth."

If he hadn't already been seated, his knees would have buckled beneath him. His gut understood something that his mind couldn't quite yet comprehend. "When?" he croaked.

"A few months after she arrived."

His lungs refused to draw breath. *A few months after she arrived.* It could mean only one thing. "And the child?" he found himself asking. "Was it buried with her?"

A sly smile playing about her mouth, Mrs. Ditch reached for the bag of coins. He'd had enough. He slammed his hand on top of the pile as he leaned menacingly across the table. "Enough games, woman. Tell me all. *Now.*"

She swallowed. He'd rattled her. *Good.* "The child, he survived."

If someone had taken a knife to his gut and slashed though, Jamie would have felt no differently. *He...a boy...a son.*

"Bring him to me." He hardly recognized his booming voice. He never raised his voice. *Never.* That was the sort of thing his parents did. Never him. *"Now."*

"The boy isn't here," Mrs. Ditch stammered. "He disappeared five, maybe six, years ago."

"*Disappeared?* Children don't just vanish into thin air." He was being loud and unreasonable, he knew it, but he couldn't seem to stop.

The matron gave a dry laugh. How he'd come to loathe this woman. "Now, there your thinking is all wrong-side-up, milord. That's exactly what imps do in London. Vanish into thin air every day." She jerked her chin toward Hortense. "Ask that one. She knows."

Hortense's hand wrapped around his arm. "Let us go."

"She knows more than she's telling," he insisted, not budging an inch. "His name. What's the boy's name?"

"His mum named him James Rafferty before she passed. Everyone called him Rafe."

James. The name struck Jamie like a blow. Mollie had given the boy his father's name. It was the final confirmation he needed. The boy was his son.

Hortense's fingers squeezed, nails digging through cloth to skin and muscle. "We leave. *Now.*"

At last, her words cut through the wool in his ears. She was correct. Nothing more was to be gained from Mrs. Ditch, whose avaricious gaze kept darting toward the bag of money beneath his palm. He unceremoniously dropped a few coins on the desk. "For your time." He wouldn't thank her.

But that didn't prevent her from shooting to her

feet and expressing her effusive gratitude. "Anything I can do for you in the future, milord—*anything*—I would be most willing to oblige."

Jamie controlled the rise of bile in his throat and vacated the room, Hortense at his back. In a matter of minutes, they were outside, and his lungs began operating again, even if his mind was having difficulty. Through the gates they strode, the driver calling out, "Where to, my lord?"

And, like that, his mind snapped to. There was but one destination. "Take us to the Cross Bones."

The driver frowned. "The burial yard?"

"Aye."

Jamie found Hortense already settled inside the carriage. He took the bench opposite her and Sir Bacon, who'd already curled himself into a ball on her lap. The vehicle jerked into motion.

He stared unseeing at London squalor blurring past the window. Mollie was dead. He'd known that. But to have it confirmed was another matter. A few other questions had been answered, too—the how, why, and what—with a single word: childbirth.

Mollie had given birth to a boy. A son. Jamie's son. *James Rafferty...Rafe.* Who had disappeared. A fact that struck him at hard angles.

His gaze flicked over to Hortense. She'd kept her tongue silent and her eyes upon him. She'd never seen him like this. Well, that made two of them. He'd lost control in that room, and he was having difficulty regaining it. She would wait, her eyes told him, until he was ready.

Soon, the murky length of the Thames stretched alongside them, and the carriage was stopping. To the other side lay the Cross Bones Burial Yard. In a matter of minutes, he was striding across the grounds, nary a headstone in sight, only small wooden markers strewn about, a nosegay here and there, a noisome breeze swirling off the river. Fitting that.

His fury had not faded as a feeling snuck in alongside it. A sadness that felt fathoms deep. Here, Mollie rested in an unmarked pauper's grave. She'd deserved better.

"I need to know something," said the woman at his side.

He sensed a question weighing heavy on her and braced himself. "Ask."

"Did you know she was with child?" She was watching him closely.

"No." The truth needed no embellishment.

She gave a slow nod, but he detected belief in her eyes. Relief shot through him.

"If I had known," he said, "she wouldn't have ended up here."

"How did you not know?"

"Where do I start?"

"At the beginning."

He could tell this woman; that he understood. This thing that had sat heavy on his chest for fourteen years, he could speak aloud to her.

And no one else in the world.

CHAPTER SEVEN

$\mathcal{A}$ breeze signaling a coming storm began to whirl about them, freeing tendrils of hair from the tight chignon at the nape of Hortense's neck. She resisted the sudden urge to take Clare's hand in hers. This aristocrat who she'd viewed as magnificent and untouchable looked in need of comfort and friendship, two kindnesses she sensed he hadn't experienced in a great long time. The solitary nature of his life struck her as strangely similar to her own.

A thought, like her hands, which she would keep to herself.

"I was bored," he said.

The offhand way he spoke those words brought a dry laugh and a rejoinder to her lips. "A bored aristocrat is nothing new under the sun."

The shadow of humor that flickered in his eyes was gone in an instant. "One day, I was in Covent Garden and stopped in Pett's Coffeehouse. The young woman serving me struck up a conversation. She had a smile entirely lacking in artifice. A winsome smile. When she asked a question, she was genuinely interested in the answer and treated everyone that way, from pauper to duke. I'd never met anyone like her." He ran a hand through his hair, attempting to tame the errant lock that insisted on flopping over his forehead. "I went back every day after. Soon, I was taking her out for strolls and buying her new bonnets or whatever struck her fancy."

"She was special."

He nodded. "She was. She had a big laugh, and a personality larger than her."

This memory of Mollie brought a light to his eyes. It was clear he'd been besotted with the woman. A fact that reflected well on him, she couldn't help thinking.

Bitterness twisted about his mouth. "I couldn't marry her," he continued. "I knew it. She knew it. So, I established her in a flat of rooms in Cheapside."

"And that didn't sit well with you," she finished for him.

He flashed her an annoyed glance. "Do you always have to be so deuced intuitive?"

She shrugged. "Occupational hazard."

"I had a kept mistress, just like—"

"Just like?" Hortense prompted. He needed to keep talking. Not for her—she'd already deduced much of this story. It wasn't a new one—but for himself.

"Just like my father."

As they walked through the burial yard, which was as wretchedly sad a place as one was ever likely to encounter—so many hopes, dreams, and souls lost and forgotten by time—the only sound was the muffled crunch of boot heels on dirt. *Just like my father.* Those four words, the way he spoke them, only confirmed the nature of the relationship between father and son. A son who didn't admire or want to emulate his father, but rather the opposite. Over the years, she'd had the same idea about Nick.

"I didn't see much harm in it, either," he said. "I wasn't wed, and I had a genuine liking for Mollie."

"Then one day she was simply gone?" That math didn't add up to her.

"Not precisely. Our family has a far-flung Scottish estate that my father wanted to make grander with a new manor house. He asked that I go north to oversee the final stages of construction and meet his retainers and tenants. Collect annual rents, that sort of thing. He claimed it was the business the heir to a marquessate needed to learn." He scoffed, a bitter sound. "Not that I ever witnessed my father conducting any such business, mind you. His estate agents managed all that was loathsome to Father about the title, like rents and repairs and the tenants themselves."

She nodded, understanding at once what he wasn't saying. "It was a ruse to get you out of London."

But *why*?

"I should have known." Rage simmered below the surface of Clare's words. "Father hadn't the slightest care for what sort of marquess I would be, for he hadn't the slightest care for the marquess *he* was." His gaze cut to hers. "But the truth was I didn't mind the diversion. Scotland was a welcome relief from Town, so I stayed for nigh on half a year. I wrote Mollie the occasional letter, but her reading and writing weren't strong enough for her to write back. Anyway, I felt useful in Scotland, unlike my half existence in London where I waited to inherit a title with not much to do. There, I was able to see something take shape and flourish under my guidance. There, I mattered."

"Couldn't you have stayed?" she asked. "Why return to London?"

"I am an Englishman. As much as I was accepted on the estate, I would never be a Scotsman. But I did return with the intention to make a better life in London, one more useful than that of a wastrel heir. And if not here, then maybe at our family estate in Hertfordshire."

"But that didn't happen."

"When I returned, Mollie was gone. I could find no trace of her. Not in the Cheapside flat. Not at Pett's." He appeared to be weighing how to proceed, perhaps whether or not to do so. "I was on the verge of hiring a runner," he continued, "when Father and Mother paid me a visit. I saw them together once a year, during the Christmas holiday, so it was notable."

"They paid her off while you were in Scotland," Hortense said, certain.

"She accepted the money and ran away."

Just as she thought.

"Except it was a lie," he said. A beat passed. "One I believed until a few days ago."

"It does seem to be the truth. She did leave, after all."

He shook his head. "But not with coin."

Of course. "Or why would she have needed to enter the workhouse?"

His jaw tensed. He was reining in emotions that wanted their head. "I believe after Father and Mother found out about Mollie, they had us investigated and discovered my attachment to her. So, they devised a reason for me to leave Town. Then they must have paid her a visit and found her with child. Perhaps they feared I would do something rash like—"

"Marry her?"

"Aye."

"Would you have?"

"Perhaps." A beat of silence, leaden with regret, passed. "They intimidated her into leaving."

"How was that possible?"

"The Honey Lane apartment is a property of the Asquiths."

Hortense nodded.

"And, Pett's wasn't likely to take Mollie back, not in her condition."

Mild shock traced through Hortense. "This is something you believe your parents would have done?"

He didn't prevaricate. "Yes."

A question came to her, one she must ask. "Then why did you believe the lie?"

"I grew up watching them betray each other year after year, scandal after scandal."

"Why would you expect anything else?"

As the question hung in the air, she understood something fundamental about this man, something she wasn't sure she had the right to know. He'd revealed the elemental value that formed his impressions of the world. He'd revealed his vulnerability. In her work as a spy, this was the element about a person she always sought, for it gave her the weapon she needed to exploit their weakness.

But, here, now, with this man, it was too much.

He'd been hurt by those who should have loved him all his life. As a result, he'd come to expect it. Why wouldn't the woman he cared for accept money and leave him? It had been inevitable, no? His parents made it easy to believe love would turn to betrayal.

"What happened next?"

"Father and Mother proceeded to sit on opposite sides of the room and lecture me about suitable mistresses."

And she'd thought it wasn't possible for him to shock her further.

"No shop girls. No coffee house girls. They recommended finding a mistress among the ranks of expensive courtesans. Or a married lady for spice. *'But not the sort of girl who makes you heartsick. Not like your father gets on occasion.'* My mother laughed. My father turned scarlet."

"Your parents were—" Hortense searched for a word.

86

"I can help you, if you're at a loss for adjectives."

"*Beastly.*"

That was the word, the perfect one, and she saw in his eyes he agreed.

He cleared his throat. "Then they proceeded to hold forth on my duties as heir. I had only two. The first was to find a suitable wife. The second was to continue the line with an heir and a spare."

"Isn't that the duty of all firstborn aristocratic sons?"

"From love and respect come a sense of duty and obligation." He snorted mirthlessly. "I decided at that moment I owed them, and the title, nothing."

Although she happened to agree with that sentiment, a feeling of portent strummed through her.

He faced her. "I wouldn't be marrying, and I certainly wouldn't be continuing the Asquith line."

"So you began drinking."

"And gaming." A hesitation. "For years. I'd shown an inclination toward becoming a wastrel before Mollie, I perfected the art after her."

"Then, five months ago, your parents died in a carriage accident."

"And the compulsion died with them."

That struck Hortense as odd. "It is rare for someone to lose their taste for drink once they've acquired it."

Clare's mouth curled into the approximation of a smile. "Oh, the taste for it has gone nowhere. At first, the urge was so strong my body wanted to curl into a tight ball with need. But days, then weeks, then months passed, and the urge faded, which isn't to say it doesn't still rear its head at times." He stared out across the burial yard that grew more bleak as a heavy bank of clouds rolled in. His eyes shone with the blankness of one who had suffered a shocking loss. "Mollie is dead," he said aloud, for his own benefit. "And buried here, possibly beneath our feet."

"I am sorry for it." Hortense meant every word. Yet she must say something more. "Our investigation is now at an end."

Clare's brow furrowed. "At an end? How can you say that?"

This was familiar territory. At times, clients had difficulty accepting an unsatisfactory end to an enquiry. "We found out all there is to know about what happened to Mollie."

"But how can you say this is the end?" He looked entirely nonplussed. "If anything, it's the beginning."

"*Beginning?*"

"There is the matter of the boy."

Hortense's stomach dropped to her feet. *The boy.* In all this, she'd lost sight of him.

"*Disappeared,*" Clare said. They reached a low retaining wall overlooking the river. "That was the word Mrs. Ditch used. Not dead, but *disappeared.*" He released a harsh, frustrated breath. "Where could he have disappeared to?"

Hortense wanted to collect her money and put this day—and this man—behind her. What she didn't want to do was answer that question. The next words she spoke, she weighed carefully. "He could have gone anywhere."

"But he didn't go *anywhere,*" Clare pressed. "He went somewhere." His eyes, gone silver with emotion, narrowed into thin slits. "That woman back there"—he pointed in the general direction of St. Mary Magdalen —"she remembered you."

Temptation pulled at Hortense. She could turn tail and lose herself in the dark warrens of Southwark in a flash—this aristocrat would never catch her. But she must resist. She wasn't sure if it was obligation or the desperation in his eyes that caused her to relent with a "Perhaps."

The word emerged curt and pettish. This man had no idea what it cost her speak it.

"You were a child who disappeared, weren't you?"

She went very, very still, even as her heart threatened to hammer through her chest.

Clare released a frustrated groan. "Don't you understand what it means that Mollie bore a child? One that she named *James* Rafferty?"

Hortense nodded. She'd noticed.

"My son is alive and out there. *Rafe*," Clare said, hesitant, as if testing the weight of his son's name.

She waited. She knew what words were coming next.

His hands clenched into fists. "He must be found."

There. He'd said it.

He grabbed both her hands. The intensity within his eyes only grew. "Will you help me?"

Hortense shifted on her feet. A war waged within her. The right course for him and the right course for herself were two completely separate entities and very much at odds with one another.

Clare's eyes went bright with sudden understanding. "You know where the boy is, don't you?"

"I cannot be entirely certain."

A truth only in technicality. And they both knew it.

He ignored it. "Just like you didn't want to return to St. Mary Magdalen, you don't want to go back."

If only the truth was that simple. If only he knew what he was saying.

"Know this," he began, desperate to convince her.

His gaze had captured hers so completely, that she felt in thrall to him. She couldn't look away, though she knew it would be best if she not only looked away but reclaimed her hands and ran away, too.

"You will not be alone. I shall be there." He released one of her hands to tuck an errant tendril of hair behind her ear, and the moment leapt out of the bounds of time.

His touch, the delicious, earthy scent of him... She fought the impulse to sway into his fingers.

"As will the full power of my title," he finished.

This brought Hortense back into herself. She took a distancing step backward, breaking contact. There was so much this arrogant aristocrat didn't understand. "There are places in London where even a lofty marquess holds no power."

An irritated moan emerged from him. "You are too young to know what you know about the world."

"The life we live is an accident of our birth."

"Oh, more wisdom from the oracle," he said, testily. "Don't you tire of it?"

"Tire of what?" she asked, not entirely pleased with his tone.

"Of always being correct," he shot back, ticking his fingers down with each ensuing point. "Of always being in control. Of always being wise. Doesn't life sometimes call for a bit of intrepidity? Sometimes, the unwise course is the morally right one."

She couldn't deny it—the man was correct. This matter was about a child who was likely his son. Knowing where the boy had likely gone and the life he was likely leading, wasn't it her responsibility to pursue the unwise course? Had she a choice, if she wanted to live with herself?

Stormy silver eyes stared out at her, within them the gamut of human emotion—fear, uncertainty, anger...hope. She couldn't turn him away. "I might know where he is," she said, her voice ragged and resigned.

He searched her eyes for a few rapid heartbeats of

time, then the air around him released with relief. They crossed the short distance to the coach and four. Sir Bacon's front paws perched on the window as he watched them approach.

"Where shall I have the coachman take us?"

"I shall be returning to Little Peter Street," she responded.

"Your lodgings?" He wore an expression of utter befuddlement. "Aren't we going to find my son?"

"I understand your haste." She'd expected as much. "But not today."

Nonplussed, he demanded, "Why the deuce not?"

"A few reasons. First, you aren't dressed for it."

"I'm wearing my best, as instructed."

"We can't go where we're going and ask questions with you looking like"—she waved her hand up and down, indicating his entire person—"*this.*"

"Like what, precisely?" he demanded.

"Like *you.*"

"And who else would I resemble?"

"You look like a lord."

"What else would I look like? I am a—"

"*Nob.* I know." A beat. "But you can't look like one. We need to procure other togs for you."

"Let us do that now."

She shook her head. "Tomorrow. I, um"—why was she hesitating?—"I have an engagement tonight."

He flinched, as if she'd struck him. "Another client?"

"A personal engagement."

His shocked expression would have been amusing if it wasn't so perplexing. Did the man think he was the only person in her life? That he'd been too far off the mark wouldn't bear up beneath close scrutiny.

"Allow me to retrieve Sir Bacon, and we can part ways here."

She needed to ready herself for tonight. But she also

needed to ready herself for what tomorrow would bring, for tomorrow she would be taking Clare to Flick Doyle, two worlds she was none too keen to see collide. *Bloody hell.*

"I shall see you to your lodgings," Clare said, determined.

"You must stop this."

His eyebrows knitted together. "Stop what?"

"Treating me like a woman."

"But you are a woman." He said each word slowly and deliberately as if he were speaking to a simpleton.

"I am most definitely *not* a woman for the purposes of our relationship. I am someone you've hired to run an investigation for you."

A fraught instant later, he gave a reluctant nod.

Her message hadn't sunk in. "You are a blasted frustrating man. Has anyone ever told you?"

"Yes."

She didn't think anyone spoke thusly to aristocrats, particularly not marquesses.

"My brother."

Ah, Nick. Bless him.

In silence, Clare handed her up into the carriage, and they were soon on their way, a clearly annoyed Sir Bacon curled on the squabs beside Hortense, the little terrier refusing her lap in protest of her having deserted him, twice.

Gaze hooded, she watched Clare. His jaw tensed and untensed. Sir Bacon wasn't the only occupant of this carriage annoyed with her.

Clare's head cocked. "You aren't thinking of reneging, are you?"

Yes, she didn't say. Instead, she said, "I shall see it through. You have my word."

On the carriage trundled through London, across pitted thoroughfares and through traffic composed of pedestrians, carts, carriages, and all manner of conveyances getting on with various days. As a spy doing England's work both officially and unofficially, when necessary, she'd visited every major city on the Continent, and not one teemed with the life that vibrated through London. London was a beauty. London was a beast. London was a two-headed glory that would never be tamed.

At last, they arrived at Number 11. She placed her hand on the door handle, but hesitated before she pushed. "Tomorrow. Arrive here at ten of the clock."

"In the morning?"

"*Night.*"

"Why—"

"And bring more coin with you." It was worth a try, though she knew from experience Doyle didn't place much value on money. She scooped up Sir Bacon and hopped to the ground before Clare's gentlemanly instincts bade him assist her.

He leaned forward, his broad shoulders filling the opening. "Until tomorrow."

At her nod, he pulled the door shut, and the carriage lurched into motion. Relieved, she sighed. She needed time and distance from that man.

While Sir Bacon located the perfect patch of wall on which to relieve himself, Hortense's mind worked. The objective had been achieved: they'd discovered Mollie Rafferty's fate. Tragic, that. Then had come the news of the boy, and not just any boy, but a son. It struck her that just as she'd been breaking free of St. Mary Magdalen, Rafe was being born into it and Mollie spending her final days. Young Amelie would have had no notion of them, but life was ripe with such strange overlappings.

And that motherless boy was the illegitimate son of

a marquess. *Right*. And tomorrow she would lead the man to Doyle and attempt to pry the boy away.

Right.

Doyle wouldn't make it easy, that was certain.

A sudden frustration streaked through her. Just as she'd begun to form the notion of disentangling herself from Doyle's spiderweb, she found herself tangled tighter. For there was no doubt in her mind that whatever deal they struck for the boy—*if* they struck a deal —Doyle would expect a separate tax from her, even a bigger tax than she'd yet paid.

Logic demanded she step away from this, that she send her regrets by post and have nothing more to do with the Marquess of Clare and his problems.

But logic had naught to do with the matter. Her heart demanded she help. Here was the opportunity to redeem one boy from Doyle's grasp. There was no choice.

And she would pay whatever tax Doyle demanded.

She knew that, too.

But that was tomorrow. Today was Monday, her favorite day of the week, and tonight was her weekly dinner with Nick, Mariana, and the twins.

She would leave tomorrow for tomorrow.

It would come soon enough.

CHAPTER EIGHT

"*I* know Cuvier and Lamarck hold oppositional views on the beginnings of humankind, but I'm not sure either of them has the right end of the stick."

From her place on the opposite end of the settee, Hortense sipped sherry and let Mariana's words fill the room unimpeded. Nick's wife possessed many a view on the subject of scientific progress, and most subjects in general, and Hortense was content to listen in silence, for the woman was well informed on a great many subjects.

And Hortense, well, she wasn't. While she contained a deep well of information, much of it couldn't be found in books or museums. Most of it, she'd happened upon in dark alleys or in grand corridors whilst wearing servant's garb. Education arrived in many forms.

Mariana wasn't finished yet. "I simply cannot adopt Cuvier's view that the world was formed by one catastrophe after another, or Lamarck's that animals transmutated from one generation to the next." Her brow furrowed. "Something is missing."

"Dearest, if you put your mind to it, I've no doubt

you will find that missing link." This from Nick, who was sitting on the floor with his son of thirteen years, Geoffrey, the two engaged in a riotous game of tug with Sir Bacon. The little dog weighed barely a stone, but, pound for pound, he was strong as an ox. Lavinia, Geoffrey's twin sister, sat quietly on a chair near the fire, engaged in needlework, a smile curving her mouth as her eye kept wandering toward her father, brother, and Sir Bacon.

"But I would likely have to travel the world," continued Mariana, "and I cannot leave you and the children for such an extended period of time. I'm afraid some clever chap will have to do that legwork, and I'll have to content myself with reading his scientific extract. I hope it's within the next decade or two, is all."

"Patience, my dear."

Mariana sighed dramatically. "It never was my virtue."

Monday nights with Nick's family settled and set Hortense's week to rights. Although, this picture of connubial bliss hadn't always been so perfect. For a decade of their marriage, Nick and Mariana had been estranged, living completely separate lives and only occupying the same room for the sake of their children. Then, a few years ago, they'd reconciled in Paris. She didn't know the exact details, but they hardly mattered when the two were so clearly besotted with one another.

A small, sharp pang of envy shot through Hortense. She'd never shared that sort of bond with anyone.

"Aunt Hortense," said Lavinia. "Would you like to see my needlework project? It's a pattern from the latest issue of *The Lady's Magazine.*"

"Of course," she said. Being called *aunt* never failed to stir something joyous inside her.

The girl extended her hoop. It was a delicate sprig

that wound elegantly round and round, splashes of yellow, red, and blue flowers here and there. Hortense's only surprise was that a horse wasn't grazing in the background, for Lavinia was mad for horses. Hortense held the fabric to the light, inspecting it closely. "Your stitching is quite uniform and intricate." She handed the piece back to the girl. "Well done."

Lavinia blushed with quiet pleasure.

"Lavinia," began Mariana, "I have shared the writings of Mrs. Wollstonecraft and Mary Lamb on the subject of needlework with you. They refer to it as a technology that oppresses the intellectual advancement of women. Neither I nor your school require it as part of your education."

The girl set the hoop down and met her mother's eye. "I enjoy it."

Lavinia may have been a sweet and quiet girl, but so, too, was she possessed of a backbone of steel. Her parents would need to keep a close eye on her. Those still waters ran deeper than they likely suspected, and, at thirteen years of age, the girl was already developing into quite a beauty with her honey-colored hair and complexion to match, like her mother, but silvery gray eyes like her father's.

And her uncle's, offered a stray thought.

"Auntie," interrupted Geoffrey, who had stopped playing tug with Sir Bacon and was now beckoning Hortense over to the games table in the corner. At nearly six feet tall, Geoffrey was looking less and less like a boy these days. It was easy to make out the man he would be. The spitting image of his father.

"What do you have here?" Hortense asked, taking in the impressive spread of weaponry.

"It's my knife collection." The boy's eyes shone bright with pride.

"And a superb one at that." Particularly for a boy who recently entered his teen years.

"They're from all over the world."

"Can you name each blade?"

"Of course." He sounded offended, and she couldn't help smiling. "This one"—he picked up a petite knife with an ivory handle and thin, double-edged blade that narrowed to a sharp point—"is a stiletto Papa picked up in Italy." He laid it down and reached for another, this one more weighty, with a wickedly curved blade that meant business. "And here is my favorite. A kukri knife from Nepal that Mama found in Paris a few years back."

"I hope you don't have plans to use it any time soon."

Geoffrey's expression took a turn for the thoughtful. "Who is to say? If an intruder breached our house, I would be ready. I keep them beneath my bed." The boy was most definitely his father's son.

"Do you know how to use them in such a case?" she asked, interested in the answer. A weapon could easily be turned against its owner if the owner didn't know what he, or she, was about.

Geoffrey grabbed a knife and took a wide stance.

The spy inside Hortense sprang to life and scanned the boy with a critical eye. "Your feet are how they should be, but your hold on the knife is wrong."

"Oh." He looked crestfallen.

She picked up a knife. "Like this." She demonstrated how best to hold a knife if an attacker was advancing. "You don't want them to be able to disarm you."

"I've heard that if someone attacks you with a knife, and you have no other option, you should grab the blade."

She opened her left hand, palm facing up. "See that?"

The lad's eyes went wide as his gaze followed the long, red scar bisecting her palm. "You did it?"

"I'm alive."

"It had to hurt."

"Like the devil."

Sir Bacon gave a single bark, drawing Hortense's attention across the room. There, in the doorway, stood Clare, his gaze locked upon her open palm. Clearly, he'd heard that last bit. His eyes lifted and met hers. Her lungs refused to move or do anything useful, like breathe.

"Oh, Jamie, you're arrived," called out Mariana. "I'd begun to despair of you. But, Nick, why didn't Bartlett announce him? Has he been hitting the gin again?"

"I told Bartlett not to bother," said Clare. "It's only me."

From her place at the table, Hortense watched him become swallowed into the embrace of his family as Nick stepped forward to shake hands, followed by an embrace from Mariana. Geoffrey and Lavinia rushed forward to greet their uncle, who bowed to his niece and shook hands with his nephew. Sir Bacon soon joined in the greetings, circling the grouping round and round, tail wagging, barks flying.

Only she hung back. She'd been startled to see him, but then this was Nick's house. It was his prerogative to invite whomever he pleased, even his brother.

A flare of annoyance blossomed inside her. Was it too much to ask that she be free of the man for one evening?

So, too, was it vexatious that he somehow managed to become more handsome with each additional meeting. Viewing the brothers side by side, their similarities were all too apparent—tall, dark, handsome—but the differences foregrounded themselves, too. Clare, while arrogant and commanding, lacked the hard edge of

Nick. It was something deep within Clare's eyes that she'd noticed, but hadn't been able to articulate, until this afternoon. It was a melancholy. One that had likely begun in his youth, given what she now understood about his upbringing. Then there had been Mollie Rafferty, and now there was a boy. His son. *Rafe*.

And, tomorrow, they would attempt to strike a deal with Flick Doyle for the boy.

She quelled the nerves that threatened to jangle out of her veins whenever the thought inevitably circled back around. It was the sun around which much of her mind revolved this evening. Clare and Doyle, in a room, together. It was one matter to bring Doyle a little brass horse to pay her tax, as she had last night, but another entirely to bring him Clare. Clare was no inconsequential trinket.

Again, his eye caught hers, and she couldn't look away. Her heart banged out three hard thumps. Though they surely shared little in common, she couldn't shake away the feeling that she and this aristocrat understood each other on an elemental level. Bloody confounding, that.

"I take it you are acquainted with Miss Marchand, Jamie?" said Mariana, mischief in her eyes.

He took half a beat too long to acknowledge Mariana's question. "Um, yes." He offered a stiff bow in Hortense's direction. "Miss Marchand."

"Lord Clare," she returned.

The moment stretched long. Long enough that Nick cleared his throat. "Does anyone mind if we commence with supper? I am famished."

Mariana rang a bell and instructed a servant that they were ready to dine. The doors to the dining room swung inward, and everyone began to move in that direction, including Sir Bacon who pranced jauntily forward, taking the lead as if he might demand a seat at the table. Mayhap that was the custom in Lady Fortescue's household. Nothing about the private lives of aristocrats surprised Hortense.

Candles were lit about the room, but not the grand chandelier overhead. While many aristocrats had their children take their meals in the nursery, not Nick and Mariana. When Geoffrey was home from Westminster School, he sat at the table with his parents, as did Lavinia.

Every Monday, Hortense soaked in the meal and company, but, tonight, course after course passed with her hardly noticing. Conversation moved around her, and she even took part in it, but she couldn't have told anyone later what they'd discussed. Her attention, if not her direct vision, was concentrated entirely upon Clare. Observing him. Taking in his mannerisms.

She understood what she was doing. She was studying him like a mark.

And what did she find?

His eyes lit up when Geoffrey and Lavinia asked questions of him. He adored his nephew and niece. So, too, did he have the same reaction to Mariana. With Nick, he was more guarded, which showed he knew his brother. She'd so long regarded Nick as not only a mentor to her, but as an older brother, that it was a bit surprising seeing him as younger brother. Most men naturally deferred to Nick's sharpness and intelligence. Not Clare. To him, Nick would always be the little brother.

It was a question that Nick asked of Clare that pulled her back into the conversation.

"So, brother," began Nick, "now that you're out and about again, will you take up your seat in the House of Lords?" The question could be viewed as offhand were it not for the intensity of Nick's gaze.

Clare settled his fork on his plate. "I cannot imagine I would have any initiatives worth pursuing."

"I'll happily provide a list," Mariana said. "There's no shortage, I can assure you."

Before Clare could reply, Nick continued, "What he's really saying, dearest, is that he cannot be bothered."

"Why not?" Hortense found herself asking. All eyes swung around and landed directly on her, a feeling she'd never particularly enjoyed. But she wasn't finished. "Take workhouses, for example, they could use reform."

Clare winced. Her words had hit their mark.

"Indeed, they could." Leave it to Mariana to take up the banner. "It's the children that break my heart."

"What children?" asked Geoffrey around the spoonful of tart lemon ice in his mouth. Dessert had arrived.

"Orphans, my love," said Mariana. "They are taken in, and to earn their food and bed, they are made to work. Their small hands and sharp eyes are useful to the unscrupulous."

"That's horrid," Lavinia said with such a vehemence that one could catch a glimpse of the woman she would someday become. One very much like her mother, love of needlepoint notwithstanding.

Hortense, meanwhile, held Clare's gaze, steady. "Some are born there, and it's the only life they know. They will do anything to escape it for a taste of freedom."

She was speaking to the room at large, but only to him in truth. When they went to Flick Doyle tomorrow night, it was vital Clare understand this about his son and the life—one of sticky fingers and petty crime—that he'd chosen over the workhouse.

A servant's hand reached in to remove her un-touched dessert dish. Dinner was over.

"Shall we continue our conversation in the drawing room?" asked Nick. "I believe Sir Bacon would appreciate a lap to curl within."

At his name, the canine gave a determined little bark that had Geoffrey and Lavinia chasing after him. Mariana rose, and the gentlemen followed her lead. Even in this informal setting, certain manners were adhered to. Hortense followed the group toward the doorway, all too aware of Clare on the opposite side of the table doing the same. The room could be pitch black, and her nerve endings would be able to locate him. Unsettling thought.

She was about to exit the room when an arm appeared at her side. A forearm. *His* forearm, to be exact.

"May I provide you escort?"

Her gaze flew up to meet his. "I'm certain that won't be necessary. 'Tis no more than a few feet away." Oh, that telling rasp in her voice.

"When have humans ever been content with what was merely necessary?" he asked, the rumble of his voice possessed of the same telling rasp. "We're too full of wants and desires to reach satisfaction so easily."

She wasn't certain she'd ever been struck speechless in her life before she'd met this man. And now it was happening daily.

Of its own accord, and entirely unnecessarily, her hand slid up and settled itself upon his forearm. She inhaled, and her body went flush with heat. There it was, the scent of him. This man...he conjured feelings in her. Sometime in the last few days they'd snuck in, though she couldn't locate the precise moment. But here they were, swirling inside her. Feelings, wants, desires, and, oh, most definitely necessity.

But this need was no mere or simple thing, she was beginning to suspect.

How had she let it happen?

* * *

THROUGH LAYERS of linen and superfine wool, her light touch was enough to set Jamie's skin alive. The vibrancy within Hortense was that potent.

As they navigated the short distance from dining room to drawing room settee, it was all he could concentrate upon. He darted a glance down, but her gaze remained fixedly ahead. Once they'd maneuvered around Geoffrey, Lavinia, and Sir Bacon engaged in a rowdy game of fetch, she offered a murmured thank you and took her seat near Mariana. He moved to stand at the fireplace and rested his arm on the mantelpiece. He found Nick's gaze steady upon him. Little brother had been watching. Hortense was family here, that was clear.

Only a few hours ago, he'd arrived at Asquith Court to find Nick in his study, waiting. He'd been gutted from the afternoon's discoveries, and in no mood for Nick, who looked to be harboring a grudge. Well, Nick wasn't the only one with a grudge. Considering it was Nick who had inserted a spy into his household—even if that spy now occupied his thoughts night and day—he felt his grudge superseded his brother's. "Miss Marchand?" he'd asked, gruff, annoyed.

"I hired her," Nick said, cool, unapologetic. "I didn't know what had come of you." A beat passed. "And I needed to know."

That instant, Jamie released the grudge for two reasons. His brother cared. And there was the not insignificant fact that he would have never met Hortense otherwise.

"Will you come to dinner tonight?" Nick asked without preamble.

Jamie's first instinct was to refuse. Then he considered if Nick could put forth the effort, then he could, too. "Will there be other guests?" If so, he wouldn't go. Socializing *en famille* was one thing, with the *ton* quite another.

A smile twitched about Nick's mouth. "We have but one guest every Monday evening. I believe you are acquainted with her."

A feeling of portent stirred in Jamie's gut.

"Rather recently, in fact."

And he knew. *Hortense.* "What time should I arrive?" It would be mortifying if he sounded half as eager as he felt.

"Half past seven should do."

Long after Nick was gone, Jamie thought about the look in his brother's eyes as he'd spoken those words of parting. For it had definitely been *a look.* What had he revealed to his too observant brother?

Just now, Nick called out from the opposite end of the room. "Would you care for a brandy, brother?"

There Nick stood, at the drinks cart, decanter in hand. Every cell in Jamie's body screamed *yes.* "No," he said firmly and felt the usual tremor in his hand. The mention of spirits tended to have that effect.

Nick stoppered the decanter without pouring one for himself. Relief traced through Jamie. He hadn't relished the idea of watching Nick savor a snifter of amber oblivion.

Finished with their Sir Bacon japes, Geoffrey and Lavinia had cleared the gaming table of Geoffrey's knife collection and were already engaged in a competitive game of backgammon.

Now it was only the four adults. Jamie waited as Nick took a seat in the chair opposite the settee, done in the same blue damask. He had a question to ask. One that had been plaguing him these last few hours, since Nick's visit. And with Nick and Hortense occupying the same room, he mustn't miss his chance. "How did the two of you meet?"

It was a simple question, really. Except the look that passed between Nick, Hortense, and Mariana wasn't simple at all.

"Oh, I do love this story," said Mariana. "But, Hortense, it is yours to tell. And only if you like."

Jamie's instinct was to take his words back, even as curiosity burned inside him, for he sensed her hesitation. Still...how had she come to be a spy for his brother?

Just when he'd accepted she wouldn't answer, she spoke. "I was attempting to pick his pocket."

Jamie caught his jaw before it hit the floor. "You were a pickpocket?"

"Amongst other talents," she said, dry as desert sand.

"Where was this?" Now that the dam had been breached, he wanted every detail.

She glanced at Nick. "Piccadilly, wasn't it?"

Nick nodded.

"My fingers had just latched on to that shiny gold pocket watch of his," she continued, "when a hand clamped around mine like an iron band."

"And?" Jamie's jaw tensed.

"And she exclaimed—*Mon dieu!*—in perfectly inflected French," Nick said. "And I knew."

"Knew what?"

"She was no ordinary guttersnipe."

Guttersnipe...which meant she would have been young. *Very* young. "How many years had you?"

"I'd just reached my fourteenth year."

"And where did the French come from?" He'd been wondering this since the night they'd met.

She gave a one-shoulder shrug. "It is part of my past."

He sensed falsity in both gesture and words. It meant something that she spoke French.

"How did you come to be a pickpocket?" he asked, but he knew the answer before he'd finished the question. It had to do with where they were going at ten of the clock tomorrow night. Where they would find his son.

"Another part of my past," she responded, and the moment held for a few beats of time.

"And that is quite enough of the interrogation portion of the evening," said Mariana. "Come, Hortense, I would like to show you the new book of botanical illustrations I recently purchased. This one flower from Amazonia matches the blue of your eyes perfectly."

Unable not to, Jamie's gaze followed Hortense. A feeling of protectiveness surged inside him. He didn't like that she'd experienced the lives she had—life in the workhouse, life as a thief, life as a spy. Or that they had forged the woman—tough, scrappy, and canny—he knew today. He didn't like that she had to be so.

Nick cleared his throat. He'd joined Jamie at the hearth. "What do you have going with her?" It wasn't necessary for Nick to clarify who *her* was.

Jamie followed his first instinct, which was to deny. He wasn't ready to share this part of his life with his brother. "What gives you such a preposterous idea?"

"The eyes in my head."

Further denial wouldn't do. "I've hired her for an investigation."

A hard glint shone in Nick's gaze. "Plenty of people can do that work in London."

"I wanted *her*," Jamie said, lordly and implacable. Was he deliberately provoking his brother? Possibly.

But every few years, Nick needed to be set in his place. This was one of those times.

Nick untensed his jaw long enough to say, "For the job only."

"Of course." The assurance slid out of Jamie as if the subject held not an ounce of interest. He felt the lie down to his gut.

Nick wasn't finished. "Do you understand what that story says about her history?"

"I am certain you will tell me, little brother." Jamie flicked a strand of lint off his sleeve. Nick would not rile him.

Nick pitched his voice low, ensuring it would carry no farther than the two of them. "She has no one. She's alone in the world." He shook his head. "Actually, that isn't true. She has Mariana, the children, and me."

"I can see that."

"Know this: I will protect her from anyone, including—"

"Me?" Jamie finished for him.

Nick nodded, his gray eyes silver with intensity. "Aye, including you."

An unexpected wave of anger surged inside Jamie. "Is that so? And *you* never put her in harm's way?"

Nick's mouth snapped shut. An emotion flickered in his eyes. *Guilt.*

"As I thought." Jamie pushed off the mantelpiece. He needed to be gone from this room before he said something regrettable to his brother. "You will have your carriage return her to her lodgings?"

"Of course. As I do every Monday night."

Jamie crossed the room and spoke his good-byes to his niece and nephew before thanking Mariana for the pleasant evening. She stood and took him in a sisterly embrace. Her brown eyes, warm and inquisitive, stared up at him. "It is good to see you, Jamie. You are always welcome in our home."

Jamie wasn't quite sure her husband felt the same. His gaze shifted and found Hortense. "Until tomorrow?"

The moment held longer than made him comfortable. Then she nodded, and he could draw breath again.

He turned on his heel and strode through the townhouse. *Tomorrow.* Tomorrow she would lead him to Mollie's son. *His* son. *Rafe.* What sort of boy would he be? Only a day remained between him and the answer.

His feet struck slick cobblestones outside, and rain drops hit the back of his neck, heavy and refreshing. It was as well he hadn't arrived by carriage. He needed the walk.

Nick certainly had some nerve. But, even so, Jamie couldn't help feeling glad Hortense had picked Nick's pocket, for it was apparent she had no family in this world other than Nick, Mariana, and the twins.

And him.

He understood it with a certainty, swift and sure. She had him.

Her parting glance gave him pause, for he'd detected a flicker of something at the mention of tomorrow. *Fear.*

Who would they encounter that had the power to spark such an emotion inside the most fearless woman he'd ever met?

CHAPTER NINE

*H*ortense sank back into a shallow alcove, tetchy, alone. She'd left Sir Bacon with a dubious Mrs. Hayhurst. The guinea she'd paid the woman had assuaged the few remaining doubts. She couldn't bring him tonight. She needed no distractions.

A familiar coach and four slowed to a stop at the agreed-upon corner. Speaking of distractions…

The carriage door swung open and out jumped Clare. He was a fish out of water in these surroundings. More like a peacock outside the forest. She suspected he was wearing his plainest clothing, but it made no difference. The man looked expensive.

She would wager a year's pay he'd never ventured to the parts of London they would see tonight. Sure, he'd spent years trawling gaming hells of the highest and lowest order, but, like all nobs who indulged in those proclivities, it was a lark. They might have stepped one foot inside the East End, but the other remained solidly rooted in Mayfair and St. James. They knew the low pleasures offered in St. Giles and Southwark, not the realities. Tonight would be an education for the marquess.

"Return the carriage and horses to the mews," he

called up to the coachman. "I won't be needing them again tonight."

The man's eyebrows lifted to the sky. "Ye want me to leave ye here?"

Even in the shadows of fallen night, she could see Clare's gaze narrow on the man. "Indeed."

Instead of offering further protest, the coachman called out a command to the horses, and the carriage lurched into motion. Clare was master here.

"You truly don't like to be nay-sayed, do you?" she called out.

He faced her in a neat pivot. "Does anyone?"

She fought the half smile that wanted to curl at the corner of her mouth.

He gave her a quick up-and-down. "Back to the trousers tonight?"

The obvious didn't warrant an answer. "We walk."

She could see he was about to offer his arm—like a gentleman—so she struck out into the crowd and began wending her way through, leaving him no choice but to follow at her heels.

Once they reached a point where the crowd had thinned, she allowed him to draw abreast with her. "How was the rest of your evening last night?" he asked.

"I left soon after you."

"No other personal assignations?"

"No." Not that she owed him an accounting of her evening. "I spent much of it cleaning up after Sir Bacon."

"Is he very much trouble?"

A bemused laugh escaped her. "Quite."

"I'd posit you've come to rather like the dog."

"Perhaps."

"And your morning?" he asked. "Was it a fine one?"

She cut him a sharp look. "What are you on about?"

111

He spread his hands wide. "Making conversation. Have you never heard of the concept?"

Perhaps she was being unduly rude. "My morning was, um, yes, decent."

"Do your lodgings offer a fine night's rest?"

"They, um, do."

"No one ever asks these questions of you or enquires into your life, do they?"

She didn't like what she detected in that question. *Understanding.* They were coming to know one another rather well. Too well.

"Where, pray tell, are we going?" He glanced around as if he'd only now taken in his surroundings.

"To a pawnbroker."

"A pawnbroker?" Surprise and concern sounded in his voice. "Are you in need of coin?"

Exasperated, she shook her head. "I am not. But *you* are in need of other clothes, and the pawnbroker is where we shall procure them."

In silence, they wended their way through the East End, the streets growing narrower and narrower until they began to resemble a rabbit warren. Buildings stacked close together, the sky was smaller here. Putrid smells wafted around every corner. Sir Bacon's nose would have been tempted every other step. Raucous shouts sounded all around, impossible to distinguish between surprise, anger, or joy. Only those directly involved would know. To say it was all very different from a marquess's world would be vast understatement.

They turned into the darkest, narrowest alley yet, crowded with passersby coming to and fro, some at a rush, others at a crawl—beggars, street urchins, buyers, sellers of all sorts. A tobacconist to the left. A gin seller to the right. Hortense pointed ahead. "That's us."

"The sign with the three golden balls?"

."The sign of the pawnbroker," she confirmed, fist already pounding on the shop's locked door. She wiped a thick coating of grime off the small window and pressed her face to the clear spot. From behind a curtain at the back of the shop emerged the proprietor, Haley, licking his fingers before wiping them on his trousers. They must have disturbed a late supper.

He recognized her and unlocked the door. "If it isn't Maggie!" he exclaimed, the door swinging wide, a bell tinkling overhead.

"*Maggie?*" came Clare's murmur in her ear.

She ignored the question and followed Haley into the narrow shop. From floor to ceiling, it was bursting with all manner of items, giving it a cramped, overstuffed feel. One wall was all bedding. Stained linens, pillows, coverlets, pads. Cutlery on one shelf, flatirons and occupational tools on the next. Mostly, however, it was personal items that populated the shop. Paste jewelry and shoes, yes, but the majority of space was occupied by clothing of every sort—men's, women's, and children's. Dresses, shirts, trousers, overcoats, smalls. Boots lined the baseboards along one length of wall.

"What brings you here?" The pawnbroker grazed a quick eye over Clare. He would have calculated the worth of those fine clothes in an instant. "With such a distinguished guest."

Hortense understood this game. This was the part when Haley sized Clare up as a nob and tried to rake him across the coals.

"Surely," the man continued, "I am honored to have such a distinguished lord in my humble establishment. If I might enquire as to your name?" A beat passed. "Or, perhaps, title?"

She hoped the avaricious light in Haley's eye only confirmed for Clare how right she'd been. His clothes marked him as moneyed wherever they went. It was all anyone would be able to see.

"That is none of your concern, Haley," she said, her tone final. "He needs different togs."

The avaricious light in Haley's eyes grew into a full-blown expression of greed. "I can certainly provide any number of splendid vestments for such a grand gentleman. Only yesterday, a lady brought in all manner of fine toggery. You see, her husband passed a fortnight ago, but the rogue left naught but debts and a widow to pay them." He shook his head. "A sad business."

Hortense cleared her throat, loudly, thereby ending the story of the debt-ridden widow. Haley could go on and on. "Nothing fine," she said. "Nothing splendid. He needs working man's clothes."

Haley cut Clare a sharp glance, less awe-struck than he'd been seconds ago. "Fallen on hard times, have you?"

Two sets of expectant eyes upon him—albeit for different reasons—Clare had no choice but to reply. "Something like that."

Haley shifted to Hortense. "For purchase?"

She noticed a quizzical, slightly bemused light in Clare's eyes. They were talking around him, which would be a thoroughly novel experience. Generally speaking, as a marquess, he was the highest-ranking individual in most rooms and was deferred to as such. But, here, in this room in the East End, he was discovering a different reality.

She caught his eye. "How much coin have you?"

"Enough."

"Coin?" cut in Haley. "Now, we're old friends here, ain't we? The clothes on his back will do."

"Now, wait a minute," Clare began.

She held up a hand, staying his protest. "You have a bargain."

Haley took her hand and shook it. "One for one?"

She nodded.

"Surely you can't be serious," Clare exclaimed.

"We cannot bring them with us tonight," she explained, patiently, as to a child.

Mutiny in his eyes, he shut his mouth, her point conceded.

Haley clasped his hands together with a glee fit for a girl of teen years. Clare winced, and Hortense inhaled a snort. It was distasteful behavior for a man of middling age. The pawnbroker began zipping about his shop, plucking up a few shirts here, a pair of trousers there. "Will milord be needing boots?"

"Yes," she said at the same time Clare said, "*No.*"

Their eyes clashed. "Not my boots," he said. "They took two years to break in, and I'm not parting with them." A man had to make his stand somewhere, Hortense supposed. Boots seemed a reasonable place.

She released a resigned sigh. "I reckon a chunk of coal will do."

"For what purpose?" he asked, warily.

She pointed at his rather dashing boots. "They're too shiny. They need a bit of roughing up."

"Like their master?"

She gave a wry snort. "Something like that."

"Milord?"

Haley stood at the back of the shop, one arm full of clothes and the other sweeping back a curtain with a flourish. Dust filled the air. "For your convenience," he continued, "you may use this room to exchange your clothes."

Clare cast a parting glance at Hortense, who couldn't help smirking up at him. This was the moment of decision. He would proceed to exchange his fine clothing for the rags in Haley's arms, or he wouldn't. And if he didn't, the job was off.

Jaw tight with decision, he closed the remaining distance to Haley, took the clothes, and stepped inside, securing the curtain behind him.

She followed, her ear attuned to the muted sound of his broad shoulders knocking about the tiny room fit for a broom closet. Once the noises settled a bit, she pressed her mouth to cloth long gone dingy with must. "I'll take your discards."

A midnight blue frockcoat shot through a thin part in the curtains. "That coat alone is worth the contents of this entire shop."

Her thumb rubbed across the velvet collar appreciatively. It was of the latest style, she reckoned. He was likely correct.

"One for one, milord," sounded Haley at no far distance. "That's the agreement."

An indistinct, muffled grumble sounded from behind the curtain. A few seconds later, a black silk vest appeared, then a white silk cravat. A white lawn shirt and gray cotton twill trousers followed another flurry of movement. The man must be down to his smalls.

A frisson of heat flushed through her at the notion.

His hand appeared again, this time empty. "Trousers."

Haley transferred an armful of clothes to her, and she passed the requested item along.

"These won't do," came Clare's voice, brimming with irritation, which, in turn, irritated her.

Without properly considering the consequences, she poked her head inside the tiny room, a scold at the ready. "This is hardly the time to be concerned with quality or appear—"

Her gaze fell, and the remainder of her admonishment died on her lips.

He was shirtless.

Her mouth went dry. Had it ever been this dry?

She couldn't remember.

She wasn't sure she could remember her own name.

For there, not six inches from her face, was Clare's bare chest in all its full glory. She knew him to be tall, broad shouldered, and generally well formed, but the formation of this specific man extended beyond generalities. The muscles of his chest were corded and defined, and down they went forming into the hard, segmented ridges of his stomach, a fine dusting of dark hair narrowing from his chest, leading her eye across that ridged stomach and lower to the fall of the trousers, which wasn't fastened, revealing his smalls and a—*oh*—bulge.

A throat cleared.

His throat.

Her gaze flew up to meet his. What she saw there sent heat flushing through her. *Knowledge.* She'd been ogling him, and he knew it.

Oh, the mortification.

And, worse yet, her eyes begged to be indulged again.

* * *

"What is, um," she stammered. She cleared her throat and tried again. "What is the problem?"

If Jamie were to say he felt badly for Hortense's flushed cheeks and generally flustered state, he'd be lying.

That he could—well, his bare chest—render her speechless spurred a wave of gratification he was powerless to control.

"If you lower your gaze," he began, unable to keep the self-satisfaction from his voice, "you will notice these trousers are about eight inches too short."

She closed her eyes for a pair of seconds, as if

steeling herself, before glancing down. Then she nodded and allowed the curtain to close.

"Too short?" asked Haley.

She must have given a silent nod, for seconds later her hand was shoving another pair of trousers through the curtains, as if she didn't dare peer through them again. "Try these."

Disappointment pinged through Jamie. He wanted to watch her go speechless again.

The second pair was little better than the first. "The waist is loose."

Her hand reappeared with a third pair. "If these don't fit, we will use a belt."

He jerked them on. "They fit."

"Thank heavens," she said. Was that relief he detected? Did she *need* him to be clothed?

A few minutes later, he emerged wearing the clothing of a laborer: gray coat, brown trousers, shirt that had once been white, and red neckerchief, all rendered in rough cloth that would easily blend into a crowd. To his eye, he looked the part, but Hortense must have seen differently, for her brow had lifted into an expression that could only be characterized as skeptical.

"What is it?"

"Slouch your shoulders."

"Why?"

"You look too—" She searched for the right word. "Lordly."

He obeyed, even as he snorted. "Anything else?"

"Your face," she continued. "It looks too hand—" She caught herself mid-word. "Clean," she finished.

"My face is too clean?"

"Plenty of dirt to be had outside," chimed Haley.

Jamie only noticed she held an object when she extended it toward him. "Wear this."

118

He turned the gray woolen flat cap over in his hands a few times. "Must I?"

"Is there a problem with it, milord?" asked Haley, wringing his hands.

"Might it have nits?"

"Nits? Nits? *Nits?*" asked Haley, his volume, and presumably his outrage, increasing with each repetition of the word. "I'll have you know every article of clothing and bed linens have been boiled in lye for three full minutes before you see them in my shop. I'm known for it, ain't I, Maggie?"

A smile twitched about her mouth. "He is."

"*Right.*" Jamie couldn't help sounding doubtful. Even so, he stuck the cap on his head and got on with it. In for a penny and all that.

"I believe our business here is concluded." Hortense was already moving toward the door. "Your assistance was much appreciated tonight, Haley."

"Any time, Maggie," Haley said to their backs as they exited the shop.

The walls growing ever closer, the dank and damp seeped into one's bones as they slipped through the darkest recesses of Whitechapel. He kept half his attention on their surroundings, the other half on the woman at his side. Her mind was imprinted with a map of every twist and turn, he would wager.

She cleared her throat. "You aren't going to like what I have to say."

Jamie stepped around an unconcerned mongrel dog that wasn't about to move for him. "Say it." She didn't need to play nice with him. It ranked at the top of what he liked best about her.

"We'll be dealing with a man who goes by the name of Flick Doyle. When we arrive, you keep your mouth shut."

"I beg your pardon?"

"*There*," she said, as if she'd caught him out. "Don't you hear it?"

"Hear what?"

"You can't help sounding like a lord. The instant you open your mouth, the negotiations will become, um, *difficult*."

"Difficult how?"

"One never knows with Doyle. That's my point."

The cryptic aura surrounding this Doyle chap was beginning to grate on Jamie's nerves. "Who is this Doyle, anyway?"

"You'll know soon enough."

"A criminal?"

"Aye."

"A criminal has my son?"

"Likely."

"How do you know this?" He'd been wondering.

"Doyle likes to pull his eels—"

"*Eels?*"

"Lucky eels. It's what he calls his pickpocket gang."

"My son is a lucky eel, a...*thief*," Jamie said slowly, his brain trying to absorb these baffling, yet likely, facts.

Hortense nodded, understanding in her eyes. "Doyle likes to pull them from St. Mary Magdalen, because it's the other side of the river and harder to trace back to him."

Ah. "Like you."

She gave him no confirmation. Not a nod. Not a grunt. Not a corroborating flash of the eye. Nothing.

Onward they strode, keeping to the winding alley-ways in silence, until, at last, she slowed her step. She jerked her chin toward a building ahead—musty gray, ramshackle, and listing subtly to one side. To all appearances, the edifice would be a pile a rubble in a matter of days, if not hours.

But it wasn't the building Jamie had a care for. It was Hortense. Even in the uncertain light, he detected an unnatural brightness shining in her eyes. She held a fist to the door, poised to knock, and hesitated. Once she knocked, she would be committed to the events which would follow.

As much as he wanted to spare her this, Mollie's boy —*his* boy—might be within these walls. He couldn't leave it be. Now that he knew about Rafe, Jamie would claim him and take him to his new home, his true home.

Her hand hadn't yet knocked. Instinctively, Jamie closed the distance, so only a few inches stood between him and her. Low words were emerging from his mouth of their own accord. "You will not be alone in this."

She blinked. She recognized them as the words he'd spoken yesterday, yet the jitters didn't completely clear from her eyes. He gave her a steadying nod.

She knocked three soft raps, waited ten seconds, rapped two more times, waited five seconds, and then one short, sharp knock. A code. One she still knew. Curious that.

Thirty fraught seconds passed. She wiped her palms on her trousers.

The door barely squeaked open. A boy's canny eye appeared in the scant sliver, landing on Hortense, then Jamie. "'Oo's this?"

"Tell Doyle it's Hortense and"—she hesitated—"an associate."

Without acknowledging the command, the boy shut the door.

Jamie glanced around the ramshackle building. "Will Doyle want coin?"

"One never knows with him, but likely not."

"This place could use a bit of coin to prop it up."

"It won't be coin."

Again, the door opened, its rusted hinges screaming with the effort, this time wide enough to admit both of them into a dark corridor, lit only by the meager light of a small, dirt-crusted window. Through close corridors the boy led them. As Jamie's eyes adjusted to the nearly complete dark, he was able to form impressions of the surroundings. Narrow walls moldering with damp. Small table jutting into the walkway that he jostled with his right thigh. Around corners they curved, his broad shoulders clipping the walls. He would have a few bruises after tonight.

It wasn't long before they reached an opening, even darker than the corridors they'd just traversed. Hortense's arm swung out, preventing him from proceeding through. "There is a staircase," she said in a rushed whisper, saving him from a tumble down rickety stairs that would have likely resulted in a broken neck at the bottom.

As they descended, the light grew brighter, and soon they were inside a room lit by the dim, flickering light of a few tallow candles. The walls of the room were undecorated, rough, and streaked with black mold. It looked as if it had been dug out by hand and left half unfinished. Five or six boys were scattered about, all staring out at them in silence.

Hortense's gaze, however, was fixed on a point straight ahead. There, seated behind a large, square table, hands resting on its top, each finger adorned with a bejeweled ring, could be none other than the man known as Flick Doyle. All manner of ill-gotten goods lay scattered before him—handkerchiefs, pocket watches, snuff boxes, coin, papers, any and every thing that might fill a gentleman's pockets.

Doyle settled back in his plush, red velvet chair and pushed round, wire-rimmed spectacles up his nose.

"When the boy told me he heard Hortense's knock—but it weren't just Hortense, but Hortense and an *associate*, I thought to meself, Flick, ye got to meet this *associate* of Hortense." He spewed a hearty bark of a laugh. "Now what ye be wantin' from me, pet?"

CHAPTER TEN

"*Now what ye be wantin' from me, pet?*"

Hortense's jaw tensed, and her hands clenched into fists.

Pet.

After all these years, her body still had a visceral reaction to Doyle calling her by that sobriquet. She was no one's *pet*.

When she didn't offer a reply, he snorted. He knew she didn't like being called pet. She took him in with fresh eyes, the ones Clare would be casting over him now. Doyle was essentially the same as the first time she'd ever laid eyes on him. Hair maybe a little thinner and grayer, but still unkempt and greasy. Actually, those words sufficed to describe his entire person, inside and out. He jerked his chin toward Clare. "Who's this *associate* ye've brought fer me perusal?"

She darted Clare a suppressive glance. Under no circumstances was he to answer the question. But here he was opening his mouth. She let the first lie that came to mind roll off her tongue. "He can't speak."

Doyle cocked his head. "Mute, ye say?"

"Aye." She kept talking for some unfathomable reason. "And simple."

She didn't need to risk another glance at Clare to know a storm had gathered on his brow. A hysterical giggle wanted to bubble up, which she instantly quashed. She had serious business to attend in this room. A boy's life hung in the balance.

Doyle must have sensed her shift. "What ye here fer, pet? Somehow, I don't think it's to have a laugh o'er yer new man."

"He isn't *my* man," Hortense shot back, rising to the bait before she could catch herself. Doyle's mouth curved into his rogue's smile, and she could kick herself. "We're searching for a boy," she said, stating it flat.

"Lots of lads trollin' 'bout these streets."

"This one has been misplaced."

He spread his hands wide, conciliatory. "Lads lost, few found. That's the sad truth of this ole world."

"Around thirteen years on him," she pressed. "Tall for his age." It was all conjecture, of course, but she quickly realized what she was doing. She was describing her imagining of how Clare would have looked as a thirteen-year-old lad. "Grey eyes," she continued. "Dark hair with a tendency to curl on the ends."

"'E got a name?"

"*Rafe*. He came from St. Mary Magdalen."

Doyle shifted forward and began sliding a watch chain through his fingers. "Ah." His gaze narrowed on her. She'd been the recipient of that particular look a hundred times over. And even today it stirred uncertainty within her. "Rafe," he called out.

"Aye?" sounded a young, raspy voice.

"Come 'ere now, won't ye?"

The lad stepped out of the shadows and into dim, flickering light. Hortense inhaled a gasp. He was the eel who had summoned her a few days ago. Further, she'd described him precisely to the curled-up ends of his hair.

She stole a glance at Clare. His features had transformed into a mixture of shock and belief, with a large dollop of burgeoning determination turning them to granite. He'd understood in an instant this boy was his offspring.

"Ye mean, like *this* Rafe?"

Clare took a step forward, the look in his eyes hard and focused. Hortense grabbed his arm. The stakes had increased tenfold. This must be handled with delicacy, not force, for she understood two facts at once: the occupants of this room were the only family the lad had known for years. Clare might think Rafe would come with them and be grateful. But she understood the situation differently. He might not want to leave this place at all.

Then there was the second fact: Doyle would want something in return.

She nodded. "Aye."

Doyle's head cocked, his gaze gone canny. "Ye know what I find interestin'?"

The question emerged light as air, even as it landed on her shoulders like a lead weight. "What?"

"Here is Hortense askin' 'bout a boy. But, really, when it comes to it, ye and yer associate be askin' me fer a favor, no?"

"Perhaps. Depends on your point of view."

"That's what I thought." He leaned forward. "Here's what strikes me to the cockles. Ye'll be wantin' a favor, but what are ye prepared to do fer me?"

Ice shivered through her veins. *What*, indeed?

Doyle's forefinger tapped thin, chapped lips. "So ye've found this Rafe ye've been searchin' fer, now what is it ye want with him?"

"You know what we want." It was obvious to anyone with eyes that the man standing at her side was the boy's sire.

"So ye think ye can waltz in here and ask all nice and I'll let ye have him?"

"I suffer from no such delusion."

He barked out another laugh. "Hortense and her fancy words. That smart mouth o' yers always did have somethin' to say. Now, what's it goin' to say to me today?"

"How much for him?" She might as well get to it.

An exaggerated frown pulled at Doyle's mouth. "*Tsk-tsk-tsk*," he chided. "Now yer disappointin' me. *How much?*"

The mockery in his voice was unmistakable, even as his gaze shifted toward Clare, giving him a thorough once-over while sucking his teeth. Even though Clare wasn't wearing the finery of an aristocrat, Doyle wasn't fooled. The marquess couldn't help being, well, a *marquess*.

"She thinks she can ask *how much*, and I'll just name her a price like that?" he said to the room at large. He snapped his fingers, and his head cocked to the other side. "But I do be wondrin' why she brought ye along. What's all this to a big strappin' man like ye?"

Clare's hands clenched and released.

"One thing I can tell ye, ye won't be gettin' nowhere with yer fists."

"Your price. Name it," Clare ground out.

"He speaks," Doyle exclaimed. "And what an interestin' way of speakin' ye got. Ye speak *nob*, if me ears ain't deceivin' me."

"It's me you're dealing with," Hortense said. She had to right this conversational ship, or it would sink before it was out of the harbor. "Let us parley."

Lips pursed, Doyle gave her a long, assessing look. "Aw'right, me eels, out wi' ye."

The eels didn't need to be told twice as they slipped from the room. At the top step, Rafe cast a curious glance at Clare over his shoulder. Perhaps the boy, too, had noticed the family resemblance. Then he was gone, and it was only her, Clare, and Doyle.

Doyle's gaze again landed on Clare. "What do ye know about yer *associate* here, eh?"

"Doyle, let's get on with it," Hortense said. No good could come of the conversation going down that road.

He slammed his fist on the table. "Yer on my turf, and it'll be on my time," he roared before immediately settling back in his chair, his face now a mask of placidity, as if his outburst hadn't occurred.

"You will not speak to her that way, do you understand?" Clare stated low and hard. He wasn't truly asking. It was clear he needed only an excuse to slam a well-aimed fist into the man's face.

"Well, I'll tell ye a little about her that I'd wager honest money, if I had any"—Doyle never could resist a good, long laugh at his own jokes—"that ye don't know. Hortense here, she was me best. Luckiest eel that ever slid through the streets or slipped a hand inside a nob's pocket. Never nabbed once, were ye?"

"Once." She glanced at Clare. He had a face like a thunderstorm. *Nick*, they both knew.

A stillness came over Doyle, and a familiar reptilian look entered his eye. "I will release the boy."

She knew enough not to let relief worm its way into the moment.

He hadn't named his price.

"On one condition."

"Whenever you're ready to name it."

"Ye always were a saucy one."

She held her tongue and told Clare with her eyes to do the same.

"Ye pull a job fer me."

Here it was, the catch. A job for Doyle. *Another* job for Doyle. Would there never be a last one?

Her stomach tangled itself into a dozen fluttery knots. How quick one's return to the gutter, if one wasn't careful.

A throat cleared at her side. Clare, his eyes fast upon her, gave her a subtle nod. He was telling her to say yes. But, unlike her, he didn't know the world he was entering of his own free will. No one chose this path. Save this man who would so obviously do anything to get the lad.

The lad who was so obviously his son.

For that is the sort of man he is, entered a small voice. *Determined. Implacable. Honorable.*

It was a voice she didn't want to hear.

The seconds having dragged out into a minute, she, at last, nodded. "What's the job?"

"I won't tell ye 'til ye've agreed to it. Yer agreein'?"

Disbelief shuddered through her. How had she descended so far, so fast? For that was the truth of it. One tax at a time, she'd slid by small increments back into Doyle's world, a world only a few short years ago she'd vowed to leave behind forever, until she'd fully reimmersed herself. Now, on top of the taxes, it was a job.

But she had no choice. Clare wasn't leaving here without a way to have his son. He might even insist on taking the boy by force. That was what his stormy eyes were telling her.

And where would that leave her? Doyle would lose no time naming her as an eel and a thief and destroying her reputation among her upper-class clientele, leaving her with nothing.

She must agree.

She could retch.

"Aye," she said, at last.

Doyle clasped his hands together, a smile that would have done a snake proud spreading across his face. "Would ye like a seat? This'll take a while."

"We'll stand."

He shrugged. "Iffin ye can believe it, I was once a wild, young lad, who had a propensity fer dice. One night, I found meself in the house of a duke. Ye can't imagine such a mansion." He jutted his chin toward Clare. "Well, I imagine he can. Prob'ly lives in one himself."

That Doyle wasn't wrong grated on Hortense.

"So, after goin' through all his coin," he continued, "this duke started gamblin' anythin' he laid eyes on. His snuffbox. His silk handkerchief. A candlestick. One bloke even won a talkin' parrot off him. Filthy mouth on that bird, I'll tell ye fer free. Make a sailor blush. Still alive, that bird." Doyle shook his head in wonder. "Anyway, the hours were gettin' small and the duke was gettin' right desp'rate. Kept thinkin' his luck was 'round the corner, so he kept goin', but anyone could see we were up to the end o' it. The mood had turned rotten. There's always that moment with the dice. Best to get gone, 'specially if there's a nob in the mix. They ne'er lost anythin' in their lives, so some of 'em don't take nicely to it. I could see that's where this duke was. Then he looked me square in the eye and said he'd be takin' all his back off me. Real quiet like, I asked him how he planned on doin' that. I never did like squarin' up to a gent, and a duke no less, but I had a pretty pile sittin' in front of me and I wasn't 'bout to give it up easy just because some spoilt nob was cryin' in his milk. He said somethin' to one of his fancy servants and it wasn't a minute before the man was back with the sparkliest thin' I ever did see."

"What was it?" Hortense asked. Doyle had paused for the question just so she would ask, and it was his game they were playing.

"A tiara."

Clare's eyebrows lifted in surprise. "Unexpected."

Doyle snorted. "That's exactly what I told him. He said that tiara fer all me winnin's. His mam got it off a Russian princess. All sapphires and diamonds. Never seen nothin' like it. Now, just so ye don't think I'm all rogue, in me defense, I did hesitate. I didn't want to give up all me winnin's, but I saw I didn't have much choice in the matter. I wasn't gettin' out of that house without one more throw of the dice. And, what more, the duke had the mark of the loser as clear as if it was writ on his fore'ead. So, I rolled."

"And you won," said Clare.

"I collected me tiara and winnin's and got out of that house like the hounds of hell were nippin' at me arse. I knew it was only a matter of a minute before that duke came to his senses and robbed me of me winnin's. Nobs got everythin' in the world, and they don't like to part with a ha'penny of it. 'Bout a fortnight later, a pair of runners showed up at me door, demandin' the tiara."

"And?" Hortense couldn't help asking. She was anxious to know the end of the story. The scoundrel always did have the gift for a compelling tale.

A wily look entered Doyle's eye. "I gave 'em *a* tiara, that's sure."

She caught the distinction. "But not *the* tiara?"

"Eh, I knew it wouldn't be long before a runner was at me door. So, I had one made."

"You had a tiara made?" asked Clare, his brow knitted in bewilderment. He truly wasn't part of this world.

Doyle gave a dismissive flick of the wrist. "Oh, yeah, nothin' to it if ye know the right people."

Sudden understanding walloped Hortense. "*Paste.* And that's the one the duke received."

"Pet, ye always were quick on the uptake."

"And you still have the real one?"

He nodded, smug. It was no small satisfaction to pull the wool over a duke's eyes.

"You have the genuine tiara. What's the job?" she asked slowly, her mind racing. What was she missing?

His smile slipped. "Years ago, ye met me mam."

Hortense gave a slow nod. "She lives?" The woman must have reached her ninetieth year by now. Hortense remembered her as both frail and steely.

"Aye, she's yet among us," he said, his reptilian mask falling away entirely. He doted on his mam. It was his one good quality. "I always thought she was royalty and deserved to be treated like such. She wears that tiara every evenin' to take her tea, she does. But she's gettin' up there in years, and she reckons 'tis time to give it back. Attack of conscience, she calls it."

"And you can't simply return a tiara to a duke without confessing your crime," Clare cut in.

"That would be the sticking point," said Doyle, his gaze steady upon Hortense.

At once, she understood. "Impossible."

"What is?" asked Clare.

"He wants—" She detected confirmation in Doyle's eyes. "He wants me to switch the genuine tiara for the fake."

"Eh, the Duke of Rothesbury wouldn't stand a chance goin' 'gainst the likes of ye."

Clare's eyebrows drew together. "*Rothesbury?*"

"Ye know him?" asked Doyle.

Clare gave his head a shake that would convince no one. He truly wasn't very good at being anyone other than himself.

"You want me to switch the tiaras under the nose of this Duke of Rothesbury?" Hortense asked. It was best to be clear.

"Yer the only eel with fingers slip'ry 'nough to do it."

"There is but one problem."

"And what is that?"

"I do not have access to the Duke of Rothesbury."

"Oh, pet, ye've always bin a clever girl. Always know the ins and outs of what ye put yer mind to."

"One doesn't simply sneak into a duke's jewel vaults. It's an impossible task."

Clare cleared his throat, as if to remind them of his presence. "In three nights, there is a supper party."

Doyle snorted. "I reckon yer lot has a dozen of those ev'ry night."

"At Apsley House."

Doyle whistled through his teeth, the sound high and reedy. "The Duke of Wellington's house, eh? Well, *la-ti-da*. Wrong duke."

Clare captured Hortense's gaze. "I have an invitation to attend."

"I'm not sure how it will help."

"Rothesbury will be there," Clare continued with a fervency she had difficulty understanding. "He and Wellington are long-standing friends."

"Well, that's just braggin', innit?" Doyle laughed.

A terrible thought came to Hortense. "You're not suggesting we rob a duke's palace while he's at Wellington's supper?"

"It occurred to me, but no. In addition to his London residence, Rothesbury has a ducal estate in the country and a number of other properties. The tiara could be anywhere, if he even still has it."

"Ye better pray he does," said Doyle.

Clare refused to release Hortense's gaze. "I have a different idea." He hesitated. "You can attend Wellington's supper with me."

She shook her head. "I cannot. Dukes do not allow the likes of me into their midst unless there's an exchange of services for coin, of one variety or another." As distasteful as her words sounded, they were true.

Clare cleared his throat. "There is a way."

"And what way is that?" She was growing exasperated. "I do *not* fancy playing a maid."

The air went still and heavy, as if weighed down by the words Clare had yet to speak. Portent stole up Hortense's spine, and she braced herself.

"Marry me."

CHAPTER ELEVEN

M *arry me.*

  Had he truly expressed the idea aloud?

Judging by the parade of emotions marching across Hortense's face, he had.

The idea that had been forming in his mind had weighed on the tip of his tongue, as substantial as a solid object, composed of but two small words.

Two small words to alter the trajectory of a life.

Her first instinct had been a jittery smile. Then came a disbelieving widening of the eyes when he didn't respond in kind. At last, she settled into shocked silence.

No care for the silent drama playing out between Jamie and Hortense, Doyle rocked a few times in his chair before shoving to his feet. He shuffled to a corner and pushed a chest of drawers out of the way to reveal a safe. A few moments later, he returned to his place at the table and set two items before him.

First to grab Jamie's eye was the tiara.

Even in the dimness of tallow candles, its diamonds and sapphires caught the murky light and threw it sparkling in every direction, its platinum settings glittering white and sharp. It was a costly piece that would have fetched hundreds, if not thousands, of pounds. Yet this man—*Flick Doyle*—who lacked decency, honor, and principles, had held on to it. Jamie doubted not the man's love for his mam.

It was then he noted the other item on the table. A bottle of rotgut. The variety didn't much matter. It was all the same in the end.

Twin ribbons of dread and desire slithered through him when Doyle reached into a drawer and pulled out three mismatched teacups. Jamie knew what was coming next.

"I do not drink spirits." He needed that to be clear, most of all to himself.

Doyle's head cocked. "The way I see it is I'm puttin' more faith in ye, than ye are in me. And I don't put faith in ye if I ain't slung back a glass with ye."

Hortense pinned Jamie with her intense blue gaze. "We can walk away."

That she understood his struggle, well, it stirred something to life inside him. But, no, they couldn't walk away. The lad—*Rafe*—was his son. It was clear to anyone with eyes. He wouldn't walk away from the boy.

Doyle sloshed a few fingers of the spirits into each glass. As if outside himself, Jamie reached for the cup. He noted a slight tremor in his hand as sweat coated his body, the acrid, sickly smell assailing him with its familiarity and promise of oblivion.

Doyle held up his chipped teacup and indicated they do the same. "To old wine and young women." He gave Jamie a wink before slamming his drink back.

What precisely was Doyle implying?

Jamie stopped himself there. If he didn't, he might

have to consider the old rogue was implying a few thoughts he'd perhaps thought himself.

Right.

"Think nothing of it," Hortense murmured. "That's what he always says when he starts getting into his cups."

She tipped hers back, and Jamie followed suit. It was like fire going down the throat. It was like a drop of rain in the desert. Of a sudden, his body demanded more. A single drop—or an ocean full—would never be enough.

On a wheezing cough, Doyle barked one of his laughs that didn't quite sound jolly. Untrustworthy, that laugh. "That'll grow fur on yer nethers." He plunked his teacup on the table, chipping off another piece of porcelain. "Ye have a fortnight. Me mam has been poorly, and I want this done before she's off to meet her Maker with a clear conscience."

Jamie caught the man's shifty gaze. "And I have your word about the lad? You'll let him go?"

Doyle had the temerity to snort. "If the word of an old scoundrel means anythin' to ye."

"It doesn't," Jamie said. "We'll do it your way, *once*. But there are other methods for getting the boy, if you choose to go down that path."

Doyle spread his hands wide in a gesture of peace. "It won't come to that, milord." His gaze slid toward Hortense. "Once a eel, always a eel, pet."

She flinched, as if winged by a hard object. Jamie grabbed her arm in case she needed steadying. Her gaze met his for a flash, but what he saw surprised him. *Fear.* When he'd first met her, he'd thought her immune to the feeling. Yet, somehow, he sensed it didn't render her weak. Instead, its weight informed her every decision and made her stronger.

She pivoted neatly on her heel and was already

halfway up the stairs by the time he caught up to her. On their progress through the house—or whatever function this structure served, he suspected it had many—they encountered boys scattered about here and there. But it was one boy he sought. Not three feet ahead—for that was as far one could see—he detected a lanky form, and his stomach gave a lurch. It was the boy. *His* boy.

Without thought, he stepped in that direction. Fingers wrapped around his arm, staying him. He glanced down to find Hortense's cerulean gaze steady upon him. "Now is not the time," she murmured.

"What is to stop us from taking him now?"

"Me, fer starters," the boy said in a voice that was pure guttersnipe as he dug a shoulder into the wall and shifted his weight against it. "I ain't goin' nowhere with ye."

Rafe stared out with the same thick-lashed, gray eyes that Jamie encountered in the mirror every day. But these eyes held an impudence, a hardness, that one didn't expect to find in one so young. First the workhouse, then Doyle, when had this boy the luxury of being a child?

"Let us leave now," Hortense said, low, steady.

Still, his feet remained rooted in place, stubborn.

"*Jamie,*" she said, a plea weaving through his name.

She'd never called him Jamie.

It was enough to pull him into reality.

It went against every fiber of his being to leave the boy—*his* boy—behind. Through the door. Into the chill London night. Just as Hortense had led them here through the warren of Whitechapel streets, alleys, and byways, she led them out. It wasn't until they hired a hackney on Fleet Street and were ensconced in its noisome interior that she broke the silence from the bench opposite. "Marriage?"

The whirl of Jamie's racing mind came to a complete standstill. *Marriage.*

He'd proposed marriage to this woman. Panic should be rioting through his body. But of all the twists and turns and matters weighing heavily on him, surprisingly, this wasn't one of them. "Aye."

Her head canted to the side. "Surely a false one."

"Nay."

"I know a document forger who can make anything." She was utterly serious.

"It will need to be real." For whom wasn't quite clear.

Her eyes went wide with incredulity. He'd flummoxed her. "But...but *why?*"

"Nick would not stand for me besmirching your honor. He would have my head on a pike." It was the truth. It might still be the truth even after the marriage.

"Nick can be talked around."

"Society will know if it isn't real. The rumor of a special license for the Marquess of Clare will spread through Society like wildfire."

She released a long breath before nodding slowly. "Giving us a little notoriety and panache."

"Aye." There was yet more on the subject of their marriage that needed to be said. "In name only. It doesn't need to be more than that."

"I never planned to marry," she said.

His presumption struck Jamie hard. Marriage was nothing to him, but he hadn't considered it might be something to her. "But you might someday. If you met the right man."

Why was he trying to talk her out of it?

She shook her head. "I'm a thoroughly independent woman, I'm afraid. No man would tolerate me. I can't cook. I can't clean. No interest in needlework beyond darning the odd stocking. I'm useless as a woman."

"I'd hardly say that." A beat of time slunk past. "I might find some uses for you."

Sudden tension snapped through the air, his implication clear. A ray of moonlight streamed through the window at her side, and he thought he might detect a blush-stained cheek.

Her gaze met his and held. "But you already have, my lord."

"Oh?"

His cock thickened, and his mouth went dry. The directness of her gaze did that to him.

Yet another reason for his marriage proposal occurred to him. And this reason wasn't simply *another*, but possibly *truer*. As his wife, her direct gaze would be his. Not as a possession, but to possess. He wanted to capture it and hold it and transform it with desire. He wanted it to bend to him, but not break.

"I've been very useful in locating your former lover, and now your son."

Right. *Right.*

Of course. *Of course.*

Her words were the splash of cold water he needed.

"Now I shall put the question to you." Her eyes narrowed. She'd recovered herself and was now on the offensive. "If you're married to me, then how will you marry someone else?"

"As I've explained, marriage has never been high on my list of priorities."

"You might change your mind about the lineage of the marquessate sometime in the future. We humans can be mercurial."

He snorted. "I don't give two tosses about continuing the Asquith line. Nick has a legitimate son. The family line is secure as far as I'm concerned. Geoffrey can carry it forward."

"But—"

Impatient with this line of questioning, he cut her off. "That was my *son* in Flick Doyle's lair."

The light of knowledge shone in Hortense's eyes. She knew it, too.

"He is the spitting image of me at that age."

"You need to understand something," she said slowly. "Doyle and those other boys, they are his family."

"*I* am his family."

She gave her head a slow shake. "He won't see it that way."

"I shall remove him from there."

"And you will do anything?"

"*Anything.*"

"Even marry a guttersnipe?"

The way she posed the question struck him like a blow. For she wasn't accusatory or bitter, but completely and utterly matter of fact.

"You are more than that, Hortense. You know how to read. You speak French." He searched for more —*better*—words. "You're *you.*"

He hesitated, unsure he had the right to ask the next question. But he must nonetheless. "What is the story of Hortense Marchand? Or is that Amelie?"

"How do you know—" Realization lit across her face. "Mrs. Ditch used the name."

Jamie nodded. "How did that little girl who spoke French and could read end up in the workhouse and in Flick Doyle's pickpocket gang? What is the story of *you*?"

Her gaze fixed on the window, seeing nothing but her past, he suspected.

"My parents escaped the Reign of Terror in the spring of seventeen ninety-four," she said. "They were master weavers who supplied fine fabrics to the French nobility. In the beginnings of the Revolution, they had been safe, but then the winds changed. Anyone who conducted trade with aristocrats were suspect and imprisoned as sympathizers. They fled to England and set up their business in London. Several years later, I was born, their little Amelie."

"That's what they called you?"

She nodded.

"Then how did you—" He shut his mouth. It would be wrong to rush her along. This story didn't end well.

"How did I end up in the workhouse?" Her eyes went dark with a deep sadness. "Cholera began making the rounds of Spitalfields. Papa and Maman contracted it and succumbed."

"You weren't infected?"

"I was, but it was milder for me."

"How old were you?"

"I'd just reached my seventh year."

Shock traced through him. So young to be alone in the world. "And you were taken to St. Mary Magdalen workhouse?"

She nodded.

"What was it like?" He needed to know. The place had affected those who he cared about most in the world, including the brave woman sitting opposite him. He wouldn't dwell too long on that, only it was the truth.

"It houses about two hundred children. We were kept separate from the adults."

"What was the work?"

"Mostly picking oakum for shipbuilders, and some shoe work, too. Tasks requiring small, nimble fingers and sharp eyes. We were fed three times a day, had a pallet for sleeping, and a roof over our heads."

Her eyes had gone flat in the telling, as if she needed distance from her own story.

"How did you get out?"

"One day, I saw one of the workhouse boys—*Ned*—talking to another boy through a crack in the wall."

"One of Doyle's eels?"

"Doyle wanted the matron's strongbox lifted."

"Not our Mrs. Ditch by chance?"

Hortense laughed drily. "The same. I shoved Ned aside and said I would do it."

"And you pulled it off?"

"Aye."

"You have nerve."

"Lugged that box all the way to a hole dug beneath the wall. Once outside, I was one of Doyle's gang, a lucky eel. The first and only girl."

He intuited something important here. "And you weren't called Amelie?"

"That was Papa and Maman's name for me. I could no longer be her."

"Hortense had to be a different sort of girl."

She nodded.

"Then how did you get out of the eels?" A shadow darkened the blue of Hortense's eyes. Before she could speak, he had the answer. "You picked Nick's pocket."

"And spoke French."

A possibility occurred to Jamie, one that had him clenching his hands into fists. "Did Nick threaten you with arrest if you didn't go with him?"

Her eyes went bright with alarm. "It wasn't like that."

"Then why did you agree?"

"Because he offered me—"

Jamie found himself hanging on her every word.

She cleared her throat. "Fair monetary recompense," she finished, her voice gone hard and unyielding.

He would have sworn she'd been on the verge of saying something else. "Just like you and me."

She winced. He wasn't trying to wound her. But

that wince told him something. Fair monetary recompense was the truth, but not all of it.

"In name only?" she asked without segue. They'd circled back to the original topic.

"You have my word."

"I can't imagine we suit."

"We can lead separate lives."

The instant the words were out of his mouth, he wanted them back.

She stared through him with those keen blue eyes of hers, head canted. "That's the way your kind do it, isn't it?"

He didn't like this turn in the conversation, and it didn't help that he'd precipitated it. "It was how my parents did it."

"I know nothing about being a marchioness."

"If my mother could be one, you certainly can. You're a sight more clever than she."

"The bar is set that high?"

He shifted forward, on pins and needles. "Will you? Or won't you?"

"You were dead bored when we met." A beat. "Am I an exotic adventure for you?"

Fair question.

"You are a person," Jamie said. *And I've grown surprisingly fond of you*, he didn't say. "I feel it's *right*. To save Rafe, to save—"

"*Me?*" A fiery spark lit within her eyes. "I don't need saving."

"Myself," he finished.

"Oh." Her countenance settled.

"Using the marquessate to marry you and free my son is the best use I've ever had—or ever will have —for it."

She went stone still. Weighing her options, he suspected. He felt balanced on the tip of a needle. If she said no...

"So, we marry," she said softly.

He allowed a relieved breath to release from his lungs.

She extended her hand. He took it in a handshake but held on a beat too long. It was simply that her hand was so much smaller than his, the bones delicate, but not fragile. This hand was capable and strong. Yet he felt the sudden resolve to protect it. With great reluctance, he let go.

"And after you have Rafe?" she asked.

"You can lead whatever life you choose." He didn't like the pang in his gut.

"As can you."

He had to clamp his mouth shut, or risk scaring her away. He might say something like the life he'd chosen before he met her wasn't much of one.

That his life was better with her in it.

But he couldn't say that.

The carriage began slowing. They were approaching 11 Little Peter Street. "Shall I hold on to the tiara?" he asked.

She nodded. "Return for me three days hence."

"Why not tomorrow?"

"I have affairs to put in order, and you have a special license to procure. Settle that tomorrow and let the news circulate a few days before Wellington's supper party. It should attach a good bit of notoriety to us by the time we make our debut as the Marquess and his new Marchioness of Clare."

He saw the soundness of her reasoning, but he hadn't gone a single day without seeing her since they'd met. Now it would be three? "Then, Saturday?" he asked, albeit reluctantly.

"Sir Bacon and I shall be ready." She reached for the

door handle and hesitated. "One more matter before I go."

"Yes?"

"The drink at Doyle's..."

Like that, he could smell it, taste it...*crave* it. "I'd thought never to touch the stuff again."

"Sometimes one drink leads to the need for another," she said. "Has the need returned?"

He shook his head. "I don't think so."

"Do you want—"

"Do I want what?"

"Do you want someone to sit up the night with you?"

The question hit Jamie flat-footed. Its content. The concern in her eyes. He could say yes and keep her with him. But he didn't want her that way. He wanted her of her free will.

In more ways than one.

He'd been avoiding it in himself for days, but he could no longer. He wanted Hortense. No qualifications to the statement.

Which, of course, didn't mean he would have her. He'd assured her of that, and he wouldn't break a promise to her. No matter what it cost him.

"I shall see you three days hence," he stated.

"Until Saturday." She pushed the hackney door open, hopped to the ground, and was off.

The night went gray without her presence. For that was what he'd noticed these last several days. When she left, she took all the vividness of life with her, leaving behind a world gone drab at the edges.

She was capable, intelligent, and strong. She was also small and alone. He understood Nick's ferocity regarding her, for the same ferocity now coursed through his veins.

Just now, he'd lied by omission. It was true he

wanted to use his power and resources as a marquess of the realm to save his son and, by extension, himself. But he would also be able to use it to protect her when, on Saturday, he made her his wife.

In name only.

So help him.

CHAPTER TWELVE

*H*ortense stood before the moldering door for the second time tonight and tapped out her special knock.

This time, it was her alone. The terms Doyle had agreed to with Clare weren't the only terms, she was certain. It wouldn't be as simple as trading the paste tiara for Rafe. There would be a tax.

Further, Doyle hadn't revealed his and her continuing arrangement to Clare. She would have to pay for that, as well.

The taxes kept stacking up.

The door cracked wide enough for a suspicious eye to appear, then opened to admit her. Not a minute later, she was standing before Doyle exactly where she'd left him two hours ago.

"I knew ye'd be back. Gettin' predictable in yer dotage, pet." He roared his vile, phlegmy laugh.

"What's my tax?" She didn't see any reason not to cut directly to it.

"Can't I be doin' somethin' from the bottom of me heart?"

"No."

Again, he laughed. "No tax, pet."

"Why did you agree to the deal?"

"Me dear, sweet mam, 'course." He was definitely toying with her.

She wasn't having it. "You never agree to let one of your eels go, not until they're too big, too old, or too incarcerated to serve your purposes anymore. So, why Rafe?"

"Oh, he's servin' a purpose. He's how me mam's soul will be able to rest in peace."

Hortense believed that bit, but there was more. Doyle's eyes shone with a canny light. He wanted her to puzzle it out. Of a sudden, it struck her like a thunderbolt. "You're not giving him up."

A beatific smile broke across Doyle's face. "I knew ye'd get there. Ye always were too clever fer yer own good."

"What's the game?"

"It'll come in right handy to have an eel on the inside of a lord's palace, ye ken?"

The fear and anger that had been building inside her broke like a dam. Rafe would be used as a weapon against Clare. "No," she stated, clear and direct.

Doyle's eyebrows lifted. "*No?* Last I checked, ye don't be givin' the orders 'round here."

Her mind raced. *Think, think, think.* She couldn't let this happen. Clare and Rafe would never have a chance of a true, father-and-son relationship. Further, Rafe would never be free of Doyle. *Think, think, think.*

The solution came to her. "Use me instead." Such a terribly simple solution.

Doyle's eyes narrowed behind his spectacles, and his smile faded. "Don't be spoutin' words ye don't mean."

"I'll be the wife of a lord."

"Yer gonna become the nob's wife, in truth?"

"Aye."

"Is it love?" There was no missing the sarcasm in the question.

"Hardly," she shot back. The reply was surprisingly difficult to speak.

Doyle tapped his forefinger to his mouth. "I saw the way he looked at ye."

"You're mistaken."

Doyle snorted. "Ye could run circles 'round that lord and rob him blind and he would ne'er notice. That's how he looks at ye."

Hortense shrugged. She wouldn't give Doyle the satisfaction of rising to his words.

"Yer gonna stay married to him?"

"Doubtful." Which was only true.

"Ye and me, Hortense, we could rule o'er London town."

And another lightning bolt struck her. "It was me you wanted all along." His reptilian smile only confirmed it. "But why? I've paid my taxes."

"I want more of ye, pet. *All* of ye."

She felt suddenly winded. "I will not be your mistress." The very idea brought sick up her throat.

Doyle looked genuinely affronted. "What do ye take me fer? An old lecher?"

Best to steer the conversation back in the other direction. Still, no small amount of relief coursed through her. "I'll agree, but only if you let the boy go. Free and clear."

Doyle sucked his teeth. "Now, how can I trust ye'll follow through?"

"I'm a woman of my word."

Skeptical eyebrows lifted. "Oh? Ye didn't tell me 'bout yer dealin's with that nob ye brought in. Makes me wonder what else ye be holdin' back."

He had her there. "What surety do you need from me?"

Doyle allowed a few beats of time to tick past. "His ring."

"Pardon?"

"All those nobs got a fancy ring," he continued. "A ring that says they're more important than the rest of us. Ye bring me his."

Doyle wanted Clare's signet ring. Now that she thought about it, she'd never seen Clare wear it and hadn't the faintest idea where it was. But, no matter. She could figure out the details later.

"What's to stop him from calling the watch on me when he discovers it gone?"

Doyle snorted. "Call the watch on his wifey fer thievery? That would be right humiliatin' fer a nob. Ye see men, and 'specially nobs, they don't take too well to humiliation of the public variety. He won't breathe a word of it, ye kin be sure."

The truth rang through Doyle's words. There was only one thing left for her to do. She nodded her assent.

Doyle spit into his hand and extended it. After a repulsed hesitation, Hortense did the same and shook hands. It was a bargain sealed. The real bargain. The one he'd been after all along.

"You'll have it after I get the tiara and you hand over Rafe."

Doyle nodded, and she turned on her heel.

"Once a eel, always a eel," he called after her, the words following her up the stairs and haunting her step across London and into her bed.

She'd made the right choice. The *only* choice.

She repeated the words in her head as dawn stretched its long golden fingers across the sky and until they took on the weight of truth. At last, she fell into a fitful slumber, Sir Bacon snugged into the crook of her legs.

* * *

Four hours later

A haranguing of the door leading to the alley, muffled but distinct, jerked Hortense awake. That, and Sir Bacon's barking response.

She scrambled out of bed, her eyes only very reluctantly squeezing open, and pulled on the item of clothing nearest at hand, which was her overcoat. Who could possibly need inside her rooms this badly?

She snatched the dagger off her bedside table and dropped it into a pocket. It could get her out of whatever situation lay on the other side of that door. Or, at least, a galloping start.

It was only when she found herself at the bottom of the staircase that she realized she hadn't as much as glanced into a mirror.

She jerked the door open, and her exasperated greeting froze in her mouth. Mariana stared out at her, expectantly. "That happy to see me?" she asked as she swept past Hortense and up the staircase. Even Sir Bacon appeared bewildered as they obediently followed.

Hortense closed the bedroom door with a quiet click and slowly turned to find Mariana taking in every inch of her surroundings and drawing her own conclusions.

"What are you doing here?" asked Hortense. It was the only logical question.

"I hear there is to be a wedding in two days," Mariana replied with a bright smile.

"Well—"

"We are to be sisters." Mariana closed the few feet between them and took Hortense into an embrace that she had difficulty returning with a corresponding intensity.

"The future Marchioness of Clare." Mariana slapped a newspaper on the room's central table. "It says so right here."

Hortense took the paper, gingerly, as if she was in danger of being scalded by its contents. *The London Diary*. A scandal sheet. There, on the lower right corner of the front page was a blind item that would leave no member of the *ton* in the dark as to its subject:

> *What is the saying? Marry in haste...*
> *Oh, Cl*re, have a care!*
> *But the real question is...*
> *What lady would dare?*
> *She would need to be spirited...*

She slapped the paper down with more force than necessary. Eyes solemn upon her, Sir Bacon gave a little whine, sensing her distress. But, oh, gossip rags did their dirty work fast.

It wasn't the main content that upset her. In fact, it was the perfect introduction for a couple looking to generate a little notoriety upon their Society debut. It was the last line that had her jaw tensed. *Spirited...* Spirits. Clare's wastrel past was a well-known fact in those circles. But the casualness of the line, well, it seemed unnecessary, and cruel.

"I take it Jamie procured a special license last night?" Mariana asked.

"He must have." So quickly. Hortense would never not be amazed by how quickly doors opened for the aristocracy.

Mariana strode to one of the room's two threadbare chairs. "May I?"

Hortense snapped to. Where were her manners? "Of course."

Mariana clasped her hands in her lap and waited, an

expectant expression on her face. "That means you, too."

"Oh, yes, of course." Hortense hurried over to the other chair and perched stiffly on its edge. Mariana wasn't the sort of lady to gad about, wasting her time. She was here for a reason. "I'm not usually so—"

"Scattered?" Mariana finished for her. "The twins will be so excited to attend their first wedding."

The twins? *Oh, no, no, no.* "You must not invite them."

Mariana made her eyes innocent.

Hortense knew the ploy well enough to brace herself.

"But why ever not? They love their uncle, and they love you."

Blast. Mariana was *good.*

"It's simply better if they're not involved," Hortense said. *It would be too difficult to explain later,* she left unsaid.

The expression in Mariana's eyes said she'd heard it anyway. She sat forward in her seat, her brown eyes suddenly black with intensity. "What is truly behind this marriage?"

And now the lies would begin. While Hortense didn't relish the idea of playing a role for a beloved friend, she couldn't see she had a choice. This was Clare's private business, and if he hadn't seen fit to tell his family, it certainly wasn't her place.

And then there was her deal with Doyle. She didn't want that slipping out. Nick and Mariana must never know. It was too shameful.

So, she calmed herself in the way she always did before uttering a necessary lie. "We fell madly in love."

Mariana laughed, heartily, as only Mariana could, from the very depths of her belly. Hortense felt slightly envious of that laugh. She'd never been able to laugh so freely in her entire life. Well, maybe that wasn't entirely true. There was a time before Papa and Maman's deaths—a time she never allowed herself to dwell upon.

Oh, how the past had been conjured these last few days.

"You will have to do better to convince me of a mad, all-consuming passion," said Mariana.

Hortense lifted her eyebrows and pressed her lips together. Mariana was her friend, it was true, but she didn't have to explain this. It wasn't her story to tell.

"If I may be so bold," Mariana continued, undeterred, as ever, "you lack the specific madness and agitation of the wretchedly in love."

Oh. Mariana would see that. "I..." This was uncharted territory in Hortense's canon of lies. "I would think wretched love takes many forms."

Mariana snorted. "Not bloody likely." She exhaled a resigned sigh. "You may keep your secrets, but you must know this. Beneath all Jamie's titles and general lordliness beats a true and steadfast heart. A good, thoughtful man hides inside him. You can trust it."

"I trust nothing," Hortense retorted, the words a reflex, one that felt less true now than it did a mere few days ago.

Mariana leaned forward and placed her hand on Hortense's knee. "We all need someone we can believe in. Someone we can trust. That trust fills our hearts."

Hortense swallowed around the lump that had formed in her throat. She was encountering rather too many of those these days. "My heart is not constructed that way."

"Oh, it is." Mariana pinned Hortense in place with her unrelenting gaze. "But you must brave the wild brambles to find the center. And, my dear, it is worth it."

Hortense knew nothing of hearts. The brambles,

however, were all too familiar. "Shall I ask my landlady to send up tea?"

Mariana flicked a dismissive wrist. "Oh, we don't have time for that."

"We don't?"

"Show me your wedding dress."

Hortense opened her mouth and closed it, the command catching her quite flat on her feet. "I...um..."

Mariana nodded in confirmation. "Just as I thought."

Dread ribboned through Hortense. "What did you think?"

"You don't have a special dress for your wedding day."

"I have a perfectly suitable dress for the occasion."

"Perfectly suitable?" Mariana scoffed. "*Perfectly suitable* simply won't do for one's wedding."

Hortense pointed toward a dress draped over the back of a chair at the opposite end of the room. "That would do." Not impressive for a future marchioness, but no matter. She wouldn't be one for long, she was certain of it.

Mariana's eyes went wide with incredulity. "No, no, my dear. You are *not* wearing gray on your wedding day."

"I'm not?"

Oh, this marriage farce was truly beginning to grow legs of its own.

Mariana shot to her feet. "Lucky for you, you have me as your sister."

Hortense wasn't sure she felt lucky in the least as Mariana dashed across the room. "Where are you going?"

"To my carriage," Mariana said, hand on the door handle, "to retrieve a few items, and people."

CHAPTER THIRTEEN

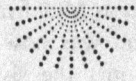

*P*eople?

But Mariana was gone before Hortense could ask. She sank back in her seat. A whirlwind had swept through the room and would soon be doubling back to wreak yet more mayhem. All she could do was wait.

She glanced down at Sir Bacon, who had hopped onto the bed and was now resting his muzzle on his front paws, content to watch the proceedings from a distance. "Wise choice."

Soon—*too soon*—footsteps began ascending the staircase, more than one pair. What did Mariana have planned?

The door swung open and in tromped Mariana, arms full of what appeared to be fabrics, colorful, *fine* fabrics. "Have you turned dressmaker?"

"No, I leave that to the professionals. Today, I'm simply a delivery woman."

It was then Hortense noticed the figure entering the room behind Mariana. Small of stature with lustrous sable hair and large dark eyes set within a face of delicate beauty that belied the steel beneath the surface, the woman swept in with great bustling energy as she settled her bags on the floor and directed the girl at her heels to do the same. "Nell," came the woman's soft, yet firm, Spanish accent, "retrieve the stand from the carriage."

"Yes, Señora Galante."

Señora Galante? Hortense had only met the woman once, but she knew her as Mrs. Eva Gardiner, the sister of Isabel Galante, who was now Lady Percival Bretagne. Hortense had met the sisters last year when Percy was helping them through a precarious family situation. Although the woman had a small child, Hortense suspected the widow story was a complete fabrication.

"Señora Galante is one of the owners of Galante: Dressmakers Extraordinaire and has graciously agreed to work up a bride's dress for you on short notice," explained Mariana.

Hortense met Señora Galante's eye. "We are acquainted."

Mariana's brow furrowed. "Acquainted?"

"We were briefly introduced at Gardencourt Manor last summer," the dressmaker replied, "And you must call me Eva."

Mariana smiled in understanding, the air suddenly ripe with the events of a late June day. A shadow crossed Eva's face, but in the next moment, she was squaring her shoulders. At once, it was clear she would be taking charge. Her assistant stomped into the room, a little out of breath, carrying a large, circular stool. "Where should I put this?"

Eva pointed toward the room's single window, coated with the dust of a few dozen years. "There will have to do." Clearly, the woman was none too impressed with Hortense's abode.

She contained a snort. Her lodgings were functional

and clean. Her domestic skills didn't extend any further.

"Well, if everyone is settled, I must away," said Mariana, slipping her fingers into her kidskin gloves. "The headmistress of Lavinia's school has called for an emergency meeting of the board of directors, which consists of myself and my sister. Apparently, the school's French cook is being too French. Mrs. Bloomquist's words." She shrugged. "What time shall I send the carriage for you, Eva?"

All business, the woman consulted the silver time-piece hanging from a chain at her waist. "One hour hence."

Mariana tossed a wink toward Hortense and exited the room.

"Nell," said Eva, "please move the mirror to the window as well." As the girl set about her task, Eva gestured toward Hortense. "And you," she began, "disrobe."

Hortense blinked. She wasn't sure what she'd expected to emerge from the woman's mouth, but it wasn't that. "Entirely?"

"Of course," Eva replied, absently, the majority of her attention concentrated on removing the tools of her trade from the various bags strewn about the room.

"Oh...um..." Truly, she couldn't think of a response.

Eva swiveled around "Have you never been fitted for a dress?"

Only the truth would do. "No."

"And you're to be a marchioness in two days?"

"Aye."

An assessing glint entered Eva's eye. She'd intuited an intrigue afoot. Yet she chose to leave it and again bent to her task. "While you disrobe, Nell and I shall ready your new attire for the fitting."

Well, this wouldn't take long, as Hortense was only

wearing two articles of clothing. She slipped her over-coat from her shoulders and folded it neatly before placing it on the bed. Sir Bacon leisurely rose to his four feet and gave the garment a good sniff before deeming its voluminous folds a worthy resting place for his nap. As the other women went about their business of setting out pins, needles, scissors, fabrics, and a few dresses that looked already mostly constructed, Hort-ense stood, awkward, wearing nothing but a chemise.

"Shall I move to the platform?"

"If you will." Eva cocked her head. "The chemise, too."

"Surely, I can wear my own—"

Eva held up her hand, staying the words in Hort-ense's mouth. "The innermost layer of our clothing is as vital as the outermost. It is what lies next to our skin that gives us the most pleasure, no?"

Hortense's mouth wanted to gape open. "I've never once in my life formed such a thought."

"Well, slip this on"—Eva held out a bit of ivory muslin—"and tell me it doesn't change your mind."

Cheeks flaming, Hortense shimmied out of her well-worn chemise and accepted the new garment from Nell. A giggle on her lips, the girl wouldn't quite meet her eye.

The new chemise slid over her head and down her body, reaching the middle of her thighs. Until this very moment, Hortense hadn't been aware that cotton could feel so silky. Never had she experienced such luxury against her skin.

Eva's mouth curved into a knowing smile. "You see?"

As Hortense accepted and donned layer after layer of clothing—chemise, stays, stockings, slippers, all constructed of the finest silks, satins, muslins and leathers—she could hardly countenance the change she observed in the mirror. To her stunned eye, she was truly beginning to embody the role she was to play.

Marchioness.

Eva held up a silk gown of pale blue silk shot through with silver. It was the most exquisite dress Hortense had ever beheld. "I am to wear *that?*" she heard herself ask.

"Indeed."

"I've been betrothed"—how strange that word felt in her mouth—"to the marquess for less than a day. How could you possibly construct such a...a—"

"Masterpiece?" asked Eva, disingenuousness dancing in her eyes.

That hadn't been Hortense's next word, but it fit. The dress was a glory. "But to sew it so fast. I don't see how that's possible."

"Oh, it ain't," said Nell, who surely recognized Hortense from that long-ago June night. "It were goin' to another lady."

Eva shrugged. "She can wait."

"You mustn't lose business over me. I'm sure some other dress will do."

Eva's mouth curved into a smile that contained no small amount of guile. "You strike me as a woman who knows the workings of the world."

"I like to think so."

"Then you should appreciate that the other lady is the wife of a minor lord and you will be a marchioness in two days."

Ah.

"The finery you see before you is the result of aristocratic connections and money, the full power of which you have at your fingertips."

Eva Galante was, first and foremost, a business-woman. Hortense understood the decisions that made one a success. "Lady Mariana can certainly be a force when she puts her mind to it."

"It wasn't Lady Mariana rapping on my shop door first thing this morning," said Eva.

"No?"

"It was your betrothed, the Marquess of Clare."

The Marquess of Clare...her betrothed. It beggared belief.

"He was quite clear that you are to have the best. When he saw this garment hanging on a dress form, he insisted it be yours." She tapped her mouth with her forefinger. "And I can see why. It suits your coloring perfectly."

Hortense fought the urge to squirm. Never in her life had she been the recipient of such attention. No, that wasn't true. Although she could hardly call to mind the curves and contours of Papa and Maman's faces, the care in their eyes had never left her.

And the dress Clare had chosen for her—had *insisted* upon—was fit for a princess.

The very notion was too bright, too bold, for her to face directly. She had to turn away from it. This was part of the ruse they were selling to the *ton*. That was all.

A whine from Sir Bacon caught the room's attention. The little dog had come to a stand and was wagging an impatient tail. She knew exactly what that meant. "He needs to go outside."

"Surely, he can wait."

"Hand me my dress."

She made to step down from the stool. Sir Bacon hadn't had an accident indoors all day yesterday. He was a smart fellow, which led to a single explanation for his indoor incontinence. No one had ever taken the time or had the patience to teach him his manners.

Eva held up a staying hand. "Nell, take the animal outside, if you will."

Nell's face lit up. "Happy to."

"His lead is beside the door," said Hortense, but Nell had already located the length of white silk and was slipping it over the dog's neck. The girl was out the door in a matter of seconds.

Now just the two of them, Eva met Hortense's eye. It was obvious the woman had something to say. "Before we continue, I feel I must clear the air between us." She was referring to last June.

"There is entirely no need," said Hortense. "I can assure you."

Eva had a look in her eye that said she wouldn't be dissuaded. "Thank you for saving my life."

Hortense went suddenly hot, a blush rising to the surface of her skin. It was the rare occasion that she received gratitude for her services, and it sat at an odd angle inside her. "It wasn't your life that I saved."

Eva's eyes narrowed. "*Sí*, it was."

It was clear neither of them wanted to revisit the June summer night when Hortense had only just deflected the shot Eva had fired at Lord Bertrand Montfort. Although she'd been able to prevent the bullet from hitting its target squarely, it had wounded and paralyzed Montfort. Not that the man hadn't deserved it. But if he'd been killed, well, the consequences for Eva Galante would have been beyond Hortense and Percy's ability to cover up.

Eva held up the dress, her gaze shifting back and forth between Hortense and the garment. "Oh, why must you be so small?"

"I haven't the choice, I'm afraid. If I did, I can assure you I would be considerably larger."

Eva heaved a resigned sigh. "This dress will need to

be taken in a great deal. You are no more than a scrap of a woman."

"I believe I have all the necessary parts."

Eva sized her up from head to toe. "But look at the lean muscles on your arms. You are strong, too. Now, let us see what we are working with."

Hortense did as commanded and slipped into the dress. Eva cinched and bound her into the garment, before carefully placing pins where alterations would be needed.

The bodice pinched in at her waist in the latest Parisian style, and that wasn't its only French quality, for the bosom was cut scandalously—*perilously*—low. She attempted to hike it up, but to no avail. It really was determined to expose her at the slightest hint of a deep breath.

And she'd wished to wear a silk dress on a job for once. She must be more careful with her wishes.

Yet she couldn't deny that, even with her hair pulled back in a severe chignon, she looked more feminine —*felt* more feminine—than she had in all her life. Femininity was a luxury she'd never experienced.

She hardly recognized herself. She'd played many roles as spy, but never *lady*. Could it really be she who stared back at her in the looking glass?

"Does the dress have to be so…"

"*Revealing?*"

"That would be the word."

"I was given explicit instructions that you are to have the latest Parisian fashion. And you are wearing it." Eva's eyes dared Hortense to protest as she set about loosening ties and buttons. "I have all I need. You may remove it now."

Hortense allowed the dress to fall and stepped out of the pile of delicate silk at her feet. She prided herself on the fact that there was no role she was unequal to, but the suspicion was growing that she may have reached her limit with the role of marchioness.

"The alterations will take me no more than a few hours," continued Eva. "I shall have this and two more dresses ready for you on the morrow, and a riding habit, too."

A riding habit? "I do not ride."

Eva raised a skeptical eyebrow. "*You* do not ride?" She emitted a little laugh. "I thought nothing was beyond your capabilities."

"Well, that is," Hortense amended, "I do not ride like a lady."

This time, Eva's laugh reached her belly. "Now, *that* I believe." The woman held up a few yards of a coral-colored silk. "With your coloring, crisp hues for you, I think." She picked up another swath of fabric, this one a silk saffron. "Too muddy." She cast it aside and reached for a half-finished crimson silk gown. "With your pale skin and black hair, perfection."

The door swung open and in strode Sir Bacon with Nell only a few steps behind. "Lawks be, he wants to sniff the world, don't he?" the girl exclaimed, her cheeks bright and rosy.

Hortense smiled wryly. "The curiosity of his nose knows no bounds."

Truly, she'd grown very accustomed to him. She might even go so far as to say she'd begun to enjoy him. But he wasn't hers, and, soon, he would be returning to Lady Fortescue. She must remember.

"Nell," began Eva, consulting the timepiece at her waist, "can you help me gather our things? Lady Mariana's carriage will return within the quarter hour."

Hortense realized she was still standing on the stool, clad in nothing but a chemise, corset, stockings, and slippers. "I take it you'll want these back as well."

Eva waved the idea away. "As they fit, you can keep

them." She carried on replacing unused pins in a small pouch. "And I shall consent to make your presentation dress, as well."

Hortense hardly noticed when Eva and Nell spoke their good-byes and closed the door behind them. Other matters had pushed into the forefront of her mind.

Presentation dress?

The very notion snapped her back to the purpose of the finery surrounding and clothing her. She was being prepared for a role. She would enter and charm Society. And...

Use all her wiles to woo the Duke of Rothesbury. She and Clare hadn't discussed this, but surely he understood.

How else was she to get close enough to a duke to discover where he kept a jewel such as a diamond and sapphire tiara? Likely, he had a dozen.

But to accomplish it, first, she would marry Clare. Until now, the idea hadn't truly taken root in her mind. A portion of last night's conversation returned to her. He'd asked why she'd left Doyle's gang to join Nick's operation, and she'd told him for coin. But money hadn't been the first or even second reason she'd agreed.

Family, she'd almost confessed. A family different from Doyle and his lucky eels. One that didn't include a swift knock to the head when she did something wrong or said something pert. Nick's was a *family* to which she'd belonged and that served a purpose higher than lightening a nob's pockets. Nick gave her the opportunity to be a worthwhile person.

And she had been...for a time.

She could have said all this to Clare. Part of her had wanted to. But doing so would reveal so much of her. Too much of her.

She might even feel compelled to confess that she hadn't quite left the eels behind. Which would surely lead to one form of disaster or another—for Rafe, for Clare, for her. She must stay the course.

Yet a feeling related to those unspoken words had begun to unfurl inside her when Mariana spoke of him and, again, when Eva told her it was he who had banged on her door at the crack of dawn. It was a feeling Hortense hadn't experienced in years.

She couldn't trust this feeling. If she remembered correctly, it was composed of rare and elusive elements: security...safety...*hope*.

A dangerous element, that last one. It might lead her to think everything might come out all right in the end.

She shooed the feeling away. She couldn't trust it.

It lurked in a corner of her soul, patiently waiting for her to allow her guard to slip, which she quite simply couldn't do.

It would be the height of foolishness.

CHAPTER FOURTEEN

$\mathcal{A}$s discreetly as he could manage, Jamie wiped damp palms on his trousers, pretending to attend the conversation being held up mostly by Nick and the Bishop of London. He'd never spent such a nerve-riddled three days as the ones since he'd last seen Hortense.

The very thought of her had his eye flicking down the center aisle of the family chapel. Light streaming through a small rose window that was over five hundred years old illuminated the gray-veined white marble floor in a heavenly glow. But it remained empty of her. He couldn't quell the doubt she wouldn't put in an appearance.

"*Jamie,*" cut into his preoccupation.

He glanced over to find Nick regarding him as if expecting an answer. "Can you repeat the question?"

"Have you the bridal ring?"

Jamie patted his waistcoat pocket. It was there. He grunted in the affirmative.

Nick's brow furrowed. "One of Mother's?"

"Of course not," Jamie retorted with too much force.

The Bishop's eyebrows lifted in a straight uninterrupted line, a bushy caterpillar on his forehead. The thing was, since Hortense had tiptoed into his life with all the quiet of a hurricane, his emotions were all too big, as if they'd somehow grown in size and were spilling out of him at every opportunity.

He dug the ring from his pocket and held it up for Nick, who studied the piece of jewelry for a good, long thirty seconds. For whatever blasted reason, Jamie's breath suspended in his chest and the rate of his heart kicked up a notch.

"That is quite a stone, brother."

"Is it too much?" It very possibly was.

"I doubt she'll be able to lift her hand."

Jamie grunted and again glanced toward the center aisle. Still, no Hortense.

The jeweler at Rundell's had explained that he knew any number of ladies who would gladly give up a first-born son for a sapphire of that size and clarity.

"Doesn't it need some diamonds around it, or something more?" Jamie had asked. The simple gold band had looked rather plain to his eye.

The jeweler had pinned him with a long look. "When one has a large, perfect stone such as this, one lets it sing its aria alone."

And, now, looking at the ring, Jamie was glad he'd listened to the man. Hortense wouldn't want an ostentatious ring. Or, at least, not one more ostentatious.

Nick clapped him on the back. "She will be the envy of every lady of the *ton*."

With her jaded eye, Hortense would view the gift in exactly the same light, except from a different angle. It would be part of their ruse to sell their story of impetuous love. Notoriety was bound to follow.

Yet Jamie viewed it in neither light. Simply, he'd seen the ring and known in an instant that she had to have it. That was all.

"Well, everything seems to be in order. We simply need the bride."

Jamie caught a tone in his brother's voice. Nick had his doubts.

Three nights ago, after he'd left Hortense at her lodgings, he'd gone straightaway to see Nick.

"You wish to marry Hortense." Those had been the first words out of Nick's mouth upon receiving the news. "*You* wish to marry *Hortense?*" He'd frowned. "Does *she* wish to marry *you?*"

Jamie had snorted. He hadn't been able to help himself. His brother truly didn't have a high opinion of him.

Then Nick had narrowed his eyes. "What's this all about?"

"You'll know soon enough." Jamie didn't owe Nick the explanation his brother thought he did.

Nick's face had gone like thunder. "I'll know now. If you think to dally with Hortense, think again."

"I wouldn't treat her so."

"Will the marriage be a true one?"

"On my end, yes."

Nick searched Jamie with his gaze. "You'll need a special license."

"That's why I came to you."

"When is this wedding to take place?"

"Saturday." When Nick hesitated, Jamie asked, "Is it possible?"

"For the Marquess of Clare? Of course."

Something nagged at Jamie. "And a dress. She will need a dress." A beat passed. "Make it a whole new wardrobe."

"I know of someone." Nick wrote a name—*Galante: Dressmakers Extraordinaire*—and an address on a piece of paper. "Tell them it's for Hortense."

"Hortense knows a dressmaker?" Jamie was

shocked. "She's not exactly wearing the latest Parisian creations."

Nick rolled his eyes. "Just tell them."

Now, Jamie couldn't help anticipating how she would look in the dress he'd chosen. He'd only seen it on the dress form, a confection of powder-blue silk and silver. It looked entirely composed of clear mountain sky and crisp sunlight.

She wouldn't feel at ease in the dress, as such a garment placed a woman at the very center of a room's attention, a place she wasn't too comfortable occupying. She spent the majority of her time hiding herself away.

The sound of rushed footsteps click-clacked across marble just outside the chapel, and Jamie felt muscles tensing, bracing themselves. Mariana breezed through the open doorway, and the tension released from his body. His feelings were all up and down and no in-between. Deuced irritating.

Mariana dashed up the aisle, mischief in her eyes. Seating herself in the front pew, she said, "Your bride is on her way."

Next came a rapid *clickety-clack* against marble, and Sir Bacon appeared at the end of the aisle, drawing laughter from all, even the dour bishop. The terrier raced toward Mariana's outstretched hand. She scooped him up and settled him on her lap.

But one person remained to arrive.

The perspiration that had been relegated to Jamie's palms broke out across his entire body. This was it, the moment his future would change.

If she appeared.

She had every reason and right to bolt. He wouldn't choose to be saddled with himself, given the option. He was arrogant and stubborn, a trifle argumentative, and wholly intent on his goals once he'd set his sights on them. In no small part were he and Hortense similar on those points.

In name only.

A promise he intended to honor.

At the end of the short aisle, she appeared, and all past promises, all words, faded into the inconsequential. The sight of her stole his breath away. She was a small woman, but what hadn't been apparent were her feminine curves. *Until now.*

She should wear nothing but such dresses—she was made for them—for such a dress only highlighted the fact that Amelie Hortense Marchand—with her lithe figure, her silky black hair, and penetrating cerulean eyes—was a diamond of the first water.

From the corner of his eye, he noticed Mariana swipe a tear away. Nick leaned in and murmured something in his ear, but the words didn't register. It was only when Nick took a seat next to Mariana on the front pew that he realized his brother must have been excusing himself. Nick was unconvinced of the wisdom or validity of this marriage.

That last bit mattered not to Jamie. *He* was convinced. He wasn't sure any moment had felt more right in his life than this one, *here...now.*

Hortense took her place at his side, her light scent of fresh lemon drifting up to meet him. Unable to help himself, he breathed her in.

Her gaze flashed up to meet his.

"You look..." he found himself murmuring, but the perfect word wouldn't come. What word perfectly described a goddess?

"Like a nob?" she finished for him.

Definitely not. What was a better word for beautiful? That had been his next word, if he'd found it.

The bishop cleared his throat. "Dearly beloved, we

are gathered here in the sight of God to join together this man and this woman in holy matrimony..."

Jamie knew he should be facing forward and attending to the bishop's words, but his gaze couldn't resist sliding left, and landing on the elegant curve of her neck. He wanted nothing more than to lean down and press his lips to the patch of pale skin where beat her rapid pulse.

"...Therefore is not by any to be enterprised, nor taken in hand, unadvisedly, lightly, or wantonly, to satisfy men's carnal lusts and appetites..."

Jamie came to. The way he'd been following the curve of her neck to the line of her collarbone to the dip at the base of her throat, well, words like *carnal* and *lust* and *appetite* might apply.

"...Like brute beasts that have no understanding..."

The phrase hit uncomfortably close to the matter, if his physical response was any indicator.

"...Duly considering the causes for which matrimony was ordained. First, it was ordained for the procreation of children..."

Since there would be no consummation, there would be no children. His conscience could rest easy on that score. Except...

What a mother Hortense would make. He had no doubt any children of hers, be them male or female, would be forces in the world.

"...Secondly, it was ordained for a remedy against sin, and to avoid fornication..."

How had he not known the Church of England's marriage vows focused so tightly on sexual congress? He glanced down and found a smile twitching about the corners of Hortense's mouth. He had to fight the urge to kiss those delicately plump lips to see for himself if they tasted like cherries, as he'd thought the night they met.

"...Therefore if any man can show just cause, why they may not be lawfully joined together, let him now speak, or else hereafter forever hold his peace..."

The chapel went silent. Jamie couldn't help glancing behind him at Nick, whose mouth was pressed together in a firm line. Doubt shone in his brother's eyes. He didn't give a fig, as long as Nick didn't give voice to it now.

The bishop turned to Jamie. "Wilt thou have this woman to thy wedded wife, to live together after God's ordinance in the holy estate of Matrimony? Wilt thou love her, comfort her, honor, and keep her in sickness and in health, and, forsaking all others, keep thee only unto her, so long as ye both shall live?"

Jamie didn't hesitate. "I will."

His mind understood this marriage was a show, but a part of him he couldn't allow himself to explore had a different understanding of the matter.

It wanted to protect her.

It wanted to bed her.

It wanted to never let her out of his sight.

He'd never meant two words more.

The bishop turned to Hortense and repeated the words. In the space between the bishop's question and her reply, Jamie lived a lifetime, his throat tied into a knot, his heart a hammer in his chest.

"I will," she uttered at last.

He could breathe again.

The bishop directed his next words to the chapel, empty but for Nick, Mariana, and Sir Bacon. "Who giveth this woman to be married to this man?"

A silence ensued that only grew more uncomfortable with every second that beat by.

"Me," Hortense said, a comely blush spreading to the tips of her ears. "I give myself."

"That is most irregular, I daresay," the bishop huffed. His voluminous robes shuddered in agreement.

"The pouch in your pocket is there to ensure any *irregularities* will be overlooked," Jamie said, adamant.

It was the bishop's turn to blush. "Now repeat after me."

Jamie faced Hortense. "I take thee, Amelie Hortense Marchand to my wedded wife, to have and to hold from this day forward, for better for worse, for richer for poorer, in sickness and in health, to love and to cherish, till death us do part, according to God's holy ordinance, and thereto I plight thee my troth."

He'd never spoken more important words in his life.

When she spoke the vows, he held her gaze. He could see it wanted to skitter away, but he wouldn't allow it.

"Do you have the ring?" asked the bishop.

Jamie pulled it from his pocket and suddenly felt shy of it. It truly was obscenely ostentatious, exhibitionistic even. And he could see from the widening of Hortense's eyes that she had the same thought. She took an unconscious step backward, and he couldn't help smiling. "It doesn't bite," he murmured.

A small laugh escaped her like a much-needed release of nerves.

He took her left hand. Small and delicate within his, he only just realized that she wasn't wearing gloves, and neither was he. Her skin lay bare against his. Warm, soft, a subtle hint of moisture. As he slid the ring on to her fourth finger, he said, "With this ring I thee wed, with my body I thee worship, and with all my worldly goods, I thee endow."

He would wed this woman, worship her, protect her, to his dying breath.

It felt true.

It felt right.

"Those whom God hath joined together let no man put asunder," the bishop declared.

Silence descended on the chapel as Jamie held Hortense steady with his gaze. In those cerulean depths skittered uncertainty. But what he didn't see was doubt. Her faith stirred him. He wanted nothing more than to be worthy of it.

From the front pew, a throat cleared, discreet, expectant. What the deuce were they expecting?

It hit him. *Oh.*

Understanding had dawned on Hortense, too.

Cautiously, unconvinced he wouldn't scare her away, Jamie took a step, close enough that the banked heat of her body reached out and invited him nearer. Intuitively, he cupped the side of her face, and she swayed toward him. His head lowered, and he felt the breath from her upturned mouth in the heartbeat before his lips touched hers. The kiss was to be naught more than a touch, a formality. Then she breathed a sigh into his mouth, and a spark lit through him. His free hand couldn't help finding her lower back and pulling her into him. Her eyes fluttered shut, and she surrendered to his kiss. A single, fundamental understanding of himself came into perfect clarity:

His entire life had been moving toward this moment.

The moment his lips touched hers.

Again, a throat cleared, and a fluttery giggle echoed through the chapel, pulling a resistant Jamie from the depths of the kiss, depths he hadn't yet begun to properly explore. Not one to be far from the center of attention, Sir Bacon barked. Hortense's eyes flew wide, and she startled back, fingertips touching her kiss-crushed lips, chest rising and falling with shallow breaths. Stunned eyes stared up at him, and she bit her plump bottom lip.

He followed the movement. *Carnal...lust...appetite.* Words from his vows. Words that all applied to his state of mind. He wanted to take that lip between his teeth. It was all he could do not to go back in for another taste of her cherry sweetness.

Next he knew, Nick was clapping him on the back, and Mariana was gathering Hortense into a tight embrace. While congratulations where being offered and received, Hortense never left his field of vision. She was his *wife.* The idea filled him with equal parts dread and joy, and he couldn't decide which was more unreasonable.

He'd told her that she didn't truly have to be a wife to him. That they could lead separate lives. Nothing more was promised.

But, oh, what more he wanted.

He wanted all of her.

Sudden regret shot through him. There wouldn't be a wedding night.

And he wanted one. He wanted to explore every nook and cranny of her kiss and find out what more it offered, where it could lead...

He stopped himself there.

The kiss could lead nowhere.

He'd made a promise, one he would keep, even if it killed him.

"Shall we dine?" Mariana asked. "Join us for a celebratory supper tonight."

"Thank you for your offer, but we—" Hortense began.

"We have other plans for the evening," Jamie finished. Nick and Mariana gaped in unison, and he knew what they'd assumed in an instant. "Not like that."

Next, their brows furrowed. If not *those* plans, then what?

It was Nick who spoke next. "Dear brother, please explain."

"We have a previous engagement." Jamie was employing the aristocratic hauteur that so drove his little brother mad.

"With whom, pray tell?" In turn, Nick had adopted the infuriatingly patient tone that did naught but reveal his deep impatience with the subject at hand and dig beneath Jamie's skin.

"A supper party at Apsley House."

"You're choosing to spend your wedding night with the Duke of Wellington?" Nick sputtered.

"That old *roué*?" Mariana added for good measure.

"Indeed, we are," said Jamie.

Nick's eyes narrowed. "What precisely is *this* all about?" He waved his arm to include the chapel and the bishop, who was now halfway down the aisle. The man gave an indifferent wave of farewell, and said, "Everyone sign the register at your convenience. Have it delivered by morning."

Jamie opened his mouth to instruct his brother to mind his own business, when Hortense beat him to it. "Nick, it doesn't concern you."

"Like hell, it doesn't," Nick protested.

She didn't bat an eyelash. "Husband," she said, turning toward Jamie, "I believe you and I shall be late, if we do not leave soon."

"Don't forget your gloves, Lady Clare," Mariana chimed in, placing a staying hand on her husband's forearm. Nick's eyes had gone the hue of a thundercloud. "And be sure to put your ring on the outside of the glove. When one is in possession of a sapphire visible from the moon, one wants to throw it in everyone's faces, just a little."

With that parting message, Mariana dragged Nick

from the chapel, but not before Nick tossed Jamie one last glower that said this wasn't over.

Which left Jamie alone with Hortense.

His *wife*.

An awkwardness pervaded the air between them.

"Mariana called me Lady Clare," she said, stunned.

"That is who you are now."

She blinked, picked at the blue silk of her skirts. "This dress…"

"It's perfect on you." He could say more, but he would leave it at that.

"And the ring…"

He could see this woman who was always so cool and composed was rattled. "Nothing is too grand for the Marchioness of Clare."

Something in her eyes shifted, and he saw her withdraw into herself. Gone was her vulnerability. She nodded. "That is who I shall be tonight."

"That is who you *are*."

Disbelief shone in her eyes. "Shall we go?"

He held out his arm to walk her down the aisle. As man and wife.

Or something like that.

Even though this was a marriage of convenience, they were now bound to each other by something more tangible than handshake agreements and secrets.

They may not have had love, but they did have respect for one another.

Many marriages were based on less and worse.

Like that of his parents.

On, into the uncertain night he would walk with this woman.

It felt as if his life had only now truly begun.

CHAPTER FIFTEEN

"*J* take it that was a spoil of war?" Hortense stood at the foot of Apsley House's grand spiral staircase, transfixed by the nude statue of Napoleon styled as a Roman god holding a golden orb.

"Ah, yes, *Mars the Peacemaker*," said Clare, lightness in his voice, even if his impassive expression gave nothing away. "Along with the Battle of Waterloo, one of Napoleon's more questionable decisions. Prinny purchased it from the French government and pre- sented it to Wellington about a decade ago. One could hardly refuse such a gift."

"It does make a statement." She was relieved to be sharing this small bit of drollery with Clare. Ever since his mouth had touched hers two hours ago, she'd felt shy of him. That kiss... It had lasted no more than a handful of seconds, but her lips still tingled.

In a daze, she'd signed the marriage register, and they'd personally delivered it to the Bishop of London on their way to Apsley House. Clare had insisted.

Which made it official: she was a marchioness, an outcome she couldn't have predicted given a dozen lifetimes. In her finery and jewels, people deferred to her, *bowed* to her, and it was unsettling. This outrageous statue served as the release her jangly nerves needed.

"Shall I show you to the striped drawing room?" came the butler's polite tones.

Clare nodded and held out his arm. "Shall we?"

She placed her left hand on his forearm—a forearm whose tensile, masculine feel was becoming all too familiar. The ostentatious sapphire on her fourth finger winked up at her. With that stone and this dress, to all outward appearances, she was one of *them*, a nob.

Over the years, she'd done near anything to achieve her objectives. Lie. Cheat. Steal. Extort. Blackmail. She hadn't been above any of it if she believed her cause just. But to marry a man?

Her eye caught on his right hand. She'd never seen him wear his signet ring, but he was tonight, which made sense. It was an object central to who he was—a lord, a marquess. He likely didn't see it so due to the loathing he bore his father, but it was true.

And she would treat him no better than anyone else she had stolen from, or would steal from in the future, and take it.

Once a eel, always a eel.

Yet she'd never gone this far.

Which begged the question: why this far with this man? Or...

Was this man why she'd gone this far?

The question rattled her to her bones, for she rather suspected the answer lay within the question itself.

With each step they ascended toward the next floor, the volume of the party grew louder and more dense, the buzz of conversation intensifying, serious tones mixing with the light and happy. It sounded as if all of London Society was here.

For her new husband, this house and gathering would be somewhat commonplace, boring even. At least, that was what his expression communicated. It wasn't lost on her that the circumstances of this job had entirely flipped on its head. No longer were they navigating her world, but his.

As they followed the footman down one corridor, then another, they passed dozens of curious eyes. A few gentlemen nodded at the Marquess of Clare and their ladies offered up bright, flirtatious smiles before directing their attention toward the new marchioness. Then it was a quick narrowing of the eyes, an arch, assessing cant of the head. They couldn't yet place her in Society, but tonight they would.

They entered a room with twenty-foot ceilings and red-and-white striped sofas and benches, the walls filled with gilt-framed paintings of but one subject: the military glory of the Duke of Wellington and his generals. It was a room intent on inspiring awe in its occupants, and she would be damned if it didn't succeed.

The butler's voice rang out, "The Marquess and Marchioness of Clare."

For the space of three heartbeats, all fifty sets of eyes turned in a single, unified direction. As in the corridors, they widened with surprise before narrowing in assessment. Clare placed his hand on top of hers and squeezed. "Are you ready, *wife?*" he murmured.

Those were the words she needed to snap into her role. She was the Marchioness of Clare, the bride the besotted Marquess of Clare wanted so badly, so intensely, he had to obtain a special license to have her. Now, it was up to her to show the *ton* exactly the sort of notorious marchioness it had on its hands.

She gave the room a perfectly calibrated, saucy smile, and it burst into a buzzing hive of gossip in an instant, which was precisely the stir Clare had predicted. He knew these people. And why wouldn't he? He was one of them, through and through.

That last bit rang untrue, even unfair. He was one of them, but more, too. He was a man who would do anything to save a guttersnipe son about whom most men in this room wouldn't give two tosses. *He's better than the lot of them*, came an unbidden thought.

The spy in her took the lead as her gaze roved the room. "Do you see Rothesbury?"

Clare scanned the crowd. "There."

She followed his eye line and landed upon a lean man of middling height and sixty-something years with a head of thick, dark-brown hair, which appeared incongruous with the deep lines of his face. "Is he wearing—" She couldn't finish the question around the sudden giggle that had bubbled up.

"A wig?" Clare finished for her, his face impassive. "The man's vanity is boundless."

Information she would certainly use and exploit.

"He was a close companion of my father's."

Clare's jaw tightened, and she knew he would speak no more on the matter. She resisted the urge to give his arm a reassuring squeeze. She was his wife in name only. She wasn't here to offer him comfort. She was here to help him recover his son. Why was she finding it so difficult to keep the two separate?

As parted the Red Sea for Moses, so did the assembled for the couple making a direct line for them. The identity of the man was unmistakable, as various versions of his visage littered the four impressive walls surrounding them. "Clare," said the Duke of Wellington on a nod. "Good of you to make it out. It has been some time since you've graced Society with your presence, but"—his hawkish gaze landed on Hortense—"rumor has it you've been busy."

"Duke," said Clare, "may I introduce my bride, Lady Clare, to you?"

"You may, indeed." Wellington bowed over Hortense's hand. She felt not quite in her body. The *Duke of Wellington* was kissing the back of her fingers. "And, Lady Clare," he said, "may I introduce my friend, Mrs. Arbuthnot, to you?"

A small woman with chestnut hair and lovely dark eyes stepped forward and offered a curtsy. "Lady Clare, I am most pleased to make your acquaintance."

Unsure of the proper etiquette, Hortense gave a small curtsy in return.

"Please avail yourselves of the Duke's hospitality," said Mrs. Arbuthnot as she snatched two champagne coupes off a passing tray and offered them to Hortense and Clare. He refused. She accepted.

So, the whispers were true. Mrs. Arbuthnot was the mistress of the Duke of Wellington. A de facto wife, it appeared, as Wellington's true wife preferred the bucolic joys of the countryside to Town entertainments.

"Now," the woman continued, her authority clear, "it simply isn't done for a husband and wife to remain tied to one another for the duration of a supper party, so speak your farewells here," she finished on a tinkling laugh, her arm winding through Hortense's.

"Can you manage without me, dear husband?" Hortense asked, all flirtatious delight.

"Certain parts of me cannot, I'm afraid."

Mrs. Arbuthnot gave a giggle of faux shock and swatted Clare with her closed fan. "Oh, you are very bad, I fear. Lady Clare, you must divulge all your secrets for having harnessed him to the straight and narrow path. Many a lady had given him up for a lost cause."

"Oh, the straight and narrow was never for me," Hortense said, tossing Clare a parting glance over her shoulder. "I rather like the twists and bends."

Although she and Mrs. Arbuthnot walked side by side, Hortense understood she was being led through the drawing room as a curiosity on display. She'd only ever been in the presence of such a gathering of *ton* luminaries in the role of servant. Sparkling jewels—draped around pale necks, wrapped around delicate wrists, dripping from attentive ears—winked their combined brilliance as their owners cast alternately shy, bold, hard, or giggling glances her way.

"Let us take a rest," said Mrs. Arbuthnot. They approached a centrally located sofa upholstered in the same distinctive red and white fabric as the wall hangings and the benches lining the walls. Mrs. Arbuthnot chose the place strategically as any lady could observe or approach the new Marchioness of Clare. "Now, my dear, your time has come to run the gauntlet." She shot Hortense a shrewd glance. "I sense a bit of steel about you. Now would be the time to employ it."

As if a subtle cue had been dropped, the ladies began to approach, sometimes singly, sometimes in pairs, to make the acquaintance of and goggle at this mysterious woman who had managed to capture the elusive Marquess of Clare. It wasn't long before Hortense found herself abandoned by Mrs. Arbuthnot to the horde of inquisitive ladies who had no intention of holding their curiosity at bay. She also found that yet another full coupe of champagne had appeared in her hand. Her third.

"No one ever thought to see Clare a married man," said one lady.

"Rumors about his, ahem, *abilities* did abound," said another.

"Oh, pish," said yet another, "no one would ever believe such piffle about a man like Clare. Just look at him."

All eyes swung toward the marquess. Not a breath stirred the air as the collective gaze roved up and down his profile from afar. Hortense understood why. Her husband—with his dark tousled hair, stormy gray eyes, broad shoulders, muscular thighs that showed to particular advantage in his black superfine trousers, and quietly arrogant demeanor—was the sort of man who made a lady's breath catch in her chest. There was no question as to his, ahem, *abilities*.

All eyes swung back to Hortense.

"So, the question is—" began one.

"How did *you* manage to catch him—" continued a second.

"Where so many others failed?" finished a third, unblinking.

Hortense tried a dismissive giggle, but the ladies were unwavering in their sincerity. They silently demanded an answer. *Now.*

Anyone who said aristocrats were soft as butter had never met these ladies. The Spanish Inquisition could have used their services.

She gave her throat a delicate clearing and began twirling the sapphire ring Clare had placed on her finger but a few hours ago. The movement had started as a nervous tick, but once she saw several gazes alight upon it and widen with envy, she used it as a tactic and kept twirling. Mesmerizing, all that sparkle.

"My parents were of minor nobility in France," she began telling the story she and Clare had agreed upon and leaned heavily into the French accent she usually tried to minimize. "They had to flee the Revolution or lose their heads." She gave a quick slashing motion across her neck.

This elicited a few shocked gasps from all save one lady, whose eyes had narrowed. "Oh, I understand now."

"Understand what, pray tell?" Hortense asked. The look in the lady's eye bade trouble.

The lady glanced about the group. "She's French."

186

The tension evaporated, and the ladies' faces creased with knowing smiles. Hortense knew enough to keep her mouth shut and allow a knowing twinkle in her eye to do her talking. If that was what they wanted to think, she wasn't here to argue with them. It would only enhance her and Clare's notoriety and increase their chances of catching the attention of the Duke of Rothesbury.

"Then you must know the meaning of the French word *enceinte*, no?" asked one lady with wide, innocent eyes and eliciting more than a few titters.

"Oh, we French have letters for preventing such an occurrence," Hortense returned, eliciting no fewer than five shocked gasps.

"Lady Clare, you are a bit of a scandal, aren't you?" No small amount of delight sounded in the question from yet another lady who had joined the expanding group. Hortense felt herself becoming quite the sensation.

She was opening her mouth to reply when a familiar form caught her eye and tugged on the edge of recognition. It was a lady she'd seen before; she knew it. But who was she...

If the lady's identity had been a solid object, it would have plonked her on the head. *Lady Fortescue.* And the lady was now offering a shallow curtsy.

Hortense froze. It would appear the ruse had reached its end. For in a matter of seconds, Lady Fortescue would recognize the woman she'd hired to rescue her not-so-beloved pup from a disgruntled former lover.

Hortense's heart skipped along in unsteady beats inside her chest. If ever she would lose her nerve, this was the moment. The lady made fleeting eye contact, murmured her felicitations, and kept moving along, her face betraying no hint of recognition, as cool and indifferent as ever.

Hortense released the breath that had hitched in her chest. Lady Fortescue didn't know her. She could bellow with wild, giddy relief. They'd only met the once, several weeks ago when she'd been hired. For the duration of the interview, the lady hadn't glanced up from her needlework once. At the time, it had felt bloody insulting.

Now, well, she'd never been so happy to have been insulted.

Mrs. Arbuthnot stood before the open double doors at the far end of the room. "Supper is served."

A figure appeared before Hortense. The Duke of Wellington held out his crooked arm. "As a most special guest, please allow me to serve as your escort."

She betrayed not a hint of shock as she gave a flattered giggle. Her gaze flitted about the room until she found the eyes she sought. Clare gave her a tight nod.

Saucy smile upon her lips, she said, "It would be my honor, your grace."

A more magnificently appointed dining room she'd never beheld. A glittering chandelier, dripping from an opulent gold rose medallion, hung centered above a long, polished table that could comfortably seat everyone in attendance. Along its length ran a silver dinner service comprised of multiple serving platters, bowls, candelabras, and even dancing nymphs that appeared to have some relation to Greek mythology. Yet another spoil of war, no doubt. She'd never seen so much gold, silver, and crystal displayed in one room. This was life lived at its most ostentatious.

She spared a glance for the sapphire ring on the fourth finger of her left hand. This ring had been created to be worn in such a room.

As she lowered into her seat, she noticed Clare all

the way at the other end of the table. Aristocratic couples didn't sit near each other to dine. She remembered this from times she'd been a servant at such suppers. From what she could tell, aristocratic couples had as little to do with one another as humanly possible. For all the wealth displayed in this room, she couldn't help thinking their lives rather uneventful and small. This was splendor in its most elevated form, but she couldn't see where the appeal lay.

"My dear marchioness," began the duke. "Are you acquainted with the supper partner to your right?"

Hortense turned to greet the man, who had taken his seat late, and her smile slipped. *Rothesbury*. Up close, his wig looked even more ridiculous. Further, he had the look of a predator. In her years as a spy, she'd encountered no small number of such men. Lascivious gaze. Oily smile. She tried not to shudder when he took her hand and pressed it to his mouth.

"Lady Clare," said Wellington, "may I introduce the Duke of Rothesbury to you?"

"*Enchanté*," Rothesbury murmured against her skin.

This was the man she would be wooing with her feminine wiles. This time she did shudder.

"'Tis no wonder Society hasn't seen Clare in months," said Rothesbury, leaning around Hortense to speak directly to Wellington. "He had all the sweetmeat he needed for the winter."

Hortense fought back nausea and smiled blithely as if his double entendre had passed over her head.

Wellington's eyebrows gave the waggle of an aging *roué*. "If you don't mind me saying, Lady Clare, your husband never could resist involving himself in the odd bit of scandal."

Rothesbury slung back a large gulp of red wine. "A branch off the old tree. The Asquiths always did possess a wildness of the blood." He leaned in. "So, you're French, eh?"

"In a manner of speaking," she began, trying—and failing—not to inhale his breath of rotten garlic. "I was born in England, actually."

He must not have heard or cared, for he next addressed Wellington. "I always did particularly enjoy the French tongue." He paused for effect. "Those chits always seem to know what to do with it."

Here it was again—*revulsion*. Which she instantly tamped down, for the mark had all but landed in her lap. She must be charming and pleasing and the best liar in the room.

"Always preferred the Spanish ones myself," said Wellington, eliciting a few manly snorts from nearby gentlemen and a roll of the eyes from their ladies.

"Like father, like son," continued Rothesbury. "The late marquess always did like himself a French bit."

For the next several minutes, Hortense sat between the two lechers, smiling, eating, drinking, nodding, giggling, and generally pretending to enjoy herself. Still, every once in a while, she found her gaze straying toward the opposite end of the table, sneaking a glance at her husband.

Her husband?

Somehow, it was true, although she suspected it never wouldn't defy belief. She had a marquess for a husband. For now, at least.

It might have been the fourth coupe of champagne she'd imbibed but, really, all she could think about when she looked at him was how very, very, very handsome he was in his evening black and whites. Objectively speaking, he was the most handsome man in the room. And the ladies to either side of him knew it, as each vied for his attention. His evident boredom only seemed to attract, rather than repulse, them.

She experienced the flare of a novel feeling, a feeling that sat hot and testy inside her. It made her want to spring up from her chair and...and—*what?*

Could this feeling be—*oh*—could it be jealousy?

She shoved the notion away. *Impossible.* What should she be jealous of? The man was her husband, yes, but not truly. Yet...

She felt the overwhelming urge to walk to their end of the table and clack those ladies' heads together.

Which wouldn't do.

"So," came a voice in her ear, "where did Clare find *you?*"

Hortense willed steel into her resolve. She was attracting Rothesbury. She should feel relief. "Well, you see I have a very naughty little dog," she began, her smile bright. "One morning, on our daily walk, the scamp slipped his lead and led me on a merry chase. It was the marquess who caught him for me. The rest, as you English say, is history."

"Have you been in London very long?"

"Oh, no. That was my very first day. I am not familiar with London at all. And a supper party like this —" She gave her head a little shake and bit her bottom lip.

His pupils flared with desire.

"It is maybe too much for me. I do not know anyone."

"What you need, my sweet, is a guide." Even his laugh was lecherous. "We wouldn't want you to lose your way, now would we?"

She should giggle. She should give his arm a flirtatious swat. And she should say, "Oh, your grace, whoever could show me the way?"

And she did.

Then she felt it on the side of her face. *His* gaze. She followed the feeling and met stormy gray eyes boring into her. The breath in her lungs suspended mid-breath. Never had a man made her heart race by the sheer force of his gaze.

Not until this man.

Her husband.

Right.

CHAPTER SIXTEEN

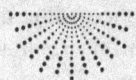

A dark force built inside Jamie—his blood burned with it—as he watched Rothesbury's gaze rake across Hortense like she was his for the taking.

His jaw tensed, his hand clenched a glass of water until his knuckles showed white, the compulsion to do violence to both Rothesbury and Wellington threatening to propel him across the room.

"Lord Clare, it isn't polite to stare at one's wife," came a pouty, feminine voice to his right.

The lady to his left giggled. "One would think you besotted with her."

He was about to offer up a protest when the first lady gave his arm a light swat with her fan, her eyes flashing flirtatiously. "And *that* most definitely isn't done in polite society," she said. "To love one's wife? *Tsk-tsk.* So *de trop.*"

"Of course, you did marry her by special license," observed the second lady.

"And the marriage was only this week?" asked the first.

"Quite." He would keep private the fact that he and Hortense had wed only a few hours ago.

"And she's French?" A return of the poutiness.

"She was born in England."

"But good as French, *non?*"

He shrugged, weary of this conversation. Rothesbury was now listing to the side, like a crusty old battleship, and encroaching into her space. His stomach roiled. He understood intellectually that, by charming Rothesbury, she was succeeding at tonight's objective. She was drawing him into their web. What he hadn't anticipated was his frustration and nausea at the sight of it.

The ladies to either side of him exchanged a glance loaded with meaning. Though he offered them no encouragement, they weren't finished with him quite yet.

"Tell me, Lord Clare, what is it they have?" one of them asked. It hardly mattered which.

He heaved a sigh. "Who?"

"French women."

He rolled his eyes. Could their conversation be any more banal or utterly, fixedly stupid? In unison, they turned speculative glares on Hortense. "Her black hair is nice," said one.

"And her blue eyes are fine, I suppose," said the other.

"A bit showy, truth be told."

"I'll allow that she is pretty."

With her silky, jet-black hair and eyes the color of a clear Mediterranean sea, his wife was a diamond of the first water, he didn't say. Saying so would only arm these two vipers with more poison.

He was only counting the minutes until this supper was over, and he could take his wife home. Away from aging roués who had no sense of a lady's personal space.

And the thing of it was—the thing that most set his teeth on edge—she didn't appear to mind. Not one bit.

Actually, she appeared to be enjoying herself immensely.

He'd never seen her smile so, her eyes flashing back and forth between Wellington and Rothesbury. She was the loveliest, most vibrant woman in this room. In any room. Gone was her customary intensity and reservation. In its place was sparkling light.

Strangely, he didn't prefer this Hortense.

He liked her intensity.

Then she met his eye, as if she'd known all this time that he'd been watching her. He detected a flash of her intensity, and that was all he needed. Heat shot through his body, and another sort of tension wove through him. All the *carnality*, *lust*, and *appetite* spoken in their wedding vows pushed forward and made themselves known.

He shot to his feet, and his dinner partners emitted thrilled cries of astonishment and gossipy delight. Next, he was striding around the table, wide eyes and amused titters following him to his clear destination. He had no care for a single person in this room, save one.

Save the one who set his blood alight.

"My love," he said upon reaching her, the endearment flowing from his mouth all too easily, "you look flushed. These close environs are too much for your delicate constitution. Mayhap a cooling stroll on the terrace is what you need."

"I can assure you, dear husband, that I am quite well." Her narrowed eyes told him in no uncertain terms to return to his seat and stop his foolishness. "I've just been acquainting myself with Lord Rothesbury and would hate to interrupt our fascinating conversation."

A different sort of heat streaked through Jamie. The heat of humiliation. He'd been a fool. She'd only been doing the job he'd hired her for: lure Rothesbury into their web.

How had it never occurred to him that this was the way she would accomplish that goal? By using her beauty and wits to charm the man silly. But...

What else was she planning to use?

Red flashed before his eyes, and the feeling was now speeding through him with a momentum of its own. He was powerless to stop it. And neither, it appeared, could he stop playing the fool, for he held out his hand. "I must insist."

Her eyes snapped with pique. She wasn't happy with him. He didn't care. He couldn't watch her flirt with that reprobate a minute longer.

"It's gone cold with the night out there, Clare," said Rothesbury. "Have a care for your bride's creamy shoulders." The duke's gaze slid up Hortense's arm and across her clavicle.

Jamie took a threatening step forward, which only made the duke smile. "I'll not be looking to you, Rothesbury, for advice on how to treat one's wife," he said through clenched teeth.

Rothesbury froze at the mention of his long-deceased wife, who had died under mysterious circumstances at a far-flung estate. The man emitted a tight laugh, but no warmth entered his eyes. "Gallant young men and their brides."

Jamie held out his hand, and Hortense took it. The buzz of the room quieted to a dull hum. They tended to have that effect. The scatter of muted laughter chased at their backs. They'd definitely given the *ton* something to talk about on this night.

But he had no care for that. What he needed was to get Hortense alone and...

What?

An idea hadn't fully formed in his mind. He was operating on instinct.

As they strode down a dim corridor, empty of all but a few servants, he tested the first door at hand. The room behind it lay empty and dark, but for the light of the moon streaming through a window. Instinctively, he pulled her inside. The door shut behind them, muting the cacophony of the supper party that now seemed long ago and far away. Silence would have prevailed but for the sound of their uneven breath.

She stared up at him, her cherry red lips parted a fraction, her body removed from his a hairsbreadth, so close he could inhale her clean lemon scent. Intensity and truth shone in her eyes. This was the Hortense he knew. How detached he'd felt from that other Hortense, the one who could charm two dukes with the merest bat of an eyelash.

But this Hortense...he needed to connect with *her*.

His lungs refused to draw air. This woman, she shifted his center of gravity. Into the intimate space between them entered their wedding kiss, of his lips touching hers, his hand on the small of her back, its sweet curve fitting perfectly into the palm of his hand. Reserve and restraint had pulled him away then. He wasn't sure they would come to his rescue a second time.

She reached up and caressed his jaw, light fingertips tracing its line. The tip of her tongue ran along her bottom lip. What he saw in her eyes...

Could it be?

If he touched her again, there would be no reserve, no restraint.

Her eyes told him she understood all this, and, like him, she wanted more.

On a low growl, he cupped one hand at the nape of her neck and fitted the other into that sweet spot at the small of her back. His head angled down, and her breath met his in the heartbeat before his mouth was upon hers, tongues tangling, fitting together with a carnal *rightness*. Her arms slid around his neck, and her body stretched up the length of his, the taut nubs of her nipples felt through gossamer silk, her feminine curves in perfect sync with the hard lines of his.

Her hands found his chest, and she pushed and pushed again until she had his back against the wall.

This was madness.

This was desire.

This was all their pent-up longing crashing into each other.

Never had he experienced passion like this. Her sweet body against him, his hard cock throbbing against her stomach. She swiveled her hips, applying delicious pressure. Through layers of wool superfine and dupioni silk, he ground against her.

"Hortense," scraped against his throat as he grabbed her waist and swiveled her around. Now it was her pushed against the wall. On instinct, he shoved her dress up. His fingers found her thighs and began trailing higher. *Creamy...soft...*and—*oh, yes—wet*. On a ragged moan, she wrapped one of her legs around his waist, granting him access to the sweet slit he sought.

She pulled her mouth away and exhaled a long moan against his neck. "I want you." Fingertips traced the implacable ridge of his cock. "I want *this* inside me."

He could have her here. Against the wall. In the Duke of Wellington's mansion. And he would be giving her what she wanted. But was it what he wanted?

Yes, he wanted her to bursting.

But was it *how* he wanted her—the woman who was his wife—for the first time?

The *first* time?

Wasn't this marriage to be in name only?

With a resolve he hadn't known himself capable, he pulled back—or attempted to. Her leg was still wrapped around his waist. And there was the matter of her cunny. It was wet and inviting and in need of a good stroking.

He couldn't think about that and hold his resolve.

"We can't do this," somehow emerged from his mouth.

"Oh, but we can," she whispered against his neck, her hot words skirring across his skin, inciting his cock to more madness.

"We agreed the marriage would be in name only." Through blunt force of will did the reminder scratch across his throat.

Again, he attempted to move away. Again, her leg tightened around him.

"We could make an exception."

This woman knew what she wanted. *Him.* And, oh, how he yearned to give her every last inch.

Yet he found himself shaking his head. There was a line here, one he mustn't cross. If he had her once, that would be it for him, for he would need to have her a second time and a third and a fourth until he'd inextricably lost himself inside her. She didn't understand that about him, but he did. Someday soon, she would want her freedom, and he needed to be able to let her have it. No matter what it cost him.

Of a sudden, her leg released him, and her dress slid down her body. He took a step backward that felt no small bit drunken. Though he'd imbibed no spirits tonight, intoxication pulsed through his veins. He was drunk on her.

Across the three feet separating them, frustration flashed in her eyes. She wasn't exactly pleased with him.

Well, he wasn't exactly pleased with him either.

Then, at last, she nodded curtly, and the moment turned. She wouldn't push the matter further.

He'd gotten what he wanted. Relief should be pulsing through him. Instead, he felt tetchy and cross. "Let us leave. I believe we've gotten out of this night what we came for."

Her eyebrows lifted toward the ceiling. "Oh?"

"We've established contact with Rothesbury and left him wanting more."

"And he's the only one left wanting more?"

Saucy minx. He would leave those words in this room, where she'd dropped them. He dared not carry them into the night, or his resolve would crumble. He was only a man, after all.

He strode to the door and pulled it open. "After you, my lady," he said in the most condescending, aristocratic voice he could muster. He needed distance from this woman, his wife.

Otherwise, she and her fresh scent and her sweet cunny would haunt him all the night.

Otherwise?

He snorted. It was a given. He would be haunted.

Through the ride back to Asquith Court and until she'd disappeared from view up its grand staircase, they spoke not another word. From the set of her mouth and the flash of fire in her eyes, he could see she was angry with him.

So be it.

He could handle her anger.

Her desire, on the other hand, was a whole other beast.

One that cut through all resistance and immunity.

One that could bring him to his knees.

CHAPTER SEVENTEEN

*I*t was too blasted hot in this bed.

Hortense spent the next few minutes kicking and untangling her legs from several layers of covers. Sir Bacon gave a little growl of annoyance before heaving himself up and vacating his place. From his new spot curled up in a plush armchair on the other side of the room, he shot her a baleful glower.

"My apologies for disturbing your beauty rest, your royal highness," she groused.

Madness. Agitation. Wretchedness.

Those were the words Mariana had used to describe the madly in love.

She could think of another condition those words quite accurately described:

Mad, agitated, wretched *lust*.

It was those hot kisses.

And the man who had delivered them.

He'd set her alight.

Her back against the wall, his lean, hard body pressing into hers, his thick cock straining against her stomach. His long masculine fingers first clutching at her, then sliding along her throbbing, wet quim.

Oh, how she'd wanted those fingers inside her.

Then he'd stopped.

She was possessed of willpower, but none like that, for here was the thing: he'd wanted her, too. She'd seen the wanting in his lust-glazed eyes, felt it in the clutch of his hands and in the press of his hard cock.

In name only.

He must have remembered and gotten a case of scruples.

Wrongheaded scruples.

Irresponsible scruples.

The more she thought about it, the more annoyed she became. Really, someone should explain to the blasted man that was no way to behave in a chaste marriage.

And she was just that someone.

And the sooner, the better.

As in *now*.

She hopped off the bed, her feet landing on soft Persian wool. With only the banked fire in the hearth illuminating the room, she marveled anew at its splendor. In her capacities as spy and investigator, she'd navigated homes of fortune, but she'd never been entitled to them, and as the Marchioness of Clare, that was precisely who she was: a woman entitled to the best of everything life had on offer. For now, at least.

The softness of the bed. The slide of silken sheets. The plush wool beneath her feet. The fire in the hearth, providing constant warmth to the room, and which didn't have to be stoked by her to stay aflame. To lead such an existence was the heart of luxury that aristocrats took for granted every day of their pampered lives.

Silently, she crept across the short corridor separating her bedroom from his. With each small step, her nerve threatened to give way. He hadn't invited her. In fact, he'd done the opposite. But…

If he wanted the opposite, then why had he pulled her into that room and kissed her to the point of utter abandon? Truly, she'd never been kissed so thoroughly, so *skillfully*.

Oh, how she wanted to be kissed so again. The center of her went liquid at the very thought.

That was what she needed to tell him. Well, not the last bit, but that he mustn't kiss her so again.

Or she couldn't be held accountable for consequences, which very likely involved her doing everything in her power to seduce him. After all, it had been he who had spoken the words *in name only*. Her mouth had remained shut.

She gave the door a testing push. She half expected it to be locked. Instead, it eased open on smooth hinges.

Like her bedroom, his was lit by the low fire in the hearth, casting slow-moving shadows about the walls, and a window overlooking the back garden. Before it stood an armchair and a side table piled high with various books. Beside the pile, she saw it. The signet ring, its gold absorbing mellow firelight. So, this was where he kept it, a knowledge she would hold on to until the night that would be her last in this house, which was arriving soon.

She gave her head a clearing shake. Tonight, she had other business to attend.

Her heart racing in her throat, she located the bed and began moving in its direction. Yet as her eyes adjusted to the darkness, she saw its coverlet was yet undisturbed. The bed lay empty of him.

She exhaled a huff of frustration. *Of course.* The man was likely in his beloved study, reading about corn laws or some such. She wasn't too keen on creeping through the mansion in the nightdress provided by Eva Galante, being fairly certain the outline of her nipples could be detected through diaphanous muslin. She would just have to dig out her well-worn overcoat from the bottom of the wardrobe. Her lady's maid, Smith, had gone wide-eyed and flummoxed when she'd insisted on keeping it.

She had just turned to vacate the room when she heard it. A splash, muted, but distinct.

Following the sound, she detected a faint orange strip of light at the bottom of a closed door. Without thought, she tiptoed closer, closer, so close she could reach out and grab the handle. A nudge, and the door was opening. Again, her heart was in her throat.

He was near. She could feel it.

If a quick glance didn't confirm it, her sense of smell would have attested to the fact that she'd entered his dressing room, surrounded as she was by his delicious, masculine scent. She located another strip of orange peeking from the bottom of another door. Like a magnet, she was pulled toward it, her heart deepening its rhythm into a heavy throbbing of anticipation. Her body moved as if independent of intention.

At the door, she stopped, her breath suspended. Another splash sounded. She counted down from ten and lightly pushed at solid oak. The hinges obliged her by opening in complete silence. She poked her head around the corner. She had but a fraction of a second to contain her gasp of surprise.

Across a black-and-white checkered floor, reclined the Marquess of Clare, engaging in a leisurely soak in a plunge tub surely constructed for five fully grown adults. Only in bath houses on the Continent had she beheld such a tub. He faced away from her, his arms propped up to either side of him, holding him aloft. She could only view him in profile—the strong line of his jaw, the relaxed curve of his mouth, fringe of thick eyelashes resting on high cheekbones. Beads of sweat dripped down the side of his face, running down the rivulets of his neck, curling the tips of dark hair at his nape, sheening his arms and back.

A demigod in repose.

This sight of him wasn't helping her mad, agitated, wretched lust. She should quietly retreat and return to her room and leave the man in peace. By staying, well, she was being a bit of a voyeur, wasn't she?

Yet she found herself widening the crack in the door and slipping through, her bare feet padding softly across tile slick with steam.

Of a sudden, shoulder muscles that had been re-laxed bunched in tension. She froze in place, painfully aware of how wrong it was for her to be here. His head whipped around, his gray gaze immediately finding her. She detected not the relaxation she ex-pected to find in those depths, but rather the turmoil of a storm.

Like as not, he saw the same turmoil reflected back at him from her eyes.

She swallowed. She must ignore the knowledge that their turmoil sprang from the same source. *Wretched-ness. Agitation. Madness.* Such feelings weren't to be al-lowed their head.

"A midnight soak?" Her voice emerged reedy and high and irritatingly unlike itself.

He shrugged a shoulder, bunched muscles rippling just beneath his skin. "Such is the prerogative of a lord."

"I'm certain your servants appreciate that." At least, she could take pride in the tartness of her observation.

Again, he shrugged, as only an entitled, self-assured lord could.

It was damned attractive.

"They are well compensated."

She couldn't deny this. The pay she'd been offered as a scullery had taken her by surprise. It was a more generous amount than most households offered girls who surely had no other options if scullery was the job they sought.

"It's better than a bottle of brandy."

He'd made a stab at lightness, but she wasn't fooled. The heaviness of past misdeeds weighed the words down.

"If you wouldn't mind too much," he said, "could you walk into my natural line of sight, so I don't give myself a neck strain?" He only sounded slightly annoyed. "I'm certain you'll state your reason for being here."

Even as her body urged her to obey his command couched in a request, she hesitated. To do as he asked, she would have to walk deeper into this room, steamy with heat and humidity and him, *naked*, thereby fully committing herself to this foolish path she'd set upon. Truly, she should turn tail and run.

Instead, her bare feet did as bid, sticky against damp tile. She inhaled deeply of air dense with sumptuous oils that had been added to the water. *Birchwood... patchouli...him.*

As she passed him to enter his line of sight, so help her, she darted a quick glance down. Blessedly—*frustratingly*—she saw naught below the water due to the blessed—*frustrating*—combination of steam and glare from flickering candlelight.

When she turned to face him, however, what she saw above the water was enough to steal her breath away. This wasn't the first time she'd seen a man's bare chest, or even this man's bare chest, so what was this wobble in her knees?

It was quite simply the sum total of him: the day's growth stubble of his dark beard, the muscles of his arms and shoulders, his tight, ridged stomach, the light sprinkling of dark hair on his chest that led down... down...*down*, the rest of him cut off by the waterline.

He cleared his throat, and her gaze lifted to meet his. Faint amusement shone out, but something else, too: assessment.

Right.

Gaze hooded, he took a slow appraisal of her night-dress, stopping right about where her nipples stood hard as cherry pits. Now, it was her turn to clear her throat. His eyes lifted to meet hers. She detected no apology in those depths, but rather a blazing desire that corresponded to her own.

"I'm waiting," he said.

Her mouth went dry. Her body knew what it hoped he was waiting for. Best to ask for clarification. "Waiting for what?"

"For you to state your reason for invading my privacy. You've rather made a habit of it."

Oh. That. "I, um, I came here to speak with you."

"I gathered as much." His tone was patient.

Somehow, though it was he who was naked and in the prone position, he possessed all the power in the room.

It was this implacable lust of hers. It made her weak and vulnerable to her desire. She could resent him for it.

"About tonight." Her voice had gone to gravel. It could be from a lack of sleep, but she knew the truth. It was him. And his effect on her.

"Ah," he exhaled and slipped deeper into the bath, his ridged stomach sliding from view.

Was he aware of how very desirable a man he was? She licked her bottom lip. A nervous tell that she tried to keep under control, but some moments it wouldn't be contained. Like this one.

He followed the slide of her tongue, and an arrow of lust shot straight through her.

She stiffened her spine and squared her shoulders

and attempted to summon an ounce of the outrage that led her here. "You simply cannot do that."

He cocked his head, questioning. Was he deliberately showing off the strong line of his jaw?

"I cannot do what?" His voice emerged a velvet rumble.

"Pull me into a room for a kiss."

Oh, it had been so much more than a simple kiss, and they both knew it.

"My apologies if I offended your sensibilities." Neither his eyes nor his tone conveyed contrition.

"Offended my—"

The rest of her sentence was cut off by what started as a dry laugh. It instantly transformed into a gale of laughter rising from her belly. Long and loud, unguarded, she hadn't laughed so in years, in all her life mayhap.

She'd finally begun to exhaust herself when he asked, "Have I got it wrong?"

"I think you know you do."

"Pray tell, how did I offend you?"

All remaining traces of her laughter faded. Anticipation took wing and fluttered through her. Now she would voice her grievance, and everything would change. Her heart sped into a wobbly rhythm. There would be a *before* and an *after*. She felt the certainty deep in her bones.

But, deep in her bones, she wanted the *after*. What had brought her here was mere pretense.

"By stopping."

The words hung in the air between them, palpable, laden with unmistakable meaning.

An alert stillness slid over him, and he swallowed. She followed the subtle undulation of his throat, the muscles that led to his chest. She detected discomfort in the movement. *Good.* She had no intention of making this easy for him.

"Has it not become obvious to you?" she asked.

"What is that?"

"The solution."

"What are we solving?" He yet resisted what she took as inevitable.

"This pull between us," she said. "There is only one way we're going to get it out from between us."

"It isn't part of our agreement." A war of emotions sounded in his protest.

"Agreements can be amended."

"But—"

"I won't tell, if you won't."

His head cocked. "It isn't that anyone else would know."

Her breath hung in her chest.

"It's that I will have had you," he said. "*I* would know —" He considered her, saw into her. "*You.* Every line, every curve. Every moan, every sigh."

Within her, places stirred that she hadn't known existed.

"And that nightdress…"

"What about it?" she asked. Somehow, she was capable of speech.

He gave a dry laugh. "It does naught to hide you from me. It only whets my appetite."

His movement sudden and swift, he shoved to the edge of the bath, water sluicing around him, pouring over the sides, and reached out, his hand grabbing the hem of her nightdress. He angled his head back, and eyes hazed with desire met hers. He gave the hem a testing tug—testing *her*—and she followed, surrendering. He pulled again, and, again, she inched closer. It was a little game they were playing. Tit for tat.

Once her thighs pressed against the side of the tub, he reached up and cupped the back of her head, silky hair sliding through his fingers, as he pulled her down. Face to face, her lips an inch away from his, their eyes locked.

"If you have any doubt, now would be the time to speak it. For you aren't the sort of woman one tastes, then simply walks away." A rakish smile pulled at the corner of his mouth. "Not a second time."

CHAPTER EIGHTEEN

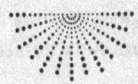

*Y*ou *aren't the sort of woman one tastes, then simply walks away. Not a second time.*

Where had he learned to speak such words?

They stole her breath away. They deepened her intention.

Assurance in her femininity and desirability blossomed inside her. "I'm going nowhere."

Her hands clutched his shoulders for balance as she stepped one foot, then the other, inside the sultry water, its heat penetrating her down to muscle and bone, a fitting companion to the desire pulsing through her. Lowering into the steamy pool, her nightdress floating around her, she released his shoulders before pushing backward. She submerged entirely in the water, letting it flow across her skin, through suddenly weightless hair. When she emerged, the nightdress clung to her every curve.

In harmony with not only their own desires, but each other's, she and he moved, slowly, deliberately, erasing the distance between them, eyes locked on to each other. She wasn't sure if it was the hour of the night or the heat of the bath or, quite simply, the inevitable, but it was like a sensual dream from which one didn't want to awaken.

She knew full well this was no dream, and that coming here was likely a bad decision, but just tonight she would shut off the part of her brain that evaluated potential consequences for actions, for what if she was right? What if this was the only way to get this implacable desire out from between them?

It didn't matter now.

It might matter later.

She would leave later for the future.

Only the present—and this man—mattered.

Her gaze fell to his mouth. Firm and assured, that mouth. A mouth that knew how to devastate her. Her focus singular upon that mouth, she leaned forward, cutting all distance between them until his mouth was the scantest hairsbreadth from hers.

It isn't too late.

Oh, but it was. For her.

Her lips touched his in a kiss that could have been sweet were it not for the pent-up lust driving it. Her body wanted more than his kisses. It wanted everything he had to offer.

On a groan, his hands found her bottom. As he pulled, she floated through the water, offering surrender as she straddled him and strained up against him. His cock—thick, hard...*ready*—pressed against her, the only barrier separating her most intimate flesh from his, a thin scrap of muslin.

"Are you fond of this garment?" he muttered against her mouth.

She shook her head.

He took the flimsy fabric in both hands and rent it in two. Greedy eyes roved across her bare arms, her breasts, every inch of revealed skin.

"Don't," he commanded.

"Don't?"

"Don't cover yourself."

She only now realized she'd been lifting her hands to do just that, a reactionary impulse. She'd always thought herself too small, unfeminine. But the way this man was regarding her with appreciation—nay, *lust*—sent a hot blush rioting through her. Instead, she used her hands to run through his hair.

"You're as beautiful as I imagined." He spoke into the whorl of her ear, nipping the lobe, a testing nibble. She arched into him, wanting more of pleasure that teetered on the edge of pain. Then she felt it. His rigid manhood, slick and hot, against her slit. Instinctively, her hips ground down, the head of him rubbing against her nub. An intoxicated animal groan poured from her.

He clutched her hips, fingertips digging in. "Do that again." His pupils had pushed his irises into thin gray rings. *Desire.*

She could deny this man nothing. The thought would unnerve her at any other moment. At this one, with obedience came the promise of pleasure. Denial wasn't an option.

She swiveled her hips, and his gaze flickered. "I need you inside me."

"Need?"

She reached down, and her fingers trailed across his manhood. "You're so—" She caught herself.

A devilish smile curled about his mouth. "I'm so—"

She couldn't help a sheepish laugh. *"Big."*

She squeezed, and his smile transformed into utter, serious intention. She positioned him at the opening of her sex, and he grabbed her waist. He entered her with one long, slick thrust, her tightness giving way to his hardness. Her hands on his shoulders, she collapsed into him as he steadied her.

"Am I too much?" he asked, his concern unmistakable.

"Yes," she breathed.

He tensed below her.

"And no." She angled back to meet his eye. "It's—*you're*—sublime."

He began to move, slowly, testingly. Oh, the feel of him...slick and hot, he slid in and out of her, her hips finding his rhythm, a force beginning to build inside her, a force unlike any she'd ever experienced. An urgency to have more of him began to overtake her. Eyes drifting shut, she became enslaved to sensation, unwilling, unable, to form an impression beyond the feel of this man inside her.

"Hortense," he said, her name a ragged exhalation.

Her eyes fluttered open.

"I'm too close."

His words confused her. "Too close to what?"

"Release, my love."

Swiftly efficient, he withdrew—provoking a cry of protest from her—gathered her into his arms, and stood, water sloshing and splashing on marble tile in forgotten drops as he carried her into his bedroom and lay her on his bed. As he stood above, she couldn't but marvel at the male beauty of him, as if he'd been chiseled from marble by Michelangelo himself. Except none of those statues depicted a cock like his, hard and rigid and full to bursting. A demigod, indeed. And the way he gazed upon her, with raw lust, sent shivers skittering across her skin.

She sat up and grabbed his hand. "Have I told you how much I like your hands?"

His gaze burned down at her.

"They're so big, and the fingers are so long and masculine." Driven by instinct, she took one, then two, fingers inside her mouth and sucked, her tongue moving in lazy circles tasting the salt of his skin.

"Hortense," he uttered, her name a plea.

She slid his fingers from her mouth and began guiding his hand down her body, slowly, deliberately, until he reached her mons pubis. "I wonder what they would feel like—"

His thumb grazed the nub of her sex, and she gasped. A knowing smile tipped at his mouth. "Inside you?"

He took over, which was just as well as she collapsed back on her elbows, watching him as one, then two, fingers slipped inside her. Her knees had no choice but to spread—one foot finding his chest, the other digging into the bed—as those masculine fingers slid in and out, expertly delivering pleasure with each stroke, his gaze concentrated upon intimate parts of her no one—not even herself—had ever seen.

"You're as beautiful as I imagined."

He'd been imagining her...like this?

She couldn't think upon that now, but she knew she would later. Now, she had only this moment, the feel of him stroking her, his rhythm assured, deliberate. The tension in her sex again building, she reached over her head, pulling pillows, sheets, whatever she could grab hold of, as she arched into his hand, her hips tilting to receive more of him, long moans turning into frenzied gasps. Her eyes slitted open to find that wicked smile curving his mouth. "I need," she began and couldn't finish, the idea of this need floating just out of reach.

"This?" His thumb again pressed on the nub of her sex—his fingers working their magic on her cunny—and that was all it took for her body to burst into an explosion of sensation, stars behind her eyes, filling her with light and air, as if the universe pulsed inside her, shooting fluttery comets through her veins.

Eyes closed, lost to the world, a kiss on the instep of her right foot coaxed her back. Next came a kiss to her inner thigh...her navel...her left nipple...the indent at the base of her throat...her ear...his every breath sending sparks of desire shimmering through her.

"Open your eyes," came his whisper. She found a question in his gaze. In answer, she wrapped her legs around his back and tilted her hips up, taking him in inch by sublime inch. Just when she thought he filled her, he had yet more inches to give.

He began moving in a rhythm that she met stroke for stroke. Though she'd only just found release, a wildness began to overtake her, a hunger for more making her greedy. The same relentlessness reflected at her in his eyes. He reached under her, grabbing her bottom, angling her hips so she could receive more of him.

"*Oh*," she moaned against his neck, corded tendons straining against the skin. He thrust again, and a shout poured out of her. Oh, the way he was using her body... she couldn't get enough of it. And, like only a few minutes ago, release began clawing at her, insisting she surrender to it. Another hard thrust of his cock, and there she was, tipping over the edge into climax, her quim pulsing against his cock that yet drove into her. Then off the precipice he followed her into the oblivion of release on a shout, his head arched back. He collapsed, careful to keep most of his weight off to the side of her.

Never in her life had she suspected it could be like this.

Oh, the man was bewitching her body and soul, something she should consider...

Tomorrow.

For now, she would close her eyes, feel the sticky press of his body against hers, and sink into the splendor they'd wrought together.

Life didn't deliver many such moments.

* * *

JAMIE'S BREATH slowed and settled into a rhythm at one with hers. He'd never felt so at-one with another person.

He rolled fully off her and slid one arm beneath her head, tucking her into the curve of his body. Unable to resist, he nestled his face into her hair, damp and scented with the oils from his bath. They combined well with her lemon sweetness.

Lazily, he began to reenter his body, and layers peeled away from the bud of an idea, before revealing a fully formed thought. Hortense wasn't precisely experienced with the act of love, but neither was she *not* experienced. "You weren't a virgin," he muttered into the top of her head, without thinking.

She didn't pull away. "I haven't been a virgin in a good many years." She stated it as a fact, carefully devoid of emotion.

Discomfort, even foolishness, traced through him. This woman had lived a dozen or more lifetimes in her short number of years on this earth. Of course, she wasn't a virgin. "I have no right—"

"I was a spy for eight years."

The words, and the implication that lay within them, struck him at a wrong angle. Before he knew what he was about, he bolted upright, hardly able to contain the sudden storm raging through him. She rolled on her back and met his eye.

"Did Nick order you to use your body to obtain intelligence?" Although framed as a question, it was a demand. Silently, he vowed Nick would have hell to pay.

"Never." She pulled herself upright and sat against the headboard, her hair a tumble about her shoulders as she gathered the covers to her chest. She was a spent goddess. One who was weighing her next words carefully. "After the first time, it was my choice. Not that there were many."

It was as if wool had been stuffed into his ears, for he wasn't able to hear anything that followed *after the first time*. He went cold with fury. "What do you mean by that?"

"By what?"

"*After the first time.*"

"The first time was not by my choice."

Breath refused to enter or leave his lungs. "You were raped," he ground out.

"I was in a household, playing the maid as usual," she began, the words emerging mechanically, as if she'd removed herself from her past.

"An aristocrat's household?"

She gave a curt nod.

"Which one?" There would be reprisals.

"It wasn't in England," she said. He thought she would speak no further on the matter, but she continued. "It was early morning when servants are up and the nobs are still abed or are only arriving home for bed. I hadn't considered the latter possibility when I was hauling a bucket of wood up the servants' staircase. It was dark." Her gaze lifted, and all he saw was hollowness. "From start to finish, it couldn't have lasted more than three minutes. I doubt the lord ever gave it another thought, or that it occurred to him he'd done anything wrong." She shrugged, masking an event of life-altering significance with indifference, which only made Jamie want to howl with rage. "Most lords are that way. I got better at taking care of myself after that."

Helplessness charged alongside his fury. "It isn't your responsibility to make certain a man acts like a gentleman."

Her brow lifted in disbelief. "That hasn't been my experience of matters."

He needed this woman who was now his wife to understand something. "You shouldn't have to *take care of* yourself."

Her jaw tensed and released. "Every person on God's green earth has to take care of themselves. That is what it is to be alive and out in the world. There is no escaping it."

"Did you tell Nick?" If his brother knew about this and didn't take measures—

"He didn't need to know."

He supposed Nick's thrashing could wait. "Why didn't you quit the spy work?"

"I didn't need to."

"What do you mean?"

"It taught me something."

Bile rose at the very thought, at its pragmatic necessity.

"The world would always be bigger and stronger than me, but I could be quicker and smarter."

He took in her words, giving them the consideration they deserved, for they had the sound of a mantra. These were the words that ruled her life. Her person was small and petite, and as beautiful as he'd imagined, but also strong, the muscles showing beneath her skin. Even her stomach was ridged. She'd created this body so as to use its every advantage, to protect herself.

"Hortense, you're my wife now. I'll take care of you." They were the only words he had, and they felt ineffectual, worthless.

How could he make her see?

By proving it. Which would take time. In the more immediate future, he could do something else.

He reached out and gathered her in his arms. At first, she tensed against him, but he held her secure, determined to hold on for as long as it took. At last, she released a breath and relaxed, her cheek soft against his chest as his arms fully encircled her.

No one would ever hurt her again. He wouldn't speak the words aloud, for she wouldn't believe him. He would show her with action.

Inside his embrace, he felt her breath grow even and regular in the cadence of sleep.

It felt like surrender and like the sweetest gift.

One he wouldn't take for granted.

He found her left hand and gently turned it over. Cutting across the palm, from pinky to thumb, was the knife scar, jagged and red. Instinctively, he pressed it to his mouth, protectiveness—*ferocity*—rearing up in him. Never again would she have to defend herself thusly.

Never again.

CHAPTER NINETEEN

Sir Bacon lifted a leg against a purple willow bush, and Hortense experienced no small amount of satisfaction, even glancing around the garden in case someone witnessed this not insignificant triumph. The fifth morning in a row he'd made it all night without piddling indoors.

She would have to return him soon, now that she knew Lady Fortescue had arrived back in Town. Surprisingly, she didn't especially look forward to it. Somehow, Sir Bacon had grown into a fond companion. She rather liked it in the night when he hopped into her bed and curled his little body into the crook of her legs.

Not last night, though.

Last night, she hadn't been in her bed.

She'd been in bed with Jamie and had stayed there until the sky turned pink with the first rays of dawn.

And there she'd left the marquess—*her husband*. She'd simply been unready to face him in the light of the new day. Not just yet.

So, she'd treaded the succession of Aubusson carpets to her bed, and lay there awake, staring up at the ceiling until Smith arrived, bearing a tray of toast and tea. She'd only taken her fourth or fifth sip when the maid returned with box stacked upon box, each imprinted with the insignia *Galante: Dressmakers Extraordinaire.*

After selecting a day dress—the ivory muslin printed with a lovely twining leaf motif—she submitted to Smith's ministrations on her hair. The woman she viewed in the mirror looked exactly her part—fashionable marchioness—and was utterly unlike the Hortense she'd known since, well, since she'd become Hortense.

Marchioness of Clare.

And not in name only.

She shook her head as if she could as easily shake the truth of last night away.

What a twenty-four hours that had passed. Truly, even for the up-and-down life she'd lived, it was a remarkable whirlwind that had blown through.

What had possessed her?

Lust. No point denying it.

She'd never harbored a particular desire for lords, not like so many of her sex. In her experience, they were fussy and too full of themselves to tolerate for long. But Clare, well, he was a different sort of lord.

Her dealings with the man only grew more complicated with each passing day. Too complicated.

As if her thoughts had the power to summon him into the garden, he emerged from the set of double doors. If she looked every inch the marchioness, he looked every inch the marquess.

Watching him approach, she saw last night had been inevitable. It was only a wonder that it hadn't happened sooner.

Yes, he was handsome and tall and possessed of all the physical features women found desperately attractive, including long, skilled fingers. An echo of last night's desire skittered through her. Yet more lay within the foundation of this handsome man.

It was the look in his eyes. A seriousness. A determination. And when one found oneself the recipient of that gaze, well, one's breath was likely to be stolen away.

Like now.

Never in her life had a man stolen her breath away.

Until this man.

He stopped within a few yards of her. She waited for him to speak first. If she opened her mouth, she might go straight to last night, and, well, that wouldn't do.

"Have you broken your fast?" he asked after a few interminable seconds.

"Tea and toast," she replied. She'd never given much thought to what husbands and wives might say to each other in the morning, but this sounded about right.

"The kitchen offers more variety if you so desire."

"It's my usual morning fare."

He nodded slowly, reluctantly accepting her choice.

In the distance, Sir Bacon began alternately scratching at the back gate and squeezing his nose beneath the bottom edge and the ground. When neither of these actions yielded the desired result, he stood back and began barking.

"Sir Bacon!" she called out, already on the move. "Never a dull moment."

"St. James's Park isn't far," Jamie said, close at her back.

"Oh?" she asked over her shoulder.

"Would you care for a stroll?"

That brought her up short. "Sir Bacon certainly would." The little terrier's ears had perked up at his name. Big brown eyes staring up, he emitted an impatient whine for good measure. "I reckon it's early enough that no one would see us."

Jamie cocked his head. "I assure you it's perfectly acceptable for a husband to take the morning air with his wife, even in civilized society."

His dry tone pulled a bemused laugh from her. "The possibility hadn't occurred to me."

His humor fell away. "You've become so accustomed to living in the shadows, you no longer know how to live in the light, do you?"

The question sliced through her with the precision of a straightedge, stopping the breath in her lungs, cutting too close to the core of her. That he'd seen this truth about her so clearly, more clearly than she saw herself, was startling and disconcerting.

She glanced away on the pretext of keeping an eye on Sir Bacon. "Shall we go?"

Jamie held out his arm, and she hesitated, even as she understood that, of course, she must accept his offer. They were a married couple, the fiction they were selling to the *haut ton*. Of course, Lord and Lady Clare would walk arm-in-arm.

She threaded her arm through his. Birchwood and spice...his heat...*him*—all of it washed over her and set her heart into a light sprint. A single word came to her and circled around her mind in obstinate refrain.

Mine.

What a word. What an idea. It wouldn't let up. This man was her husband. In the eyes of the world, he belonged to her.

And last night in his bed... There, he'd been hers, too.

"We may regret having left his lead behind," he observed as Sir Bacon raced ahead. It was as if the little dog had intuited their destination.

Although it was a Sunday morning, the short route

to St. James's Park was already beginning to bustle with morning activity. Grocers setting out their wares. A wagon here and there trundling up the lane. Pedestrians shouldering past, intent on this task or another. Hortense had always liked this about London. Its industry. Its sense of purpose and importance.

For all the city cacophony racketing about, silence persisted between her and Jamie as they strolled on, careful to keep Sir Bacon in their sights. They reached the wide mall leading into the park, orderly colonnades of plane trees providing a verdant border between the park and the city. At least, Sir Bacon must have thought so as he ran free and loose, alternately scaring up flocks of pigeons and scurries of squirrels. Even his antics couldn't distract from the beauty of the park with its wide avenues for strolling lined with oak and mulberry trees and flower beds bursting into bloom at the insistence of spring. St. James's Park was an oasis.

"Do you know much about the park?" Jamie asked as they approached the canal that served as a pond.

She shook her head. "Preserves of peace and loveliness don't figure much into my line of work."

She might have imagined him tensing his jaw, but then he continued, "As it happens, I came across a short history of the park recently."

"Let me guess. In your study?"

Half a smile tipped up the corner of his mouth. "Not much has happened in England, Scotland, Wales, or Ireland that isn't accounted for in its collection." He pointed toward the pond. "What do you see?"

She squinted across the water. Upon its surface floated a group of large white birds. "Swans?" she guessed.

"Pelicans."

"*Pelicans?*" She squinted again.

"Their ancestors were a gift from the Russian ambassador almost two hundred years ago."

"What a thing," she marveled.

"On a more scandalous note, King Charles the Second courted his favorite mistress, Nell Gwyn, here."

"I would venture Hyde Park would have been too near the watchful eye of his queen."

"But what we see today will soon be changing," Jamie said.

"Surely, there are no plans to build here. That would be a shame."

"Nothing like that. The king has commissioned the landscaper John Nash to redesign the entire park and make it less formal and more naturalistic."

"Wild and free. I rather like that idea."

"They say it will be done next year. We'll have to return."

Had he hesitated before adding that last bit? She held her tongue. She wasn't at all certain they would be strolling anywhere together a year from now.

Truly, she would be content listening to him speak on this or that subject for hours on end. His deep, mellifluous voice. His knowledge that came from between the covers of every book under the English sun. He was learned in ways she wasn't, and she appreciated that in a person, for while she could read, write, speak two languages fluently, and two others passably, she lacked all formal education beyond what Papa and Maman had taught her before their untimely deaths.

As they approached the reedy banks of the pond, she noticed areas on its surface where the morning mist hadn't yet dissipated, casting a magic over the water. Sir Bacon ran up to the edge of the bank and came to a sudden stop, his gaze casting a wide net of suspicion. He must have seen something that needed investigating, for he started barking and charged off.

She couldn't help laughing. She'd never experienced such an enjoyable walk. Mostly, when she was walking London streets, it was to travel from one place to another. The idea of strolling for pleasure's sake was a novel one, and she let it all soak into her—trilling birdsong, the tiny splash of water from a fish jumping, the soughing of the breeze through the newly emergent leaves of the canopy overhead.

"About last night," said Jamie, his voice pitched low.

The pleasantness of the morning faded, replaced by the low buzz of discord. She unwound her arm from his, her body gone tense in anticipation of the conversation ahead, and set her gaze across the pond. She couldn't touch or look at him. "We might not need to discuss it," she said. It was worth a try.

"Why is that?"

She didn't need to look at him to know his brow had furrowed into a deep line.

"Because now we have it out of the way," she said, her voice light and breezy. "We solved the problem."

How convinced she sounded. She'd always been a good liar.

"That was what we were doing in my bed last night?" A tetchy beat passed. "Solving a problem?"

She angled her head so she could meet his eye when she spoke her next lie. "Yes."

* * *

JAMIE DETECTED a flicker of something in her gaze. She didn't quite believe her *yes*.

"More was shared between us than two bodies solving a problem," he said, careful to keep his voice even. Otherwise, he might find himself shouting at the deuced frustrating woman.

"How can you know that?" asked the deuced frustrating woman. "Desire can be very deceiving."

"This isn't a question of desire. It's a question of l—"

Her eyes flew wide, stopping him mid-sentence. Which was for the best, truly. What L-word had he been about to say? *Lust?* Or an altogether different L-word?

She covered her mouth, and he realized her shock had naught to do with him, but rather a point over his shoulder. "Oh, no," she said, panic replacing shock. She brushed around him. "No, no, no, no, no." Her feet gained momentum with each *no*.

"What is it?" he called at her back, alarm setting in. The woman was near imperturbable. What could be upsetting her?

"Sir Bacon," she called over her shoulder.

That would account for it.

His gaze swept the area, following the sound of barking to the far side of the pond. There was Sir Bacon at the bank, wading through a clump of reeds and becoming increasingly worked up over the group of pelicans, which he seemed only now to have noticed, his entire body straining with the effort of his barks. Hortense was jogging now, calling out to the feisty, little beast, who was decidedly ignoring her.

To watch this perpetually composed woman become a sprinting, shouting harridan, well, it was a sight. Just as she reached Sir Bacon, the dog jumped into the water and began swimming.

Standing on the soggy bank, she shouted, "Come back here, you blasted dog!"

Sir Bacon simply swam on toward the pelicans, who had started taking notice of the scrappy interloper. As he joined Hortense at the water's edge, Jamie thought a silly smile might have overtaken his face. He hadn't smiled like this in...days, weeks, months...*years?* Had it been years?

Her voice transitioned into a wheedle. "Sir Bacon," she sing-songed, "if you wouldn't mind returning to shore, it surely would be appreciated."

On Sir Bacon swam.

Hortense flashed Jamie a hopeful glance when he drew abreast with her. "Would you happen to be carrying a breakfast meat with you this morning?"

"Afraid not."

She planted her fists on her hips and let out an exasperated huff.

Meanwhile, a scene began to unfold on the water, and all they could do was watch, helpless, as Sir Bacon caught up to the pelicans, his little legs working like pistons. Since ignoring the little pest hadn't proven effective, the pelicans began flapping their wings in warning. Intuiting where this scene was heading, Hortense started calling out to the stubborn dog with yet more serious urgency, interrupting herself to say, "Who knew he could swim like that?"

"A dog of many talents," Jamie said equably.

Unfortunately, said talent appeared to be breaking through the pelicans' natural peaceableness and working them into a royal tizzy. As one, the birds switched direction and aimed directly for the dog. He must have seen the error of his ways, for he made a sharp reversal, now making for the shore as fast as his little legs could swim. The pelicans, however, weren't content to let him get away without consequences for disturbing their morning meditation. A lesson was to be taught.

The chase was on.

Hortense crouched low as she waved him into shore with her whole body. "Swim faster, Sir Bacon!"

Even Jamie found himself calling out to the dog. The birds were gaining on him.

The dog's paws touched land just as the pelicans caught up. Understanding his life was in imminent danger, Sir Bacon bolted past Jamie and Hortense without even stopping to give his fur a shake. In the nick of time, Jamie grabbed Hortense's hand and pulled her out of the way of fractious pelicans bent on avian revenge. The next instant, however, the birds wearied of their vendetta and pivoted on the water, their long beaks set at composed angles, their ruffled feathers coming to lie placid and flat. It was as if nothing of note had disturbed their morning.

Sir Bacon, however, was another matter. He'd begun charging around trees and shrubs in circles and figure eights, kicking up mulch in flower beds, eyes wild, tongue lolling out the side of his mouth. In short, he was one het up dog.

"Sir Bacon, you come back here this instant," Hortense shouted, not one bit returned to her usual composed self.

Her words must have cut through the fog of mayhem clouding the dog's brain, for, across the distance of some twenty yards, he stopped dead and met the eye of his mistress. Then he charged forward, and all Jamie could do was watch in unfolding horror as, a few feet from her, the dog leapt up, her arms only shooting out at the last second to catch him.

The dog was a wet, muddy mess, and within three seconds, Hortense was, too. He began licking her face and continued making a general spectacle of himself. She sputtered and fussed and finally got him back on the ground, at which point he streaked off again. Arms held out from her body, she stood before Jamie, hair askew, a soggy, dirty, disheveled mess. Undoubtedly, she smelled of London pond. He may have just caught a whiff.

She met his eyes, a bewildered moment held, then, as one, they burst out in laughter. The sort of laughter that swept through a person's entire body and left one enervated and heaving for breath. It wasn't that this was better than what they shared last night, but it was different and novel, and he wanted more of it, more of this Hortense.

Increasingly, he wanted every part of her.

At last, the laughter faded, but not the lightness left in its wake. She picked at her sodden dress and pelisse. "I think the gods might be telling us it's time to return home." Too quickly for Jamie's liking, she corrected herself. "To Asquith Court, that is."

He caught her gaze. "It is your home, too."

"We both know that isn't quite the truth."

He opened his mouth to contradict her, but Sir Bacon came to a racing stop at her feet, his little chest huffing and puffing. "All done with your mischief?" she asked, not quite achieving the scold intended.

Too soon, they'd arrived back at Asquith Court.

Inside the receiving hall, Hortense faced Jamie, her customary seriousness returned. Already, he missed her lightness.

"Did you have a purpose in seeking me out earlier?" she asked.

"I did," he said reluctantly. He reached inside his greatcoat and dug out the missive. "I received this."

She accepted the note, turning it over, noting the broken seal. The broken seal of a duke. "When?"

"This morning."

She took in the contents without batting an eye. It was from Rothesbury, inviting the Marquess and Marchioness of Clare to his private box in Vauxhall Gardens for tonight's entertainments.

She returned the invitation to Jamie. "That was re-markably fast."

"Rothesbury isn't known for curbing his appetites once they're whetted."

She caught his gaze. She'd detected the note of anger in his voice. Rothesbury wanted Hortense, and the man intended to have her. Jamie would be damned to the farthest reaches of hell before that happened.

And here it was again, rearing its head, protective-ness...*possessiveness.*

The latter feeling must be curbed. Hortense wasn't the sort of woman who would stand for being pos-sessed by anyone.

"I know the sort of man Rothesbury is," she said. "He can be handled."

Her confidence from last night stirred the air. It hadn't always been so, Jamie wanted to protest. But it would be wrong of him, and, further, insulting to her. She'd learned how to navigate the world of men like Rothesbury. Yet she hadn't been able to handle that long-ago man...

Never again would she find herself in such a position.

Never.

"You stay in my sights at all times." His tone, forceful and autocratic, brooked no opposition.

"That will slow our results."

"At all times," he repeated, very nearly growling.

She nodded, slowly, understanding in her eyes, as if she'd intuited his thoughts.

Likely, she had. So much had passed between them in the week since they'd met. It struck him that he and she knew each other about as well as two people ever did, if not better.

He'd never particularly wanted to be known, but now he did. By her.

"I suppose I should begin readying myself for the night, starting with a bath." She picked at her clothes and wrinkled her nose.

"I could help." The words had left his mouth before he could give them a second thought, or any thought for that matter. "A return of the favor from last night."

She blinked, opened her mouth to speak, closed it, then opened it again. "I do not think that would be—"

"Wise?"

She nodded, the movement tight. "I shall see you here when it is time to leave."

And she was gone.

He pivoted on his heel and made directly for his study, unable to trust himself upstairs with the knowledge that she was bathing only a few doors away.

He came to a dead stop and called out, "Stinton, send to the mews for my dappled stallion." He had another idea. His most rational one of the day. "And have my riding clothes brought to my study."

He needed to vacate Asquith Court altogether. Perhaps a hard, sweaty ride through Hyde Park would cool blood that wanted to run hot at the merest thought of her.

Merest thought?

He snorted. He'd had her.

And still he wanted her.

But wanting wasn't the same as having. He could have her myriad ways, but, truly, he wouldn't *have* her, not the way he wanted. Not just with his body, but with his soul. This morning, when he'd awakened, alone, he wasn't sure his bed had ever felt so empty.

He gave his head a clearing shake. What treacly, mawkish rot.

But...

Was it untrue?

CHAPTER TWENTY

O ars sluiced through the inscrutable Thames, night having fallen hours ago. From the Westminster side of the river, Jamie had hired a wherry to row him and Hortense to Vauxhall Gardens. Across the water floated sounds of revelry, its volume growing in intensity as they drew near. The boatman, indifferent to all but the river, kept his sharp eye on the murky water, managing the current and the odd scrag of debris with a sort of stoic aplomb, pipe ever clenched between his teeth.

"Do you think your lady's maid will be able to handle Sir Bacon?" Jamie asked in an attempt at small talk. They'd been awkward with one another since setting out from Asquith Court. The woman certainly had no quarrel with a lengthy silence.

"I have my doubts." She didn't sound particularly concerned.

"His antics with the pelicans aside, he does seem better behaved within doors."

"All he needed was attention."

Again, tetchy silence descended. He'd given it a think on his breakneck ride through Hyde Park and determined he shouldn't have offered to help with her bath. That had been a mistake, which had bungled their pleasant morning as a result. Why had he done it?

The answer was simple.

Because he'd had her last night—in his tub, in his bed—and the wanting followed him into the day. His blood couldn't stop running hot with her.

"Have you ever visited Vauxhall Gardens?" he asked, ignoring his hot blood.

"I have." She drew her blue fur-trimmed, velvet cloak close. With the clear night had descended a northerly chill.

"It doesn't seem like the sort of place you would frequent."

"Not as a guest."

Of course. "As a spy."

"If you insist upon that word, then, yes, as a spy. But more as a serving wench than anything."

"I take it you've played the servant on more than a few occasions in your chosen profession."

She heaved a beleaguered sigh. "I wouldn't mind it so much, but..." she trailed with a slight grimace.

"*But?*" he nudged. She was on the verge of a confidence, and he would have it. He would have all of her.

"Well, a woman has to *be* a servant to *play* a servant, doesn't she?"

A wry smile found its way to her mouth, and he found himself responding in kind. She was such a serious person, and he could admit to being a fairly serious person himself. But together, they made each other smile. He liked that about them.

"Perhaps we should visit the lodge in Scotland. Well, it's more of an enormous manor house these days," he said to keep the banter going. "Something tells me you would be quite useful in a pinch."

This time she laughed, and gratification soared through him. "No doubt about it. I'm one of the Continent and England's great luggers of buckets and starters of fires."

Although it had begun as half a joke, he found he'd like to take this woman to Scotland. It was his favorite place, and he'd like to share it with her.

With that arrived a sobering thought. They had a marriage arrangement, not a marriage. An important distinction, and one he found himself chafing against the more time he spent with her.

She must have sensed his shift in mood for she, too, cast her gaze across the water, fragmented light dancing on its surface with every stroke of the oars. Jamie couldn't help keeping half an eye on her profile. How beautiful she was in the moonlight. It wasn't only her new clothing, its color and fit suiting her to perfection. Or her lady's maid's skill with her hair. Those were superficialities that did nothing to enhance beauty that reached deep into her bones. She would be exquisite in a potato sack.

And desirable.

Another sobering thought.

Last night, at the Duke of Wellington's supper party, he hadn't been prepared for how the *ton* would react to her, like she was their newest, shiniest bauble. Tonight, he would handle his reactions better and not let his emotions get away from him.

Rothesbury was their target, and their success in rescuing Rafe from Flick Doyle relied heavily upon Hortense securing the confidence of the duke. Last night, she'd achieved just that.

He should be pleased.

Yet he couldn't quite summon the feeling.

She cut a sharp glance his way. "Shall we review tonight's objective?"

"To get closer to Rothesbury, correct?" There was no mistaking his disgust.

She nodded slowly. "That's the means, but not the end. Tonight, we must gain an invitation to his residence so I can access his vaults, and pray the tiara is there."

It hit Jamie. "You're not simply good at your profession. You're the best, aren't you?"

"Amongst them."

She made the acknowledgement without arrogance or braggadocio, but rather as a statement of truth. This quality, her quiet assurance, was damned attractive.

As if she needed to be any more attractive.

"I take it you have a plan for how to achieve the objective?"

"Flattery," she said quickly, then hesitated. "But I must warn you."

"Of what?" He knew enough to be wary of what might next cross her lips. The woman didn't give idle warnings.

"Tonight won't be pretty."

"I don't follow."

"I shall be appealing to Rothesbury's vanity, and you will be the foil."

Jamie found his jaw tensing, for he understood two facts at once. He would be playing her fool tonight. And he would have to keep a tight rein on himself.

Not like last night when he slipped the bit and lost all control.

She watched him, expectant, assessing what substance he was made of. She needed his agreement.

At last, he summoned every shred of grit he possessed and nodded.

Oars continued steadily slicing through the water, and she finally nodded back. Reserve hung about her. She had her doubts.

That made two of them.

As their boat slid into Vauxhall's water gate, he

would have missed the subtle changes in her demeanor had he not known her so well. A spark twinkled in her eyes. One corner of her mouth curled into a playful smile waiting for a witty rejoinder to tip into full bloom. The set of her shoulders wasn't so square any-more, but rather relaxed into an openness that sug-gested invitation to a dalliance. She'd fully slipped into the role of coquettish marchioness.

She flashed flirty eyes at him. "Are you ready, my husband?"

The dark feeling from last night slithered through Jamie. He didn't like this version of her.

He jumped from the boat and noticed the boatman's subtly extended hand. Jamie dug into an inner pocket and slipped a gratuity into the meaty palm, while keeping six shillings ready for their admittance into the gardens. Hortense took the boatman's hand, stepping from the boat and onto the landing, a coy tilt to her head as she stared up at him through her eyelashes. A sheepish smile tottered about the man's mouth. Good gads, was he blushing?

They ascended the water stairs and were soon promenading along Vauxhall's Grand Walk, a gravel path lined by stately elms strewn with glass lanterns providing the illumination of a dozen constellations. All around were other guests seeking their pleasures in the myriad ways Vauxhall so amply provided. Foun-tains, artificial ruins, cascades, temples, grottoes, and minstrels parading about. The gaiety of the atmosphere effervesced a bit much, in truth. But when had pleasure seekers ever given a thought to *a bit much*?

Hortense's head angled back, her gaze sweeping across the canopy above. Jamie had to fight the impulse to lean down and press his mouth to the exposed curve of her pale throat.

Which wouldn't do.

Not even at Vauxhall.

"Do you know how many lanterns are strung about the place?"

"I've heard fifteen thousand," he said.

She gave a dry snort. He couldn't help feeling a bit relieved. That snort was very much in keeping with the Hortense he knew.

"This place is beyond extravagant."

"I believe they're preparing for a reenactment of the Battle of Waterloo this summer."

"Wasn't there one only a few years ago?"

"It will have a thousand soldiers and horses, complete with artillery and ammunition wagons."

"Surely not live rounds?" she asked, shocked.

"You wouldn't put anything past the pleasure of an aristocrat, would you?"

An emotion flickered within her eyes and was gone. "Nothing."

"I believe fireworks will be employed."

"I—" She began and stopped. A shyness hung about her. A hint of the genuine her. "I was interested in your history of St. James's Park."

"Oh?"

"Would you happen to know the history of this place as well?"

"I might have read an article or two."

"The study's collection?" she teased. How he warmed to it.

"Its collection on London is rather exhaustive."

"Tell me about Vauxhall, then."

He could deny her nothing. "It was established as Spring Gardens—in 1660, I believe—but it didn't become the Vauxhall Gardens we know until some chap took over the lease and did a complete refurbishment in the 1730's. It's been a pleasure garden for the rich and poor alike ever since. Nowhere else in London—I daresay in all of England—do the classes so closely mingle and share in the same amusements."

Examples of high and low London swirled around them, all intent on the same frivolities from shop girl to duchess, from costermonger to prince. It possessed a fearless vivacity that fizzed its way beneath the skin and through to one's veins.

A shout sounded from a nearby supper box, "Clare!"

Dread twisted Jamie's gut. A voice he'd known since childhood, one he would know anywhere. *Rothesbury.* In the space of a few seconds, Hortense's visage went from thoughtful and engaged to vacuous and coy, a saucy smile curling about her cherry red mouth, coquettish mischief twinkling in her eyes. He'd lost the genuine Hortense to her role for the night.

They crossed the short distance to Rothesbury's box, and she squeezed his arm. "Are you ready for this?" she asked under her breath.

No, he wanted to growl, but he bit it back. He could sit through a night of playing her fool if it meant saving his son from Flick Doyle. He mustn't lose sight of tonight's objective. Jaws were made for clenching after all. "Of course," he said tightly.

"Angry newlywed husband doesn't suit you," she said through her false smile. "Try haughty marquess. It should be a natural enough fit."

He gave a dry snort.

They reached Rothesbury's box and found six occupants: Rothesbury, a lady whose bounteous bosom was in danger of spilling from the front of her dress and who could be none other than Rothesbury's mistress, and two other couples, ladies paired with ladies and lords with lords, undoubtedly sharing on-dits from Almack's and Tattersall's respectively.

"If it isn't the Marquess of Clare," exclaimed one lady.

"And his new bride," said the other.

Deuce take it. They were his supper partners from Wellington's party.

Rothesbury's mistress batted the duke with her fan. "You said you had a treat for us tonight, you rogue." She brazenly eyed Jamie up and down. "And how you delivered."

Rothesbury paid the woman scant attention as he introduced her as Lady Selborne. Greetings continued around the box, and Hortense unthreaded her arm from Jamie's and stepped away, her gaze for Rothesbury only. Instinctively, Jamie made to follow, but halted mid-step. Haughty lords didn't follow their ladies about like green pups. Instead, he watched her settle into the open chair next to Rothesbury's mistress.

A serving girl appeared, bearing a tray of arrack punch, Vauxhall's infamous libation, the arrack a sugar and coconut liquor imported from the East Indies. Jamie waved her away, attracting Rothesbury's attention.

"When are you one to turn down spirits, Clare?" the duke asked. "Last I saw you in Pizzy's Pleasure Palace— when was that? a year ago?—you were hell bent on turning into a right old sot."

Jamie shrugged, thoroughly uninterested in Rothesbury's opinion of him. "I've lost the taste for it." Perhaps if he told the lie enough times, it would become the truth.

The duke turned his lecherous eye on Hortense, all but licking his lips at the sight of her. "And you, Lady Clare?" He lifted a cup of arrack and held it out to her, leaning across his long-suffering, all-but-forgotten mistress. "Do you follow your husband's lead in all things, like a good, little wife?"

"Oh, I'm good, your grace"—she suppressed a naughty smile—"but not at obeying my husband."

"And what is it you're so good at?" Rothesbury asked.

"Wouldn't you like to know?" she asked, all enticing primness as she accepted the proffered arrack and took a delicate sip. Her tongue darted out and licked the sweetness off her bottom lip.

Jamie wasn't the only man transfixed by the motion of her tongue. *Rothesbury.* He could punch the leer off the man's face—a quick clip on the jaw should do it— or, better yet, yank the wig off the man's head. Did he not realize how ridiculous it made him?

Settle, he scolded himself. This was exactly what Hortense had warned him against. To win Rothesbury's trust, they must keep to their roles.

Rather than the conversation returning to gossip about balls, fashion, and horseflesh, it pivoted to the political. "Can you believe George Canning replaced Lord Liverpool as prime minister?"

"Lord Liverpool must be at death's door to stand down after fifteen years."

"Canning is a good enough Tory chap, even if he is the son of an actress and a solicitor."

Titters floated around the box.

"Wellington and Peel won't serve under him. He'll split the party."

"He'll have to invite Whigs to serve in his cabinet at this rate. Won't last the year, you watch."

Lady Selborne spoke up. "This is to be a night for gaiety, gentlemen. No more of your politics."

Like that, talk returned to balls, fashion, and horseflesh.

"Lady Selborne," began Hortense, "your tiara is absolutely stunning. Is it a family heirloom?"

Only now did Jamie notice the tiara perched atop Lady Selborne's head. Platinum, diamonds, sapphires— well, paste ones.

This tiara was the replica they sought and a stroke of great good luck. It was both still in the possession of Rothesbury and in London. Now it was certain. They would be able to switch and steal it.

Hortense had likely noticed it the instant they entered the supper box. She kept her head, his wife.

Before Lady Selborne could reply, Rothesbury said on a malicious chuckle, "Oh, her family had to sell their jewels decades ago. Poor as church mice, aren't they now?"

Lady Selborne laughed along, but the humor didn't quite reach her eyes.

"No, this lovely jewel belongs to the Dukes of Rothesbury and their duchesses." No one had the temerity to point out that Lady Selborne was, in fact, *not* a Duchess of Rothesbury.

Smartly, Hortense didn't acknowledge the sour exchange, instead proclaiming, "I simply adore sapphires."

"To match your eyes," Rothesbury said ardently, as if he'd channeled the poet Keats for his laughably banal observation.

"Not remotely close to the mark," Jamie said. He'd had enough.

Rothesbury's eyebrows lifted. He was a duke. No one, save a king, nay-sayed him. "Pardon?"

"Sapphires are a dull shade compared to my wife's eyes."

Smiles twitched about mouths and eyes danced with humor. He'd just revealed himself to be utterly —*vulgarly, stupidly*—besotted with his bride.

"You've already married her, Clare," said Rothesbury. "You don't have to spout poetry at her anymore."

Jamie refused to feel embarrassed. "It's only true."

Hortense caught his gaze. Though her eyes flashed with the merriment being had by all at his expense, he detected concern. She had misgivings about his ability to hold himself together in this company. And she was right to wonder.

He questioned his ability himself.

"Lady Clare," said Lady Selborne, "you and Rothesbury have become such fast friends, let us trade seats so you can speak more freely."

"What generosity of spirit, Lady Selborne," Hortense exclaimed, making the switch. Now, no barrier came between her and Rothesbury.

Jamie had no time to stew about this development for Lady Selborne was crooking her finger at him. "Lord Clare, I find myself with an empty chair beside me." She gave the cushion three quick pats. "Shall we better acquaint ourselves with one another?"

Unable to refuse, he took the proffered seat beside the lady, yet he couldn't think of one thing to say.

Unfortunately, the lady had no such difficulty. She leaned close enough that he could feel her breath on his neck when she spoke. "You are so very earnest these days, Clare. I do not remember this about you."

"Sorry to disappoint," he said, terse, distracted. Hortense was now batting Rothesbury with her fan and calling him a naughty, naughty man. If a man's blood could boil inside his veins, Jamie's surely was.

A feminine hand on his knee pulled his attention toward Lady Selborne staring intently into his face. "Oh, I rather like an earnest man," she said. "I find they make the best—"

Blessedly, the remainder of her sentence was cut off by a sudden rustling at the back of the box, followed by a stream of servers bearing nothing less than a feast—a whole roast chicken, a dish of Vauxhall's famous sliced ham, dishes of beef, bread, butter, cheese, salad, a platter of lemons and oranges, tarts, custards, a Shrewsbury cake, another quart of arrack-punch, burgundy wine, champagne, old hock, and several pounds of ice. It was a spread fit for a king, except the excess and extravagance might make even Prinny blush.

As each new dish arrived, Hortense appeared ever more impressed by the duke, her eyes wide and appreciative. She'd turned into a vacuous, little coquette, one precisely calibrated to please Rothesbury's vanity. The way she was gazing upon the duke...how could he possibly resist her?

Standing behind her, Jamie leaned down, unable not to catch a quick sip of her clean, lemon scent. "Would you like me to make a plate for you, wife?" He couldn't seem to stop calling her *wife*.

She twisted around and stared up at him, mischief twinkling in her gaze. Whatever she was about to say, he wouldn't like it, he felt it in his bones. "What an attentive, little husband you are."

Shocked titters sounded around the box as Rothesbury roared with laughter. Jamie's jaw might never regain the ability to unclench.

Little?

Last night had showed her there was nothing *little* about him. He would be only too willing to prove it again.

"Our host has such discerning taste that I think he could find what would best satisfy me."

If Rothesbury had been a peacock, his tail feathers would have sprung into full fan.

And all Jamie could do was tense his jaw and stew and settle back as his wife made him a cuckold and a fool.

CHAPTER TWENTY-ONE

Oh, Jamie had caught that *little* crack.

And he didn't like it one bit.

Hortense shrugged off his glower. This was the operation, and it was running as smoothly as an operation possibly could. Vain, self-absorbed men were the easiest marks. Truly, the only difficulty was her husband.

Now, time to have a stab at the heart of the matter. She gazed into Rothesbury's soulless eyes. "My family lost all their jewels during the Revolution."

"A tragedy." He took her hands in his clammy ones, offering hollow comfort. She stopped herself from snatching them back. "A woman like you should be dripping in jewels."

"Yet, as you can see"—a mean smile played about her mouth—"my new husband does not share your point of view." She held up her left hand. "Only this single jewel adorns my body." She said it dismissively, like one would need a magnifying glass to see the sapphire, when she was fairly certain Mariana had been correct in her observation about the stone. Indeed, one could likely view it from the moon.

Meanwhile, behind her, she sensed her husband seething.

"Clare," Rothesbury threw over his shoulder, "don't you know anything of women? Or how to keep them?"

"I don't have to keep her." The menace in Jamie's voice was unmistakable. "She's my wife."

Rothesbury scoffed. "You have a lot to learn, and I have a feeling this wife of yours will teach you. Although, who wouldn't wish to learn at her feet?"

"Oh, it isn't at my feet where he will learn his best lessons, but rather higher up my person," Hortense quipped, eliciting delighted gasps from the other ladies.

Rothesbury only smiled. Even in good humor, the man had the mien of a pit viper. "You are a very naughty thing, aren't you?"

She shrugged, as if suddenly bored. Drawing back served to work up the duke more. A giggle, then a slap. That was how he liked it. He wanted her to be easy, but not too easy. An achievable challenge.

She leaned in and jerked her chin toward Lady Selborne. "Do all your mistresses have access to your jewel vaults?"

Rothesbury inched closer. The sickly sour-sweet smell of arrack drifted on his breath. "Of course."

She lowered her voice to an excited whisper. "Without limits?"

Half a smile tugged about his mouth. He had her, that half smile told her. How she wished she could tell him differently. "That is dependent on a few factors."

"Like?" she asked, oh-so-breathless.

"What access she offers me."

A tense moment passed, him awaiting her response with bated breath, her making him. She batted his thigh with her fan. "I fear you're the naughtiest man I've ever had the pleasure to meet, duke."

His gaze turned imploring. "Come to my masquerade."

Ah. Now, they were getting somewhere. "Your masquerade?"

"Tomorrow night at my manse." He threw Jamie a hostile glare. "Clare knows the address."

Hortense drew back, breaking the intimacy of their little *tête-a-tête*. It wouldn't do to have the man thinking her eager to accept his offer. After all, the opportunity she'd been shamelessly flirting her way toward had landed in her lap. She modulated her response to utter indifference. "Send an invitation to Asquith Court tomorrow, and I shall consider it."

A comically dumbfounded expression spread across Rothesbury's face. What sort of woman refused a duke's masquerade? He cocked his head and narrowed his eyes, and she knew. He was eating out of the palm of her hand. This duke very much wanted to find out what sort of woman.

Tomorrow night, she and Jamie would be able to pull off the switch for the tiara currently gracing the head of Lady Selborne. How incredibly fast and easily this job was nearing its conclusion.

And when it was done, they would be out of each other's lives.

A part of her that she kept trying to suppress—and mostly failing— didn't like that last bit, but she'd known it all along.

Lady Selborne leaned forward. "Are you speaking of the masquerade, Rothesbury?"

"We are."

The lady swiveled toward Jamie. "Oh, do come!"

He gave a noncommittal grunt. The man was decidedly grumpy, which annoyed Hortense. Didn't he understand how to play a role? Did he have to be so decidedly himself?

Yet at the same time, she rather liked this about him. He built up no artifice.

It was damned attractive.

But, mayhap, the time had arrived to put him out of his suffering. The night's objective had been achieved. "Husband, shall we go for a stroll about the grounds? Mayhap you could use some air."

"Ah, a splendid idea," said Rothesbury. "Shall we all go—"

Jamie's eyes narrowed to angry slits. "Not you."

The duke gave an indulgent laugh and held up hands in surrender. "Don't stray too long."

Two minutes later, Hortense and Jamie were again strolling the Grand Walk, arm in arm. Well, *striding* was more accurate.

"Rothesbury isn't chasing us," she said, her steps two to his one.

He took the hint and slowed his pace, his mouth pressed into a firm, silent line.

She wasn't having it. "If you have something to say to me, then out with it. Petty resentments can't lie between partners on a job."

Incredulous eyes rounded on her. "*Petty?*"

"Is this about that *little* bit?"

He snorted. "Did you have to be so...so—"

"Flirtatious?" she finished for him.

"*Provocative*," he finished for himself.

"Yes." Let that sit and simmer inside him a few steps. Sometimes bluntness was the only way. "I am seducing the man, after all."

A strangled noise emerged from Jamie.

That was it.

She grabbed his arm, pulled the blasted man to a stop, and met him square in the eye. "That is what he must believe tonight and tomorrow night when we attend his masquerade."

Eyes silver with frustration stared down at her. He wanted to refute her words. "That's our chance," he relented.

She nodded, relieved. "Aye."

"It must work." A hint of desperation sounded in his voice.

"It will."

"It's the quickest means of rescuing Rafe."

"It's the quickest, but not the only," she said.

"Aye," he said, dark determination in the utterance.

A shiver ran through her. This man would have what was his by means fair or foul.

"We will secure your son." She was as determined as he.

"I'm thinking the boy will be a handful."

"Good assumption. He would have spirit to have survived as long as he has."

"I might need your assistance." Jamie hesitated. "Even after I have him."

Hortense glanced away. She had to. "You'll manage without me, no doubt," she said, even as guilt surged through her. To achieve that end—of Jamie having his son—she would thieve from him. Even now, she was in the process of that betrayal. How did such a woman fit into a future with him?

Once a eel, always a eel.

The answer was easy. She didn't.

They resumed their walk, the tension between them dissipating by bits. Jamie glanced around their surroundings, which were quieter and darker than the rest of Vauxhall. "I don't know this area of the gardens."

"No?" she asked. "Well, you may know the history of Vauxhall, but I can navigate its ins and outs. That's the advantage of having played the serving wench here on a few occasions."

"Of course."

"You and I, husband, have entered one of the scandalous Dark Paths."

"Will our reputations survive intact?"

His question was lighthearted, but a sinuous note slid within. One that sent a frisson of awareness purling down her spine.

Sudden white streaked across the sky and, two seconds later, a shocking boom of thunder ripped the heavens open. Rain first came down in sporadic, fat drops, then released in a torrent. An impromptu storm had landed on top of them.

"Just around the next bend in the path," she shouted over another crack of thunder, squinting through raindrop-laden lashes, "is Wipple's Folly."

"What's a Wipple's Folly?" he shouted back, his hand shielding his eyes.

"Shelter."

He grabbed her hand, his fingers weaving through hers, and held fast, pulling her into a run. Wind whipped the rain in all directions as it penetrated cloak, dress, and chemise, soaking her to the skin. But she felt it not, for warmth radiated through her entire body from the place where his hand held hers tight.

Ahead, through the darkness and downpour loomed a brick structure, octagonal in shape with a domed roof. It had a shabby look to it, as if left unattended for a great number of years, vines trailing up walls, mortar crumbling between bricks. But one never knew with a folly. Its state of disrepair could all be for effect.

Below the shallow portico, Jamie released her hand, took the five steps in two swift bounds, before pushing the door open and poking his head inside. "Only us," he called over his shoulder.

Inside, Hortense was pleasantly surprised to find the roof had a skylight that didn't leak. It wasn't much on a night like this, but not complete darkness either. While her eyes adjusted, she leaned against a wall and watched Jamie prowl the perimeter of the small, plain room. That was the thing about follies. All style, but not much substance.

"It appears we are alone."

Her ear caught something in that *alone*. Her body caught it, too.

Above them, rain battered the dome, drowning out the night music of Vauxhall, drowning out the sound of her ragged breath. In silhouette, she watched him run his hand through his hair and flick the wet away. The room went white with lightning and her eye found his for that flash of a second. She shivered. But not from cold.

"Surely you're soaked through," he said.

"Sopping."

Another lightning burst. He was advancing, toward her. She couldn't move a muscle. With the next flash of lightning, she saw that he was nearly upon her.

"Remove your clothes."

She gaped.

"You'll catch a chill."

"We are in a public place. I'll not be removing my clothes."

Although she couldn't see the details of his face, she knew his expression with certainty: frustrated imperiousness. Before meeting this man, she'd never known that expression existed.

"Take off your cloak, then."

"The storm will tire itself out soon, and we can—"

"Your cloak."

He would be obeyed, so she did. He moved close, close enough she could feel the heat from his body, close enough she could breathe him in.

"Take this. It's dry inside." A brief rustling of fabric, then his greatcoat was settling onto her shoulders.

"Don't you need it?" she asked on a protest that

emerged weak. The truth was she wouldn't give it up even if he answered yes. The leftover heat from his body penetrated her wet clothes down to her skin, to her bones, to another place, too, the place in the center of her chest. The place she would rather not name, not even to herself. No man considered her the way he did.

He brushed a clinging tendril of hair from her face. She wanted to nuzzle into his hand. But she resisted. She must maintain some shred of control. At least, that was what she had to tell herself. How slender the space between a lie and the truth.

"I must appear a fright."

He shook his head. "It's not possible."

Maintaining his contact with her skin, he trailed his fingers lower to the line of her jaw, her throat, cupping her nape, tilting her head so her eyes met his.

"Last night was to be the last time," she uttered.

"The only time."

"But it won't be."

He angled his face, his mouth but a whisper removed from hers. "Last night was simply the *first* time."

A slow tremor snaked through her and curled deep in her sex, leaving no doubt as to the truth and inevitability of this moment. This was the next time.

"You're so wet," he murmured. "*Here.*" He pressed his mouth to the pulse point below her ear and her eyes drifted shut, her breath caught in her lungs, her knees went trembly. The effect he had on her...

"And *here.*" His lips brushed across her clavicle. "And *here.*"

Kisses trailed along her décolletage, as he pulled her dress, exposing her breasts. His mouth covered one nipple, and he sucked, dragging a long moan from her, her head arching into the wall at her back. His tongue flicked across the hard bud and a sound issued from her, a sound she was distressingly unable to control, a sound that was decidedly like a...

* * *

A WHImper.

He'd made this extraordinary woman whimper.

She'd likely never whimpered in all her life.

And here he was pulling whimpers from her.

And he would do it again.

He caught her eye, emboldened. "I wonder where else you're wet."

He grabbed her skirts and shoved them up to her waist, baring legs clad only in white stockings and frilly pink garters. He wasn't sure how it was possible, but his cock grew harder. He hadn't been able to rid his head of the image of her in Apsley House, pressed against the wall, cunny bare and ready. As if intuiting the direction of his thoughts, one stockinged leg wrapped around his waist.

His fingers slid along her slit, and her eyes fluttered shut, a sigh of utter abandon escaping her. She liked his fingers.

"Oh, you're wet, my sweet," he said into the crook of her neck.

Her nimble fingers began working the fall of his trousers. His manhood sprang free, and her eyes grew dark with lust. Her hand wrapped around him and tugged. Now it was his eyes drifting shut and ragged groans escaping him. She pulled on him again, her hand moving in slow, deliberate rhythm, drawing him closer. The head of his cock dragged along her wet cunny, and her heel dug into his arse cheek and her hips angled, opening her to him completely. "I need you," she whispered. "*More*," she demanded.

Driven by her words—by instinct—he clutched her

hips and drove into her with a slow deliberateness that had her squirming, gasping, groaning, pleading for more, *demanding* more. "More like this?" In and out, he drove into her, stroke after relentless stroke.

"Oh, yes," she cried, her fingers curling into his hair, her hips matching his rhythm as he gave her what she wanted, what she *needed...more.*

This wasn't going to be a long tup; he understood that from her increasingly sharp gasps and protracted moans and from the tightening in his manhood, release beginning to coil inside him. But not until she found hers first.

He slowed his strokes and a whine escaped her. "Trust me, sweet."

Her lust-filled eyes found his and held. "I do," she said. "I trust you—*oh*—I trust you."

He had her trust. Now to properly earn it. Again and again, he thrust in and out of her. Her fingers slid beneath his shirt, her fingernails dug into his skin, spurring him on, driving them both to the brink. Against him, she inhaled a ragged gasp and her body held. She'd reached the edge, teetering, waiting... He moved with slow intention, and she broke, her quim pulsing its release around his cock, her fingernails surely drawing blood from his shoulders, her parted mouth emitting his name on a scream of pleasure.

It was all he needed, and release was upon him. He held on to her, his hips driving with a primal abandon as he tumbled into an ecstasy only the two of them knew. Only the two of them would ever know.

Here, they stood, suspended outside time, ravished, only his larger body pressed against hers holding her upright, chests heaving, hearts pounding in union, her pulse beating against her ivory throat in moonlight that now streamed through the skylight. The storm had passed.

"Can you stand?"

She nodded, avoiding his gaze.

He moved back to give her space, and fastened the fall of his trousers, keeping half an eye on her as she made haste to return herself to presentable. He wished she wouldn't. He liked her like this, unkempt, out of control.

At last, she looked up. "That was—"

She couldn't seem to finish the sentence. He could. "Inevitable."

Her eyes agreed, even as she shook her head. "The last time."

Every cell in his body disagreed. Not if he had anything to do with it.

She began to shrug off his greatcoat.

"What are you doing?" he demanded.

"I can't wear this."

"Why not? You're my wife."

"And several inches shorter than you. It will drag on the ground and be ruined."

He shrugged. What did he care about a coat? He could have thirty more in his closet by morning. "You shall wear it."

She blinked and shut her mouth. *Good.* It was a battle she wouldn't win. She was dry and warm within it, which was all that mattered. Still, he grabbed her discarded cloak in case she got an idea to wear the sopping, woolen mess. She could be stubborn.

By land, by water, by carriage, by stairs and corridors, they returned to Asquith Court. All the while, quiet nested between them. It wasn't a tense silence, or tetchy, but one pensive and perhaps wistful. They both knew: one more day.

Tomorrow night, they would either succeed or fail to switch the tiaras, and all this would be over. It wasn't playacting for him, but it was for her. For him, this thing between them was something he wanted more of.

She was his wife.

His lover.

His.

She could remain her own woman—in truth, he wanted her to remain her own woman, for it was deuced attractive and she was deuced good at it—but he wanted her to be his, too.

He had only a day to convince her of it.

CHAPTER TWENTY-TWO

*A*s Jamie moved through his morning ablutions, he hardly noticed the motions of his body or the ministrations of his valet. His mind was singularly focused elsewhere, on *her*.

And last night.

And his resolve to have her, not only in his bed or against a wall.

After the first time, he'd considered it had been so long since he'd touched a woman that emotions were becoming confused with the sensation of sublime release. He'd doubted it, but the possibility existed. But last night...

Put that possibility to an end.

What he and Hortense shared was unique to them.

Could she see that?

Could a marriage between them be genuine?

The *Morning Chronicle* tucked beneath his arm, he strode into the breakfast room.

At the table sat Hortense, dressed in her clothes—her old clothes—tying the silk lead around Sir Bacon's neck.

The sight brought Jamie's progress to an immediate halt, his stomach flipping before dropping to his feet.

"Are you—" He cleared his throat, collecting himself to an outward show of cool indifference. "Are you leaving?" *No, no, no.*

She glanced up, and he caught a flicker of something in her eyes—a remnant of last night, mayhap. Then it was gone, a careful wariness replacing it. "Yes."

Of course. Here it was. The inevitable.

Of course, she was leaving.

But that didn't mean he wouldn't put up a fight.

"But I thought—" He shut his mouth before his inner turmoil could spill into his voice. "But what about tonight?"

She couldn't leave. She *couldn't.*

He wouldn't have it. A day yet remained to convince her to stay.

"Tonight has naught to do with it. I'm returning Sir Bacon to his owner."

Swift relief soared through Jamie. "But why are you wearing—" He gestured up and down, indicating her current attire.

"It might be best if Lady Fortescue doesn't recognize the Marchioness of Clare as the woman she hired to rescue her dog from her former lover."

"Ah." *Of course.*

He seated himself at the opposite side of the table, and a footman entered bearing the familiar silver tray with the morning's correspondence. Jamie did a quick sort through and came across a gold-embossed missive with a seal that had become all too familiar. He held it up for Hortense's inspection.

Her head canted. "Rothesbury?"

"Aye." Jamie broke the seal and gave the contents a quick scan. "It's the invitation to tonight's masquerade." He debated whether or not to tell her the next part.

"And?" She'd noted his hesitation.

"All couples are to arrive separately and not within the half hour of each other."

Hortense showed not an ounce of surprise. She'd seen it all when it came to aristocrats. A fact that set his teeth on edge.

"Which of us shall arrive first?" she asked. "You? Or me?"

"*Me.*"

"Let us consider this carefully. It would likely be more productive if it's me."

"*I* shall be the first to arrive."

Their eyes locked. When she opened her mouth to continue making her case, he held up a hand. "I won't have you alone in Rothesbury's manse."

"Hundreds of the *ton* will be in attendance. I shan't be alone."

He refused to relent on the matter.

Weary of the staring contest, she nodded. "'Tis your operation, my lord."

That *my lord* delivered the prick intended. He was being an imperious ass, it told him. On this matter, so be it. She would be safe.

"You must send a message to Eva Galante about tonight's clothing requirements," she said. "They need to be here by eight of the clock, at the very latest."

"I shall inform Stinton."

Sir Bacon gave a small whine and tugged at his lead. "Well, I must be off," she said, rising to her feet.

A spark of panic fired through Jamie at the thought of her leaving. Too soon it would be the last time. "Might I accompany you?"

He shouldn't have asked. He should have sat at his customary place at the breakfast table and commenced with his morning ritual of coffee, *Chronicle*, and toast.

But he couldn't help himself. He couldn't help acting like a besotted wretch around her.

That was the truth of it. He was completely infatuated with this woman.

His wife. His lover. His...

"You'll want to change into different clothes."

"Why?"

"We shall be entering by the servant's entrance."

Jamie held up his hand, as if, like a wizard, he had the magic to stay her feet with a spell. "I shall meet you in the receiving hall in five minutes."

She gave a nod that didn't appear as reluctant as he would have expected. "I'll be waiting."

On the way to his dressing room, he summoned Stinton and dictated a quick note to be delivered to Eva Galante. He would be a laborer again, and he didn't mind a jot. Not when he was with Hortense.

How deep the troughs. How high the peaks. He'd never experienced this riot of ups and downs dependent upon another person.

So, this was infatuation? The mercurial emotion that made fools of men. No wonder poets dedicated untold numbers of lines and rhymes to it.

It was imperative he control it.

Or he would spook her like a skittish horse.

And, then, he'd lose the chance to make her his.

* * *

HORTENSE STOOD in the receiving hall and reflected on how different Asquith Court felt now than it had the first time she'd entered through the servant's door.

The grand entrance faced a magnificent marble staircase that led up to a wide landing where the stairs split to either side leading up to the next floor. A skylight allowed the sun to shine through, illuminating the vast space in a soft glow. At carefully chosen intervals, marble statues stood displaying their ties to the ancient pasts of Greece and Rome.

Nobs never met a classical statue they could resist.

Still, she could appreciate that different Asquiths had curated elements of the house through the centuries. This sort of space had ever made her feel small and insignificant. What was she to a man who possessed all this?

Under usual circumstances, the answer was that she was a nothing. Yet the man who owned all this had sought her out, repeatedly. And, two days ago, he'd made her his wife.

In name only.

Right.

That horse had already bolted from the stable.

Twice.

Her body had never felt so deliciously used.

She heaved a great sigh. How was it she kept falling into sexual congress with the man she should be viewing as a mark?

Her body refused to heed her mind was how.

The rapid clip of boot heels clicked smartly against marble. She turned to find Mrs. Blanche approaching. The woman who had hired her as a scullery over a fortnight ago hadn't batted an eyelash when she'd become the marchioness. If Mrs. Blanche had an opinion about the strange turn of events, she'd kept it to herself.

"Do you require anything, my lady?"

My lady.

Instinctively, Hortense opened her mouth to correct the woman, then closed it. As much as it defied all belief, and for as long as she resided in this house, *lady* was her identity. "I do not, Mrs. Blanche. I am awaiting the return of his lordship."

Mrs. Blanche wasn't quite finished. "Mayhap before tea we could consult about the week's menu?"

"That would be most agreeable, Mrs. Blanche."

It wouldn't. Hortense knew naught about food beyond the sustenance it provided. Further, she likely wouldn't be here to eat it.

Oh, that her gut didn't twist at the thought. It would have to accustom itself to that reality sooner or later.

Her face neutral, Mrs. Blanche nodded and took her leave, continuing on with the myriad duties a housekeeper faced in the course of morning, day, and night.

It wasn't long before another set of footsteps sounded, their tread heavier, but no less crisp and clipped. She would know the step of her husband anywhere. Sir Bacon's tail began wagging, and she turned to watch his approach.

She gave herself a mental shake. Best not to dwell on her husband's handsomeness, but rather focus on the task at hand. "How is it you manage to look aristocratic in what you're wearing?"

He lifted empty hands. "A special talent?"

A planter in the corner caught Hortense's eye. "You need a little mussing."

She scooped out two fingers of dirt, and before he could gather what she was about, she strode up to him and smudged it on both of his cheeks.

"What on earth?" he sputtered, stepping back.

"Now rub it in and make sure to get some in your hair. You're simply too clean for a laborer."

"You expect me to walk through Mayfair with dirt on my person?"

She gave a little shrug, one designed to wheedle its way under his skin. "I can always go alone. Besides, no one will recognize you."

"Why is that?"

"Because no nob is looking for the Marquess of Clare to be striding around with muck on his face."

With a bemused shake of his head, he did as he was

told, even though he clearly didn't like it. For all his airs and titles, the man truly was a good sport. She liked that about him.

Soon, they were on their way, companionably traversing the streets toward Lady Fortescue's townhouse. "Have you ever entered a house through the servant's entrance?" she asked. She already knew the answer.

"Never."

"Follow me, then." She slowed her step at a townhouse painted in the same white with black trim as its neighbors and opened a low wrought iron gate at the head of a short flight of stairs. She descended, Jamie two steps behind. She raised her fist and gave the kitchen door three quick raps.

The same kitchen servant she'd dealt with last week opened the door. "Oh, it's ye," the girl said with no amount of joy as she glanced down at Sir Bacon, who barked by way of greeting.

"Fetch the housekeeper and tell her I've returned Lady Fortescue's dog," Hortense said, the voice of authority. It was the only way to deal with a servant who looked on the verge of slamming the door in one's face.

Just before she turned to her errand, the girl's eye caught on something over Hortense's shoulder. Her gaze widened, and a blush pinked her cheeks. She'd noticed Jamie.

Hortense cleared her throat. "The housekeeper?" she said, giving the girl a nudge, even as she understood. Jamie was a difficult man to remove one's eyes from. Just one more quick glance back and the girl was gone.

"Shut the door behind ye," came a rough voice, "and 'ave a sit down with one of me fresh biscuits." It was the cook. "If I know that lass, ye'll be waitin' a tick or two."

For Jamie's eyes only, Hortense held a quieting forefinger to her mouth, telling him in no uncertain terms to keep his mouth shut. They each took a stool at the kitchen table, Sir Bacon settling at their feet, his face upturned in the eternal hope of a dropped scrap. Cook cast a baleful eye the little dog's way.

Hortense felt compelled to speak up for him. "He's trained to go outside now."

Cook responded with a disbelieving, "Harrumph."

At last, the efficient rustle of skirts approached, and the housekeeper swept into the kitchen. The woman wore what Hortense suspected was a permanent frown of vague offense. "Her ladyship will not be requiring the dog any longer."

Alarm shot through Hortense. "What does that mean? He's her dog. The one she's paying me to fetch for her."

"As to that..." The housekeeper held out a pouch, coin clinking inside. "Here's your payment. Now, if you will please take the animal with you when you go."

Neither Sir Bacon nor Hortense was dismissed so easily. "Doesn't she care what happens to him?"

"Not particularly. She procured a new pup in the country."

"He's trained to go outside now." Hortense couldn't help feeling defensive. "He's truly a good little—"

Jamie's fingertips trailed down her upper arm, staying the remainder of her defense. In bruised silence, she accepted the pouch from the housekeeper's hand. Then she pivoted on her heel, brushing past Jamie, who had opened the door. Sensing fractiousness in the air, Sir Bacon barked at the household at large for good measure. They may have seen the last of him, but they wouldn't soon forget him.

Once they were back on the sidewalk, Jamie shot Hortense an amused glance. "It appears you have a dog."

She glanced down at Sir Bacon, thoroughly befuddled. Big brown eyes stared up at her, awaiting their new direction. He was...*hers?*

"He cannot possibly be mine." It had to be said.

"I'm not sure he knows that."

Sir Bacon remained uncharacteristically indifferent to the sights and smells of the world around them and singularly focused on her. A strange feeling ribboned through Hortense. This little animal was dependent on her, and...she might like it. What an unsettling development.

She started walking and changed the subject. "Are we clear on the plan to switch the tiaras?" Work, always a reliable—and safe—topic.

The moment's good humor fell away. "Aye."

"'Tis the only way," she said, answering what he'd left unspoken. He didn't like the plan.

"I'm sure there are others."

This again. "Short of outright theft, it's the most efficient way."

Jamie's mouth pressed into a firm, silent line, and he spoke not another word until they entered Asquith Court. The man truly wasn't at all equipped at not getting his way.

"Until tonight?" She could be a professional, even if he couldn't.

"Tonight."

She pivoted on her heel, leading Sir Bacon away. The heat of Jamie's gaze scorched her back all the way up the grand staircase. After what felt like an eternity, she reached the landing and rounded the corner, and out of his view. Inside her bedroom, she shut the door and was, at last, able to release her held breath. Her mind wandered through too familiar thoughts.

After tonight, their objective would be achieved and the farce of their marriage would be over. She would give him permission to have the marriage annulled any way he saw fit. It was only fair, and the only way that made sense. That the two of them could have a shared future was utter nonsense. Girls from the workhouse didn't share their futures with marquesses. It wasn't done.

She suppressed a pang of emotion at that last bit. Emotion it was becoming ever more difficult to deny. Emotion that contained a trace of—oh, what were Mariana's words?

The specific madness and agitation of the wretchedly in love.

How melodramatic.

Jamie had hired her for a job. She was doing that job. And, tonight, if all went well, they would switch the tiaras, secure Rafe, and she would betray Jamie. In that order.

And then he, like she, would see that what they shared last night, and the night before, was naught more than illusion brought on by danger and intrigue.

And then she would return to her old life.

Without him.

CHAPTER TWENTY-THREE

*J*amie propped against an unobtrusive stretch of wall, his gaze trained on the front entrance of the Duke of Rothesbury's mansion. Soon, Hortense would be arriving, and he wouldn't be letting her out of his sight once she did.

Vibrantly colored silks hung in draped swathes from the high ceiling of the receiving hall, which along with half-lit candelabras and chandeliers, created an atmosphere of mystery and intrigue. The effect was dim and dramatic as a lilting waltz from the ballroom swirled through on the scent of pungent spices and perfumes. As befitting a masquerade, all guests were masked. Some wore simple dominos, like himself, while others went all out for elaborate, even grotesque, Venetian masks.

A naughtiness very conscious of itself pervaded the atmosphere. A flimsy mask seemed to be all the permission his fellow aristocrats needed to be their most uninhibited, scandalous selves, as if it could hide their multitude of sins. Wives ran ungloved fingers invitingly across jaws that didn't belong to their husbands. Husbands' hands roamed freely across the backsides of wives who weren't their own. Excess was the word of the night. Which, of course, was no great shock.

Father and Mother would have been here. The realization struck Jamie sudden and hard. They weren't ones to miss an entertainment whose sole purpose was excess and debauchery. They'd been rather well known for it.

There was a time, not so long ago, when such a thought would have had him racing away from here as fast as a coach and four could carry him. He may have been a wastrel, but he was no lecher. He understood the distinction, even if most didn't.

The crowd parted a sliver and through the opening Hortense slipped, coy smile pasted on, fingers wrapped around a champagne coupe. A jewel in sumptuous crimson silk, she drew more than a few leers, all speculating about her identity. She wouldn't appreciate the attention this dress, with its showy opulence and low décolletage, afforded her. Her free hand moved to discreetly coax the bodice higher, but there was no more fabric to be had. How very little of her breasts the dress left to the imagination.

She should only wear such dresses. In his bedroom.

Next, she touched her fingertips to the beauty patch adorning her left cheek to ensure it remained in place, then to secure her black velvet domino. All done in a matter of seconds.

When she began to move, he pushed off the wall to follow, deciding not to reveal himself just yet. He would rather watch her navigate the room. She finished her champagne, and another coupe appeared in her hand within seconds. She would have to watch that. Champagne was a dangerous minx.

Into the ballroom, she followed the stream of string quartet music and aimed for the periphery, avoiding all eye contact and never stopping. If she did, she could draw unwanted impertinence, and it wouldn't do tonight's operation any good if she broke a lord's hand for laying it on her.

He snorted. She would.

All the while her feet moved, her eyes never stopped either. She was searching for someone. *Rothesbury.*

The duke's oily, leering smile shouldn't be too difficult to locate. Except her gaze landed on the man, rested for the flicker of a second, and moved on. She was searching for someone, yes, but not Rothesbury.

And Jamie knew.

She was searching for *him.*

Unable to resist, he circled around, so he was directly behind her. Slowly, he approached, closing the distance between them with care. He wasn't sure what precisely he was about. He would let the moment take them where it led.

Close enough for his breath to disturb the fine hairs of her nape, he angled his head and murmured low in her ear. "Forgive me, my lady, for being so forward, but have we met?"

She inhaled a quick sip of air and went still. Instantaneous heat pulsed through him, firing up his blood, causing his heart to perform a neat, little flip.

Oh, they had met.

She met his gaze over her shoulder. Beneath her domino, her eyes were lined with kohl, imbuing them with an otherworldly blue. "I think not, my lord," she said, engaging in the game he'd only thought to start the instant he asked the question. "I think I would remember *you.*"

Her gaze roved over him. He couldn't miss the appreciation therein.

"'Tis you who is the memorable one," he said, feeling

a suggestive smile curl about his mouth. "No lady in this room is more bewitching."

"Surely, you flatter me." Within the protest, did he detect breathlessness?

"I never flatter."

Surrounded by a profusion of frivolity and falsity, here they two stood, speaking truths to one another they never dared speak outside these walls, even as they played strangers to one another. Here, he was experiencing a freedom with her he'd never thought to have. He could be both stranger and...lover.

"May I be so bold as to ask your name?" he asked, following the possibility that lay down this road.

"Boldness does seem to be the order of the evening." She tapped her mouth, as if considering his worthiness. "You may call me Madame Coquette. And you are?"

"Lord X will suffice."

Her smile told him she rather liked that. "A man of mystery."

Possibility, indeed.

The opening notes of another waltz struck up, and he extended his hand. "Would you do me the honor of this dance?"

She foisted her empty champagne coupe into the nearest stranger's hand and placed her fingers in his. All he could think as she followed him onto the dancing floor was that these fingers had been wrapped around his cock, and he wanted them so again. That might be too much truth to speak aloud.

They entered the flow of the dance, their bodies at one with the rhythm, at one with each other, as they stepped to the *one-two-three* of the dance. He pressed at the base of her spine until her lithe body strained against the length of his. His mouth found her ear, raising goose bumps along the column of her neck.

"Why is a confection like you wandering about a party alone?"

She angled her face up to meet his eye. "I was trying to locate my husband."

He lifted his brow in mock disbelief. "You are wed?"

"Very much so."

Very much so.

Were they *very much* wed?

"You should hope he doesn't see us," she continued. "I wouldn't put it past him to punch you directly in the nose."

"A violent man?"

"Possessive, it turns out."

A smile tipped about her mouth, adding lightness to her words. But they weren't wrong.

"What man wouldn't be with a wife like you?" he returned. "My only surprise is he doesn't keep you to himself under lock and key."

She gasped. "He wouldn't dare."

"He might." The eyebrow he lifted wasn't quite ironic. "You might not want to test his limits."

"And you, my lord?" she asked. "Have you a wife?"

Turnabout was fair play.

"Let us not discuss husbands and wives. Let us speak of you and me." He wasn't sure if it was the whirl of the waltz or their conversation that dizzied through him and made his chest go light. "And *us.*"

A seriousness settled about her. "Lord X, there is no *us.*"

But a note sounded in her voice, an uncertainty, as if she could be tempted into belief.

Then let him be Lucifer.

"There might be," he said.

Her step faltered. He caught her without missing a beat.

"But why—" Opaque emotion flickered in her eyes. "Why speak of the future when we have tonight?"

Even as the part of him that wanted to realize a future with her demanded he press forward, another part —namely, the carnal—wouldn't be deterred from exploring the possibility of this flirtation.

The future could wait.

He swirled them through the throng of other couples to the edge of the dance floor. His mouth met the cup of her ear, his hot breath surely sending a shiver purling down her spine. "It's rather loud in here, don't you agree?"

* * *

THE INVITATION RUNNING below his words...

The promise...

All Hortense could do was nod and not let go of his hand for anything as he led her past the crowd and down a long, quiet corridor devoid of all light, save that streaming through open curtains, night music at their backs. She knew—*felt*—where he was leading her, and she wanted to be led.

He poked his head into the first dark alcove they encountered. "Occupied."

As was the second.

But the third was the charm. He pulled her inside and closed the curtains behind them. A long window allowed the moon to illuminate the small space in a silvery glow. How shadow and light caressed the angles of his face.

Shivery and hot, she pressed back into the corner where wall met window. Dark lust shone from his gaze, sending a sinuous wave of desire glittering through her. "I've never wanted a man like I want you."

Oh, that she hadn't spoken thusly to him, this stranger, her husband.

She couldn't be sure if it was courage or foolhardiness inspiring her to speak those words aloud, but she cared not. She'd gone heady with champagne and *him*.

With deliberate intention, he moved forward, and she became prey held in thrall to a predator. Powerless against him. Powerless against herself... against her desire. One hand planted on the wall beside her face, the other cupped her nape, as his mouth met hers, his lips firm and soft, pressing, searching, deepening the kiss as he touched his tongue to hers. His knee wedged between her legs up to her sex, which strained against him with exquisite pressure. She squirmed, writhed, mindlessly stretched toward the promise of release any way she could find it.

His hands slid down her body and began gathering up crimson silk, until he had her skirts bunched around her waist, her throbbing quim waiting for him. She reached down, her fingers trailing across his hard and ready manhood. She used the leg wrapped around his waist to bring him closer so she could work the closure of his trousers.

His mouth broke from hers. "I want to taste you."

"Isn't that what you've been doing?"

Wickedness flashed in his silvery eyes. "*All* of you."

Through the blinding haze of lust entered confusion. "What are you on about?" she asked, her frustration with the man very genuine.

He let his actions answer for him as he fell to his knees before her. He grabbed her foot and lifted. "What is this?"

He'd noticed the dagger strapped above her ankle. "One never knows how a night will go."

"Truer words..." His gaze returned to her sex as he

placed her satin slipper on his shoulder. Clutching her hips, he pulled her forward.

"Why—"

His mouth found her quim, and she lost all capacity for speech. His tongue stroked along her slit, slick and hot and utterly, utterly devastating. With one hand, she grabbed the curtains, and with the other, clutched his hair, hanging on for dear life as pleasure unlike any other swept through her.

She'd had a great many experiences in her life, but never *this*. She'd never once conceived that a man would do *this* to her...*for* her.

His cunning tongue stroked, caressed, laved, by turns firm and soft, butterfly flickers and kisses driving her beyond pleasure to the point of madness.

"Oh, you clever man," she cried, her hips angling for more of what he had to offer. In the grip of this wildness, she entirely abandoned herself as climax bore down on her, taunting, teasing, hovering, so, so, so near... Until, of a sudden, it closed in and pulsed through her quim, shooting pleasure through her veins, delivering it to every last nerve ending, until she was naught more than a quivering bundle of satiety.

He gave her one last kiss before settling back on his haunches and tugging her skirts down. Fortuitous that he had a care for her modesty, for she hadn't. She would become the most immodest hoyden in all of London to have him do that again. She might not ever get over it. Jamie, and his tongue, had turned her to jelly and rendered her speechless.

He'd made a habit of both.

"Clever man?" he asked with the lift of a single eyebrow.

There had been a time when she'd wanted nothing more than to wipe that arrogant smile off his mouth. Not now. He'd earned the right to that smile. "Very," she said, her voice near unrecognizable to her own ears.

He stood and held out one arm. "Shall we return to the dance?"

"But aren't we going to—" She pressed her mouth shut. She sounded petulant and spoilt. But, truly, weren't they going to finish what they'd started? She ached for it.

"That was for you. We wouldn't want to muss you up too much."

"I believe I'd let you muss me up anytime."

So much truth spoken tonight.

They didn't speak again until they were halfway down the corridor, passing this and that paired off couple seeking a discreet encounter. Slowly, by increments, she returned to herself. She suspected, however, she would never make a full recovery. These last three nights—what he'd done to her body—well, it might have imprinted on her soul.

"What are you thinking, Hortense?"

She detected a note beyond curiosity in the question. *Concern.*

"It's Madame Coquette, remember?" She couldn't address his concern. She might turn to jelly, again, and that wouldn't do.

"*Hortense,*" he insisted, low and definite. "Or do you prefer Lady Clare?"

"In name only," she said, because she had to. The moment required it.

A dry laugh was his response. "Oh, I think we put paid to that notion."

What could he possibly mean? Was he implying their marriage was now real?

Before she could ask, a voice that made her skin crawl sounded behind them, "Tsk, tsk, you know the rules of the night."

Her stomach plummeted with dread.

Rothesbury.

She couldn't be Hortense, Madame Coquette, or Lady Clare. She was an investigator hired for a job. Jamie had a way of making her lose sight of her objectives.

Tonight's operation had just begun in earnest.

CHAPTER TWENTY-FOUR

*H*ortense chanced a quick glance at Jamie just as he said, "I never met a rule I particularly liked." His face had turned to stone, inscrutable. A shiver raced through her.

Rothesbury sidled to her other side and took her arm. His wig tonight was truly something special, abundant with curls and powdered a vivid fuchsia not found in nature. "A husband mustn't monopolize all his wife's attention."

Even as she smiled, Hortense shot Jamie a look. This was it. The job was on. The muscles of his jaw tensed by way of response.

"Your wife's cheeks are quite flushed," said Rothesbury, unaware of the unspoken conversation being had around him. "Be a good boy and fetch her a glass of punch."

Hortense broke into a wide smile. Her laughter was that of the ever gay and carefree marchioness, merciless. "Oh, yes, be a good boy, dear husband, and play fetch. I am positively parched."

"I wouldn't want to leave you wanting, sweet wife," he returned.

A sudden wave of hot lust rolled through her, for that was precisely what he'd done.

And he knew it.

And now he knew what else he must do, though she sensed him hesitating. He needed a nudge to play his role—the cuckold. "Well, dear husband?" she prodded. "The punch won't fetch itself, now will it?"

Rothesbury's loud guffaw contained no small amount of cruelty. Stoic, jaw clenched, Jamie pivoted on his heel and strode away. Hortense felt the loss of him like a physical ache. Her body—and mayhap other parts of her, too—wanted him back in the alcove, finishing what he'd started.

"Are you enjoying my little gathering?" Rothesbury asked. The man was ever self-satisfied. She wasn't even sure what he expected she could do for him.

"I've never experienced such a party," she said. The truth, in more ways than one.

"What a little innocent you are," he said. Oh, his condescension was near insufferable. "Perhaps you need someone to help divest you of that innocence?"

How many times had he uttered that line?

She could retch at the idea. Instead, she batted her eyelashes at the vile man and asked, "And are you that someone, duke?"

His chest puffed out like a randy fowl. He liked having his title acknowledged and brandished about.

"Perhaps we could go someplace quieter and discover for ourselves?" His leer was so comical as to be a parody of itself. All he lacked was waggling eyebrows.

"If you must know," she said, "one part of our conversation from last night keeps niggling at me."

"Oh? Which part?" This time, he did waggle eyebrows powdered a pink to match his wig.

"About your jewel vault." She bit her lip, drawing his eye. "I have a confession to make."

"You may confess all your sins to me, my pet."

Pet. Doyle's nickname for her. She didn't like it from this man's mouth any better. A shiver of revulsion wanted to streak through her, but she repressed it, instead gazing up at him through her eyelashes. "I've always wanted to wear a tiara."

"Surely, Clare could dig into the family vaults and find one or two."

Mayhap she'd taken her poor, woebegone act too far?

Rothesbury's conceit, however, saved her. "Of course, the vaults of a marquess would be nothing to a duke's."

"A duke's jewel vault," she said dreamily. "I can only imagine its wonders. Gold, platinum, silver. Rubies, diamonds, pearls...sapphires." She gave a dramatic shiver of delight. Gads, she was irritating herself, but Rothesbury couldn't seem to get enough. "And, oh, to behold such wonders would make me feel so incredibly grateful. I would absolutely need to prove my gratitude in any way. Nothing would be taboo."

He swallowed as if his mouth had gone suddenly dry. "Nothing?"

"*Nothing.*"

He picked up the clip of his step, all but pulling her along now. "I keep a vault in my dressing room. It isn't my largest—that one is at Aberthorpe Palace, the family seat—but I think you'll find something here to entice you. And"—a suggestive note the consistency of rancid oil entered his voice—"it adjoins my bedroom."

"Oh, how delightful." She giggled to keep from gagging.

Through the party, he led her, ignoring all calls for his attention. He was a man on a mission. Hortense was glad for the dagger strapped around her ankle. She trusted Jamie would do all in his power to keep her safe

—she doubted it not for an instant—but a wise girl always had a contingency plan. This night wouldn't go the way Rothesbury thought it would, not if she had anything to say about it.

And, truly, she was relieved to be passing through the fray of the party, for in her and Jamie's absence, more inhibitions—and articles of clothing—had been shed, more closely resembling the decadence of an ancient Roman orgy than a proper English aristocratic ball. What permissions a simple mask allowed.

All too soon, they entered a room that could only be described as an unchecked explosion of gold and aubergine. Of course, Rothesbury's bedroom would resemble a bordello. He snapped his fingers at the valet nodding off in a chair. "You are dismissed for the night." A sly smile curled about the duke's fleshy mouth. "And shut the door behind you."

The servant sprang to his feet, offered Rothesbury a low bow, and vacated the room before Hortense could blink. The duke crooked his finger at her, and she followed him into his dressing room, where he removed a small painting from the wall, revealing a square black vault. He twisted the key in the lock, and the breath froze in her chest. The entire operation hinged on the sapphire tiara being in that safe.

"I know the perfect trinket for you, my delightful little marchioness."

His hand slowly emerged...holding the sapphire tiara. She exhaled a sigh of relief that could have easily been mistaken for one of pleasure. "Oh, your grace, you can't mean—"

"I saw how much you admired it." He moved closer, the tiara held out before him.

Hortense willed her body to remain in place. Four minutes. That was the amount of time she and Jamie had agreed would be enough to secure the jewel. Still, she noted all the exits. Two doors and a window. She could escape one way or another. Her hands bunched into fists at her sides, ready, in case quick action was needed. She would aim low. He would never see the blow coming.

"Would you like me to remove my mask?" she asked, sweet and submissive.

"Oh, no, my pet, that's part of the fun."

Of course it was.

He settled the tiara on her head, and she let out a squeal of delight. "The delicious weight of all those jewels," she exclaimed. "I must view myself in a mirror."

He indicated the dressing room mirror, but she gave her head a shake. "I noticed a splendid gilt mirror in your bedroom. I would like to see myself in that one." She needed to get out of this small, isolated room with him. She was too vulnerable in here.

He gave a chuckle equal parts salacious and indulgent. "After you."

On light feet, she traipsed across the room, all giggly delight, and began preening before the mirror. Narcissus would have nothing on her for vanity. Rothesbury came up behind her, and every muscle in her body instinctively constricted. She hadn't realized until this very moment how much bigger the duke was than her.

But she was quicker and smarter.

Right?

Right.

And she had a dagger strapped to her ankle. It had never once let her down, and it wouldn't tonight, if needs must.

Yet when his hands trailed down her arms, her fingers again curled into fists. She might very well need to break role and fight this man off. She would be ready.

Had it been four minutes yet?

"I've never seen a more delectable temptation than your neck, Lady Clare. I must sample a taste."

He lowered his head, clearly intent on pressing his fleshy lips against her skin. She was readying herself to deal him a blow to the nethers he wouldn't soon forget when the door flew open and Jamie stormed into the room. "What in the blazes are you doing with my wife?"

High color on his cheekbones, metallic fury in his eyes, the anger radiating off Jamie wasn't for show. He charged across the room and grabbed Rothesbury by the collar, forcibly pulling the duke away from Hortense. The next instant, it became clear that neither the duke nor her husband had ever engaged in fisticuffs, as they faced one another, each clearly calculating what to do next.

Rothesbury struck first, delivering a rather effete slap to Jamie's left cheek. Jamie responded in kind, except his slap whipped Rothesbury's head around. Hortense found herself stifling a chortle. She'd been itching to do that since she'd first met the man.

Enraged, Rothesbury latched on to Jamie's hair, which only drew Jamie closer. The duke appeared to be trying to lock Jamie's head beneath his arm. Interesting strategy.

On a roar, Jamie used his superior strength to pull away—minus a small handful of hair—and grab both sides of Rothesbury's face. Then he jerked his head forward on a quick snap and butted Rothesbury directly on the forehead, eliciting shouts and groans as both men staggered backward, momentarily dazed, hands to their respective foreheads.

It was obvious Jamie had never butted anyone with his head in all his life. There was a correct way of doing it, and an incorrect one. He'd done it incorrectly. Truly, she should have given him some fisticuffs tips before tonight. She simply hadn't considered the necessity.

The next instant, the men were back at it. Hortense sprang into action as the tussle continued, stepping behind Jamie, just as they'd planned, and flung the tiara off her head. "Oh, dear, the tiara!" she exclaimed, falling to her hands and knees as if to retrieve the jewel. She tugged at his cloak, all the while imploring, "Stop this instant, Clare! Stop!"

He'd received her signal, for the cloak fell to the floor. Unerringly, she felt along the interior lining until she came upon a jagged lump. Half an eye on the brawling men, she slid her hand inside the hidden pocket and pulled out the genuine tiara, and slipped the fake one into its place. She sprang to her feet and tapped the small of Jamie's back three times in quick succession, thereby giving him the second signal. She'd made the switch.

But he wasn't finished. He drew back his right fist and clipped Rothesbury directly on the nose. A bright red spray of blood shot forth and began streaming down the duke's face.

Livid and plugging his nostrils to no avail, he shouted, "Out of my house!"

Jamie wasn't done. He grabbed Rothesbury's wig, snatching it clean off the duke's head. "You're fooling no one with that pathetic thing!" Out, the mess of furry fuchsia sailed through an open window.

For what could have been a pair of seconds, a pair of minutes, or hours, time stood still as three sets of eyes stared at the window, the import of what Jamie had done sinking into the air. Rothesbury's hand flew to his head, which had but twenty or so white natural hairs populating his rather bulbous dome. His face contorted with rage and humiliation, but mostly rage, while with one hand he held his bleeding nose and the other his head.

"Get out!" he shouted.

Jamie grabbed Hortense by the wrist, even as she made a big show of straining toward Rothesbury. "I will not abandon you, my duke," she cried, the mawkish words leaving a sour taste on her tongue.

"And take your little trollop with you!" Rothesbury's blood dripped on the Persian carpet. "The tiara stays here!"

Only now did Hortense realize she yet held the real one. She dropped it on a console table on her way out and cast the duke one last tearful glance over her shoulder.

"Out!" he shouted, sounding entirely deranged, his free hand shooing her away.

The man had been humiliated in front of a woman. He wouldn't be able to tolerate such a thing.

Within a thrice of minutes, she and Jamie were exiting the mansion and summoning the coach and four. She swiped at her tears before removing her beauty patch and domino. "Have you a handkerchief?" She suspected kohl was running down her cheeks.

He reached inside his cloak and dug out a square of white linen. Quiet stretched between them as she dabbed at the kohl. "Did I get it all?"

He searched her face. "Here, allow me."

She closed her eyes as he gently wiped a few spots. She swayed into his touch, unable to help herself.

"There," he said, too soon. "You look like yourself again."

Her eyes blinked open, as his hands fell away. "In Rothesbury's bedroom…"

"Yes?"

"There were a few seconds—" She shook her head. "It matters not."

"You thought I wasn't coming?"

"I knew you would come."

"But you thought you might have to fight him off?"

"Possibly."

He tucked his thumb beneath her chin, lifting her gaze to meet his. "I was outside the bedroom door the entire time. I gave it exactly four minutes, as we planned. You were never alone with him, not truly."

She swallowed back a sudden surge of emotion. Of course. Jamie would never leave her stranded. A smile pulled at her mouth. "The wig." A laugh bubbled up, no restraining it. "Do you think Rothesbury will ever recover from this night?"

Jamie snorted. "Not bloody likely."

"Good."

The levity of the moment faded, and his hand fell away, his eyes growing serious. "There will be no changing of clothes or other distractions. We go to Flick Doyle *now*. My son is coming home tonight."

As she'd expected. She hoped for Doyle's sake that he didn't have any further games planned, for Jamie wouldn't tolerate them.

Then it would be done.

And, not long after, she would take the signet ring, and *they* would be done, too.

CHAPTER TWENTY-FIVE

"*T*he instant you see us emerge from that door" —Jamie pointed toward Flick Doyle's establishment—"make ready to leave."

"Aye, my lord," said the coachman, positioning himself on his perch so the door remained in his line of sight.

Once they stood outside Doyle's lair, Hortense caught Jamie's eye and said, "I just want you to know that no matter where this night takes us, I've come to enjoy knowing you."

Her sudden statement took him slightly aback. He didn't know whether to feel flattered or insulted. A little of both, perhaps. "You will know me after this night, Hortense."

She stared silently up at him, tense and on edge. Something in her look rattled him. He couldn't read it. "You stay out here," he said. "I can take the tiara and get Rafe, alone."

She shook her head. "I must go and see the job through to the end."

Her words hit him like a punch to the gut. *To the end.* The end of the job. The end of them. The irony didn't pass him by. In gaining his son, he would lose

Hortense. For he suspected that though he'd given her pleasure after pleasure, he hadn't given her *enough* to stay.

She tapped out the special knock. The door opened a crack, and a boy's dirt-smudged face appeared. "Oh, yer back." The boy stood aside and waved Jamie and Hortense inside.

The interior was as dark and grim as the first time, but tonight Jamie felt its impact more sharply. This was where Hortense had lived. This was where his son now lived. In this squalor, in this pit of despair—for although it was deepest night, surely no light ever shone within these walls, other than cheapest tallow—the two people who meant the most to him in the world lived beneath Flick Doyle's thumb, subject to the power he wielded in his little fiefdom.

No more.

Not while breath remained in Jamie's body.

Down into the underground room, they descended, its rough environ exactly the same as it had been five days ago, complete with Doyle sifting through the day's take—coin, watches, chains, rings, handkerchiefs—and looking very much like the slum lord of his realm.

His head popped up. He pushed his spectacles up his nose as a reptilian smile spread across his face. "Why look at ye two, all fancied up fer the night."

Jamie supposed he and Hortense were rather conspicuous in their masquerade ball finery. He shrugged. He didn't give two tosses.

Doyle's eyes narrowed into assessing slits. "Now, what ye got fer me?"

Jamie pulled the tiara from his cloak and plunked it on the knife-scarred table. Doyle slid the lantern close and retrieved a magnifying glass from a drawer. Hunched over, glass to his right eye, he flipped the tiara over, inspecting it closely for a full minute.

Jamie stole a glance at Hortense. Her entire body was a tight ball of tension. He itched to reach for her hand, but he resisted. He understood instinctively it was the wrong move in this room and with this audience.

Doyle straightened, setting the magnifier and tiara down. "Now me mam can rest in peace. It be the imposter."

"You had a mark placed on it." This from Hortense.

Of course.

A guffaw rumbled from Doyle's gut, bringing up a gob of phlegm he spent ten full seconds disposing of. "This ain't me first stroll 'round the block. Ain't me last neither, pet."

Her jaw tensed. She didn't like being called *pet*.

Jamie's patience had its limits. It was time to finish this. "Where is Rafe?"

Doyle's eyebrows lifted toward the ceiling. A ceiling which threatened to tumble down on top of them at any moment. How on earth was this edifice staying upright, anyway?

"Don't like to be kept waitin', do ye? Ain't ye a right proper nob."

Hortense spoke up. "That was the agreement." She flashed Jamie a warning glare. He was to keep his temper quiet in his mouth.

Doyle sucked his teeth. "Oi! Rafe," he bellowed.

A handful of seconds later, footsteps came tromping down the stairs. Jamie didn't know much about children, but the boy was tall for his thirteen years. Thin, too. And filthy.

His son would never know another filthy, flea-bitten day.

"Rafe," Doyle said, "yer to go with them."

"What fer?" Rafe asked, managing an impressive glower at Jamie and Hortense. That glower would serve the boy well as the man he would become someday.

Doyle shrugged. "Not me business."

Rafe's eyebrows drew together, and he blinked. "But, I live 'ere." The boy's voice cracked on the last word, his panic unmistakable.

Doyle shook his head. "Yer replaced easy enough."

Rafe flinched as if he'd suffered a physical blow. "Back to the work'ouse?"

"If they say."

Hortense stepped forward. "Not to the workhouse. To a home."

"'Oo's 'ome? This nob's?" Rafe asked, distrust and a budding anger flaring through the question.

"Aye," Jamie said, hoping the word offered a measure of reassurance to the boy who was suspicious—and rightly so—of this entire situation. Building a relationship with his son would be no instant thing. He could flatten Doyle's nose for needlessly inflaming the matter. His fist seemed to have developed bloodlust tonight.

"Now, off with ye." Doyle picked up the magnifying glass and returned his attention to the tiara.

Jamie met Hortense's eye and nodded. Taking his meaning, she led the way up the stairs. Jamie gestured that Rafe follow. Pugnacious set to his jaw, the boy remained rooted in place.

Before Jamie could figure out how to handle an intractable lad of thirteen, Doyle barked, "Go, and don't darken me doorstep again."

Alongside the distrust and anger flickered hurt in Rafe's eyes. At last, the boy followed Hortense. Jamie brought up the rear as they vacated the shambles of Doyle's lair. Outside, the coachman sat upright on his perch, reins in hand, ready.

Rafe hesitated at the carriage door before seating

himself beside Hortense. Jamie took the bench opposite and gave the ceiling two taps. The carriage lurched into motion, and he released a relieved breath. He had his son. A son he didn't know, and who didn't know him. A sullen and circumspect son whose glower had returned with burning intensity.

"Are you"—Jamie searched for something to say, for the *correct* something to say—"comfortable?"

Rafe shrugged.

That had gone over well.

Jamie was opening his mouth surely to make another blunder when Hortense turned to the lad. "What's your position?"

Position?

Even if Jamie had no idea what that meant, Rafe seemed to know, for his eyes narrowed, but his mouth remained silent.

"I was the pick," she said. She understood more about his son than Jamie ever might. She spoke his language.

Rafe's eyes lifted, betraying a measure of respect. At last, he'd taken a bite of the bait Hortense was laying. "Lookout. I weren't e'er good enough fer pick."

She nodded with understanding, even camaraderie. "Your hands are too big and you're too tall for a pick."

"Yeah, that, too. Doyle always said."

"Did you like it there?"

He gave a shrug of indifference. "Better than the workhouse. I never was much on pickin' oakum." His eyes darted between Jamie and Hortense. "And least I know whut's whut with Doyle." His cautious gaze landed on Jamie like a punch to the gut.

"This is a better arrangement, trust me," said Hortense.

Rafe scoffed. "Trust ye? I don't know ye. I only seen ye 'round Doyle's."

Hortense thrust her hand forward. "I am Hortense."

Warily, he took her hand and gave it a shake. "I'm Rafe."

"It's nice to make your acquaintance, Rafe."

He jerked his thumb toward Jamie. "Is 'e a real nob?"

"He is."

"And 'e's me da?" He still wouldn't look at Jamie.

"You're the spit of him, I'd say."

At last, the boy's eyes shifted toward Jamie, taking him in, sizing him up. "I reckon." He didn't sound too excited about the prospect.

Soon, they were pulling to a stop before Asquith Court. Rafe pressed his nose to the carriage window, eyes wide. "This yer digs?"

"Aye."

"Lawks be," the boy muttered with no small amount of wonder.

That any child of his should feel such awe at his father's house sent a fresh infusion of rage spiraling through Jamie. While Rafe would have never been in line to inherit Asquith Court or the title of marquess, the boy would have grown up no stranger to luxury. That boy would have hardly batted an eyelash at Asquith Court. But this boy...

Well, he was an altogether different proposition, one Jamie wasn't at all sure how to handle.

They were met in the receiving hall by Sir Bacon, who wouldn't stop barking and running excited circles around Rafe. A smile broke across the boy's face, the smile of an equally excited child. Something resembling happiness surged inside Jamie. He knew nothing was truly solved, but this was a start. A good one.

Having caught wind of the ruckus, Mrs. Blanche joined their rowdy, little party. While Jamie might not have had the first clue as to how to proceed with Rafe, she did. She took one look at the lad, quietly drew her own conclusions as to his identity, and took charge. "Let's get you to the kitchen for a bite, then a"—clearly the woman was using all the self-restraint in her arsenal not to wrinkle her nose at the stench coming off the boy in waves—"bath."

Rafe allowed himself to be led away, Sir Bacon at his heels.

Jamie found himself alone with Hortense.

"You will need someone to keep an eye out for him," she said, breaking the silence.

"He has me."

She laid her hand on his arm, empathy shining bright in her eyes. "I know, but to ensure he doesn't try to run back to Doyle."

"Ah."

"You must go to him now. Talk to him."

"I don't speak his language."

"You must learn it. And—" She held his gaze. "Teach him yours."

Now that he had Rafe, Jamie hadn't the faintest notion of what to do with him.

Hortense must have sensed his misgiving. "You must put in the effort. He needs to see that, even if he doesn't know it yet."

Jamie sensed she was correct, but something else prevented him from leaving just yet. "Will you—" He had no right to ask.

"I'll be here," she said, rightly intuiting his question.

Jamie walked away with a shred of hope in his heart. There was still time to convince her to stay.

But it was running out.

CHAPTER TWENTY-SIX

Ninety-eight...ninety-nine...one hundred.

Panting and with sweat dripping down the side of her face, Hortense collapsed on her stomach. Unable to wait calmly for Jamie, she'd decided to put her body through its paces, which usually quieted her mind and set it to rights. Not on this night. So, she was doing two rounds.

Having placed her masquerade finery in the wardrobe, she was down to a simple chemise. If she donned the plain black trousers she planned to leave wearing, Jamie would instantly suspect her intent. She had, however, taken care of one vital piece of business: she'd taken the signet ring from the side table in his bedroom and hidden it in her trouser pocket.

Eventually, he would miss it and deduce it was she who had taken it. He could come after her, but she doubted it. It held no sentimental value for him, and he could easily have another made. He would, likely and rightly, see he was well clear of her.

And he would have Rafe, free from her and Doyle's like. The boy would have the opportunity to fashion a life of his own creation. The son of a lord, no one would have power over him.

An enviable life, that one.

Midway through her stomach curls, the door between their bedrooms opened. In Jamie walked, only stopping when he noticed her on the floor. Instead of settling back on lush Aubusson carpet, she sat all the way up and crossed her legs in front of her. He didn't take a seat in the chair, but rather lowered himself to the floor and faced her. The man looked exhausted and utterly, utterly wrung out, his face drawn, his mouth tight. The enormity of this night must be sinking in. It always happened after a job was finished. She should have warned him.

"Where is Rafe?" she asked.

"Submitting rather gracelessly to the ministrations of Mrs. Blanche."

"And Sir Bacon?"

He gave a weary laugh. "He seemed very intent on joining Rafe in the bath." All traces of humor faded from his face. "The lad's naught more than dirt, fleas, skin, and bones."

Hortense swallowed. It was painful to see the effects of squalor and deprivation up close, especially in a child. There was no preparing for it. She wrapped her arms around her shins to stop herself from reaching out and offering comfort. "Mrs. Blanche will have all that well in hand."

"By the time I left, he'd already stuffed three shortbread biscuits into his mouth. I explained to him the biscuits weren't going anywhere, and if we ran out, all he had to do was request more." Jamie shook his head, disbelieving. "He couldn't seem to comprehend the notion."

"It will take time for him to see his new world. For him to believe in it."

Jamie caught her gaze and held. Knowledge shone within. Her words were about more than Rafe. "And you?" he asked. "Do you believe? What would it take to gain your faith?"

Her gaze slid toward the embers of the fire. She couldn't answer such a question, not without giving too much of herself away.

"So this is how you do it," he said.

"How I do what?"

"Make your body so strong."

Ah. "Every night."

"That's quite a discipline."

"The last few nights, I skipped," she confessed.

"But you felt the need to resume the practice tonight."

They both knew what she was leaving unspoken. After tonight, she would be returning to the life that required her body to be a weapon.

"I'll never be the biggest or strongest in a match up, but I can be quicker and smarter."

"You're a marvel, Amelie Hortense."

Amelie.

It had been so very long since she'd been called by that name, the name she considered her truest, the one writ upon her heart. That this man spoke the name Amelie felt right.

She found herself leaning forward, and him matching the movement, both driven by mutual instinct until only a hairsbreadth of distance separated her mouth from his. She inhaled a sip of air, breathing him in. This air, it was precious to her, for she understood it was the last time.

He reached out and cupped the back of her head, his fingers tangling through her hair, drawing her forward. Her entire being felt concentrated in the places where his skin met hers, the light pressure of his fingertips, the brush of his lips. It was a moment that longed to be more than a simple, sweet touch.

A surge of carnality pulsed through her, and she was unknotting his cravat, unbuttoning his waistcoat. Next his shirt went over his head, and his chest was bare. Such a gorgeous specimen of man.

He unfastened the fall of his trousers and soon was tossing them aside. She pulled her chemise over her head, and again they faced one another, naked not simply in body, but their souls bared to one another.

Even as he leaned into her space, he held her secure as he lay her down. He stretched naked along the length of her body, the firelight casting him in its warm, flickering glow, his fingertips tracing her skin with slow intention that lit a flame inside her. His dark gaze drank her in, and the urgency of the last few days was replaced with a feeling deeper, and more meaningful. What they were about to do was about more than physical pleasure and release. It would be an expression of all they felt and could not say with words, but with a language their bodies spoke intuitively.

He angled his head and pressed his mouth to hers in a kiss that blossomed with intention with every rapid beat of her heart. She wrapped her arms around his neck and brought him closer, her tongue a tangle with his, wanting—*needing*—to deepen the contact with him. She *needed* the solid mass of his body, the delicious weight of him pressing her into the carpet, grounding her to the earth, to this moment.

Forearms planted to either side of her head, he hovered over her. Her legs spread, answering the question in his eyes. In a long, slow, deliberate thrust, he entered her, his head arching back, his eyes drifting shut with pleasure. With each of his measured, relentless strokes came a sense of completion, as if she was only whole when she was at one with him, her body sticky against his.

Sweat dripped down the side of his face as he drove

into her, her hips meeting his thrust for thrust. Her hands roved across him—his face, broad shoulders, muscular arms, ridged stomach, taut arse—feeling him, savoring him, memorizing him. "Oh, Jamie," she sighed, her mind beginning to fragment with the bliss he was delivering.

Intense silver eyes met hers. "Can I do something"—a thrust, a hesitation—"different?"

A frisson of anticipation slid through her. "You can do anything to me."

He angled back, withdrawing from her—eliciting a groan of protest—grabbed her hips and flipped her over, to her stomach. She went utterly and completely still.

"Are you agreeable?" he asked, heedfulness in his tone.

"I—" Now she was here, face down in the carpet, she wasn't sure. Then again, this was Jamie, and she'd meant her words. *You can do anything to me.* "I am."

The sensation of having made herself entirely vulnerable to him skittered through her. She sank into the feeling that should have unsettled her. It didn't evoke fear, but rather relief. The release of a burden she'd been carrying without realizing it. To be completely vulnerable to this man was freedom.

Supported by one elbow to the side of her head, and the other at her hip, she felt his long length hover above her, the air between their bodies pulsing with desire. Then, inch by inch, he sank into her, his long, hard cock stretching her, her back arching so her sex could receive more of him. Without the distracting sight of him, she was able to become naught but a bundle of sensation. This surrender... It was true intimacy.

Breath hot and humid, his mouth found her neck, sending goose bumps racing across her skin. With every thrust, her short gasps met his rasped grunts in the age-old symphony of lust and pleasure. She shifted to pull her knees under her and lifted to her forearms, her bottom raised, his strong hands now clutching her hips, his cock impaling her with a rhythm that gained ferocity with each thrust.

Along with tenderness and intimacy, she needed this, too, this animal drive, this pleasure that skated the edge of pain, sometimes tipping over into it, as her sex began to coil with a tension that had become—*oh*—so deliciously familiar. "I'm so," she cried out and gasped with his next stroke, "so—" She couldn't seem to finish the sentence.

A knowing chuckle sounded behind her. "Close?"

She released a long moan in response. So close, yet so far out of reach.

One hand firm on the small of her back, he reached beneath her, finding her slit, sliding along its wet opening, driving her into a wild frenzy as her bottom slammed into his cock. His thumb found a spot—the same spot his tongue had found earlier tonight—using her wetness to glide over it, over and over, making her gasp in short bursts. "Are you toying with me?" she asked, frustrated, the question a demand.

Another dark, knowing chuckle. "Oh, yes, my love," he whispered in her ear, his voice a velvet rumble that tightened her nipples, curled her toes. "But now"—he applied more pressure, his thumb moving in tight, deliberate circles, driving her past the point of sanity—"you are going to come for me."

And...and...and there it was. Her body tensed and held in limbo—slave to the swirl of his thumb, to the relentless drive of his cock—release crashing down upon them, drowning them in quick spasms of pleasure, their bodies at once nothing more than physical sensation and somehow existing outside it.

In this infinite moment, they were one. That it

could stretch forever.

She collapsed on her stomach, and he collapsed on top of her. She matched the rise and fall of his chest. Every breath he drew, a gift.

Too soon, he slid off her, and she nearly groaned at the loss. But she didn't. It was but the first loss of the night, a small one to prepare her for the larger one. She rolled to a curl on her side, facing him, her eyes following every line and angle of his beautifully formed face.

"You don't have to do that, you know."

"Do what?" she asked, slightly taken aback by his tone.

"Memorize me." His gaze refused to release hers. "I'm not going anywhere."

* * *

SHE FLINCHED.

Good.

She needed to hear it. She needed to *understand* it.

"This doesn't have to end." He trailed light fingertips along the smooth curve of her hip. She wanted to sway into his touch, he could see by the flare of her pupils, the blue of her eyes pushed into thin rings. "*We* don't have to end."

In a sudden flurry of activity, she scrambled back, breaking contact, grabbed her chemise, and pulled it over her head. Slowly, he sat up and found his shirt and trousers. The coming conversation called for clothing.

Once dressed, he found her perched on the edge of the bed, determination on her face.

"Has it occurred to you that we don't have to end our marriage?" he asked, shifting the chair before the fireplace so it faced her. Better to be seated than loom over her like a brute. Or, worse yet, try to seduce her into compliance. That would be a very, very bad idea. And, also, very, very hard to resist.

"Not once," she retorted, her voice infused with a bravado that didn't quite reach her eyes. He detected uncertainty there. She'd considered the possibility, her eyes told him. "We've known each other hardly any amount of time."

"And yet," he said without hesitation, "you know me better than anyone on earth."

Lightly spoken, the words landed heavy and immovable. They contained the weight of truth.

"You don't know me."

"Then tell me about you."

A swirl of emotion shone in her gaze, and within it he saw temptation. "Once a eel, always a eel," she said.

"Doyle's words."

"They are."

"I don't care about your past."

"It's not only my past."

"What do you mean?"

She shook her head. "It matters not."

Jamie sensed it did, but before he could press her, she said, "The feelings you're experiencing have more to do with the novelty and excitement of the last fortnight. They aren't genuine or lasting."

"You've experienced what's between us with someone else?"

Not bloody likely, he left unspoken.

Yet she pressed on. "The feelings will fade as your life settles into regularity."

"*Regularity?* I wouldn't know how to begin having a regular sort of life," he scoffed. "And why would I want one?" Did he have the bollocks to speak his heart? He did. "Now that I've met you."

"That is precisely what I'm speaking of," she said, exasperated.

Let her be exasperated. These beliefs of hers needed to be challenged.

"What you're feeling is born of our circumstances and proximity."

He shoved forward in his chair, elbows on his knees. "*Proximity?* That's what you're calling it?"

She was truly beginning to try his patience. Why was she refusing to see what was before her?

Them.

A future.

"It won't last," she said, so certain. "It is very typical of all we've experienced together. It will pass."

"*No.*" It wouldn't. He understood that to the marrow of his bones.

"We share little in common." She held up a hand and began ticking off differences. "First, there's our disparity in class."

He snorted. "That matters not to me. Besides"—he had her here—"you're a marchioness, so I'd say we're equals in that regard."

"*You* were born an earl and future marquess. You took your first steps in a palace. *I*"—she jabbed her thumb into her chest—"was born a nobody. I spent my childhood picking oakum in a workhouse and thieving on London streets." She held up a second finger. "You have immeasurable wealth at your disposal."

"At your disposal, too. Need I keep reminding you that you're my wife? Whether you like it or not, *you* are a marchioness."

Implacable, she held up a third finger. "And education. You know everything a marquess ought, and more. You have book learning. I only know what I learned on the streets. I know nothing of needlework, menu planning, or dance steps. The simple matter is that I can play the marchioness for a few days, but no more. I simply do not fit into your world."

He was losing this battle, he could feel it. Not because he believed her reasons, but because she did.

"We have everything that matters in common." He didn't like the whiff of desperation in his voice.

"There is more to marriage than sexual congress."

"I want to be a husband to you in more ways than simply in bed." Or on the floor, or against a wall, or in a bathing tub, he didn't say.

Instead, he stood and closed the distance between them. When she didn't lift her gaze to meet his, he tucked his thumb beneath her chin until she had no choice. For the truths about to emerge from his mouth, he needed to be looking her in the eye. "I want to protect you. I want to cherish you. I want to spoil you until you're rotten and insufferable. For the rest of our days."

She shook her head. "It's but a phantom feeling."

"Who are you trying to convince? Me? Or yourself?"

He saw rawness and vulnerability and fear in her gaze, not of him, but of this unknown future he was presenting her. A future that very much collided with the view of the world she'd formed in her three and twenty years on this earth. A view formed not of natural preference and inclination, but of necessity and self-protection against the world.

What he saw was doubt. The sort of doubt that embedded deep in a person's soul, ensuring they would never believe in good fortune or lasting security.

She wasn't trying to convince herself of anything. She was a true believer in her view of the world.

"How much time?" he asked, taking one last stab at turning the moment.

Her eyebrows met. "Pardon?"

"You say there hasn't been enough time, then answer me this: How much time needs to pass before you know what exists between us has substance?"

Wide eyes fixed upon him, she didn't seem able to

answer. Only blasted, frustrating despair shone out at him.

"A day?" he pressed. "A fortnight? A month? A year?"

"I...I do not know."

At last, she'd shown uncertainty. Mayhap that was the crack his argument could slip inside and penetrate. What he must say next had to extend beyond logic and come from his very soul. It was his last chance. "Does the heart understand time?"

"I..." He'd flummoxed her. "I wouldn't know the workings of the heart."

"Don't you?"

She jerked her chin away from his touch and refused to meet his eye. He let his hand fall to his side. He knew what he must say next. "Leave," emerged from his mouth.

Shocked eyes met his. She'd expected him to keep fighting. "Tonight?"

"You can wait until morning, of course." He stepped back. Away from her.

A battle was waging behind her eyes, he could see that. But it was one he didn't have the power to decide, only her.

She cleared her throat. "I'll go tonight. It will be less confusing for Rafe that way."

Jaw tight, Jamie nodded. "My deepest appreciation for all you've done to recover my son." He'd retreated into the haughtiness he hadn't employed since the night they'd met. "Payment will be delivered to your residence on the morrow."

He turned on his heel and strode toward the corridor connecting their rooms. As he exited, his body wanted to hesitate. It wanted to look back and leave with one last image of her. But his will was made of stronger stuff.

He walked on.

CHAPTER TWENTY-SEVEN

$\mathcal{A}$s dawn stretched golden rays across the morning sky, Jamie checked Rafe's sleeping form one final time before making his way to Hortense's room.

She was gone.

From his study window overlooking the square, he'd watched her leave an hour ago. An hour spent wrestling with the urge to go to her bedroom. In the end, his will was no match for his heart.

Here he was.

The bed stood smooth and untouched. The fire flickered low in the grate. In her dressing room, her new finery remained. Stately and cold, her rooms retained no trace of her, only a stir of her scent. Soon, that, too, would be gone.

He'd had no choice but to tell her to go. Even so, he'd been as shocked as she that he'd spoken the words. But he knew the feelings pulsing through his heart with every beat. It was more than admiration, infatuation, and lust. The only word for it was love. And he couldn't force her to trust him or feel for him or love him back. That was what he'd understood in the seconds before he'd told her to leave. He couldn't be around her, feeling the way he did about her, without her returning the feeling.

And, of course, she wouldn't. How could he think he was enough for a woman like her? The truth was she'd seen into him and found him lacking. What was he to her?

In his room, he didn't find his bed, but, instead, spilled into an armchair before the window overlooking the back garden. Desperate to rid his mind of her, even if for a moment, he reached for the stack of books on the side table and grabbed the one on top. *A Treatise on the English Workhouse and Its Conditions for Work and Living.* He'd pulled it from the study days ago, after the visit to St. Mary Magdalen.

He flipped to the table of contents and gave it a quick scan, falling deeper into the subject with each word read. Hortense, Mollie, and Rafe—arguably the three most important people to enter his life—had been subjected to the workhouse, their destinies shaped by its vagaries and conditions. Perhaps the time had arrived to understand their lives, and the factors that had shaped them.

That Monday night, at Nick and Mariana's dinner, talk had centered on Parliament and workhouses. When Hortense had spoken, it was to the room at large, but truly to him. She'd believed he could make a difference.

Just now, from the corner of his eye, he noted the absence. He turned to fully take in the contents of the side table. His signet ring. Where was it?

Hortense. He knew it. But why?

Once a eel, always a eel... It's not only my past.

Doyle.

The old rogue wasn't in her past. That was the answer.

Before he knew what he was about, Jamie shoved to

his feet and strode into his dressing room, and jerked on his boots and greatcoat. Her insistence that they couldn't be together. That he didn't know her. Those assertions were at complete odds with the woman he'd held in his arms only a few hours ago. She didn't abscond with his signet ring because she was a thief, but because her past was also her present.

She hadn't trusted him with that knowledge. But how could she have? When had life ever shown her it was safe to trust?

Angry, determined strides guiding him down dark corridors and out of Asquith Court, Jamie found himself hailing a hackney.

No more.

Hortense would be free of Doyle before this night was through, for Jamie had vowed to protect her and he wouldn't abandon that promise. Hortense would be under his protection for the rest of his days, even if she wasn't under his roof.

* * *

JAMIE HAD NEVER APPROACHED Flick Doyle's establishment in the daylight. Even the soft, golden light of rising morning did the structure no favors as its ramshackle, haphazard appearance was enough to give one second thoughts about entering its narrow, listing confines.

Not Jamie, though. His step instinctively accelerated.

Nick's hand wrapped around his upper arm. "Let's wait and watch for a while."

Frustration flared through Jamie. He wanted this done. *Now.* But he also understood this sort of mission was Nick's area of expertise. A man didn't become a spymaster by rushing into situations like a foolhardy green youth. So, Jamie allowed himself to be pulled into a dark alcove where he and Nick watched, shoulder to shoulder.

"Are you going to tell me what this is all about?" his brother asked.

Jamie's jaw clenched. He didn't want to tell Nick anything. The idea of giving up Hortense's secrets without her permission left a sour taste in his mouth. Yet Nick had been rousted from his bed and come this far without question. Jamie owed his brother an explanation. "Hortense," he bit out.

Nick went alert. "Is she in danger?"

"Not that I'm aware."

"Then?"

"Doyle."

"Flick Doyle? Her old master? This is his place?"

"Aye." The air went heavy with expectation. Nick wanted more information, and Jamie supposed he deserved it. "I think she's back with him."

Nick snorted. "She's too smart for that."

"Not if he's holding something over her."

"What can that two-bit scoundrel possibly have over Hortense?"

"That's what I intend to find out," Jamie ground out.

The door cracked open, and a slight form slipped outside. *Hortense.* Again, Nick grabbed Jamie's arm. "Not now," he murmured. "Doyle, remember?"

Jamie gave a sharp nod as he watched Hortense glance about her without detecting him and Nick, then melt into the night. Every cell in his body clamored to follow her.

Instead, his feet beat a path to Doyle's door, Nick at his heels. Jamie rapped out Hortense's special knock. The door creaked on rusty hinges, and an eye appeared through the crack. The eye widened. Before the boy could slam the door in his face, Jamie shoved his foot into the crack. "I suggest standing aside as we have no quarrel with you," he said. "But we are coming in."

The door went slack. Jamie and Nick pushed inside, Jamie leading the way through the warren of corridors and stairs that led to the underground room, where the old rogue sat at his usual place at the table strewn with yesterday's take. He sat back in his chair, adjusted his wire-rimmed spectacles, and took in his visitors. "A little late—or is that early?—fer a social visit, wouldn't ye say?"

Jamie wouldn't play Doyle's games. "What are you holding over her?"

"*Her?*" Doyle's snake smile had fallen into place, the one that said he held all the cards. He would soon see that wasn't the case. "Ye be speakin' of Hortense, I presume?"

"Answer the question."

"Ain't ye curious what I have her doin' fer me?"

Jamie saw what Doyle was trying to do. Sow seeds of doubt in his mind. "I don't need to know."

Doyle wagged a finger at him. "Ah, but yer eyes be tellin' a different tale. Collects baubles fer me. Pays her taxes like a good eel."

Once a eel, always a eel.

Doyle's statement was only confirmation.

"What are you holding over her?" Jamie was convinced now more than ever. "It's the last time I'll ask."

"Or what?" Doyle guffawed. "Want some advice?"

"From you?"

"Leave Hortense with me. Her talents be wasted with the likes of ye nobs. That gel could rule over London, that's what I intend to teach her."

The time for argument was over. Doyle had missed his chance. Jamie turned to Nick. "Is your brother by law still involved in shipping?"

"St. Alban? Aye."

That got Doyle's attention, for he sat upright, clearly having noticed the look that had entered Nick's eyes. Ruthless and fixed and utterly ready to do what it took. The man had been a spymaster for over a decade, and it was easy to see how.

"What's this?" Doyle asked, the fight in his voice fading.

"My brother by law—one of us nobs, as you're so fond of saying—was a ship captain," said Nick. "It so happens he still has a vested interest in his family's shipping concern. And I happen to know one of those East Indiamen will be departing for southern seas within the week."

"What's it to me?" Doyle demanded, fear rather than fight driving the question.

"You will be on it," Jamie stated, low and implacable.

While Doyle sputtered and generally searched for words, a thin, wavery voice sounded in the void. "Ye'll not be takin' me Felix nowhere."

Above the room, halfway down the staircase, stood a woman whose age could have been anywhere between one hundred years and eternal as the hills, judging by the deep grooves life had carved into her face. Layers of winter nightclothes piled on her frail form, she wore a diamond and sapphire tiara atop her head. A *fake* diamond and sapphire tiara. She could be none other than Doyle's beloved mam.

"Just a jape 'mongst friends, Mam," Doyle said placatingly, scrambling to his feet and crossing the room to her, of a sudden her doting and beloved *Felix*. "Now ye take yerself off to bed, and we'll have a laugh o'er morning tea 'bout it."

The woman shot Jamie and Nick a parting glare over her shoulder as Doyle helped guide her up the steep staircase and closed the door behind her.

"I canna leave me mam," said Doyle, turning to

Jamie and Nick. He seemed to have gained a proper understanding of the situation as his demeanor had entirely shifted from cocksure to supplicating. "I'm all she has in this mean ole world. She won't survive without me."

"Accommodation could be made on the ship for her," said Nick, utterly dismissive of Doyle's concerns.

The old rogue looked stricken. "She canna survive that journey. Search yer heart, ye know it."

Jamie didn't want the death of Doyle's mam on his hands, but neither could Doyle stay in London. "You must leave London."

Nick clearly picked up on the direction of Jamie's thoughts. "Find another town."

Hope lay behind Doyle's spectacles. "Me mam has a older sister out Exeter way."

Older? How was that possible? But Jamie had no time for the mysteries of the universe. "Be cleared out of London within three days. One minute longer, and you're on a ship bound for lands unknown."

"And," Nick added, "I'll be keeping an ear out for you. Don't let me hear of any eels slithering about Exeter."

Doyle shook his head, eyes wide, hands spread, manner obsequious and pacifying. Gone was the Flick Doyle of ten minutes ago. One could almost admire the man's keen sense of keeping his hide intact. "Oh, no, no, no, it's the straight and narrow fer me, no mistake."

"You forget you ever knew Hortense," Jamie said. "You cause her no worry or trouble from this moment forward, or there will be no end of the earth you can go and know safety."

Doyle's brow creased in confusion. "Hortense who?"

"And one last thing." Jamie wasn't quite finished.

"Anythin', milord."

Jamie extended his hand. "My signet."

Doyle's expression turned sheepish. Without delay, he slid open a drawer and shoved his hand inside. Jamie shot Nick a glance. His brother stood, feet planted wide, arms crossed. He wasn't giving an inch. Jamie felt a pang of something he hadn't felt for Nick in years, something he'd been too numbed by spirits to feel— brotherly affection. Nick had his back when it counted. It meant more than Jamie could put into words.

The clunk of metal on wood pulled Jamie's attention. On the table sat the signet. *His* signet. It was part of him, always would be. It was time he accepted that fact. He slid it on the middle finger of his right hand. For the first time, the fit felt exactly right.

"Within three days," he said to Doyle.

"Don't have to tell me a third time."

With that, Jamie and Nick set off into the new London morning.

"Are we off to inform Hortense?" asked Nick, his eyes bright with purpose.

"No," said Jamie. He'd been giving this some thought.

"*No?*" Nick sputtered, incredulous. "Why the ever-loving hell not?"

"I won't have her this way."

"What way?"

"Indebted to me," Jamie said. "She now has the choice."

"Brother, you're speaking in riddles, and I can't abide people speaking in riddles." Nick was clearly exasperated. "What choice?"

"To have the life she wants."

Hortense had never had that chance, and he wanted it for her.

"She wants you, brother." Nick snorted, as if he couldn't quite believe it.

"Perhaps," said Jamie.

He hoped so. Perhaps in her new reality of creating a life solely of her choosing, she would realize it wasn't quite complete, and it never would be without him. The same way he felt about her. But she had to reach that conclusion on her own.

She came to him of her own free will.

Or not at all.

CHAPTER TWENTY-EIGHT

$\mathcal{M}^{ay}$ Hortense and Sir Bacon had only
rounded the corner onto Little Peter Street when a
scrappy rat dashed across their path, ruining what had
been up to this instant the rare walk without dramatics.
The little dog strained forward on his lead and let out a
great round of barking. Hortense stopped, exasperated.
She would gain no traction by fighting the tide of Sir
Bacon's inborn instinct. Best to let him tire himself out.

Out of long-standing habit, she glanced around, half
expecting to find an eel tipping his cap at her, summoning her to Doyle. But there was no one, hadn't
been in a month, not since she'd turned over the signet
ring. After the first week of waiting for contact, she'd
returned and knocked on Doyle's door for fifteen minutes, but no answer.

A small voice had come from behind her. "Ye
lookin' fer Doyle?"

Hortense pivoted and found a girl of seven or so
years squinting up. "Aye."

"'E and 'is mam up and scattered." Her brow creased
in thought. "Five days ago?"

"They left?" A strange feeling began to creep

through Hortense. "Did they say where they were going?"

"Wouldn't speak a word to no one."

Hortense pressed half a crown into the girl's hand and beat a quick path out of the East End, utterly flummoxed. She could only figure Doyle had come up against someone he couldn't handle so easily as a bunch of half-starved boys and one blackmailed woman. It had been bound to happen in a town like London.

But with each footstep she took another feeling blossomed and spread through her—relief. If she stopped moving, she would collapse to the ground with it, or grow wings and fly.

It had taken another full week for her to accept this new reality. Of Doyle being gone. Of him being entirely out of her life. Of her being free, truly so.

Sir Bacon tugged on his lead, eager to discover all the new smells just out of his nose's reach. He'd become a good partner, rarely interfering in her investigative work, which still consisted mostly of infidelities and the occasional theft. It was steady work, if not precisely fulfilling. But it was hers, hers to cultivate and grow. Hers alone. That was the important part.

However, there was another new reality that had come as a shock almost equal to Doyle's sudden departure. She no longer *needed* to continue with this work, or any work for that matter. Not with the sum of money that had arrived by special delivery the day after she'd left Asquith Court. It was a sum that could easily keep King George living quite comfortably for a year or two. And the accompanying note... If the money hadn't been enough to make her jaw drop to the floor, the note certainly had. It had been composed of few words, but not many had been needed.

Every year, on this date, you shall receive this sum.

Do not return the payment, as all such attempts will fail.
- J

And that settled it.

She was the possessor of a small fortune, and she hadn't the faintest idea what to do with it. So, she ignored it. She wasn't sure she would ever be able to spend it. Yet all those guineas weren't enough to distract from the lone remaining ax suspended above her head.

Every day, when she returned to her lodgings, she expected to find annulment papers waiting for her. It had been a month, and the papers hadn't arrived. But they would.

By now, Jamie would have come to his senses about their time together. He would have seen that danger and intrigue had a way of creating a heightened sense of emotion that quickly faded after the threat was gone and life resumed its normal pace. He would be thinking himself well shot of the thieving guttersnipe he'd wed. She simply wasn't marchioness material.

He would see that by now.

And her? What did she see?

It mattered not. Her feelings were best tucked away, where they belonged.

Within a block of Number 11, she noticed a coach and four. Her heart banged out a series of hard thumps. Could it be—

It wasn't. Glossy black paint shone where the crest would be. Yet she did recognize the vehicle. It belonged to Nick and Mariana. Dread snaked through her and settled in her gut. She'd skipped Monday night dinners for a month, and she intended to beg off again tomorrow. She needed time away from all people with the surname Asquith. At least, that was what her mind kept insisting.

Yet there was this part of her—a part rooted in her body at the chest level and decidedly independent of reason—that carried a soreness. If she let down her guard—let's say, in the small hours of the night—it could feel less like a twinge and closer on the pain scale to an ache. It could throb and make her chest feel heavy, as if it harbored a deep, unresolved sob. Sir Bacon could sense it, too, for he whined plaintively when it happened.

At the boardinghouse, she didn't take the alley entrance to her rooms, but instead entered through the front door. Mrs. Hayhurst stood in the corridor, worrying her hands, an anxious expression on her face. "You have a visitor," she said in a loud whisper and handed Hortense a calling card. *Lady Mariana Asquith.* "She insisted on staying until you returned. She's been here for nigh on an hour."

"Is she in the drawing room?" Hortense was already on the move.

"That she is."

Closing the drawing room door behind her, Hortense found Mariana perched uprightly on the edge of the sofa, shimmering with impatience. "Mariana," she said haltingly, wary of her friend in a mood.

"Where have you been?" Mariana would get right to it.

Hortense took her time unknotting Sir Bacon's lead, hoping her outward calm would serve to soothe and diffuse. "Working a few investigations here and there. The usual."

Mariana's eyes narrowed, tension soothed not one whit. "We haven't seen you these last four Mondays."

"No," said Hortense. She wouldn't elaborate.

"Are you planning to dine with us tomorrow night?"

"No." A direct setting of expectations was best.

Mariana flicked her wrist. "Please do sit. We have ever so much to discuss."

With no small amount of suspicion, Hortense did as her friend suggested, if suggestions were demands. This blithe change in tone didn't bode well. She had a nose for that sort of thing.

"Can you guess who *has* been gracing us with his presence?" Mariana asked, the words light, even if her eyes had lost none of their intensity. "And who will be there tomorrow?"

"Jamie, I suppose." Oh, that her voice hadn't broken just a little on the sharp edge of his name. Time should dull it.

"That's right." Mariana hesitated. "And Rafe." Another hesitation. "His son."

"I suppose that was a shock."

"It was, and it wasn't. Jamie has always been rather opaque."

Against her will, Hortense was becoming drawn in. She couldn't help it. She'd been wondering about Rafe. "How is the lad?"

"He's a little tough, but a sweet sort."

Hortense nodded. "I could see that about him." Like his father, she wouldn't say.

"Geoffrey has taken right to him."

"Geoffrey would."

Humor flickered in Mariana's gaze. "Yes, well, Geoffrey is always on the lookout for adventure, and this new cousin of his is that in spades." All traces of humor faded. "But I'm not here to talk about the boys."

"You wouldn't be." Hortense braced herself.

"Then I'll cut directly to it. Hortense, you are the bravest woman I know, which is why I don't understand something."

"What is that?"

"Why you are behaving like such a coward."

The statement sucked her breath away.

"Is it that you don't want to be a marchioness?" Mariana asked. "I could understand that. Such a life isn't for everyone, including many of the people leading it."

"I've never given it much thought." Hortense had known from the start she wouldn't be a marchioness very long.

"You are accustomed to a busy life, but in the role of lady you could find much to occupy yourself. And think of all the resources at your disposal."

"I suppose you're correct."

Mariana canted her head, assessing. "But that isn't it."

"No."

A one-word answer wouldn't satisfy Mariana. At all. She was going to try a different tack.

"Do you know about Nick and Jamie's dreadful parents?"

"Beastly."

Mariana nodded. "Because of those people, Nick had difficulty coming around to the idea of love—"

"Let us not start throwing that word around," Hortense protested.

Mariana ignored her. "He'd never seen evidence of anything lasting, especially love."

Hortense's heart became a hammer in her chest, as if it wanted to burst free and proclaim itself. Every muscle in her body clenched to contain it.

"Well into our marriage, he continued thinking that way, despite all evidence to the contrary." Mariana refused to release her gaze. "Is that what the universe has taught you, too? That nothing lasts?"

Hortense glanced away. She had to. Mariana was hitting rather too close to the mark for comfort.

"But what if the universe is now offering you a different lesson?"

"I believe I've heard everything the universe has to say. In several languages," she added. Oh, that was more than two fingers of bitters infusing her tone.

"Some things last," Mariana insisted. "Some people stay."

Hortense shook her head in denial. Rather like a child, she suspected. "Everything is temporary." A month ago, the statement would have emerged as simple fact. Now, it couldn't help sounding hollow and not a little despairing.

A kind smile formed about Mariana's mouth. That smile nearly undid Hortense. "No, my dear, that simply isn't the truth. I'm sorry you've been telling yourself a lie all these years. True love lasts."

The knot in Hortense's chest rose to her throat. She couldn't speak around it.

"Nick and I have that sort of love."

Hortense knew this. "What you and Nick share is a rare occurrence, like a lightning strike. I'm not sure it's for us mere mortals."

Mariana laughed. "I never took you for someone so sentimental, but, really, love can do that to a person."

"Please stop using that word."

"Which word?" Mariana's eyes shone with mischief. "Love?"

"That's the one."

"But, why, my dear? You're deep in it."

Hortense opened her mouth to lodge a protest.

Mariana held up a silencing hand. "I know all the signs. A particular lethargy. Dark circles beneath your eyes. Clothes hanging loose on the body from pounds shed. Love of the unrequited variety is its own particular sort of grief."

"You cannot possibly know what is in my heart,"

Hortense said, anger peeking through, along with a bit of desperation. She needed Mariana to stop talking.

"I may not know all the particulars of the *what*, but I do know *who*."

Hortense swallowed with some difficulty. "He is a marquess. My sort is naught more than an exotic lark for the likes of him."

Mariana lifted a single eyebrow. "Did he tell you that?"

Hortense shifted uneasily in her chair. "Well, no."

"I didn't think so." Mariana crossed her arms, quite irritatingly smug.

"Why is that?" Oh, why was she encouraging the woman?

A smile curled about Mariana's mouth. Definitely smug. "Because I've seen him, and he, too, has all the signs."

"They will pass." Just like hers would…someday.

Mariana shook her head. "It doesn't work that way when it's true."

Hortense had a question to ask of Mariana, one she'd kept to herself, but now needed airing. "How did you keep faith all those years that you and Nick were estranged?"

"I didn't keep faith. I used every distraction I could think of to dislodge it—I even considered taking a lover—but it wouldn't budge. It was simply a constant."

"Perhaps constants exist for you," Hortense said. "But not for me."

Mariana's gaze fell to the little dog curled on the rug between them. "And what of Sir Bacon?"

"What of him?"

"Doesn't he have faith that you will feed him and take him outside? Aren't you a constant in his life?"

"I am."

"Then why can't someone be that for you?"

321

Had Mariana compared her to a dog? She could laugh at the absurdity. Or cry at its possible accuracy. Or both. "I am perfectly capable of feeding and taking myself outside."

Mariana's mouth quirked. "A person needs more than self-sufficiency. *You* need more than that."

"He asked me to leave," Hortense said with an amount of composure that did her credit. For the admission, spoken aloud, gutted her anew. In all these weeks, its sharpness hadn't dulled a hair.

"Nick thought Jamie would break your heart, while I suspected it would be the other way around. But it seems you've done it to each other."

"Hearts weren't involved." The words sounded as hollow as they felt.

"Weren't they?" Mariana asked, gently. "Have you asked yourself why he asked you to leave?"

The question cut through the pain. Hortense hadn't once questioned it. She'd simply accepted it with an *of course.*

"Was it that he wanted you gone? Or could it have been for a different reason?" Mariana paused, holding Hortense in suspense. The woman was so very good at such moments. "Mayhap he wanted you too much."

Hortense opened her mouth to refute the very notion but was only able to produce a muddled croak that bore no resemblance to the English language, or any language at all, save that of despair.

Mariana reached for her reticule and stood. "As your friend, this is the last I'll say on the matter." She moved close enough to take both of Hortense's hands, squeezing as she said, "You must let go of your past to have the future your heart desires." She dug inside her reticule. "Oh, and Nick sent this."

She pressed a note into Hortense's hand and an affectionate kiss to her cheek before sweeping out of the room. Hortense broke the seal and took in the contents.

> *You've likely noticed that Doyle has been neutralized.*
> *You might send your husband a note of gratitude.*
> *Or, better yet, thank him in person. -N*

All the breath left Hortense's body. She sat slightly stunned, for a full minute.

Jamie—it had been him. He'd cleared Doyle out of London. Which meant...

He knew. He'd known she'd taken his signet ring almost as soon as she took it. And—this was the part currently causing all the turmoil in her insides—he'd instinctively gone to the source. He'd...

He'd freed her from Doyle.

Once a eel, always a eel.

She'd held on to that malignant belief for years. But not Jamie. If he'd believed that of her, he would have destroyed her standing with Nick and Mariana, at the very least. Jamie saw a different her, the person she wanted to be. The person she was with him.

Her old belief—that she was nothing more than what Doyle said she was—didn't have to be true any longer. That was what Jamie had done for her.

Sudden agitation surged inside her, and she shot to a stand. She began pacing, her feet unable to keep up with her racing mind.

You must let go of your past to have the future your heart desires.

The past. The past contained so many layers. The past even before Doyle, before the workhouse. The past that contained the true her. She'd always tried to shove that past behind, locking it away and choosing to move forward, ever forward. She'd convinced herself she'd shed that past with the name

Amelie, but Mariana's words resonated deep within her.

She hadn't let it go at all. In fact, she'd been carrying it around all these years, like a lead weight strapped to her back. And it had everything to do with her heart and its desires.

When Papa and Maman had died, her heart hadn't died with them. It had closed in on itself, tight and impenetrable. It had no other choice if she was to survive the workhouse and Flick Doyle and even her life as a spy. The only way to be safe was to be entirely reliant on herself. But now...

Mayhap he wanted you too much.

Now, perhaps, a different sort of safety was available to her, but one that required her to open her heart so she could take an unburdened leap toward happiness.

The unresolved knot tightened in her throat, and tears stung her eyes. She hadn't cried in over a decade, since the passing of her parents, but there was no stopping it now. She collapsed on the nearest chair and wept hard, salty tears, mourning all she'd lost—her parents, her innocence...*Jamie.*

Sir Bacon jumped onto her lap and curled into a ball, staying with her until her eyes were dry. She didn't feel gutted, as she would have predicted, but, instead, cleansed. She'd needed this cry for a good number of years. And in this new, purified light, she was able to experience a spark of something. Something that resembled hope.

There was no recovering her parents or her innocence. They were gone forever. But Jamie...

She loved him. She needed him. And that love and that need, they were safe with him.

She must go to him. Not tomorrow, at Monday night dinner, but tonight and where it all began.

And then she would open herself to him.

If his feelings were the same, she would let herself be loved, and she would love, unguardedly, without limits.

For what was the purpose of a life without love? It was but a shadow of a life. The life she'd been living for so many years.

It was time to bring her life and her love into the light.

CHAPTER TWENTY-NINE

he door clicked discreetly closed, and Jamie exhaled a slow, relieved breath.

The lad was fast asleep. He was still here.

The same sequence of thoughts he'd had every night for the past month.

His feet turned to the well-worn path to his study with the intention of outlasting yet another night. After the first few touchy days of gaining an understanding of one another, Rafe had become the only source of brightness in his day, even if this week the lad was worn out by his studies. It had taken Jamie exactly one day to grasp that Rafe couldn't read. Within a fortnight, he'd poached a highly esteemed tutor—one Mr. Carson —from Harrow for a pretty penny. Only the best would do for his son, and the best was all the boy would know from here on out.

At first, he'd been concerned Rafe wouldn't take to the notion of book learning, but the boy met the challenge with grit and determination, learning his letters in two days, sounding out two-syllable words within the first week of instruction. Most of the time, it was Mr. Carson who had to put an end to the day's studies. Rafe was ravenous for the newly opened world of knowledge. It was Jamie's hope the lad would be ready to attend Westminster School with his cousin Geoffrey next year.

The boy's guttersnipe accent? That was likely beyond Mr. Carson's abilities. An elocution expert would need to be retained before Rafe attended Westminster, or he would be subject to no end of ridicule, even if his guardian was the Marquess of Clare, for without legitimate birth, Jamie could be no more than that to Rafe in the eyes of the law.

Fewer than twenty-four hours after Rafe had arrived at Asquith Court, Jamie had retained a solicitor to obtain Rafe's birth records from the parish register and begin the process of binding the lad to him legally. Soon, he would be Mr. James Rafferty Asquith.

Jamie hoped the low-lying wariness that hung about the boy would dissolve over time. It was as if he was waiting to be told this was all a jape and be tossed out on the streets like yesterday's rubbish.

Each day, however, a different bit of his true personality peeked out. He was a colorful lad who could insert a bit of humor into most observations. A trait that had certainly been passed down from his mother.

Tonight, he'd asked about Mollie. Jamie had been wondering when Rafe's curiosity would get the better of him. "I only know I was named for 'er," he said. "What did she look like?"

Jamie told the boy what he remembered, which was more an idea of Mollie than a clear image all these years later. "She had bright blue eyes and dark, curly hair. It had a bit of auburn to it."

"What's auburn?" Rafe asked, head cocked, eyes intent. Now that the boy had been given permission to ask questions, he voiced every one that popped into his head. Jamie liked this about his son.

"Dark red." At the boy's nod, he continued, "She

possessed a quick wit she wasn't afraid to use on any-one. She took a joy from life that's rare. Her mouth was always ready with a smile, and her laugh was sudden and big. You have her laugh."

Rafe didn't crack. "If ye liked 'er so much, then why did ye up and leave 'er? Was it 'cause of me?"

He deserved these questions. In fact, he was relieved Rafe had finally asked them. "I didn't know about you. The day I learned about you, I sought you out. I would have never stood for what happened to your mother or you."

Solemn eyes continued to stare out at him, but he detected trust within them. "But," Jamie continued. He had to say this. "I was careless. I believed where I shouldn't have, and I shall regret that for the rest of my days."

A few seconds passed before Rafe, at last, nodded his acceptance of these facts and remained silent for the rest of the meal.

Now, Jamie entered his study, its sights, sounds, and smells enfolding him in their familiarity. A familiarity that was no longer a comfort. The room felt more akin to a prison cell these days. For whatever reason, tonight, he found himself drawn toward the brandy de-canter. Unable to resist, he extended a hand that tremored slightly less than it had a month ago and pulled out the stopper. He inhaled deeply. It hadn't been refilled in all these months, but that didn't mean the craving had gone away, or ever would. Still, it wasn't essential he fall down that hole.

He plugged the stopper and turned toward the low fire that the servants knew to keep burning into the night. A small movement caught the periphery of his vision, and he whipped around.

He stopped in his tracks and blinked.

The form occupying his customary chair could be a delusion borne of wanting her here so badly.

He blinked again. But there she sat, meeting his gaze with her own unflinching one.

"How did you—" Hope sprang up, which he immediately suppressed. Yet he couldn't entirely. She was here. And if she was here, then mayhap…perhaps…

"The servants still reckon me the lady of Asquith Court," she said.

That would be true, for he'd told them no differently.

Her gaze fell to his right hand. "What are you reading these days?"

He lifted the book he'd forgotten he was holding. *"Parliament's Rules, Privileges, and Proceedings in Modern Times."*

"Parliament?" She looked surprised.

Well, he'd rather surprised himself, too. "I've decided to take up my seat in the House of Lords, and as I don't wish to make a fool of myself, I'm learning its ins and outs."

Her head canted. "I thought your opinion was that you couldn't be of any use."

"I've since altered my stance on that position."

"A beneficial quality in a politician." The jibe landed with no malice.

He smiled. Oh, but it was good to see her, to have her here. Where she belonged.

"I'm not certain my fellow lords will see it in that light." He laughed wryly. "For I have a cause."

"Do you?"

"Workhouse reform."

"Oh" slid from her parted lips. The fire cast dancing shadows across her face, making it difficult to grasp her expression, but it might be pleased. Possibly more than that.

"Of course, I'm not sure how far I'll get. I'm thinking of enlisting Mariana in an advisory role."

Hortense snorted. "Those old nobs have no idea what they're in for."

"No mercy," Jamie said. Gone was his lightness.

"Good."

He weighed whether or not to speak his next words. "I've decided to be useful in the world." He needed her to know. "Instead of hiding from it."

"Workhouse reform likely wouldn't make it far without a marquess backing it."

"The workhouse has inflicted harm on too many, in particular those I love."

He watched his words land on her. She blinked. She opened her mouth. She closed it.

"I have purpose. I have my son," he said, emboldened. "I would say my life is almost complete."

"Almost?"

"Almost. It will never feel entirely whole."

An emotion flickered in her eyes, as if she'd intuited what he'd left unspoken. *Without you.*

Her gaze shifted away. "I saw you with the spirits decanter just now. Has it—have you—"

"A reflex, I'm afraid. I'm not sure I'll ever be rid of it."

She nodded with understanding.

"Mayhap you'll tell me why you're here." He took a step. He couldn't not.

She jumped to her feet, a tetchy energy shimmering off her, as if the words she'd yet to express were bursting for release. Her hands clasped tightly in front of her, knuckles white. She pointed at his right hand. "You're wearing your signet ring."

"Aye."

"It suits you."

"Does it?"

"It speaks of solidity and power. Of *you*."

The way she was looking at him. It could give a man hope.

"How did you get it back?"

She wasn't beating about the bush. They both knew how Doyle had come to have it, and it wasn't all that worth discussing. "Turns out Doyle wasn't too keen on living out his final years on the other side of the world."

"You didn't only rescue your ring."

"The ring wasn't the important part."

She drew in a deep breath and began speaking, unsteady yet determined. "I thought an eel was all I was or ever would be. So, when Doyle approached me a year ago and told me I would have to start paying taxes to him in order to keep my reputation and business, it felt terrible, but fitting."

"It was all you knew."

She nodded. "Then you came along, and we had to pull a job to secure Rafe. But I knew one-for-one wasn't all there was to it. So, I went to Doyle without you." She swallowed. "He'd planned on keeping Rafe under his control, even as your son lived with you."

"Ah."

"I couldn't let it happen. It was as if Doyle had stepped over a line I didn't know existed."

"So you offered yourself in Rafe's stead."

Her eyes shone with unshed tears. "But, then, you rescued me. You freed me from my past."

"A small payment for what you gave me."

"What did I give you?"

"A future, Hortense." His heart couldn't take much more. That she'd sacrificed herself for his son, for him... "You are more than someone like Doyle could ever understand."

A tear fell down her cheek, and she swiped it away impatiently. "You asked me how long it would take."

"How long what would take?" Jamie grew suddenly wary.

"For me to know if what was between us was genuine."

He chose to nod instead of speak. His voice would give away all the longing that had been building inside him for weeks.

"One month."

Here it was. The moment he'd been dreading since he'd watched her leave. She was here for her freedom. "I see. I've had annulment papers drawn up."

Her eyes went wide. "Annulment papers?" She looked utterly crestfallen. "Oh, of course."

A current of panic streaked through him. He'd bungled something. Now all he wanted was to make it right. He would start at the beginning. "What did it take one month for you to know?"

Somehow, he'd drawn within a few feet of her. So close he could reach out and caress her cheek.

Watery blue eyes stared up at him, open and vulnerable. "That what we felt—*feel*—was—*is*—genuine."

How was it possible she was speaking the only words he wanted to hear?

"When Papa and Maman died," she said in an uncharacteristic rush, her words all but tripping over themselves, "and I was taken to the workhouse, I lost faith in the workings of a benevolent universe. My time spent with Doyle, and even my years as Nick's spy, only reinforced the view that nothing good lasted forever."

"What other choice did you have? You had to survive."

"But life has to be about more than survival to be truly lived. I never understood that until I met you." Her tongue swiped nervously across her bottom lip. "I'll never have faith in the world. I'll always see its dark side before I recognize its light."

Jamie was no longer able not to touch her. He took her hands, warm and slick with nerves, and squeezed, when all he wanted was to wrap his arms around her and protect her from the world that had tried to defeat her.

"But I have faith in you. No longer will the past deny me the future I desire." Her voice was wobbly, but sure. "Nor do you have to be a prisoner of your past. Both of us, we are free to forge a new future, together."

Her words—their faith and trust—were the greatest gift he'd ever received. He would spend the rest of his life trying to be worthy of them.

"You are all I need in this world, and I can now see only one future."

"What is that?"

"One with love that lasts. One with you."

He reached up and tucked a silky black tendril behind her ear, his fingers lingering on the curve of her jaw. "I think I've loved you from the moment you called me less than impressive."

She exhaled a breathy laugh, perhaps a little embarrassed of itself.

"You not only showed me who you are—an independent woman who speaks her mind—but who I was, and who I needed to be to win and be worthy of you. You've made me a better man than I ever had a notion of becoming."

He could stop here. Mayhap he should stop here. But he needed to say something. And, perhaps, it was something she needed to hear and consider.

"You are determined, resilient, intelligent, and beautiful," he said. "You are extraordinary. You are magnificent."

"Please, Jamie, you don't need to say such things."

"I do, because they are true. And they make me wonder."

Her eyebrows crinkled together. "Wonder?"

"If I can be enough for you."

The words hung in the air between them, and he half wished he could stuff them back inside his mouth.

She shook her head. "You are not enough."

His heart plummeted to his toes.

"You are merely the sun rising in the east and setting in the west," she said. "You are merely the moon in the night sky and the stars in my veins when I feel your touch. You aren't merely enough. You are merely everything."

He wasn't sure he would ever draw breath again. That *she* would feel this way about *him*...

It could defy belief. But he wouldn't let it. Somehow, it was the truth.

She was his.

And he was hers.

They simply were. And it filled him with an awe from which he would never recover.

"Must I add poetess to the list of your extraordinary qualities?" he asked, a light murmur. "I love you and all parts of you, my marchioness, my Hortense, my Amelie."

"And I love you, my lord marquess, my lover, my Jamie."

He angled his head and pressed his lips to hers, all the words that needed to be spoken, spoken. He wrapped her in his embrace, vowing never to let her go. The universe could try to insert its form of chaos, but it wouldn't succeed.

For together, he and his Amelie Hortense were subjects to no world but the one of their making.

EPILOGUE

SCOTLAND, AUGUST

To either side of Jamie and Hortense stood high, uneven hills, green and purple with grasses and late-summer heather, as they lay on the bank of the river that ran through the glen. A blanket beneath them, they stared up at an impossibly blue sky dotted with fluffy white clouds floating along in their own slow time.

"This is heaven" fell from her mouth.

A lazy, low rumble of a laugh escaped him. "Rafe and Sir Bacon certainly think so."

"When did we last see them?"

"An hour or so ago."

"Should we form a search party?"

"Oh, Sir Bacon is likely on the trail of a fox. They'll return when they're hungry."

What a splendid father Jamie was to Rafe. Every day of the last few months, Hortense's heart had found new ways to open wider. It was as if once she'd given it permission, it couldn't stop expanding. And it was down to the man lying by her side.

He shifted to his hip and propped his head on his hand, so he now stared down at her. Her gaze fixated on his mouth. That talented, generous mouth of his. How she wished he would lean down and kiss her.

"I have something for you," he said.

"Haven't you already given me everything?"

He pushed to a seat and reached for the basket containing their packed tea. "My marchioness should have something special for her name day."

She gave a tiny gasp, even as a smile tugged about her mouth. "Who told you?"

"Who do you think?"

"Mariana."

"With strict instructions that I make a big fuss over it."

"Please tell me you haven't. I have everything my heart never knew to wish for."

Oh, the way she spoke these days. She supposed love did that to a person.

"Close your eyes."

"Please, Jamie, don't—"

"Eyes. Closed."

On a laugh, she squeezed them shut. Her ears picked up a shuffle, then the rustling sound of cloth. Anticipation ribboned through her, even as she felt silly for it.

"You may open them now."

She peeked one eye open, then the other. A true gasp escaped her this time. Perched upon his open palm was a sapphire and diamond tiara. Her hand flew to her mouth to control the giggle that wanted release. She wasn't at all successful.

"I seem to remember you going on and on about a deep yearning for a tiara of your very own."

"Jamie," she said, no small bit awe-struck, "this tiara has twice as many diamonds and sapphires as that other one." She wouldn't pollute the pristine Highland air with Rothesbury's name.

"Naturally."

"I cannot fathom the expense. Please tell me it's paste."

"Of course not." He shrugged. "It's only money."

She still hadn't adjusted to this part of her new life, the aristocrat's cavalier attitude toward coin. It boggled the mind.

"Lean forward, Amelie."

He'd taken to calling her Amelie. And, only for him, she was her.

Carefully, he placed the tiara on her head—it was quite heavy with all those gemstones—and after a few adjustments, sat back, assessing. "Queen of the glen."

She giggled again. She couldn't help herself. This joy provoked such frivolity. "What shall I do with you, marquess?"

"Allow me to give you another gift?"

"Another? This one is already too much. I don't need anything. You spoil me."

From behind his back, his hand emerged with the other gift, a folded cloth. She saw at a glance it was a powder-blue silk brocade with a delicate floral pattern. Something about it made the breath catch in her chest. She took it in hand and rubbed her thumb across the fabric. Sumptuous and soft. "Is it a shawl?"

He nodded.

She held it up to the sunlight to better take in its quality. Lovely. Not a speck of sunlight peeked through its fine weave. "Where did you procure this?"

"France." A beat. "It was quite difficult to locate."

A feeling formed in her chest, in the vicinity of her heart. It told her this wasn't just any fine silk brocade she held. "This was made from Papa and Maman's hands." She spoke with no small amount of certainty and awe. They'd specialized in such superior work. It was how they'd caught the eye of the French nobility.

"Aye."

The full range of emotions—from grief to joy—flooded her, but unlike in years past, she wasn't afraid to feel them as tears fell from her eyes and a smile spread across her face. "This is the most special gift I've ever received."

And now she would give him her gift. She'd been waiting for the perfect moment, and no moment had ever been more perfect. She swiped at her cheek—truly, she'd become quite a leaky bucket—and said, "It will make a nice blanket."

A slight frown tugged at the corners of his mouth. "It's rather small for a blanket."

"Not for a baby."

His eyes went wide, and a little wild, as they fell on her stomach. His mouth opened, but no sound emerged. She'd rendered him speechless. She took his hand and pressed it against her, which only in the last week had begun showing signs of roundness.

"You clever woman," he murmured as he leaned in, took her hips in his hands, and pressed his mouth to her belly.

Her laugh was pure, unrestrained joy. "It took no cleverness on either of our parts." But a considerable amount of lust and... "Only love."

"I never knew true love or happiness until I met you."

His lips met hers, tender, insistent. She'd moved closer to explore the possibilities of the urgency inspiring a wild recklessness inside her when up the glen, a shout sounded, followed by a round of barking. A few hundred yards away, Rafe and Sir Bacon were hurtling toward them with the happy momentum of a boy and his dog.

On a resigned laugh, she and Jamie pulled apart. "I'll

give you your third birthday present later," he promised.

Again, she laughed. Never had laughter been so free.

"It's quite a family we're creating for ourselves," he said, pulling her into the crook of his arm so they could take in the view, together.

Not so long ago, she wouldn't have tempted fate with such a belief. But that was then, and this was now.

This was happiness. This was life.

Her happiness.

Her life.

The past would always be a part of her, but never again would it be a burden that kept her from finding joy.

Here was love.

Here was the future.

It was enough.

It was everything.

ALSO BY SOFIE DARLING

Shadows and Silk
Three Lessons in Seduction
Tempted by the Viscount
Her Midnight Sin
To Win a Wicked Lord
At the Pleasure of the Marquess
If I Were Yours

It was Only a Kiss

ABOUT THE AUTHOR

Sofie Darling is an award-winning author of historical romance. The third book in her Shadows and Silk series, Her Midnight Sin, won the 2020 RONE award for Best Historical Regency.

She spent much of her twenties raising two boys and reading every romance she could get her hands on. Once she realized she simply had to write the books she loved, she finished her English degree and embarked on her writing career. Mr. Darling and the boys gave her their wholehearted blessing.

When she's not writing heroes who make her swoon, she runs a marathon in a different state every year, visits crumbling medieval castles whenever she gets a chance, and enjoys a slightly codependent relationship with her beagle, Bosco. Visit her website.

www.ingramcontent.com/pod-product-compliance
Lightning Source LLC
Chambersburg PA
CBHW011147100726
47899CB00010B/3199